the stories stars tell

the stories stars tell

by cl walters

mixed plate press

honolulu, hi

This is a work of fiction. All of the characters, organizations, publications, and events portrayed or mentioned in this novel are either products of the author's imagination or are used fictitiously.

Mixed Plate Press
Honolulu, HI
For information: Mixed Plate Press, 91430 Komohana Street,
Kapolei, HI 96707
www.mixedplatepress.com

Cover Art: Sara Oliver Designs

ISBN: 978-1-7350702-2-3
ISBN: 978-1-7350702-0-9 (pbk)
ISBN: 978-1-7350702-1-6 (ebook)

dedication

To all the good girls trying to be perfect: perfection is impossible, so be bad every once in a while.

To all the good boys trying to be bad: it's okay to be vulnerable. The world will be better for it.

part one

senior year
(14 days to graduation)

"I stood staring at the never-ending wasteland of the mess I'd created and decided the only way out of it was to go to sleep; reminded myself, there wasn't anything that couldn't be cured by a good, soul-sucking sleep. I just had one problem: I was an insomniac."

- unnamed protagonist, *Kaleidoscope Concussion* by Saul Annick

emma

I squeeze my eyes shut, terrified I'm about to screw this up. Three deep breaths. Slow. Steady. In. Out. The sound of my breath echoes in my head like the rush of the wind through the tree leaves in my backyard, and the fear of failure, which always sits in the front of my brain, drips down through my body into my stomach.

I could forget my part.

I could ruin everything.

I could be sick.

I picture Cameron, standing in front of his dad's red Ferrari in his khaki pants and suspenders over his dark brown shirt ranting about conquering his fear right before he kicks the shit out of his dad's car. Okay. He's a fictional character from one of my favorite movies of all time, *Ferris Bueller's Day Off*, but still. I'm going to kick the shit out of this, like, speech-Ferrari.

Breathe in. Breathe out.

"Emma?"

The sound of my name, as though it's being called through a

tunnel, draws me back. I open my eyes and look into the familiar bright blue eyes of my best friend, Liam.

"Emma? It's almost time. You're doing your breathing thing?"

He's dressed in a business suit, charcoal gray and red tie with those chic pants and shoes that make him seem like he's stepped out of a male fashion magazine. Far more fashionable than most males in these competitions who look like they're wearing their father's Sunday suits. He is beautiful. Dark haired, thin and fit, handsome and not into me at all (I'm not into him either). We've been best friends since third grade in Mrs. Hale's class.

My insides shimmy, but I nod. "Cameron. Remember Cameron."

"What?" He adjusts his black-framed, hipster glasses which he pulls off to perfection.

"Just channeling Cameron." I tug on the bottom of my matching charcoal gray jacket.

Liam reaches out, fixes my collar, and then takes both of my hands in his. Leaning forward, he presses his forehead to mine. He smells like wintergreen mint, familiar and comforting. "We've got this. We've practiced this. We know it. We. Know. It."

I close my eyes. "We do," I repeat, and my heartbeat slows to the rhythm of his words. Liam. My best friend. "Our last time in duo," I whisper. Tears threaten to fall. "What am I going to do without you?"

He pulls back but keeps hold of my hands. "Do. Not. Cry." Hand squeeze. "You have to keep your make-up looking good. Game faces. Let's kick the shit out of this speech, like Cameron did the car."

I smile, because he knows me, and I nod. "Let's do it."

Our names are called. We walk from the wings out onto the stage and take our marks.

We slay it. Of course we do, because that's who we are.

Later, Liam and I are at my house for our usual Saturday night John Hughes movie of the week. It's what we always do on a Saturday night, except for that one Saturday junior year when I went off the rails. The popcorn is made, drinks are chilling, and *Pretty in Pink* is cued up. While we wait for Ginny — our other bestie — to arrive, we both scroll through Instagram.

"Look at this one," Liam says. He's on the floor with his back against the couch. His legs — fit in cotton twill — are stretched out in front of him, crossed at the ankles. He holds up his phone.

"What is that?" I ask.

"It's Baker's house."

"Baker? As in Atticus Baker?"

He nods. "Party there tonight." He continues to examine his phone, and I watch him.

Instead of scrolling through the feed, he stops and scrutinizes Atticus Baker's page. Picture after picture, even reading the comments. It strikes me, because Liam hasn't ever expressed an interest in anyone specific (he's kind of private like that). As he looks through Atticus Baker's feed, it dawns on me how much of a risk Liam took to tell his truth. How lonely it might be in our small, conservative town. Lately, with graduation impending, I've thought about what kind of risks I've taken in my life (that one time junior year notwithstanding), and the answer has been none.

"I see you, Liam. You think Atticus is hot," I say with a giggle.

"Who doesn't? He's gorgeous."

He continues to study every single picture Atticus has posted, and I recognize familiarity in his actions. I've done it. My own phone, at the moment, is open to Tanner James's IG feed, as per usual. I press on his story and watch a video of him walking into Baker's party, but I don't show Liam. He doesn't approve of my infatuation with one of the biggest f-boys at school. I don't blame him; it's suspect.

Instead, I reach out and ruffle Liam's hair, which I know he hates. "But you like him like him."

"Stop!" He lurches forward to get out from under the destructive force of my hand and adjusts his hair back into place, not that I could have done much to those product-laced locks. "And shut up. I don't." His ears turn red.

"You are so lying." I grin and search for Atticus's IG feed on my phone. "He is really handsome," I say when I find it.

I select a gorgeous picture of Atticus and turn my phone to show him. Liam glances at it but looks away, aloof and noncommittal. Even I can't detach from the beauty. Atticus is gorgeous: tall, black, stylish, fit. He's a basketball player at our high school and got a full ride to St. Mary's in California. All of his pictures have this low-key, I'm-so-casual vibe in a matching filter, so there's no way it's casual. But, damn. "Liam. He's so hot, you have my approval," I tell him, even though I know how horrible and objectifying it sounds. Not that Liam needs my approval.

He groans. "Stop, Emma. For real. Atticus is like–" He pauses and turns his shoulders so he's facing me. "Look–"

"Mr. Liam, sir, I don't much feel like one of your lectures," I interrupt in my best patronizing student voice, because Liam is always lecturing me. Mansplaining. The jerk.

"Atticus is like — out of my league. And that's *if* he's gay." He looks down at his phone again. "I mean, I think I got some vibes, but my vibes are inexperienced. I have no idea what I'm doing. Besides, how many openly gay men do you think there are in this backwater, hick-horrible town?" He offers an old man grunt of disgust and readjusts himself with his back against the couch's seat again. "I can't wait to get out of here."

I understand his sentiment, though my prison is of a different kind: Christian family, striving for perfection where nothing real ever happens. Okay, maybe that's not fair, but it's how I feel sometimes. I can't wait to leave and distance myself from stifling expectations to experience my own version of freedom.

I try to give Liam a pep talk anyway. "None of us know what we're doing. We're all faking it. Ferris is the only one who seems to have it all figured out, and he's a fictional character. No one is like that."

"Has what figured out?" Ginny asks from behind us. Liam and I turn and watch her walk into the finished basement from the stairs. "Your dad said to come down, and he'll bring us some fresh cookies when they're out of the oven."

The third of our Bueller troop flops onto the couch next to me with her fresh-coated vanilla scent. She's been on a new kick to live as a 1970's hippie in order to explore the ideology of antidisestablishmentarianism, mostly to annoy her dad and stepmom. The outfit today: tie-dye cotton maxi-skirt she made herself and a black shirt without a bra (which is very noticeable because of her gorgeous boobs and high beams she's been very proud of since she got them). The whole no bra thing has really pushed the buttons of her stepmom which Ginny loves to do more than anything. She lays her head on my shoulder and threads her arm through mine.

"Life," I say, in answer to her original question.

"Our parents don't even have life figured out. Obviously," Ginny replies. "Case in point: my dad and step-monster. How could we — mere eighteen-year-olds? I take that back. We might have it more together."

"Something new?" I ask. The last installment of *The Life and Times of Ginny Donnelly* had her stepmother forcing her to paint her bedroom since she's leaving for college soon. Her stepmom is determined to convert Ginny's room into a fitness haven and has been taking measurements for her equipment.

"Besides Operation Kick Ginny Out of Her Room? Nothing new. I don't want to talk about them, or the fact that she made me go through my closet to consolidate everything into boxes for storage."

"Sorry, Gin." I squeeze her arm with mine. "On a happier note, we were discussing something intriguing. Specifically, Liam's crush on Atticus Baker."

He turns his back to us and resumes his stylish leaning against the couch, looking like a modern James Dean. He's got it all: the hair, the glasses, the pout.

Ginny sits up. "Atticus Baker? Man, he's hot."

"That's what I said."

"Is he gay?"

"We could run a new operation: Find out if Atticus Baker is Gay," I offer. "We could all slide into his DM, and see?"

"Emma." Liam's voice is threaded with a warning, like a brother

7

who has reached the threshold of annoyance.

I smile. "I'm sorry, Liam. Am I hurting your feelings?" I lean toward him and nuzzle his ear.

He moves to get away from me again. "No." He swats at me. "And no offense, but we know how the last operation you planned went."

I glance at Ginny, who raises her eyebrows and tilts her head. "He has a point."

I know they're referring to the junior year debacle. To be fair, if I was going to sneak out and go to a party, I was going to go all in. Especially if getting caught by my parents was a risk. I hadn't gotten caught, but I had gotten what I'd been after: a kiss — a gorgeously memorable hot kiss that I hadn't been able to forget. From Tanner James. "Everything turned out okay. We didn't get into trouble. Really, when you list out the successes against the failures, that was a win-win."

Liam looks at me like I'm delusional, and perhaps I am. "Emma, if you think you won in that situation, you're wrong. You haven't stopped infatuating about the school's biggest douchebag since. And for someone who claims to be a feminist, that's some contradictory bullshit."

I look to Ginny for backup, which I don't get. "He's right." She shrugs and flops against the couch. "It's been over a year, and you're still struggling with it."

They're both right. I sigh because I *am* infatuated with Tanner James, and I know better. "It doesn't matter. Graduation is two weeks away. We're going to kick ass, say our smarty-pants speeches, and leave for college. Which I will cry about later. Tanner James will be old news. My infatuation with him will be spent as I walk onto a college campus as a co-ed surrounded by beautiful men and women and a playground of sexual awakening."

Ginny and Liam glance at one another with saucer-shaped eyes and then collapse with laughter.

"Emma! I can't believe you just said that." Liam laughs even harder.

"Sexual Awakening. Emma." Ginny shrieks, falling away from me at her waist.

"Wow. You're giving me a complex."

When their laughter subsides, Liam climbs up onto the couch.

With me in between them, sulking, my arms crossed over my chest, I say, "You make me sound like a prude."

"That's not what we mean." Liam pats my leg. "I'm sorry if I hurt your feelings. I just—" He pauses and looks at me over the top of his glasses, reminding me of his dad. "Emma, you're pretty conservative when it comes to stuff like that. And scared about, like everything."

"What? Sex?" I say, still pouting but knowing he's right. I haven't done much in my eighteen years besides masturbate. I'm not ignorant about sex. I may have been raised with Christian parents, but they have been open and frank about sex. While the discussions have moved around the naturalness of the act, the underlying message has been an expectation to wait until marriage. Besides the junior year operation, I'd kissed a couple of other guys. Add to that my date for junior prom, Chris Keller, who tried to pressure me into sex and went so far as to grope me in the limo. I'd slapped him (so much for uncomplicated). Without a doubt, I'm curious and interested in sex, but it's clear my wiring leads to the red wire, not meaningless romps in the back of limos.

"Yeah, sex," Ginny says. "You overthink everything. Sex, like, isn't a thinking endeavor. It's all feeling."

I stand up to get away from them and their words, which I recognize as true but don't want to. "I'm not scared of sex."

Liam stands and mirrors me. "Emma — you're Claire." He points at the TV screen where *Pretty in Pink* waits for us.

I narrow my eyes at him. "I'm not Claire, who's in *The Breakfast Club,* by the way. I'm not a stuck-up, snobby, princess, tease."

"No. Not like that part. Like the sexually repressed part," Ginny says. "The one who secretly likes the bad boy but won't act on it."

"Except—" I hold up a finger for emphasis— "I went into the closet with bad boy John Bender just like she did, only it was junior year with

9

Tanner James." I want to lash out at Liam who's checking out a guy but is too scared to find out if he's gay. And Ginny, who slept with her last boyfriend because she wanted to "get over" her virginity. With my hands on my hips, ready to deflect, I pause and bite my tongue. It's petty and mean, and I love them too much.

"Emma." Ginny's chin falls against her chest, and she stares at me under her lashes. "You had to be drunk to do it."

She's right. *Operation Kiss Tanner James* required me to be drunk, because I couldn't muster up the courage to be bold. But then when had I ever? If it wasn't about church, or school, or duo with Liam — things that I could control — when had I ever been brave?

"Fresh cookies, hot from the oven." My dad with plate in hand maneuvers down the steps into the basement. He looks up with a smile when he reaches the bottom and pauses a moment, assessing the tension in the room. "Everything alright?"

"Perfect." I cross my arms over my chest.

"Those cookies smell delicious, Mr. Matthews," Liam says, turning on the couch to face my father.

Kiss ass.

"How many times have I said it's okay to call me Mo?"

Liam snags a cookie from the plate as my dad sets it on the table between the couch and the TV. "Thanks, Mo."

Dad straightens, walks over to me, and gives me a side hug.

"Thanks, Dad."

"*Pretty in Pink* night?" His eyes bounce from me to Liam to Ginny. He lingers and clears his throat. "Not many of these left, huh?"

We all mumble affirmations at him. I'm sure none of us are truly ready to come to terms with that fact yet, even if we say we're ready to leave.

"I'll leave you to it, then." He squeezes me against his side once more and then disappears back up the stairs.

After he's gone, I look at my friends feeling hurt and vulnerable. They might as well have just said I was the most boring person on the planet — and they'd probably be right.

Ginny pats the couch cushion next to her and holds her arms out to me.

I walk into them, flop forward, and lay against her awkwardly.

"Your Emma-think isn't a bad thing. It's an Emma thing. You're awesome. When you're ready — you'll know," she says. "In fact, because you're you, you'll probably have the best first experience of us all. All that thinking and analysis to make sure."

I move off of her to sit.

"And," Ginny says, "believe me. You don't want a Dean on your hands." Each of us snorts in reference to her first, the aftermath of just trying to "get over it." She shudders and takes my hand in hers. "Maybe it will be like a sexual awakening in college next year, or maybe it will be a hot someone this summer. Perhaps it will be in four years, or maybe it will be on your wedding night. It doesn't matter. What matters is YOU get to decide that for yourself, and that will make it perfect."

Liam sits down on the other side of me and takes my hand. "And I'll be there cheering you on for your first encounter with the D, or the V — whichever you prefer."

"I don't know why this suddenly became about me."

"Here. We can make it about me," Liam says. "I'm still a virgin."

"A status you'd like to change with Atticus Baker." I wiggle my eyebrows at him.

He smacks my shoulder. "Shut it, bitch." Then he chuckles.

"Let's get this John Hughes night moving already. Turn on the movie. Wait, Pretty in Pink? Maybe we should switch it to The Breakfast Club." Ginny lets me go and leans forward for popcorn. "We've got some analysis to do on that dialogue between Allison and Claire tonight, I think."

After an argument about sticking with our planned movie schedule, we watch *Pretty in Pink*. Ginny relents because Andie needs analysis of her attitudes about men: douchebags versus the best-friend. I point out one of my best friends is gay and the other one isn't; it's not an option in all circumstances. We're all in agreement that Andie should have ended up with Duckie (cue giant eye rolls), but as the movie plays, I'm distracted. I attempt to stay in it with my friends since our John Hughes movie nights are dwindling down to a handful. My mind keeps turning back to junior year. I think about how I'd played that night and the aftermath and wish I'd been braver.

tanner

We walk into Atticus Baker's party like kings: Griff, Danny, Josh and me. Senior year, three years of running the party game like professionals, and stories to never tell our kids (I'm not convinced I'm ever having any). The news of our arrival moves through the house like a sound wave. This scene used to be fun. It used to make me feel like I was relevant. We pose for someone's IG story, throwing deuces. Always the same story. Now, I'm bored as fuck, trailing behind the crew but smiling at the greetings, because that's the role I play.

"Tanner." Baker slaps a hand on my shoulder.

I look up at him. Basketball god at school, he's taller than me by at least four inches, and I'm six-one. "Hey, Baker."

We shake hands with a half hug, and then he greets the rest of my crew while I glance around the room. It's an ultra-modern place with a retro feel. The sunken living room is littered with bodies talking, laughing, drinking. Lights are low, with a moody lo-fi glow, and the air is heavy with tension. Bass pulses through the house speakers, and people dance. I hear someone scream, which draws my gaze beyond the sliding glass doors, and I watch as a girl gets thrown into the pool outside.

"This is lit, Baker." Griff scans the scene.

I look down at the floor instead of at Griff because, lately when I do, I just feel angry. For some reason, I feel like I'm in a play reciting the lines and making my set marks on the stage. The next scene has us getting drunk — not sloppy drunk, just enough to take the edge off. Then we'll hook up with whichever conquest for the night. Danny and Josh might, or they'll find stoner haven, and spend the night smoking out and talking philosophy. I'll have sex with someone because that's the role I play; it's what I usually do because by the time I'm drunk, I'm blocking loneliness. Griff will find a willing body, too, for whatever his reasons are. Our friendship isn't deep enough to have real conversations about it, so his motivation is a mystery to me. It's become a boring, predictable production.

"Glad you guys showed." Atticus directs us through the house to the booze.

Glad you guys showed. The statement hangs like a wet towel on a line in my mind. Because we're the party, I suppose, bringing the clout with us. It's the story we've written. I'm not feeling it and glance around the room at all the faces. Most of them I know. There are a few I don't. Eyes follow me. I notice mouths move, and then eyes slide back with knowing, curious, and inviting smiles. It makes me feel bored, tired, and wish I was at home reading. I started rereading Saul Annick's *Kaleidoscope Concussion* for the billionth time, and I picture it sitting on my nightstand next to my bed, waiting.

I turn my back to the telegraphed invitations and follow Atticus into the kitchen. He hands me a beer.

"Thanks." I take a sip and feel the bitterness hit my gut like acid.

I shouldn't have come. It isn't that I don't like Atticus. I do. He's a solid guy, and we've always gotten along. Hell, I get along with almost anyone. I just hadn't wanted to come, but Griff whined me into it like he always does lately. I let him, because he's my best friend. My bro. But after three years of the party life and not a whole lot worthwhile to show for it, I'm weary.

I take another sip, wondering when that began. I picture Emma

Matthews in my mind a few months ago, outside The Revolution club, breath coming from her pretty smiling mouth like puffs of magic. She'd waved at me, well, back at me. I'd inexplicably waved first. I'd raised my hand without thinking about it the moment I saw her, and that kiss junior year moved through my body like muscle memory, as if it had just happened. When she'd raised her hand, a tentative wave and a smile to match, as if she doubted I was waving at her, my lungs had tightened. I'd overheated with unspent energy despite the January cold. Emma. Her laugh. Raising my hand. Her smile. Her wave in return. Now, I shake my head as the golden liquid in the cup comes back into focus, and I take another sip.

Griff bumps my arm and nods toward something behind me.

I turn my head.

"Laura Hoff." Griff sips his drink. "She's effin' hot. You could hit that."

I turn away and lean against the gigantic kitchen island. I'm not interested in Laura Hoff. There was a time a couple of years ago, I would have been. Meaningless sex. No complications. I've grown weary of that too. "Why does it always feel like you're pimping me out?"

"What the ever-loving ef, T? You're being a bitch tonight. Did you lose your balls and grow a vagina?"

"I told you I didn't want to go out."

"My point exactly."

I don't tell him to *fuck off.* It would be a waste of my breath.

"It's senior year." Danny joins us, leaning against the island next to me. He smiles, one of those innocuous smiles that never presses anyone's buttons. "Kind of like the last hurrah before we go our separate ways." Always so positive. Danny's joining the military. He swears in after graduation.

"I don't want to invoke it, but I might have to remind you of Bro Code, T," Griff says, which sort of feels like a threat and climbs onto my back like added weight.

Bro Code is a bullshit agreement we made when we were fifteen after I lost my virginity to my mom's friend Pam (no, my mom doesn't know). I'd filled in the boys on the facts of life as I saw them (and everything she'd taught me), and the pact to support the sexual conquests of one another was born. The Bro Code: always have one another's back for the effort of a lay. The thing was, most of the time, for whatever reason, the Bro Code always came down to me leading the way. I'm a better talker than Griff, whose idea of flirting is throwing around disjointed one-liners that resemble insults. I'm funnier than all of them. Josh is nicer than me. Danny too, but he's shy. I'm the de facto lead — the first of us to pop his cherry — though Griff is our social director. In considering the Bro Code agreement, Griff has probably gained the most.

At one time, the Bro Code made me feel connected to them. All for one, one for all sorta thing. They are my family, my missing brother turned into three. With the wreckage of my family — the death of my brother followed by the explosion of my parents' marriage — being important and necessary to my boys, being wanted by women, made me feel something. Fulfilled, I guess. Now, it feels like a trap, because I can see the chains, and the bars attached. I have this horrible sense that Bro Code never had anything to do with actual friendship. That makes me feel unsettled.

I sigh and stare into the cup.

"Bro Code?" Josh says, stuffing his face with chips and salsa. "Why would you throw that out there, Griff? Tanner's always game."

Except I'm not. Not anymore, and this is a new awareness. I don't want to be here. I don't want to get drunk or stoned. I don't want to have sex with someone random. I want something else, something different, even if I'm not sure yet what *it* is. I set down my drink and walk away.

"Yo!" Griff yells at me. "Tanner!"

I ignore him and slide past gyrating bodies out through the glass door into the night. I shove my hands into my pockets; the cool night clings to my skin. There aren't too many people poolside — a few — which makes it easy to find a spot to isolate myself, to take a moment

16

to figure my shit out. Except I have a feeling this has only just begun, whatever that means.

"Hey." A voice draws me away from the darkened landscape beyond the house.

I turn my head and find Laura Hoff, no doubt sent over by Griff, who's interested in smashing with one of her friends. I lift my eyebrows in a greeting. "Hey, Laura." She's pretty: short blond hair, pretty brown eyes and pouty mouth. Petite. I glance behind me and see Griff in the window. He's talking to a girl. I look away and resume my moody contemplation of what's beyond the light of the pool deck where we're standing.

"Everyone wondered when you guys would get here." She mimics my stance, turning so we're shoulder-to-shoulder looking out into the darkness.

I notice her cross her arms over her chest to keep out the chill, or from insecurity; I'm not sure which. I wonder why she's out here. What does she have to gain from talking to the notorious f-boy Tanner James? I'm shit and have nothing really going for me except a job at my dad's construction company after graduation. Whoop-de-doo. No one really sees me. They see the persona, the party boy, because that's the legacy I've made.

"Why?" I ask.

"You guys make it fun."

I hum a response. "People can't make their own fun?" It feels as acidic as it sounds.

She isn't sure what to say to that, maybe a bit surprised by my vibe. "You okay?"

"No. I'm not."

Her face relaxes and sort of slips toward added insecurity and doubt. I see her glance back at the house and then back at me. "Griff thought you might like some company."

I sigh and shake my head, though I doubt she'd catch it. Predictable. "I'm good," I tell her in an effort to channel Danny's kindness or Josh's laissez faire approach to life. Josh would tell her more than he needed, and Danny would feel like he needed to make her feel better. I don't need to do either. I don't really know her that well.

"You want company?"

"Not really," I say and push my hands deeper into my pockets.

An awkward silence settles around us until she mutters, "Okay," and then turns and walks away.

I take a deep breath. I should leave before I hurt anyone else's feelings. Instead of leaving though, I pinch the bridge of my nose, and then sit on one of the deck chairs to hide. I'm not ready to face the inevitable conflict that will occur with Griff.

I lay back in the chair to stare at the sky. It's a clear night, and Atticus lives a little out of town, so there are lots of stars. The starry sky settles me.

Before Rory died, we'd sneak out onto the roof of our house to stargaze. Well, Rory did. I just followed my older brother, content to bask in his shadow. He'd tell me about space stuff he learned, and thought was cool because one day he was going to be an astronaut. Then — because I was little — I'd ask him to tell me star stories. He did. Made up stuff about pretend planets, aliens, monsters, and all of the adventures stringing them together. I loved it.

After he died, I'd sneak into his bedroom during my parents' fights. I'd duck through the window, scramble across the shingles of the roof like Rory and I used to do on our star adventures before he got sick. I'd tuck myself into a spot near a dormer — the farthest we could venture onto the steeply pitched roof. If the sun was still up, I'd watch the neighborhood. Watching the cars drive past on the street or walkers meander by blocked the yelling of my parents with all the walls between us. They never looked for me. Never knew where I was.

If it was dark, I'd look up at the sky to find Rory's and my favorite star, broken hearted because I wasn't sure which one it was. I hadn't thought to ask my big brother to clarify because I'd been too little. So I just looked up into the sky and hoped I was speaking to the right one. I'd tell him about Mom and Dad. I'd cry, staring up at the vibrant sky, feeling alone and invisible.

The sound of approaching footsteps interrupts my thoughts, and I brace myself for Griff, pissed that I sent Laura away. I mentally prepare to tell him to sleep with her himself if he thinks she's so hot, but it isn't Griff who draws up a chair next to me and sits down. It's Atticus.

"Yo."

I give him a head nod.

"Can I join you?"

"Your house, dude."

He smiles and hands me a cup. "Thought you might need a refresher."

"Thanks." Silence walks around us for a bit. "What're you doing out here?" I finally ask.

"Didn't really feel like a party."

I look over at him, confused. "It's your house, Atticus."

He shrugs, smiles, and takes a sip of his drink. "Teammates wanted a spot tonight, and my parents were out of town."

"Could have said 'no.'" And I realize I could have tried harder to stick to my 'no.'

"What's one party? I figure everything's about to change." There's something in the way he says this that is heavy with what has remained inside of him.

"You good?"

He doesn't answer right away. Waits. Then he says, "Everything good with you? Isn't like you to be at a party, turn down the prettiest girl, and then sulk in the dark."

I chuckle. He's right. "I just didn't feel like a party," I parrot back to him, then add, "I'm just over it."

"I feel you."

"Really? How's that?"

"Probably most of us are carting around shit inside that won't make it out into the light until we start the next book of the series."

I nod, though I realize my next act is here. I won't be leaving, still stuck between my parents and their perpetual war. He's got a scholarship to play basketball at the collegiate level and the grades to keep it. "You feel like talking about it?"

"Do you?"

It's my turn to be quiet, but eventually I say, "Party shit is old, and Griff wants everything to stay the same."

"And he's your boy."

"Yeah."

Atticus takes another sip and then stares intently at the cup. "I don't think my boys would get who I really am."

"If they're your real boys, then they will." I hear the wisdom in my words that I hadn't considered. If Griff, Danny, and Josh are my real friends, they'd respect any changes I want to make, right?

"Sounds easier than it is, though."

I nod. "Yeah. Who knew things would feel so complicated?"

We sit for a while, listening to the party happening behind us, lost in our own thoughts.

"Maybe living the truth is all we got though." Atticus's voice slices through the comfortable silence. "Like anything less is frontin'."

"And anyone who matters is going to understand."

Atticus nods.

There's a loud crash from somewhere inside the house.

"Shit. I better check on that." He stands up. "Good talk, T." We slide palms and finish with a fist bump.

I stay a while longer in the darkness pondering his claim: anything less than living our truth is a front. I suppose he's right as long as one knows what their truth is. I'm untethered from whatever the want is and instead chained to an expectation.

junior year
(a little over a year earlier)

"The truth about routine: it's fucking boring. Change that shit up! The bullshit of my drab monotony of grays was rooted in the drugs dealt by my psychiatrist pusher: 'Take this. Take that. It'll fix you right up.' Only I still couldn't sleep, and when I melted into the routine of not taking those little, dull, white pills, I started seeing brilliant colors which my jagged mind cut into like a stained-glass kaleidoscope."

-unnamed protagonist, *Kaleidoscope Concussion* by Saul Annick

tanner

I was at the crossroads of just enough to drink and too much, so I waved off Griff's offer of another. Penelope Jordan had been staring at me earlier, practically gave Deb Sheffner a lap dance and watched me while she did it. The invitation had been clear. Not the most original tease, but enough for me to figure she was DTF. That was what I did, after all, fuck. It sounded bad, but it was working for me on a couple of levels. First, there was the superficial level of enjoyment and release, but it wasn't just the alcohol or even the sex. That was the second level: the momentary numbness and visibility. Here was the thing: I'd found myself tired of the whole predictable game, and in the quiet moments by myself, was beginning to realize I was sad more than happy.

I stood. "I'm going," I told Griff, who had a girl sitting on his lap I didn't know.

He smiled over her shoulder at me and presented his knuckles. The girl whispered something in his ear, and Griff laughed. She was attractive. Dark haired.

My mind drifted to Emma Matthews (which was strange since we weren't friends). I'd seen her the day before with her friend, Liam, hanging a poster for some club or function in the hall after school, heads together about something. Under usual circumstances, I wouldn't have noticed, but in this case, I had because I'd noticed Emma and how cute she was. I had noticed her for a while, but she was out of my league.

Emma wouldn't be partying like this. She definitely wouldn't be sitting in Griff's lap, and if she were, it would piss me off, but I didn't consider why. She was probably at home, doing something productive, like homework, or a group study session. Perhaps she was doing something fun and wholesome, like a movie with her friends. I wondered if she went to the movies. Though I wasn't exactly sure why I wondered, because I wasn't a big movie goer (too boring to sit in one spot for too long).

Why was I even thinking of Emma at all?

It wasn't like we talked. Sometimes, I thought she might be looking at me in the cafeteria at school or in the hallway as we passed one another. Her pretty eyes always slid away, but they made me curious. What color were they? Was she just glancing at me, or was she looking? I used to think about her. A lot. That started in the eighth grade when she yelled at Cole Butler in science during a lab. She'd been so fiery and funny. The memory still made me smile. We hadn't had many classes together — one or two, maybe — because she actually tried at school.

I shook my head to get my errant thoughts about Emma out of my mind. Leaving Griff and Wannabe Emma behind, I walked through the living room.

Deb stopped me with a hand on my chest. "Hey, Tanner. Want to dance?" An invitation.

The message was clear: I could have stayed there with her and gotten laid, but it made me tired. Instead I said, "I'm looking for Penelope," and even as I said it, I was hoping she'd already left.

Deb shrugged, because that was as much as I meant to her. "Upstairs," she told me and returned to grinding to the music with her group of friends.

I moved through the crush of people toward the stairs, even though I wasn't sure why I was going through these motions. A different choice seemed an impossibility, though I couldn't articulate why that was so. Josh and Danny were sitting in a group smoking weed, and they offered me a head nod as I passed. I gave them an eyebrow raise in return and started up the stairs.

Near the top, I almost tripped on someone sitting on the steps. "Whoa." It was a girl folded over on herself, and because I'm not a complete douchebag, despite what I know has been said about me, I leaned down and asked her, "You okay?"

The girl tipped her head up to look at me, and suddenly, I was looking into the face of...

"Emma Matthews?"

She smiled, and it lit up her eyes — dark blue with swirls of gray — like stars in a dark sky. "Tanner James."

"Are you drunk?" I asked. I was too, but not enough to help me forget that Emma was the object of my secret fantasies, along with the fact I'd just been thinking about her. I shook my head to make sure I wasn't dreaming. There wasn't anything in our experiences that should have contributed to our paths crossing, and yet, there she was, as if I'd conjured her. "What are you doing here?"

"I'm feeling really good." She smiled again, and I remembered feeling that smile in my stomach like a lead weight had melted into molten liquid.

"Why are you sitting here on the stairs?"

"Waiting."

"For what?"

"You." She giggled.

That made no sense. First, why would Emma Matthews be at this party? Second, why would she be drunk? And third, why would she say she was waiting for me? I wondered if someone was playing a joke on me and even looked around, but it was just the two of us in the hallway. I slid down the wall and sat next to her. "You're definitely drunk if you're waiting for me."

"Did I say that?"

"Yeah."

"Oh. That's a secret." She pressed a finger to my lips, and that touch dove all the way from the top of my neck to the base of my spine like I'd been zapped with electricity. "I'm supposed to find Liam." Then she moved her finger from my lips to hers, her dark blue eyes — flecks of green and aqua too — never leaving my mouth. "Shh."

My heart pounded in my chest, excited by the form her lips took against her finger. "Damn, Emma. I didn't know you drank."

"Me either."

I attempted an inconspicuous adjustment of my pants, because I started feeling that tingle in my crotch and needed to calm that shit down. I chuckled, amused, because I hadn't caught wood from just a look and a touch since I was, like, fourteen. I decided the honorable thing to do was help her find her friend, which led to the decision to dump looking for Penelope. I hadn't really wanted to be with Penelope outside of sex anyway, and that left me feeling dirty. "Shall we go look for Liam?"

Her eyes roved over every inch of my face. She reached up and touched my lips with her fingertips again; it was tender. "You have a nice mouth, Tanner James."

My stomach tightened. I tried to remember that reaction. It was a hungry craving, the anticipation of the satiation of a voracious appetite, but it was also so distant. I hadn't been aware I'd been missing it until it resurfaced inside of me.

"You want to hear a secret?" she asked and leaned closer to me, though I had the impression she thought she was whispering. "I've wanted to try and kiss it."

Her admission made me smile, and my heart thumped a little more. I realized that while I'd been fantasizing about her, perhaps she'd thought about me too. Knowing that made me feel buoyant. "You have? Well, I could remedy that for you, but I'm afraid you wouldn't remember it. I would want you to." It was a truth. I wanted Emma to remember me.

"I would," she said, wide-eyed, and nodded. "I promise."

I stood up, needing the distance, because I was afraid I might kiss her. As I did, she held my arm, and I almost toppled onto her. I self-corrected and took her hand to help her up. Once upright, she stumbled against me, and I caught her waist with my hands while her other arm wrapped around my neck. My heart was now knocking against the wall of my ribs. She was so close, so pretty, so pressed against me. I looked at her mouth, heart-shaped pink. She licked her lips, and my belly buzzed. I wanted to kiss her so badly, but I chickened out, which was part of why I didn't; it also felt wrong on some level. I could take advantage, but I didn't want to. On the other hand, I wanted to extend my time with her, so when I said, "Come on. Let's go look for Liam." I took her deeper into the house instead of down the stairs, which was probably the more likely place to look. I wasn't being altruistic.

She put her hand in mine.

I noticed how soft her skin was, and I wondered about the rest of her.

"I don't want to find Liam," she insisted as we walked down the hall. "I want to wait for Tanner."

"I'm right here." I looked over my shoulder at her.

Her eyes brightened again, the outside corners scrunching with joy. "Oh! It is you."

"How much did you have to drink, Em?" I asked.

She held up four fingers. "Two."

"We should get you some water. Let's find a place for you to sit."

I started testing doors in the hallway. Honestly, on one level, I knew what I was doing. I wanted to be alone with her, even if I didn't want to cheapen the moment. I think I justified it to myself. I needed to find her a place to sober up. Deep down, though, it was a lingering understanding of a latent wish buried in the darkness of my fantasies attached to what she'd said: *Waiting. For you. You have a nice mouth. I've wanted to try and kiss it.*

26

Emma Matthews was waiting for me.

The knowledge made my heart swell even if I couldn't believe it. Even if I didn't — couldn't — trust it. I wanted to keep the idea close, to remember it, to hold it tight. I knew the moment this was over, it would slip away.

"Em?" I asked as I tested another door.

She made a moaning noise to indicate she'd heard me.

"Why were you waiting for me?"

"I like Tanner. I want to be brave."

My brain wasn't quick enough, because it was slugging through the marsh of alcohol. I understood what she was saying, but I didn't quite comprehend it. "You like me?"

She nodded emphatically. "I saw him."

"What did you see?" I asked her as I tested another door.

"He helped Connor. At lunch. I saw him. I see him. Everyday. He helps Connor."

Lunch time. Connor Festner, a kid I help with his tray. Griff gives me shit for it, but Connor is pretty badass and probably beats Griff's butt playing Duty online. Connor's given me tons of gaming pointers.

She had been watching me at lunch. I'd known it. My expanded heart compressed, constricted in my chest with a pressure that somehow made me feel like I might be floating off into space without oxygen.

I tested another door. This one opened. The bedroom was empty, and I took a deep breath. Relief. "Here." I helped her sit on the bed. "Let me have your cup, and I'll fill it with water."

She handed me her red cup, and I took it into the bathroom. I rinsed it out and put in water. Before I walked back into the room, I glanced at myself in the mirror. I stared into my own eyes and whispered to my reflection: "It's Emma. Don't be a dick."

When I returned to the room, she was curled up on the bed, eyes closed. "Here, Em."

She turned her head, looked at me and smiled as if it was the first time she'd seen me that night. "Tanner!" She reached for me, and I

27

had the impression she wanted me to stretch out next to her.

Don't be a dick, I reminded myself and helped her to sit back up. "Drink some water."

She took a sip. "Liam says I'm dumb."

"That isn't nice of him." Her statement annoyed me. I sat down next to her, suddenly absolved we weren't looking for him.

She shook her head. "No. Not like that." She stopped and took another sip. "Because I wanted to come to find you."

"Why?"

"I'm scared."

"Of what?"

"Of everything." She took another sip and then leaned her head against my shoulder.

I could smell her — a nice scent that was clean and slightly sweet, like vanilla or cotton candy. I resisted the impulse to press my nose into her neck to find out for sure, or to run my tongue across her skin to taste it. Instead, we sat like that for a long time — her head on my shoulder, my hands in my lap and my brain chastising me for smelling her like a freak.

The doorknob wiggled several times as people tested the door; I was smart enough to lock it. Habit. I tried to tell myself it was because I was trying to protect Emma from my reputation, but it was also the temptation to maybe just get to kiss her once. I didn't make a move though, and that was unfamiliar — and kind of exciting — territory for me.

"Tell me what you're afraid of," I said eventually, ending the silence, and also because I wanted to know if she'd fallen asleep. I needed to keep my mind occupied with other things besides thoughts about kissing her. I was beginning to feel more coherent and sober.

"I told you. Everything." Her hands flailed out, and when they settled, one landed on my thigh. My skin tingled under her touch, and heat spread like radiant light from a lightbulb to illuminate all the dark parts of me.

I swallowed and closed my eyes to focus on her words. The words.

28

"Well, name me one thing."

"Failure."

"Everyone's afraid of that." I looked down at her hand. Casually rested. On my thigh. Emma's hand. Her fingernails were painted a bright green and matched her hoop earrings.

"Disappointing my parents," she said. "Disappointing God."

I looked at her then, the candor of her statement running through me almost as hot as her touch. It wasn't practiced. It wasn't her act of being flirty or a ploy to seduce me. It was just an honest statement. Maybe I couldn't relate to either of those, even if I wanted to. My parents were so blind to me outside of the tug-of-war they played, using me against one another. And God? Never experienced that in my life, unless having an orgasm counted as prayer. "And?"

She moved her head from my shoulder and turned to look at me. "Never kissing Tanner James."

My stomach did another of those nose dives into my body, toward my groin. The heat of her hand still warmed my leg. I noticed her eyes, fringed in thick lashes, rove over my face. They came to rest on my mouth. Under different circumstances, I probably wouldn't have cared and would have provided what she wanted. I wanted it — bad — but I'd found some weird sense of honor I hadn't been aware I had. "I can't, Em. You're drunk." These were those different circumstances. Emma represented a different kind of life I didn't think I deserved.

"You don't like me." She moved back, slumped a little, her shoulders rounding, and folded her hands in her lap. "It's okay."

I missed the weight of her hand on my leg. "It isn't that." I leaned forward to try and meet her gaze. "I do like you."

She sat up quickly, her eyes big and bright. "I got it! I will kiss you. Then you don't have to kiss me. I'll do the kissing."

This made me laugh, because I thought it was one of the cutest things I'd ever heard. And she was so excited by the prospect, as if she'd discovered something new. I couldn't remember having more fun on a Saturday night.

"Unless, you think I'm — ugly." Her eyebrows arched over her wide eyes, but now she couldn't look at me.

I shook my head. "Nope, Emma. I don't think that. At all."

Her eyes met mine again, and she said with a slight frown, "The easiness is wearing off. We better do this fast, before I come back."

I scrunched up my face. "What?"

"If I come back–" she tapped her head– "I'll be too scared. My head will get in the way. My bravery will melt off."

"Liquid courage." I tapped her cup.

She nodded. "I made a plan. I was waiting for you."

"Really?"

"I, maybe, drank a little too much. Miscalculated."

I smiled. "And you were waiting for me. Why?"

"To kiss you." She laid her hand on my arm.

I took a deep breath, as if her touch returned a missing piece of my soul, and I needed to breathe it in. Her admission had me unbalanced, however. My usual practiced lyrics receded from the surprise. I've had girls try and lure me with their sexuality, but this? This was totally new. "Why again, Em?"

"Because I saw you. You helped Connor. That's nice, Tanner. And I think it's sexy. And I don't want Keven Bennett to be my only kiss."

I glanced at her mouth, thought about her kissing Keven Bennett, and was annoyed by it. Then I looked at my hands in my lap. She saw me not because of how I looked. It was because I helped Connor that made me sexy to her. It wasn't partying or being drunk. It wasn't a rumor that I knew how to have sex. It wasn't being smart at school. It was because I'd done something unselfish. "Keven Bennett, huh?"

She wrinkled her nose. "He has a lizard tongue."

I chuckle. "That's not good."

She adjusted her body. "So, is it okay if I kiss you?"

"Who would you be kissing? Just for clarification." I was testing the truth, not believing it.

"Tanner James. You." She faced me, drawing her knees up between us, where they pressed against the outside of my thigh. "I see you. I'm not that drunk anymore."

Her words were enough for me to nod, to give myself permission to cross the line, and indulge my curiosity. "Yes. Okay."

"You have to turn." She directed me with her hands on my arms, turning me toward her but with her knees between us.

I watched her working out the problem, completely satisfied in the moment, enjoying her and her cute pout. Her dark, curly hair fell around her heart-shaped face as she looked down at our legs.

"This won't do."

"It does seem rather awkward."

She stood. "Stand up." She remained steady, the alcohol wearing off, and held her hands out to me.

I took them and stood. When I looked down at her, my heartbeat quickened. The movement of her eyes caressed my face, and for the first time, I understood what it felt like to be seen — really seen. For me, Tanner. Not because of some rumor about what I could do, or because there was enough alcohol in my system to lower my inhibitions.

"Tanner?" She reached up and put her hands on my face.

"Yes, Em?"

"Can you bend down? Just a little bit?" She drew me closer.

I leaned forward, cataloguing all of her attributes. My heart went bat-shit crazy inside my chest. I noticed the width of her blue eyes, the fullness of her dark eyebrows, the way her bottom lip was a tiny bit fuller than the top, the way her pert nose was slightly upturned and kissed with tiny freckles that reached out across her cheeks.

I couldn't believe she didn't have a boyfriend. Did I want to be a boyfriend? Why was I thinking about that? I wasn't boyfriend material.

Her gaze flicked to my lips — her tongue darted out to wet her own — then her eyes slipped up to my eyes before sliding shut as she pressed her lips to mine.

It was a gentle kiss, soft. Her mouth was warm and pliable against mine. My heart tripped into a more intense speed. Then her lips parted, and she used her tongue to coax me to be an active participant. As much as I tried to not be a dick, that was the last straw of my self-control. I answered the tease of her tongue with my own. Suddenly, where the kiss started as one-sided and tentative, it exploded, because my whole body was an exposed nerve ending. Every sensation — her hands in my hair, her mouth, her tongue, the whisper of her clothing when she moved, the soft noise she emitted because I became involved —was enough to light me on fire.

I'd dreamed of Emma.

I lifted her.

She wrapped her legs around my waist and hugged me closer with her arms around my neck.

Our tongues moved together, and it all felt like a first time. It was. With her. Exciting. Novel.

She moaned into my mouth.

I stumbled forward until her back was pressed against the wall and then my hands wandered, molded, massaged. I forgot myself. Just let go and felt. I didn't think about how or who or why. I got lost in all of the sensations. Then I returned back to myself, because I remembered who I was kissing. Emma. She was worth more than a bang at a party. By me. She was worth more than me. "Emma," I said into her mouth, and I continued kissing her, allowing myself just a little more.

"So good, Tanner." She moaned it.

Her sound almost broke my resolve to do the right thing, but I drew back. "We should stop."

Her eyes fluttered open, and she studied my face. "Okay." She laid a hand against my cheek. "I thought I was supposed to kiss you."

I searched her face, looked for the lie but found only honesty and naivety there. "You did."

"You kissed me back." She smiled. It was shy and tentative, beautiful and endearing.

"I did."

"I liked it."

"I liked it, too." I stepped back so she could stand.

Someone pounded on the door.

We both jumped.

Something was yelled about the police, followed by retreating footsteps which pounded down the hallway.

"Shit." I ran a hand through my hair. "You're going out first, okay?"

"We can go together."

"No." I shook my head. "You know we can't do that." There was no way I wanted Emma affected because of who I was.

"But—"

"No. Em. It's better this way."

She straightened her clothes, seeming far more coherent than however long it had been since I'd stumbled upon her in the stairwell. She opened the door while I pressed out of view against the other side, but she hesitated. It was as though she wanted to say something. I waited, my breath caught in my lungs, hopeful. What did I want her to say? But she didn't say anything and instead, disappeared through the door.

I waited — counted to fifteen — and willed my heart to slow down so my head could reorient; then I left the room and closed the door, as if I were shutting off the feelings Emma awoke in me. But I looked for her as I walked out of the house, even though I scolded myself for doing it. When I got outside, I saw her across the yard. She'd found Liam and her other friend, Ginny. Emma was turned, watching people move as if looking for something — or someone. I wanted her to see me, but I knew it was impossible. I was who I was, and I would only drag her down.

I turned, cut through the flowerbed, and walked away wishing things were different.

e m m a

Liam and Ginny were waiting outside as the party surged through the front door, and the house vomited people.

"Oh my god, Em! I couldn't find you, and I got so worried." Ginny drew me into her arms.

We stood in the street like stones in a moving river as a current of bodies flowed around us.

"It was fine." I scanned the faces, glanced back at the front door, hoping to catch one more look at Tanner. Hoping beyond hope that he hadn't asked me to leave before him because he was embarrassed to be seen with me, but afraid perhaps he was. When he'd found me at the top of the stairs, I might have been too drunk, having miscalculated how much and how quickly to consume it. The whole plan could have failed, but Tanner had stopped. Tanner had stayed. Now, still buzzing but wide awake with Tanner's kisses, I'm buzzed with residual warmth from his mouth and hands.

"What happened?" Liam wasn't smiling. Instead, his eyes were over bright with concern.

"Operation Kiss Tanner James was a success."

"You had sex with him?" Ginny's voice climbed ten decibels.

"No! Of course not." I smacked her arm.

"No! Of course not," Liam said at the same time I did.

We looked at one another. "Pinch, poke, you owe me a Coke!" we both chanted. He beat me with the matching movements.

"I owe you." I looked at the house again as the sludge of partiers moved past us. "That wasn't the plan, Ginny Donnelly!"

"What happened, then?" Ginny asked, drawing my attention back to her and Liam.

"We kissed." I kept the juicier tidbits to myself to savor later.

"We should go. I heard the police are coming." Liam pulled on my sleeve.

The three of us turned to move with the flow of revelers leaving for the night. We had quite a few blocks to walk to get to Ginny's house. I glanced over my shoulder one more time to look for Tanner but didn't see him.

A latent alcohol haze remained as we walked, and I kept the movie playing in my mind. Waiting on the stairs. Tanner stopped, sat down with me in the hall. We talked and laughed. I knew I was more forward — braver than I had ever been in my life thanks to the healthy buzz — telling him the truth of what I'd planned. He hadn't been bothered by it. He'd been a gentleman. He hadn't even tried to kiss me until I'd made the move.

I wondered if my forwardness was a sin. I knew King Solomon in *Song of Songs* warned, *do not arouse or awaken love until it so desires.* I knew this because my dad and mom had recited the verse whenever we had the sex talk. But Solomon had 700 wives or something ridiculous like that. I'm thinking he wasn't a very reputable source in regard to female sexuality. Tanner didn't seem to mind my forwardness. I smiled recalling it and touched my lips with my fingertips. The moment I'd looked up into his brown eyes, and they twinkled like brilliant stars offering light, I'd forgotten to be afraid.

"So?" Ginny asked. I could hear the smile in her voice despite the darkness. A streetlamp illuminated us a moment as we continued walking. Liam had his hands in his pockets, slightly ahead of Ginny and me, head down. Ginny looked at me, her eyebrows raised, with a knowing grin.

I couldn't contain my smile. Instead of saying anything, I squealed and did a little dance. Ginny joined me.

"Oh my god."

I knew Liam was rolling his eyes. "Shut it, Liam." I turned and threw my arms around him. Then I kissed his cheek. "Just be happy for me."

He pulled away from me and wiped his cheek against his shoulder without removing his hands from his pockets. "I don't want Tanner James spit anywhere on this body."

"Uh. Are you sure about that?"

"Yes!" he said. "Ew. He's nasty. And I think you deserve better too."

"Are you slut shaming her?" Ginny asked.

"No! I just–" But he didn't finish the thought.

I stopped in the middle of the road. Ginny and Liam continued walking until they noticed I wasn't still walking with them. "Wait. Liam?"

"What?"

He turned to look at me, and if I wasn't still buzzed, I probably wouldn't have asked the question. "Do you like Tanner? Like like him a little?" Liam had come out to me and Ginny a few months prior, so I was still trying to understand his world.

He shuddered. "No. I mean, there is no denying he's hot, but I do not like him. And newsflash: he doesn't bat for my team."

"Why so adamant?"

He walked back to me. "Because, Em." He reached out and grasped the tops of my arms. "I love you; I don't want you hurt. And Tanner James — well — he isn't the kind of guy who takes care of a nice girl's heart."

"Then why did you go along with this plan?"

He dropped his hands to his sides and shrugged. "Because you need to do you. Who am I to get in the way of your journey?"

"One of my best friends." I looped my arm with his. We walked toward Ginny, and I linked my other arm with hers, me between them.

"Would you have listened?" Liam asked.

"Nope."

We all laughed, and then I started singing our anthem from *Ferris Bueller's Day Off*, "Please Let Me Get What I Want." Their voices joined me, mostly off-key, and we walked down the road arm-in-arm like Ferris, Cameron and Sloane.

On Monday after the party, I looked for Tanner. Hopeful. Though to be honest, I knew before committing to the task of *Operation Kiss Tanner James*, I was taking a risk. There was a high probability that Tanner wouldn't be as affected by the kiss as I was. I wasn't a complete fool about his lifestyle, but I couldn't help but wish he'd felt something too — like I had. In my mind, I conjured Samantha from *Sixteen Candles* and the way she'd captured hot-guy Jake's attention. I'd imagined that if I went about it the right way, Tanner would see me like I saw him. And maybe we'd sit on a table and eat a birthday cake (okay, I knew better than to fantasize that; it hadn't even been a real cake!).

When he responded to the kiss, but then hadn't wanted to walk out with me, I hadn't been prepared for the way disappointment and confusion would mar up the inside of my heart. I couldn't blame him, really. I was Emma Matthews, and he was Tanner James. It was like trying to cross a social divide like Andie and Blaine in *Pretty in Pink*. I made the assumption it was because he was embarrassed that he'd kissed me. I knew that wasn't the only possibility. It just seemed the most plausible in my mind.

Then, at lunch, when I walked into the cafeteria, and I finally saw him, all the fears rolled up into a ball and sat at the center of my chest coated in hope. He was sitting with his friends, Griffin, Josh, and Danny. They acted like their normal obnoxious selves with their raucous talking and laughter. Greta Mills squealed, reaching over Tanner's back, her boobs pressed up against him as he held something out of her reach. It was clear she didn't really want whatever he was holding away from her. She wanted what I wanted: his attention.

Suddenly, his gaze connected with mine — just a moment — and my spine buzzed with anticipation. I just wanted a smile. *Tell me you remember*, I thought. *Let me know it wasn't just me who felt something.* Then his brown eyes shifted, and he turned away, looked up at Greta to offer her the sunshine of his smile.

Nothing.

My stomach clenched with self-loathing and constricted with want, even as tears burned the back of my eyes. I couldn't stop thinking about how stupid I was being — still wanting him. I knew it. I knew it walking into that party. I knew it was a possibility, but my smarts couldn't keep my emotions from making the leap from kiss to something more. I knew there was nothing about me that would be something that would hold Tanner's interest. Yet, foolishly, I'd hoped, and that was what I got for letting my guard down and taking a risk.

I slunk over to the lunch table where I sat with Ginny and Liam, but I'd lost my appetite.

"So, I was telling Ginny," Liam stopped speaking when he looked at me. "Emma? What happened?" He reached across the table and offered me a reassuring squeeze.

"Nothing. It's nothing." I couldn't help but glance at Tanner again. Greta was squealing like a pig now, though Tanner wasn't looking at her anymore and had passed off whatever he'd been holding to Josh. Greta was still laying across his back reaching, making sure Tanner had all the feel of her he could get. I rolled my eyes.

Liam followed my gaze and turned back to me. "Emma. I told–"

I held up my hand. "Don't Liam. Don't say 'I told you so.' Please. I got what I wanted."

His eyes softened around their almond-shaped edges behind his glasses, and his lips pouted, just a little. "Did you?"

I knew what he was asking. He knew me too well. He knew I had a mad crush on the wrong kind of boy — a boy that didn't look twice at a girl like me. But like all my plans (just like all of my efforts at school), it worked. I thought if I just got a kiss, the infatuation would be served. I could let it go. Chalk it up to a great kiss. Move on. I hadn't considered it would awaken something more in me.

"He's an asshole, Emma. He doesn't care about anyone but

himself," Ginny said.

I knew she was trying to make me feel better. It didn't. It served to make me feel like more of a weakling for wanting someone who didn't want me back.

I sighed.

Counted to three.

Then with another sigh, I straightened my spine and resolved to climb back into the box of safety where I'd insulated myself. Maybe that's what King Solomon meant: avoid the physical, to avoid the awakening, to avoid the hurt. He might not have been a good source about the roles of women, but maybe he had something on emotions; he was considered a wise king, after all. Whatever. I needed to focus on what I could control: school, my extracurriculars, planning, implementing, applying to college.

"I got what I wanted," I told my friends. "I set out to accomplish a task, even if it was a bit unconventional and, perhaps, not within the scope of my usual projects." I looked up from the table to Liam and Ginny and smiled to reassure them even though I was talking myself into my feelings. "So, when viewed that way, I was successful, right?"

"When you put it that way–" Ginny held up her fork– "you gave him a taste of his own medicine." She giggled before taking another bite of her salad.

I looked down at my lunch. It didn't feel good to think I'd used him, but maybe it was the same, in a way.

When I raised my eyes again, I saw Liam smile, but his eyes watched me with his old-soul wisdom and far more knowing than I wanted from him. I offered him a bright smile to reassure him. "I'm fine. I promise. Case closed. Moving on." I pulled an apple from my lunch bag and took a bite as a symbolic action to prove it to him. Even though I knew I could say it until I was blue in the face, it wouldn't make it true just then. The thing was, I had this awesome gift: when I set my mind to doing something, I was usually able to think my way into   it.

tanner

I glanced at Emma across the cafeteria. She was sitting with her friends where they always sat, creatures of habit. I knew all I had to do was glance up and find her there whenever I needed my Emma fix. She was usually studying, and sometimes she was telling a story, but most often she was listening to her friends talk with a content look on her face. Now, she wasn't looking my way — which I knew was a good thing even if it felt terrible — and the look on her face wasn't easy to see. Instead of her usual joy, the corners of her mouth were weighted. With a cheek pressed into her hand, she leaned against the table. Her body was turned away from me.

I'd noticed her the moment she'd entered the cafeteria. Truth: I'd been hoping to see her all day. She'd stalled, and then her eyes locked with mine. In their depths: hope and anticipation. My heart moved, recognizing her look, because it matched how I felt. My heart twitched with want, but I shoved the feeling back into its cage. I couldn't go there. It wasn't safe to connect like that to anyone. I squashed any seedlings that might have been sprouting in that freshly tilled soil, looked away, and smiled at Greta, who was flirting shamelessly with me. It made me feel like shit, but that was the exact reason for not doing anything to encourage Emma or the feelings inside me.

After that kiss, I'd spent the rest of the weekend at home by myself. Griff had tried to talk me into going to a party with him the next night, but I just couldn't do it. Every time I closed my eyes, I saw her, felt her lips, tasted her tongue, heard her soft moans, reimagined the curves of her in my hands. I didn't want to lose it to anything else, so I'd holed up in my room with video games and my books content to just sit in my memory for the time being. I wasn't ready to let the moment I'd shared with Emma go. It had been — perfect.

Now, though, as my want strained toward her, I knew I needed to get her out of my mind, otherwise she was going to grow and spread. I knew where feelings led, had a healthy dose of stay-away-from-that by observing my parents. "What's up this weekend?" I said to anyone around the table listening.

"My parents are out of town," Melanie said.

My stomach turned, but I ignored it.

"Is that an invitation?" Griff looked at her.

"For you guys, yes. But we should keep it — intimate." Her smile was suggestive.

Greta, still draped across my back, wrapped her arms around my shoulders and leaned forward so she could touch my chest. I had the urge to push her off but reminded myself I had some forgetting to do.

emma

"Emma!" Shelby covered her heart with her hands. "You look so beautiful."

My seventh-grade sister's exuberance was catchy. I smiled and ran a hand over my burgundy dress. It had a sweetheart neckline with a flouncy chiffon ruffled skirt, layered and flowing to the floor. "You think?" But I knew she was right. This dress would make anyone look beautiful. I hadn't intended to go to prom, and I didn't like that it was cutting into my John Hughes routine, but since Ginny and Liam were going together and were going to meet me there, I'd made a concession. Besides, Ginny insisted this was the best way to "get over" my infatuation.

"Can I borrow it for my prom?" Shelby reached out and touched the silky fabric.

"If you want."

My mother tied the burgundy satin ribbon at the small of my back. "You might want your own," she told Shelby.

"Oh no." Her words came out in a burst of air, and then she smiled with a mouth full of braces. "It's so pretty. You'll be the prettiest girl there, Emma."

"She will, won't she." Mom met my eyes in the mirror and smiled. "Sit, so I can make sure we didn't loosen any of your hairpins."

I followed her directions and sat on the chair at the vanity in the room my mom and dad shared. The lights around the back edge of the mirror gilded all of our faces, making us seem different.

"When I went to my prom, I wore a blue dress." My mom's hand moved around my hair that had been piled into a pretty updo earlier that day to accentuate my waves and curls, but it also hid a ton of pins.

"Did you love it?" Shelby asked.

Mom looked at Shelby, "No. It was a hand-me-down from Aunt Meg." She smiled and offered an amused sound. "She was three years older than me and had worn it for her senior year. So, by the time I got invited to a prom, it was a little outdated."

"Why couldn't you invite someone to prom?" Shelby asked.

"It wasn't done that way back then," she said. "A boy always did the asking. Isn't that still the way it's done?"

I shrugged. "Mostly, but not always."

"I'd ask who I wanted." Shelby crossed her arms over her chest and narrowed her eyes.

"You say that now," I said. "But truthfully, I think most girls secretly hope the person they like will take the time to ask them." Had I secretly fantasized that Tanner asked me? Yes. Yes, I had. Did I know he wouldn't? Yes. Yes, I did. Did it keep me from hoping? No. No, it hadn't.

"Did you want your date to ask you?" Shelby wiggled her eyebrows at me.

That was an emphatic *no*. I didn't tell Shelby that, however. "No. We're just friends. Prom of convenience."

Mom helped me put on a necklace.

"Did you have a boyfriend who asked you, Mom?" Shelby asked her.

"No. I didn't have a boyfriend, but a young man — his name was Donnie — did ask me to go. I thought he was nice, and he was cute, so I said yes."

"And Grandma Polly couldn't get you the dress you wanted?"

"We didn't have a lot of money growing up with Granny being the only one working." She paused for a moment, remembering. "I made a big fuss about it with her." Her smile faded a touch. Grandma Pauline had passed away just a little over a year earlier; my mom still got misty when she thought about her mom. "Anyway — Granny Polly couldn't afford a new one — and I was such a brat about it."

When I thought about Granny, I remembered her strength, and the way she would get super focused — like she could read your mind. She'd had the greatest sense of humor and a laugh to make you feel like every moment was perfect. My mom was a lot like her.

"Like I was a brat about wanting a cat?" Shelby asked.

Mom laughed. "Kind of like that, but maybe it was worse since Granny was trying her best to raise two girls on her own." Granny Polly had been the single parent for my mom and Aunt Meg after their dad died.

"I bet you still looked beautiful in Aunt Meg's hand-me-down," I said.

My mom put her hands on my shoulders. "Not as beautiful as you do." She kissed the top of my head and then looked at Shelby. "So someday, you might want your own dress. I'd like you to know you can have your own dress." She smiled at Shelby.

"I promise I won't be a brat about that."

"My. My. Don't you clean up nice," my dad said from the doorway. He was leaning against the doorjamb as though he'd been there a while. A smile turned his eyes up at the edges behind his wiry glasses. I wondered how long he'd been standing there watching us. "The belle of the ball for sure." He smiled, proud, and I felt beautiful.

The doorbell announced my date had arrived. Chris Keller, my lab partner in AP Bio, suggested we go to the prom during a lab a few weeks ago. I agreed. Nice and easy. No frills and ridiculous promposals. I'd recently decided on a strict no-dating policy in high school, because — after the kiss debacle — it was easier that way. Chris and I were just friends. No complications.

I pictured Tanner James, and my heartbeat quickened a moment thinking about him standing at the door. Wishing it was so. Then I shoved the ridiculous idea from my thoughts, straightened my dress and reminded myself that thinking of Tanner was always a mistake. It was a fruitless endeavor. Not only would he never go to prom, he'd never ask me. *Focus on tonight,* I thought. Non-complicated Chris was the best choice.

I smiled, forcing myself to believe it.

"Ready?" Dad asked. "I'll go down and grill your date for a few moments, so you can make an entrance." He winked.

"Dad." I rolled my eyes. "He's just a friend."

"Perfect. I'll lay it on thick."

"Like you even could, Mo," my mother said after him and winked at me with a smile. She squeezed my shoulders. "There. Perfect."

When I walked down the stairs, Chris — dressed in a dark gray suit with a burgundy tie — looked very handsome. That was the thing about Chris, if I hadn't been so darned hung up on Tanner, he would have been perfect. He was smart and funny. We always had a good time in class. He did his work and had a plan (he was aiming for Stanford and was smart enough to get in. Besides he was on the swim team and could probably get a scholarship or something).

"Hi." He smiled up at me, but his smile was different. Nervous. His bright blue eyes shifted to my Dad, who must have laid it on thick.

"Hi." I made it to the bottom step. "Hold on." I held up a finger and disappeared into the kitchen to get his boutonniere from the refrigerator. I didn't return right away, and instead listened to the voices of my parents, Chris, and every once in a while, Shelby. I took a deep breath, trying to charge myself with courage for the night ahead, not content with the idea of being in a crowded place or having to function in a social setting with someone new. "Ginny and Liam will be there," I whispered aloud to myself.

"He's cute." Mom's voice made me jump.

I clutched my chest.

She chuckled. "I'm sorry, sweetie. You okay?"

I looked at her and fought the urge to cry. I didn't want to go to the prom with Chris. I didn't really want to go to the prom. I was doing it to get over Tanner. I needed to be over Tanner, but I knew it wasn't going to work even as much as I tried to make it work. "I'm okay," I said and repeated it three more times inside my head. "We're just friends."

Mom drew me into her arms. "If you don't want to go, Emma, you don't have to go."

I shook my head. "No. I'm okay." I rationalized he'd already bought the tickets. I couldn't do that to him. It was his prom, too. My parents had bought the dress, the flower. No. I wasn't going to waste it. I was going to be the perfect date. "Really." But it was comforting to hear my mom say it.

She pushed me away from her but held me at arm's length. She searched my face with her steely gaze, assessing, and then nodded. "Well, if you want me to come and get you early, I will."

Just knowing I had an out made me breathe a little easier. "Thanks, Mom."

After a flurry of exchanging flowers — me pinning on the boutonniere and him tying on the pretty wristlet amid a plethora of posed photographs — Chris walked me out to the waiting limo. The chauffeur opened the door for us, and Chris waited for me to get in. He climbed in after me. Once situated, he looked at me with appreciation and said, "You look really pretty, Emma."

His words made me blush, nervous for some reason now. I knew him in class only. Jokes about labs, fun flirting over sciencey stuff, but that was it. We were friends in that capacity, but this was outside the boundaries of our established relationship, and I felt awkward. "Thank you. You clean up nice too," I teased, trying to draw from what was comfortable in class. "Who knew."

He laughed, and the ease that existed between us in the lab returned.

The car moved.

We made it to prom.

We took awkward prom pictures.

We found our table with Ginny and Liam already waiting.

We danced.

We laughed.

We had fun.

Before I knew it, the night drew to a close with the final dance.

It was time to go home. I said goodbye to Liam and Ginny and left the venue with Chris, his hand resting on the small of my back (which felt a little possessive, but I ignored it). Once the door to the limo was closed, the ease of earlier dissipated like steam, but it didn't disappear. Instead, it lingered with tension; I felt like perhaps it was double boiling us in a pressure cooker, which seemed strange since we'd had so much fun at the dance. I made a joke to try and bring back the levity.

Chris laughed; his arm draped across the back of the seat. His fingers grazed my bare shoulder, and the outside of his thigh pressed against mine.

My body tightened as nerves stepped into my muscles. I fought the urge to scoot away, reasoning it was just the ride home, and we'd had a good night. I was still working on being the perfect date, and there wasn't much left of it to do so.

"You had fun then?" Chris ran a hand over his styled, wheat-colored hair. He'd removed his jacket, which was on the seat across from us. I focused on the boutonniere pinned to the lapel.

"I did." I looked from the flower down at my hands in my lap.

"Me too. I'm glad I finally worked up the courage to ask you."

I made a face and chanced a glance at him. With a smile, I said, "Courage? Why would you need courage? We've been friends forever."

His eyes widened, but he grinned, cutting a single dimple into his right cheek. "You're intimidating as hell, Emma."

"What?"

His smile faded, and the look in his eyes shifted toward something hazy. "Seriously. You're smart and funny and so freaking gorgeous."

In the soft glow of the lavender lights of the car's interior, I could see his eyes scan my features. My heart picked up speed and sent warmth out across my skin.

His eyes stopped on my mouth. "I've wanted to kiss you for a while now." He leaned forward, pausing a moment just before his mouth touched mine, lingering.

I went to war with myself.

He isn't Tanner.

Tanner doesn't like me.

Do you like Chris?

I don't know.

But my hesitation seemed to be enough for Chris to decide I was into the idea. His lips met mine. He was warm and smelled nice. His kiss was gentle and sweet, and nice. There weren't any fireworks, because I'd experienced those before. It was…nice. I pulled back. Smiled, feeling shy.

Which must have sent him a mixed message, because he was suddenly kissing me again. This time with more insistence. This time with tongue. As I backed away, he moved with me, until somehow my back was against the seat with him on top of me and my hands against his shoulders. The feel of his gray shirt slick under my palms.

I turned my face to end the kiss. "Wait."

He stopped, propped himself up on his hand and looked down at me. "God, Emma. You are so amazing," he said and leaned down, kissing me again — not waiting. This time his hands moved over my body: shoulders, ribs, hips, ribs, the side of my boobs.

I sort of disconnected from the physical as his words bumped and pinged against walls inside my mind: *You are so amazing. I've wanted to kiss you for a while. You're intimidating as hell. You're gorgeous.* After the last several weeks of fighting a one-sided attraction to Tanner, Chris's words hit just right, but the rest of it was outside the bullseye. His kiss, his hands. They weren't aligning with my wants and feelings. Turning my head away from him again, "Chris," I said.

Instead of stopping, he began to kiss my neck, moving toward the neckline of my dress. He hummed a response.

"Wait. Stop," I said and tried to move out from under him.

He propped himself up on his hands, his arms hemming me in on each side.

"I'm not — I mean, kissing is nice, but, um–" I wasn't sure what to say, how to say what I did want and didn't want. I hadn't had to say it before. And while I was trying to figure it out, wrestling with thoughts about being good and nice, about not wanting to hurt his feelings or make him think I didn't appreciate the effort he went to on this date, he leaned down and began kissing my neck again, offering touch and connection.

It felt nice to have a handsome boy attracted to me offering his attention.

My mind drifted to Tanner. The party. How different being with him had felt, even if I was a little drunk at the time.

Chris shifted; his knees and hands drew my dress up as he settled in between my legs.

I realized I'd wanted to be there with Tanner. I'd wanted his hands on me. I'd wanted his kiss. I wanted to be with Tanner now, too, not Chris. I had to be honest. I pressed hands against his shoulders. "Chris."

His hands reached down and slid up my leg.

"Chris." I pressed against his torso more insistently. "Stop."

His hand stopped moving, and he looked at me. His brows drew together. "What is it?" His tone sounded annoyed.

"I'm not like that," I told him.

"Oh," he said. "I didn't think you were." His lips met mine again and his hands went back to work moving up my leg. His tongue filled my mouth blocking my protests.

I clamped my knees together but with him pressed between my legs, I couldn't stop what was happening. "Stop," I told him, the words muffled by the fact his lips and tongue weighted mine. I knew where his hand was headed, and I wasn't into that with him. I knew that. "Stop." I turned my face away from his, again. Pushed against his shoulders, again, but suddenly his hand was between my legs, between our bodies, probing, and he was so heavy.

My first instinct was to freeze.

Fear moved through me, coaxing me to play dead. My mind moved through all the reasons I couldn't get away: he was bigger than me. He was stronger. He wasn't listening. He took me out on a date. I didn't have a voice.

You owe him nothing, an amalgamation of voices of all the important people in my life told me.

And I knew they were right. I fisted my hand and slammed it against his ear.

"Ow!" Chris shifted, grabbing the side of his face.

Able to find a way out from under him, I pushed him off, scrambling as far away from him as I could get. "You asshole," I said, breathing with so much anger and adrenaline I thought perhaps I was changing into a dragon. "I said to stop."

"Fuck. That hurt," he said.

"I said to stop."

"God Emma. I just thought–"

"What? What did you think?"

"I took you on a nice date. Everyone says, you know — prom night."

Tears sprang to my eyes, and I shook my head. "You were my friend."

The car had come to a stop.

Chris didn't apologize.

When the door opened, I mustered the courage to move past him, but I didn't say thank you. Thank you for what? Groping me after I'd asked him to stop? I didn't say anything. I just got out and moved through the gate toward my house.

I kind of expected Chris to follow me, to apologize because he'd realize what he'd done was wrong. I'd known him for a long time. I thought we were friends, but Chris didn't follow. When I got to the front porch of my house, the limo was already pulling away from the sidewalk. For some reason, it made me feel worse, like somehow, I ruined something with my outburst. Like maybe I should have been the one to apologize. Tears pierced my eyes, but I couldn't let them fall.

Instead, I took a deep breath to compose myself as best as I could before going into the house to face my family. Once inside, I put on a smile. I gushed about the good parts of prom. When my parents asked after Chris, I lied and said he had to get the limo back. I answered their questions with a smile on my face and told everyone the story of the perfect prom so they could feel good about it. My mom reached out and took a lock of hair that was no longer pinned between her fingers. She assessed me with her eyes and smiled, but I had the feeling she was looking deeper than the surface I offered.

When I was able, I escaped to my room. I took off the dress that had made me feel beautiful, hung it and went into the bathroom. I looked at myself in the mirror. I looked like myself except for my hair, most of it still in the updo. I pulled at the lock of hair my mother touched, unpinned.

I was unpinned and shame hit me in the chest. Where did I go wrong? What could I have done differently?

With a deep breath, I closed my eyes unable to look at myself anymore and began feeling for the pins to take down my hair. Once all of them were out, I opened my eyes but looking at myself was harder. *Who will ever want you?* I removed the makeup, and finished undressing. I stepped into the shower, submerged my head under the warm water streaming over me, and it was then I finally cried.

senior year
(a few months before graduation)

"I blinked. Hard. When I opened my eyes, she was still there with that smile on her face, like she knew something I didn't. I hated it, was sick with it. Somehow, that smile slammed the prison doors locking me inside and then blew a hole in the lock right after. I was suffering from whiplash."

-unnamed protagonist, *Kaleidoscope Concussion* by Saul Annick

emma

For the opportunity to hear *The Tinks,* I was willing to face the fear of being amidst a crowd. At least for a little while. After what happened junior year, I reinforced the seams of my boxes, and might have even skipped stepping out of them for the Tink's concert, but Ginny could be very persuasive. Besides, I loved the Tinks. Plus, I would never allow myself to step into feeling that powerless again and had done a really good job of making sure that was the case. Maybe there were broken shards of insecurity moving through me like splinters that festered every once in a while, but mostly, I'd moved forward with more control, not less.

Ginny and I found a spot in The Revolution; I stood next to a wall with Ginny on the other side of me. Safe. Once the music started, it was like the fear dripped away into puddles at my feet and freedom slid over my skin. In moments like that, I wondered why I was fearful at all. There wasn't anything that ever made me feel free like that. Check that. There was one thing: kissing Tanner James. I'd let go. I'd often wondered if it had only been the alcohol that gave me the bravery to actually follow through, and decided that yes, partially. But there had been another part of me that was so cognizant of what I wanted that I would have done it regardless. Of course, that was before prom. After was different, even if I lied myself into believing I was over Tanner.

After the concert, Ginny led the charge ahead through the crowd and looked over her shoulder at me. She smiled, "You okay?"

"I'm good." I nodded with a smile. I was.

But now I was thinking about Tanner and the kiss. The worst part about the whole operation was the aftermath. How Tanner seemed to forget or pretend — I wasn't sure which — it even happened. What made it even worse (and this had nothing to do with Tanner but my own idiocy) was how I would have kissed him again even having assumed that it meant so little to him. I suppose that he'd kissed so many people, my kiss wasn't all that memorable; I mean, I'm just me. Despite my best efforts of trying to lie myself into believing his kiss had been unmemorable, I hadn't succeeded.

That kiss.

Heart-stopping, heart-throbbing, hands moving, and breathless want rolled up into sharp stars behind my eyes, stealing my ability to think. Chills racing across my skin and deep-seated want blooming like heat in the center of me.

I sighed.

And I shook my head to reorient my thoughts. I couldn't keep going there. I'd spent nearly a year suppressing the infatuation like a virus, bolstering my immune system with all kinds of vitamins to keep it latent and hidden: school, my friends, John Hughes movie nights, speech competitions, clubs and church, plans for college. I told myself if those things stayed present, then the infatuation would just dissipate. I'd moved forward and onward, the kiss behind me, and told myself that it was enough to keep me happy. It had worked, for a while. But lately, I was beginning to understand I was lying to myself in order to protect my heart. The truth was every time I saw Tanner at school — the cafeteria, the hallway, walking across the quad, coming in from the parking lot with his friends — that infatuation kicked up and infected me with all kinds of feelings that made me redouble my efforts at controlling it. It was exhausting.

The heat in the space pressed against me along with everyone leaving. I turned my back on the thoughts of Tanner and focused on Ginny's braided hair as she led us from the club. I studied the lines of her blue and white striped shirt glowing in the blacklight. I breathed: deep breath in and deep breath out. I focused on the feel of her hand and the awareness that no matter what we had one another. But graduation loomed. College after. Then what?

The door was just ahead. I took another deep breath, relieved.

We stepped out into the cold January air. The bite was refreshing and horrible at the same time. I dropped Ginny's hand and wrapped my arms around myself. "Oh, my. It's cold." I laughed and saw my breath was steamy puffs. With my eyes closed, I took a huge gulp of air. It felt so good, cold and vibrant. I opened my eyes and blew out the breath as a huge cloud puffed out. The crowd thinned. I giggled again. Happy in the moment.

Ginny bounced, rubbing her arms to stay warm. "Where'd we park? I should have brought my coat."

"I remember. It isn't too far."

The city rose up around us, concrete and glass, lights and cars. We'd driven in to catch the show because The Revolution was the only venue that offered any bands of value. Moving to California was going to be awesome if only for the availability of good music — provided I got accepted to a school there. Ginny, Liam, and I had talked about this at length, though I was the only one who applied exclusively to California, choosing the location before the schools; I wanted to be near the Pacific. I was still crossing my fingers. Ginny was waiting to hear from the art schools she applied to, and Liam got early admission to Cornell, so he was set.

I wrapped my arms around Ginny. "We'll have to keep each other warm."

She curled into me, and we walked. I glanced up to navigate through the thinning crowd. Ten steps away, standing still and watching us, was Tanner James. He had his hands shoved into the pockets of his black jacket. He wore a white shirt, red and gray flannel underneath, a gray knit cap on his head. His dark hair curled around the edges of the cap. He smiled, which affected the stability of my belly, and the smile reached his brown eyes; they twinkled in the icy light. He lifted his hand and waved.

Like an idiot, I smiled, let go of Ginny, and raised my hand, waving back. Then, I realized maybe he wasn't waving at me and checked to see if someone was behind me. No one was there. When I turned back, he was surrounded by people I didn't recognize, and then was swallowed up by the crowd.

"Let's go. I'm so cold." Ginny's arms were wrapped around her middle, and her teeth clacked.

We walked down the street away from The Revolution toward the pay lot where the car was parked. My mind swirled with seeing Tanner in a place I hadn't expected; I'd been thinking about him, and then there he was. My insides heated despite the cold.

He waved at me.

He waved at me.

He waved at me.

What did that mean?

"Did you see that?" I asked Ginny a few moments later. My teeth rattled now, and my arms were folded around myself like hers.

"What?"

"Tanner."

"James?"

"Yeah. He waved at me."

"He should. The prick." I loved that Ginny was always my fiercest supporter. She was still pissed about his lack of response after that party and wanted to skewer his balls. I've had to remind her on several occasions that I instigated the kiss, and I knew what I was doing even if I needed liquid courage to do it. "It had been my master plan, remember?" I also reminded her that he was the one who stopped it. I might not have.

"Weird."

We made it to the car, and climbed in, our bodies trembling and shaking to stay warm. I started it and turned the heater all the way up.

"Why is that weird?" Ginny asked, shrugging into her flannel and then her jacket. She reached out and adjusted the vent even though it wasn't yet spewing hot air.

I pulled on any warm clothes in my car, layering myself into anything I could find. "Because — I don't know — because it's been almost a year since the kiss, and he hasn't even looked at me. I mean, kind of, like passing looks but those don't mean anything."

"Emma, you give yourself too little credit." She turned in her seat, arms crossed. "You're amazing. You're smart. You're pretty. Tanner James is an idiot for walking away from you because YOU would elevate him." She turned back toward the heater and placed her hands over the vents. "Where's he going in life? Probably nowhere. Which is a shame because I have him in my math class. He doesn't even try and has set the stupid curve a few times. Imagine if he actually tried."

It hurt my heart to hear her speak like that of him, even if there was truth in her words. It was true; Tanner hadn't done much at school. He showed up for class and did just enough to get by. His party-boy persona seemed more important. Regardless, thinking about him hanging out with Connor in the cafeteria always made me pause and wonder if the Tanner everyone presumed to know was the actual Tanner? Because the Tanner who was known to mess around with anyone and could have messed around with me at that party — and I would have let him — didn't.

Then I wonder: was that because of him?

Or me?

tanner

I hadn't been thinking. Emma Matthews had been at the concert, several feet away from me, smiling and laughing about something, abandoned to the moment. Cold. Pretty, like one of those artsy Instagram pictures that makes you pause, because the colors are perfect, and it's filtered just right. I didn't recognize her at first. Why would I? Being in the city where I hadn't expected to see her? She looked edgier than usual: dressed in all black. Skinny jeans. Fitted top. Different. Her smile, so disparate than when she's all buttoned up at school. My locus of control slipped outside of my body, and my animal brain took over. I realized I knew her when her blue eyes connected with mine, and the kiss rushed back into my head. My heart sped up, my stomach tightened, and like an idiot, I raised my hand and waved.

She waved back.

Josh said something. I'd turned to look at him. Glanced back at Emma, but she was gone, a river of bodies between me and where she'd been.

Now, I was second guessing my existence. Like that first line from Sartre's *Nausea*, "Something has happened to me." The discomfort of looking like a complete idiot — of Emma thinking I was an idiot —

made me fidget in the driver's seat of my truck. I hadn't been able to get the image of her out of my mind.

Josh talked about the concert.

I answered him in distracted and distant tones.

It was okay. He didn't really notice.

When he went quiet, I knew he was asleep because he'd crossed his arms over his chest, and his head rested against the passenger window. It was cool. I liked driving. I liked being with my thoughts. It was what I did.

I couldn't get the moment out of my mind. Emma. Her laugh. Raising my hand. Her smile. Her wave in return. Emma. Her laugh. Raising my hand. Her smile. Her wave in return. Over and over. A loop, as if I kept coming back around to it, because I was supposed to notice something between the actions, something more meaningful. Though, as I circled back to it, over and over, a discrepancy between my memory, and its connection to my feelings, derailed. At first, I was embarrassed because that wasn't a Tanner-thing to do, but then it hit me. I wasn't embarrassed because of what others thought. I was worried about what Emma thought. Then I wondered: why?

When we got back to town, I dropped Josh off and drove home. My house was dark but for the shallow glow of the light in the kitchen above the sink. "Mom?" No answer. She was either in bed or out.

Being alone was my norm. With mom and dad divorced for the last four years, I pretty much had the house to myself. Dad lived across town with his new family. Mom was either working or whatever she did, which I figured had something to do with a new boyfriend she was hiding. Since I was turning eighteen next month, they didn't need to bother. Not that they had since Rory got sick and definitely not since he died. At least the empty house saved me the energy of having to be the rope in their tug-of-war with one another, which was exhausting.

I opened the fridge and stood in the glowing light, not really considering what was inside but thinking about Emma instead. Seeing her. Emma. Her laugh. Raising my hand. Her smile. Her wave in return. I'd thought about the kiss. The first time I'd allowed myself to return to that memory since junior year. I'd done a bang-up job shutting it down for myself, even if that was kind of a lie, because I still had dreams and fantasies about her and that kiss. She looked even prettier than junior year — if that was even possible — more filled out. I closed the refrigerator, not hungry. Not for food anyway. I was craving something else.

A sound from deeper inside the house caught my attention.

Voices.

"Mom?" I walked through the kitchen to the darkened opening of the formal entryway. "Hello?" I called out again, my heart stalled and hung in my chest.

There was a light coming from the study, the door ajar.

Raised voices.

Mom's.

Dad's.

I froze in the dark of the entry. I'd been wrong. Mom was home. And angry.

"You don't fucking get it, Geoff." Her voice snapped in the darkness like flashes of lightning. "So typical."

I swallowed, crossed my arms over my chest, and took a step back. I was ten, eleven, twelve. Back then, I'd escape into Rory's room to hide from their fights.

"Typical? You're calling me typical? That's rich, Marna." Dad. I heard stuff being moved. Drawers or something slammed.

There were words I couldn't hear, but the tone was clear. Angry. Accusatory. Hurt.

I took another step back into the soft glow of the kitchen.

"I wasn't the one who ran out on this family. You owe us."

"I don't owe you shit. You chased me out the fucking door."

Another step away, back against the side door. Doorknob pressed into my back.

Footsteps.

"This was all I came for." Dad's shoes clacked across the marble floor. "You always have to make something out of nothing."

I grasped at my truck keys.

"Don't put this on me."

The fight continued. Always fighting. Loud accusations about who defaulted on the mortgage of their marriage.

I slipped from the house unnoticed. I was already pulling out of the driveway when the front door opened. I saw Dad's car on the street, now. I'd been too preoccupied with thoughts of Emma to notice it earlier. Now, they were arguing outside, and didn't notice me as I drove past. I don't remember the last time they noticed me.

Before Rory got sick.

Long before he died.

The last time I remember being whole was when we went to Disneyland. I think I'd been eight and Rory, ten. We'd begged to run around in Tarzan's Treehouse before going on the Jungle River Ride. Mom and Dad — still tied together by something that must have been love — watched us. Smiling. I remember running to the edge, leaning over and yelling down for them to watch. They smiled, waved and eventually climbed up into the treehouse with us. After, when we walked across the park, we'd held hands, the four of us, a connect-four line. Mom had held my hand while Dad had held Rory's, the two of us safe between them.

After that trip — hard to know how long since kid time has different physics — Rory got sick.

Our connect-four line broke. The bottom opened up. We rolled away and got lost.

It's as though everything before was erased.

The hum of the road as I drove soothed my racing heart like a song. Somehow, it calmed and quieted the emotions threatening to break me apart. I drove to my favorite place.

When I got to the access road to the north side of the Quarry, I took it, and bumped along the rough road until I was able to park my truck at the edge. I drove there a lot.

I loved sunset when the waning sun turned everything to fire. The trees, the blue-green water, the rock walls lit up in the golden light. It was difficult to stay angry or sad or lonely when that fire burned around me. Fire claimed the fire in me and cooled me back into stone. But at night, when the stars came out, it became a beautiful storied sky. I drifted into that sea and got lost there remembering Rory and my star stories.

Sometimes, I'd talk to Rory like when I was ten. I'd imagine he was an astronaut like he always said he'd be, floating past me in his spaceship. I'd look for our planet — the one we said was heaven — and found comfort in it even if I'd had to reinvent which one it was. Sitting there under the dark sky made me remember the good times. The before.

I'm not sure if that's more painful or less so.

I read a book once about the history of astronomy and learned about the constellations. Maybe I was searching for the stories, the possibility to find Rory. I don't know, and I couldn't say where the constellations were in the sky, but it was comforting somehow to look up and know I wasn't the only one who gazed at that expanse wondering, hoping, feeling, wishing. Perhaps in this giant world, maybe even the universe, I wasn't the only one running from a family that fell apart.

I thought about Emma and wondered if she looked at the stars.

It was freezing, and I wasn't sure I'd be able to stay out there for long. I pulled my jacket tighter. The sliver of yellow light streaking through the purple, blue-black sky reminded me of how I felt with Emma that night junior year. It was golden in the haze of darkness everywhere else. I tried to remember why I shoved that away. My choices, the parties, the girls, none of that serving to make me happy.

I realized, then, what it was that I wasn't able to reconcile before. Emma. Her laugh. Raising my hand. Her smile. Her wave in return. She'd waved and smiled at me, just as I had at her. I'd wanted to. What if she'd wanted to? It's an old equation I hadn't allowed myself to ponder for almost a year. She'd wanted to kiss me at that party. *I'll kiss you*, she said. And then she had.

I hadn't allowed myself to wonder about it. I mean I had. I'd thought about kissing her and liked the awareness that she'd wanted to kiss me, but it was too difficult to keep it there in the front of my thoughts when nothing could come of it. And nothing should come of it now, either. I remembered why I had shoved it away. I'm Tanner. Tanner of the broken home where love was used against you in a war. She was Emma. Smart, going places Emma. I was headed nowhere but a job with a hammer and nails. I made sure of that. She was probably going to college. But thinking about that wave — the impetuousness of it — I realized why the moment looped around in my mind. It had been unguarded and authentic. I wanted something real. I craved it. Emma was real, but she was something I didn't deserve.

senior year
(13 days to graduation)

"I was in dire need of something different, otherwise, I knew I was going to die in shades of gray."

-unnamed protagonist, *Kaleidoscope Concussion* by Saul Annick

emma

I walk into church with my family: Dad, Mom, Shelby and me. This is a Sunday morning norm. Church service, then after-church brunch. Nana and Pop Pop, my dad's parents, over to our house for Sunday dinner. I find the routine comforting, and for me, someone who overthinks everything, that's saying something. But today, I feel like I'm itching the underside of my own skin, unable to get comfortable. It's the conversation with Liam and Ginny the night before coupled with my struggle to reconcile my faith with the mixed messages. If I'm being honest — which I should be if I believe in God at all (which, for the record, I do) — I haven't been feeling this church thing for a while.

It isn't a God thing; it's a religion thing.

I follow my family into the pew and sit with them in a perfect row dressed in our Sunday best, but something that once made me feel full feels like it's leaking air.

I look around. The building looks the same, white walls, blue carpet, oak pews. The windows lining both sides of the room are tall and narrow, each of them etched and frosted with designs. At the front of the room, a dais with a gigantic plain wood cross dominating the space. A podium where Pastor Green puts his Bible and notes. Behind him, under the cross, the instruments set up for worship: a drum kit encased in plexiglass to muffle the sound, guitars on stands, a piano, an electronic keyboard, microphones.

I wonder if my struggle is a sin, but I think about Isaac wrestling with God and think perhaps it's more of a human thing. It began after Liam came out at the beginning of junior year. I remembered sitting in church and hearing people who called themselves Christians — followers of Christ who taught about not judging another's journey — judge others. I brought my confusion to the dinner table with my family because that was how we worked through big questions. I didn't tell them about Liam — because his news wasn't mine to share — but I casually mentioned the idea of homosexuality, and my struggle with religious attitudes about it.

"I know things are… different… mainstream and socially acceptable, but we can't condone what's written in the Bible as a sin." My dad scooped a pork chop on his plate.

My father — my hero — was who I'd always looked to for wisdom about the world, but this didn't sit right with me. "Well, then we shouldn't eat this pork, I guess. According to the Bible, that's a sin."

"That's different. That was Jewish custom. Context."

"Wait." My eyes narrowed, and I set down my fork; Dad stopped to look at me. "It's okay to pick and choose beliefs based on what our customs are, like whether we eat pork? But monogamous, consensual relationships between two people aren't okay? How's that different? Context."

Dad's arms rested against the table, fork and knife in hand. "Any sexual relationship before marriage is considered a sin."

"According to who?" I asked. I could feel my ire heating. "The apostle Paul, a guy from 40 AD who never got married and lived a celibate life? How would he know? Jesus didn't say anything about sex before marriage. He also didn't say anything about homosexuality."

"You're picking and choosing."

"That's what you just did! Religion does it all the time, pick and

66

choose — cut up the Bible into convenient soundbites to perpetuate beliefs. Everyone does stuff like that to promote their argument. Like fake news."

"Are you saying our faith is fake news?" Mom asked.

"No. I'm saying you can't pick and choose convenient truths. And I guess I'm asking if you do, then you must invalidate everything else, right?"

Dad set his utensils down. I could tell he'd reached a breaking point in his patience. "Emma. Christianity is the foundation of who we are as a family."

"So, you and mom waited to have sex — before you got married?"

"Emma. What has gotten into you?" My mother snapped.

That was a big no; they didn't wait.

"Are you trying to tell us you're gay?" Shelby asked around a bite of broccoli.

"No. I'm not. But what if I was?" I looked at my parents. "Would you hate me because it goes against our beliefs about what's right and wrong based on what some guy — not Jesus, by the way — said? And for the record, isn't that what makes us Christians? The teachings of Jesus?"

"We would love you no matter what," Mom said, and Dad nodded.

"Even if I was a prostitute? Or in porn?"

My dad closed his eyes and took a deep breath. "Emma? What is going on?"

"Nothing." That was a lie. I picked up my fork and pushed the food around on my plate.

"I'd still love you, Em," my sister said. "But I wouldn't want to tell any of my friends you were a porn star."

I gave her a slight smile. "You don't have to worry, Shelb. That isn't in my immediate master plan."

"Our love for you, Emmz, and you, Shelbell, is forever and unending," Dad said. "That won't change."

Except something in me had.

The struggle continued from *Operation Kiss Tanner James,* and a few weeks later — despite my attempts at perfection — prom; I was having trouble keeping my fears and doubts and wants tied up into their neat boxes for safekeeping.

And I hated it.

Now, sitting in that church pew, the doubts about everything make me feel unresolved, as if a part of me is dissolving and disappearing into the atmosphere. I watch the worship team take the stage and play the first notes of a worship song I've heard and sung a hundred Sundays. I glance at the congregation, many singing along, hands raised in worship, and I think perhaps I'm broken. I don't feel the Spirit move like that. That makes me feel silly and showy.

I look down at my clasped hands and sing, but I don't sing aloud. Instead, I sing silently in my head and stare at the blue rug marked with a golden geometric pattern and red colored dashes. I feel closest to God in moments I have with my family, or in the laughter with Liam and Ginny, or in watching Tanner sit with Connor at lunch. I feel the Spirit in the quiet of my room when the fear of failure isn't pressing against my spine, or in the beauty of a sunrise or the sparkle of the stars in the night sky. Maybe that makes me an inadequate Christian; it isn't the first time I've felt it.

After that dinner conversation, I remembered escaping to my room and standing in front of the mirror staring at my reflection. The girl in the mirror stared back at me, as if challenging me to be different. *Go ahead,* she'd said. *Go ahead and do something outside of all those expectations. You mess up, and no one will ever love you.* I closed my eyes, cutting that girl off, and sighed, wishing perhaps the weight of my skin and bones wasn't so heavy. In my mind's eye, the version of myself I saw was probably more accurate than the one everyone expected me to be. The boring perfectionist fighting to hold herself together for everyone else. *Be perfect or no one will ever want you.*

It's like Dad's praise: "Oh Emmz, you're my perfect girl. I'm so proud of you." It echoed then and now in my head like a song on repeat pushing me to be better. *Just be better, Emma,* I tell myself. *So Dad can keep being proud of you.* But the horrible thought about messing up and disappointing him loops around too. He always says he loves me. He always says he's proud of me, but what if that went away because I do something he isn't proud of?

After *Operation Kiss Tanner James*, the guilt of sneaking out, of drinking, of seducing Tanner into kissing me rusted through my insides, but it wasn't because I'd done it; it was because I'd liked it. That night made me feel alive, free, and connected to those hidden parts I've been told to suppress. When I'd allowed that girl out, it was as though I'd stepped into a truer version of myself, and she poked her head out and smiled. That version wasn't perfect, even if she was still a perfectionist. That girl was still a stress-case and fallible, but it didn't matter because she felt happy. She was still smart and competitive and even fun. She'd found a way to be brave. Every message in my life has been to hide those parts of myself for the sake of purity, of being wanted by someone else, to "save" myself. Did it mean that because I enjoyed kissing Tanner, I was bad and unlovable? Because I wanted to have sex with him, I was impure? That someone else owned that part of me?

In contrast, the *After Prom Incident* sits in the back of mind — a dangerous red balloon floating in black space reminding me to be safe. Be better. Be more controlled. Don't let my guard down because when you do, things can happen that make me feel powerless. I wasn't perfect enough. Things that would ensure no one would ever want me.

Except, Tanner had that night. Before. I told him my truth, albeit drunkenly, and he'd kissed me. Pressed me up against a wall and kissed me like our lives couldn't continue forward without it. Hands had been involved. It made my heartbeat rush ahead, leaving me behind to catch up. But then he hadn't wanted me. After, left me deflated and insecure. Then the black mark of the limo happened. Another after. The world sort of tilted, and I've spent all of my time trying to correct it, to put it back into balance. Just be better, Emma. Stronger. Smarter. More perfect.

Liam's words from last night hit me square in the chest: *You're scared about everything.*

He is right. I am.

Now, standing in church with my family, I wonder where that alive girl went? The one who'd taken the risk to go after what she'd wanted? Was she real, or is it the girl who feels like a cardboard cutout standing in church wrapped up in a nicely decorated box of dogma?

We sit after the worship. Dad then Mom, his arm draped over the back of the pew behind her back, then Shelby and me. After announcements, Shelby leaves to hang out with the youth group. I stay with the adults, freshly 18. Pastor Green asks us to turn in our Bibles to Romans. I follow the directions. Perfect Emma.

"Romans 10:4 tells us," he says and then reads, "that 'For Christ is the end of the law for righteousness to everyone who believes.'" He pauses. "Did you hear that, congregation? Christ is the end of the law for those of us who believe in Him. Christ is freedom." He stops and walks across the stage. "You see, it isn't about what you have or haven't done. It isn't about the sins you've committed or the missteps you will make, the truth of the matter is that all of us are and will always be sinners, but Christ saved us. His death and resurrection saved us. Ladies and gentlemen, you cannot earn your way into salvation."

My heart stalls in my chest a moment, as if it needs tuning to turn over properly. I reread the passage and then look back at Pastor Green, who's behind his podium pulling the reading glasses from his face. "Here's the truth. Our Father in heaven loves us. No matter what. Say that with me: No. Matter. What." The congregation echoes him. "Can you feel that freedom?"

I glance around. It isn't like I haven't heard this message before. Law versus Grace, yada yada yada. It's just even with the message, no one seems to get it. All that judgement about other people and their lives. I get it. For others. I just haven't extended that to myself.

Pastor Green comes out from behind his podium. "Jesus told us to ask, and it shall be given, yes?"

There are "yeses" and "amens."

I wonder if this excludes asking God if I can have sex with Tanner James because, yes, I still want that. I snicker at the thought and get a look from my mom. My amusement fades because lingering amidst the desire for Tanner is the insecurity too. His rejection of me, and then what happened with Chris; I can't find a way to stand up straight and say *I am enough just like this*. I'm obviously not. Not enough for Tanner to like. Not enough for Chris to offer an apology. A girl so wound up in her fear and hiding it in a perfectionist box to keep herself safe.

"Brothers and Sisters," Pastor Green continues. "In Luke, chapter 11, verse 11 in case you want to look it up, the disciples were asking Jesus how to pray. He told them — us — to ask for what we want. And then he said this: 'Which of you fathers if your son asks for a fish will give him a snake instead?' Isn't that a picture?" Pastor Green stops and looks at us over his reading glasses perched on his nose. "Fathers — I'm speaking to our fathers in this room now — We'd do almost anything for our children, yes?"

I glance at my dad, who nods.

He turns his head to look at me, smiles, and reaches to squeeze my shoulder.

Pastor Green continues stepping back behind his podium. "Romans 10:12 reiterates, 'For there is no distinction between Jew and Greek, for the same Lord over all is rich to *all* who call upon him.' Jew. Greek. Sinner. Saint. Drug addict. Thief. Prostitute. We are loved and accepted because of Christ's sacrifice. All it takes, people, is our willingness to call on him. To believe and accept what He did for all of us. It isn't about our works. It isn't about our attempt at perfection. None of us can attain it. It is a lie to think we can. God — the Father knows it. You tell me: would your heavenly Father turn you away because you messed up? Luke 11:11 or the story of the Prodigal's son are perfect illustrations to the lengths God will go for us. Certainly know, friends, that our heavenly Father wouldn't. That is Grace."

My throat dries out and tears press against the backs of my eyes like tiny needles, because I know, without a doubt, that the God I believe in, the faith I've nurtured for my entire life, wouldn't turn me away because I messed up. That realization is a sudden understanding that all the ideology the Christian Church has used to build walls around me cracks and offers rays of light to shine through the darkness of my self-imposed prison.

I glance at my dad again, his arm around my mom, rapt with attention as he listens. I know without a doubt that my dad loves me. I understand God loves me regardless of all those expectations, too. Hearing God doesn't expect me to be perfect is a sort of freedom.

He wants me to be myself — Emma.

Even if this Emma lacks the risk-taking gene because her brain gets in the way.

And even if this Emma — who is confused about wanting to have sex with Tanner James — knows he isn't interested in that with her (which is probably a good thing).

This Emma doesn't need to feel so afraid all of the time.

I take a deep breath.

It feels like the easiest breath I've taken in a long time.

tanner

Griffin pounds the front door of my house until I open it. It's loud and obnoxious, just like he is, but I still let him into the house, because he's my best friend and has been since freshman year.

"Yo, cunt."

I don't respond. This is normal, though lately instead of finding it funny like I used to, I find it annoying and abrasive. I walk into the kitchen where I'm making a sandwich. "Close the door," I yell at him over my shoulder.

A moment later, Griff walks into the kitchen. "What happened to you last night?" he asks and slides onto a stool at the center island of the kitchen.

"I left. Called for a ride."

"Right. I know. But why?"

"Wasn't into it. Came home. I'd told you that before we went out."

His light brown eyebrows scrunch together with confusion. "Why?"

"That's what I wanted." My conversation with Atticus replays in my mind.

He lays his keys on the counter and reaches across the white granite countertop to grab my sandwich. "This looks good, fuckface."

"Griff. You've been here for less than five minutes and have called me names twice."

"When did you have that sex change surgery?"

I flip him off.

He laughs. "Dude. Seriously, why are you being so sensitive."

"Why are you being such a dick?"

"T-Man, I'm just being the same old me."

This was true. Griff had always been loud, abrasive, and obnoxious. It was me who was different and feeling like my skin didn't fit right anymore.

"I just want us to finish off this year right, you know?" Griff takes a giant bite of the sandwich and makes a ton of noise while he chews it. "This is good," he mutters around the bite.

I start a new sandwich, two pieces of bread, cheese, and meat. "And what does that mean: finish the year off right?"

"It isn't just the year. It's our high school career, bro. Less than two weeks from now, we're getting our diplomas–"

"Barely."

He ignores the observation. "And then we're moving on. Danny's going into the military. You're going to work for your dad. Josh, well, he's headed to college. How did that fucker do that?"

"He studied." I add some pickles and lettuce to the sandwich. "And you?"

"Winstead Community College," he says. "I'm not ready for the total adult life yet. Besides, think of the Bro Code in college. All the pussy." He wiggles his eyebrows and takes another giant bite. When most of it is chewed, he adds, "You should come with me. We can live together."

The thought feels like a dumbbell attached to my ankle dragging me under water. "Dad's got a plan. He's starting me on the desk after graduation. School's not my thing." Even as I say it, I don't know it to be true. I love to learn. I love to read. I just don't like the pointless shit of school like tests and grading, neither of which have anything to do with learning.

"Bro. You're like smart and shit. Smarter than Josh, and he's going."

"He made the grade. I didn't," I say and slather the bread with mayo.

Griff shrugs. "Whatever. So, what happened last night? I mean, Laura pretty much said you told her to 'fuck off.'"

I shake my head. "I didn't tell her that. I said I didn't want her company."

"Same difference," he smacks. "You could have hit that."

"Has it ever occurred to you that I might not want to? That I'm over it."

"Over what? Dude. Are you gay? No guy is over getting their dick sucked or his rocks off with a hot piece of ass." He pauses and thinks about what he's said. "Even homos want their dick sucked and a hot piece of ass." He laughs.

I finish the sandwich and put away the extra ingredients. "You sound like a douchebag."

"What?" He's surprised.

I lean against the counter next to the refrigerator facing him and shake my head. "Don't you think there's more to life, Griff?" This is probably one of the deepest conversations I've ever attempted with him outside of family drama.

"Like what?" And that is the typical Griff response to conversations that require emotions. His face scrunches up in an incredulous grimace.

"More than partying. More than sleeping around? More than using people?"

He looks at me like I've lost my mind. "Who are you, and what have you done with my best friend?" Another giant bite.

I rub my right eye with my fingertips and then swipe my hand over my face. I need to shave. "I'm just not into the party stuff anymore. That's it. I fucked this life shit up." When I say it, guilt hits me square in the chest and makes it hard to draw another breath. I think about Rory who didn't get to live at all, and this is what I chose. The thought hurts, the realization I've let him down somehow.

"What are you saying then? You're just going to stop? Two weeks left of senior year — including Senior Send Off next weekend — of high school, and you're not going to party with your boys?"

I don't answer him. When he puts it like that, I see the ridiculousness of holding my ground. Like Atticus said: *I figure everything's about to change.* What's two more weeks of hanging out with them? What is two more weeks to close out the shit I've created? I sigh.

Griff stands and walks around the island. He leans against it opposite me. "Look, T. We're boys. We've been boys a long time. Let's see it through and make our last days in high school epic. The crew can't do that without you."

"Are you invoking Bro Code like last night? That was a dick move, by the way." Bro Code was used for emergencies. Griff threw it out there like my desire to stay home or not wanting to have sex with Laura Hoff was the end of the world and a slap to his face.

"Yeah. Sorry. But this isn't about that. This is about all of us making memories, you know?"

I nod, but I'm not sure I believe him. A lot of what I've been feeling is bitterness about his need to control everything. But I feel guilty even thinking that. Griff has been there for me, through the divorce and everything. Maybe I'm the one being selfish. "Yeah."

He smiles and reaches over to hit my shoulder. "Ready to play some Duty?"

"Let me eat my sandwich," I say.

"Want to know who I hit it with last night?"

"Not really."

"Imma tell you anyway: Laura Hoff." He puffs up. "Bro. It was sloppy."

"Please. I don't want any details."

He makes a slurpy sound with his mouth and then laughs.

"You leaving was the best thing for that action. Poor girl needed consolation. Why didn't we ever think of running this game before?"

I've lost my appetite. Not really sure how to get him to stop, I change the subject to the one thing that usually supersedes sex. "Let's go play Duty," I tell him.

After two hours of digital combat, a bazillion f-bombs and other uses of profanity, a couple of punches, and a short match of *uncle* to determine who really is the most virile (which I concede to Griff to end it), Griff leaves. The silence in the house is heavier after he's gone.

I walk up the stairs but stop before going into my room. Down the hallway, Rory's door is shut, like always. I stop in front of it, hand on the doorknob and push it open. His room is neat and in perfect order. Mom never cleaned it out after. Couldn't, I suppose. Then it was the fighting and then the divorce, so I suppose there never was a time. And then maybe it became about being unable to.

The twin bed is made with the red and green plaid blocks with lines of goldenrod patterned with solid navy squares. I had a matching one. The dusty desktop has an unmade Lego project with the pieces separated into neat piles. I don't know what he was making. The wooden toy box is closed, the closet doors shut. Tumba, his teddy bear sits on the bed leaning against Rory's pillows. I walk in and sit down on the floor, my back against the bed. The dresser is against the wall in front of me, random stickers on the drawer fronts. There are a few soccer trophies across the top and prize ribbons from school events.

"I'm not sure what's wrong with me," I tell Rory aloud and think that maybe I'm turning crazy. Then I decide that if I think I'm becoming crazy, I'm probably not. Who knows? "I wish you were here. I'd ask for your advice."

I pull Tumba from the bed and hold him up. His glassy black eyes shine from his fuzzy brown head. I straighten his red bowtie.

"Don't touch him. Ever," Rory had once told me about Tumba. I'd been four or five then.

I forget the sound of my brother's voice, now, and the details about how he looked. Back then, I was the annoying little brother who followed his big brother everywhere. I had a similar stuffed animal, but it wasn't Tumba. I'd wanted Rory's, because it was Rory's; I worshipped my big brother.

"I miss you." I wiggle Tumba back and forth gently as if he'll answer me for Rory.

It's been eight years since Rory died of cancer, a lifetime ago. I swallow that down and rest my elbows on my knees, Tumba hanging from my hands between them. I didn't know how to deal with it, and Mom and Dad weren't any help. My parents thought the best way for me to deal with losing my brother was to sit with a therapist who talked at me. That lasted less than a year. Then it was to put me in soccer, which made me angry because all I thought about was Rory playing. That lasted one season. Then a coding club, and a boy scout troop, karate, judo, basketball, and whatever other activities meant to fill up the loss but couldn't. Then those stopped, and the distance between my parents and me widened as their marriage fell apart.

When I was fourteen, I met Griff, and then Josh and then Danny; they filled the gaping hole of a fresh divorce still dripping with the remnants of infection. After I met them, the loss of my brother and my family felt less acute. They filled the lonely gaps for a while anyway.

Then it became the sex, drugs and alcohol.

"You think it's normal to outgrow people?" I ask Tumba.

My parents didn't outgrow one another, I think. They ripped each other apart at the seams. I don't want to do that with Griff. Or Josh. Or Danny. They're my friends.

I stand up and put the stuffed bear back on the bed where he was.

I resolve to commit to my friends. As much as I'm struggling with myself, they've been there for me, and I can go another two weeks committed to who we've been together, because like Atticus and I talked about, everything is about to change. I press the bear back against the pillows when he flops forward. "It's for the best," I tell him when he's upright again. "They're here, and you're not."

Then I back out of the room and close the door

senior year
(9 days to graduation)

"I clung to Jumbo-sized Jimbo, cried my eyes out against his man-boob chest, as though I, too, had lost an important member of my life (except I didn't have any of those). I might have been dressed the part of the grieving — all in black — but I was a liar strung out on the deadness of grays instead. Jimmy Gigantic didn't care, however. In his embrace, his tears somehow baptized my restlessness. As I cried with him, I lost a piece of myself in the community of bright — albeit painful — feeling. Crying became my deconstruction, and there, I broke up into a cosmos before the Big Bang and looked out to see the stars."

-unnamed protagonist, *Kaleidoscope Concussion* by Saul Annick

emma

"I'll tell you what—" A female voice cuts the silence of the girl's bathroom after the door squeals, announcing their entry. I'm finishing up in the bathroom stall and can tell it's Bella Noble, able to place her nasal-centric voice with a touch of melodic lilt anywhere. "Of all the guys in the senior class, I want to get with Tanner James before this is all said and done."

I freeze, not wanting to flush before hearing what's said.

The girls with her mumble their agreement to chants of "he's hot," "so good looking," and a moaning assent as if he were a morsel in someone else's mouth. I hear the reverberation of bags filled with things set on the counter or floor. One of the girls — I'm not sure who at first — says, "He's so hot. I tried to get with him junior year."

I know who it is — Greta Mills — and clench my teeth remembering that day in the cafeteria when she was draped all over Tanner. After our infamous secret kiss.

"You didn't?" someone asks. It isn't Bella.

It's quiet, which makes me wonder what Greta communicated, but then she says, "No," so I don't have to guess. My eyebrows arch with the information, surprised. I thought for sure they'd hooked up.

"I'm calling dibs for Senior Send Off," Bella says.

Her claim makes my gut tighten. First to talk about him like he's a piece of meat on a platter is offensive (though I know I have nothing to say, really. It isn't like I haven't objectified him in my own mind in some ways, but I've never verbalized it to anyone like he's no more than a food item on my plate). Second, it makes me unsettled because it brings up the limo and being made to feel like an object. Third, the idea of Bella with Tanner makes me jealous as hell, even if I don't have a right to be.

That realization alone makes me angry with myself. I'm smart — I got accepted to my top three universities for goodness sake — I just seem to be missing out on the intelligence gene that tells me to stop crushing on a guy like Tanner James, who made it clear he isn't interested. I tried to crush the infatuation, but that night in January — outside of The Revolution after The Tinks show — spun my wheels. The smile. The wave. Nothing resulted from it besides some ambiguous looks, but it hasn't curbed my memory or my imagination.

"There are quite a few things I'd like to do to Tanner James." I picture Bella leaning forward and looking at something on her face by the stretched tone of her voice.

I roll my eyes. Of course she would, and if the rumors about Tanner's whoring ways are true, she would probably be successful. Even if I'd try to talk myself into being over my infatuation — because feelings in these circumstances are irrational — her claim about Tanner has me rolling my hands into tight fists with annoyance.

I flush the toilet, announcing my presence, and emerge from the stall.

The group made up of Bella, Greta, Cora Hennig, and Siobhan Crawly have their heads on a swivel and turn to look at me.

"Tanner James, huh?" I say and pass by them to the sink. Looking at Bella through the mirror while washing my hands, she watches me and gives me one of those half smiles that seems more like a string drawing up one side of her upper lip. "Good luck," I tell her.

"I don't need it," she says with a shoulder shrug. "I'm not like you."

"Care to elaborate?" I wave a washed hand in front of the electric towel dispenser. It hums as it releases a paper towel.

"I don't think a guy like Tanner would touch you with a ten-foot pole. You're so boring." She and her minions giggle. "What can you offer someone like him? School lessons?"

They all titter together.

I nod, pasting a fake smile on my face. "You might be right, Bella," I say, self-satisfied that Tanner has actually touched me. "I guess I'll find out how boring I am at Berkeley next year. Where are you going to school?"

Her smile fades, because if rumors are true, she didn't make the grade. Too much focus on non-academic activities, I surmise. There is a tangle of self-satisfaction in saying it, at first, but I recognize the pettiness of it and feel guilty. It isn't kind or Christ-like.

"Well–" I push my arms into my own backpack and settle it on my shoulders– "have fun at Senior Send Off." I leave the bathroom with their snarky comments caught on the door behind me.

Her accusation — *you're so boring . . .what can you offer someone like him* — has my mind swirling, overthinking as I walk to my locker.

I'm not boring!

But I know it's true.

I glance at Tanner's locker. He's there, so I open mine and shove my head inside, and then roll my eyes at myself for looking at all. Except I can't keep my eyes on the perfectly arranged interior of my locker. I sneak another peek. He's across the hallway leaning into his own locker. Balled up papers slip out, and he bends to pick them up. His red t-shirt moves with his body, the hem adjusting to allow a glimpse of tan skin at his waist. I'm thinking about him without his shirt and those blue jeans hanging from his hips, hugging his behind just right.

My stomach dissolves into a sparkly mess.

Tanner stands, and with a little shake of his head gets his dark hair, a little long with soft curls around his face, out of his warm brown eyes.

He turns his head, and I look away before I'm caught staring.

I could say I don't know why my insides melt when I see him. THAT would be a lie. Of course, I know WHY I'm attracted to him. Attraction isn't the issue. It's the stupidity of allowing it. It must be a truth universally acknowledged that my book smarts have detonated my common sense, or something like that. My brain knows I'm being ridiculous and counts the ways to remind me.

First, I'm freaking out of his league. Um, Truth: perhaps, it's the other way around. Compromise: a bit of both.

Second, he only dates party girls. I'm not.

Three, he's an f-boy.

Four, my future plans don't involve a guy like Tanner James, even if for some ridiculous reason I want them to involve Tanner James. I'm just so freaking curious.

I sigh, recalling Bella's awful accusation and hate that she's right. Aside from my drunken junior year risk, I've played my entire high school experience scared and safe. I smack the locker door shut and scold myself for looking at Tanner at all.

"I don't think that locker did anything to you." Liam leans against the locker next to mine, studying me. He's so nonchalant and cool, it's annoying.

"Where did you come from, and why do you care about it?" I ask. "In a week it will be old news."

"Taxpayer dollars." His eyes curl up at the edges with his smile, showing off his perfect pearly whites. "I always meet you here before class. You're being weird."

I adjust the straps of my backpack to make it fit better and follow Tanner's walk through the hallway past me with my eyes. His warm dark brown sugar eyes slide up and meet mine, just a moment, before melting away. He smiles at something his friend Griffin says as they pass. My insides flop over.

I turn back to Liam, whose smile has faded, and whose wise eyes assess me with too much awareness. "Emma." The warning in his voice loud and clear.

"I'm good. Promise."

He knows me too well and raises a single dark eyebrow. His lips thin out with censure. "Emma."

I lean against my closed locker and ignore his warning by saying, "Bella Noble called me boring."

"That bitch. Only I can call you boring."

I smile, but it's weighted with a regret and doubt concoction cooking up in my head and heart. He and Ginny basically had said the same thing a few nights ago.

"Who's boring?" Ginny asks joining us.

"Noble called our girl boring."

"Bitch. Only I can call you boring."

"That's what I said," Liam says. They high five.

"Hey. I'm right here."

"Who cares what she thinks," Ginny offers.

"I know that rationally." I pluck a piece of lint from Ginny's arm. "I just wonder if maybe she's right. Like maybe I should have done things a little differently, you know?"

"Let's do something tomorrow, then, after rehearsal," Liam suggests and swipes at an invisible something from his shirt. He looks like he always does — casual in his nice pants that fit him perfectly, and a clever t-shirt. Today it's his gray "Nerdy" shirt, the word disguised as Chemistry elements.

"Senior Send Off," Ginny says. "Saturday."

"And forgo our John Hughes movie night?"

"That would be very John Hughesesque of us." Ginny tilts her head, her eyebrows arched over her eyes as if she's all knowing.

"We never go to parties," I say.

"You never go to parties," Ginny amends, and when I give her a look, she corrects herself. "You're right. Sorry. Forgot who I was for a moment."

Liam laughs. "We're graduating a week from Saturday."

"Exactly. We have finals. This weekend should be spent studying–" I pause hearing myself. "I am boring."

Liam scrunches up his nose and smiles with his eyes. "At this point, I think studying is a moot point. We're graduating regardless. We're into college and how much are those finals really going to matter in the grand scheme of things."

"His reasoning is sound," Ginny says.

He wiggles his eyebrows up and down. "I'm ready to start studying for college."

Ginny and I laugh but nerves move under my skin and sink their hooks into muscles. The idea of going out, being out of my routine, has the breath caught in my chest, and I wonder how I am ever going to *do college* without my best friends. So many bad things could happen.

"She's going to faint." Ginny places a hand on my arm.

"I'm not." I swat her hand away. "I just realized how much I'm going to miss you guys next year."

"That's why we need to do this," Liam says. "Together."

I notice movement behind Liam and glance beyond him. Atticus Baker, just a few feet away, steps toward us then turns away. Then he turns back and clears his throat.

"Hi Atticus," I say.

Atticus looks unsure, swallows and tries to smile, but it kind of stalls on his mouth like a grimace. "Hi." He clears his throat again and shoves his hands into the pockets of his khaki pants.

Liam freezes, his eyes searching my face, and with his smile plastered on his face turns to look at Atticus behind him. He leans casually against the lockers next to me, but I suspect there is nothing casual about the way he's feeling. "Hey, Baker."

How does he sound so cool? I wonder.

The beautiful boy nods at me and Ginny, but then settles his gorgeous dark eyes on Liam. "I was wondering if I could talk to you?" His voice sounds like velvet feels: rich, smooth, decadent.

"Sure." Liam doesn't move, which I have the impression Atticus hoped for, but now isn't sure how to suggest it.

I turn my head to look at Ginny who seems to be operating on the same wavelength as I am. She leans against the lockers on the other side of me. We look at my phone even if we aren't actually focused on my phone at all. That's about all the privacy he'll get without us walking away, which might be more awkward.

Atticus clears his throat again. "Yeah. So." He stalls, but I can't see him and suddenly wish I could. A second or so later he rushes forward, his words moving like smooth water and sand mixed together in the same container, "Would you like to go to the Senior Send Off? Like, with me?"

I see Ginny squeeze her eyes shut with excitement.

My heart sputters and then speeds up as if running downhill. Is he asking Liam out on a date?

"Oh," Liam says. "I just made plans to go with Emma and Ginny."

Ginny's eyes fly open. "Liam!" Her voice is so loud, I jump. She moves away from the lockers to save a situation that Liam's about to mess up. "We can meet you both there, or something. Right, Emma?"

"Of course." I look at Liam, trying to speak to him with my eyes.

"No way," he says. "You'll back out, Emma."

I close my eyes. He's so dense sometimes. What had I just been thinking about smarts and common sense?

"What if I drive all of us?" Atticus offers a bright smile. "Yeah." He gives a definitive nod. "I can drive."

Liam's brows shift toward one another, and then, as if he's just figured out something, raise up over his eyes. He adjusts his glasses. "Okay." He glances at me, his eyes wide.

"Maybe I can get your number?" Atticus asks. "We can plan it?"

Liam nods and pushes away from the lockers, so he stands up. "May I see your phone?"

Atticus pulls it from his pocket and sets it in Liam's open hand. He then folds his arms tightly over his chest while he waits, the blue t-shirt bunching up between them. Goodness, his biceps are gorgeous.

Liam types his information into Atticus's phone and then says, "There." He holds the phone out.

Atticus takes it; his hand brushes Liam's.

Liam blushes, the heat even turning his ears pink.

"Let me text you so you have mine."

I turn my face away to look at Ginny, because I'm smiling so big. My cheeks heat with excitement.

Liam's phone buzzes with a riff of a Beyoncé song. "Nice," Atticus says.

"It came through."

"Yeah. Cool." There's a pause, and then Atticus says — and I can hear the smile — "It's a date then."

Liam hesitates a moment, and I wonder if he's questioning it. I know he is. "Yeah. A date."

Atticus says something about going to class and leaves us standing in the hall. After he's gone, Liam looks at us, his eyes wide when our gazes meet. "Do what I think just happened, really happen?"

Ginny and I squeal, folding Liam into a hug. We walk like an amoeba down the hall to class. We're late and don't really care.

tanner

I'm slouched all the way down in the stupid desk, arms crossed over my chest, listening to Ms. Roche drone on about what to study that weekend for the psychology final. I glance at Griff asleep on the desk next to me. He's folded up his arms, face planted in the space between them.

"This is really important so get this down." Roche turns to write on the white board. "When considering locus of control." Her chicken scratch spells out the words intrinsic and extrinsic on the board.

I zone out, staring at the green cover of the spiral notebook on my desk, my mind replaying the walk through the hallway with Griff past Emma. She was standing next to her locker, hands holding her backpack straps, talking to Liam. Dressed in one of those short twirly skirts, and a fitted black t-shirt, and the backpack straps pulling at the fabric, so I noticed her boobs — which I've touched and have dreamed about touching again. God, she turns me on. I close my eyes to try and squelch the memory but can't. She's still there, in my mind, smiling. I imagine the wave from January but how she's dressed today.

When I think of you, my insides slow.

The words move through me unbidden as if inking a tattoo on the underside of my skin. I lean forward to adjust my body. I don't need a hard on in the middle of class. As much as I've tried to ignore the feelings Emma inspires in me, I can't squelch them anymore. Not since the wave. I was never very good at dousing them, but the wave — or my thoughts about it — changed everything.

When I think of you, my insides slow.

I open the closed notebook, click the pen and write the eight initial words, but then more words flow as if the pen has a mind of its own:

When I think of you, my insides slow. The inside parts that I won't let other people see. It's like time lapse photography, stretching the seconds I see you in my mind into infinite frames and highlighting feeling in the spaces I thought I'd lost. Buzzing with warmth and something probably like happiness, I ponder the hazy, distant feeling not exactly sure how to name it. I wrap the soft parts of myself around the idea of you, and long to wrap the rest of myself around you, too.

When I think about you, I smile, and have to pretend Griff said something entertaining. I do that a lot because you're on my mind. Griff isn't that funny. I'm thinking about your cute face. The way you twirl a curl of your hair around your finger when you're serious. The way you wear your backpack with both straps. The way your eyes get bigger when you're about to snap at someone. Or when you get that little line between them that has a reason I don't know but always wonder about. Your boobs. My hands tingle sometimes remembering them against your body that one time junior year.

When I think about you, I wish I were different. I wish I deserved you. I don't.

I sit up and stare at the page, the blue ink slanted left because my left hand can't follow the rules either. I reread it, and my heart races. The idea of someone seeing it makes the plumbing in my chest clog.

"Questions?" Ms. Roche asks.

A few hands shoot up.

Emma looked at me earlier, in the hallway, her dark blue eyes that I know are a cosmos, watching me as I walked to class. Griff had been talking about Kristina Burrow's ass, but I was looking at Emma and wondering if I was imagining her eyes following me. I think about the wave in January. Emma. Her laugh with Ginny and the magic steam from Emma's mouth like a visual of her laughter. Raising my hand. Her smile. Her wave in return. And now, a little while ago, her eyes following me. Could she still be interested?

The bell rings.

Griff pops up and runs a forearm over his mouth to catch the sludge of his drool.

I move to close the notebook and put it away, but Griff's eyes catch sight of ink on a page. A novelty. I should have known better. He swipes at it, catching it with his hands before I can.

"Whoa, Tanner. You taking notes?"

"Give it back, Griff." I slip the pen into my backpack and stand up, backpack open on the desktop.

He stands, glances at me and smiles. "Why? Embarrassed to be studious?" Then he looks at it and starts reading.

"Give me the fucking notebook." I reach for it, and he rolls his body away from me.

His back is to me as if we're playing one-on-one on the basketball court, the spiral notebook out in front of him, he reads: "When I think of you, my insides slow." He smiles and laughs. "Damn, Tanner did you write this crap?" His voice raises several octaves and thins out as he continues, "It's like time lapse photography, stretching the seconds I see you in my mind into infinite frames and highlighting feeling in the spaces I thought I'd lost." He laughs. "What the fuck is this shit? Sounds like something a chick would write." He throws the notebook, and it lands in a haphazard heap on the desk.

Then he walks out of the classroom.

"Everything alright, Mr. James?" Ms. Roche asks me from the front of the room where she's erasing the board. Her silver eyebrows are drawn together between her eyes with concern.

"Yeah." I grab the notebook, stuff it in my backpack and leave the classroom.

senior year
(8 days to graduation)

"Lucy grinned like she'd swallowed me whole, and I gritted my teeth. 'You think you know everything, don't you?'

'I do. You're going to ruin my set up.' I glanced at my place setting for one. 'I'm good.' I rearranged my eating utensils, shades of gray.

'Suit yourself.' She walked away.

Damn me. I couldn't tear my eyes away from her. She left a trail a million variations of the rainbow."

-unnamed protagonist, *Kaleidoscope Concussion* by Saul Annick

e m m a

The senior class erupts with movement and noise the moment Mr. Sanderson, our principal, dismisses us from rehearsal. I look for Ginny and Liam in the crowd now grouping up like separate leaves on the same tree. Lingering. I have the impression all of us are hesitant to leave; as if when we cross the entrance of the football field, we'll cross into a world none of us know how to navigate but pretend like we do.

"Excuse me," I say, moving through bodies. As I walk through the groups, keeping my eyes low, I encounter chests, shoulders, hats, hair, a few faces. I twist my body here, shoulder duck there with the "excuse me" I repeat time and again, until I face a navy-blue wall with white ink that reads, *That's a horrible idea. What time?* It makes me smile, and I look up at the face of Tanner James.

My heart speeds up, and my breath comes out in a little burst.

He's looking down at me.

I'm transported to that night junior year. He'd looked down at me, a smile on his mouth, like now. Before I'd kissed him. I shake my head to return to the present. The hat he's wearing, a red one, is backward on his head, and his dark hair curls around the edges. His eyes widen and then he smiles wider; it does amazing things to his face, brightening everything about him.

I try to say excuse me, but have to try a second time, because I can't seem to get my air or words past my dry throat. "Excuse me," finally pops out.

Still smiling, he moves so that I can pass.

I turn my body, angling it between him and someone else, trying not to brush against him as I do. There's an itch in my palm to run my hand over his chest, and I grasp the hem of my skirt, so I don't reach to touch him like a weirdo. I can't keep myself from looking up at his face just one more time. He's following me with his gaze. The smile is gone. Though, when my eyes meet his, he raises his eyebrows as if asking me a question. I'm not sure what the question is, but I wish I did know, because a glittery explosion of awareness has detonated in my chest.

Someone bumps me, and I step forward to catch my balance, right into Tanner. His hands wrap around my upper arms, catching me, holding me. His fingers are warm against my skin, hands calloused, and I like the way they feel.

My heart, suddenly full of helium, sputters around in my chest. "Sorry," I say and move away, my face hot.

He lets me go. "No apology necessary."

His voice. The perfect tone is a concoction of butter and sugar drizzled over my eardrums. Everything in me melts. I turn away, keep moving, and roll my eyes at myself as I do.

I only make it a few steps when Liam and Ginny find me. "There you are!"

"I was looking for you." Ginny wraps an arm around my shoulders.

It takes everything in me not to turn around to look at Tanner. To see if he's still there. To wish the moment could last just a little longer.

"Let's go to Marta's for shakes," Ginny says.

Liam is texting.

"Yes."

He looks up from his phone. "Is it okay if I invite Atticus?" He smiles.

"Do!" Ginny and I reply in unison with equal exuberance, and Ginny threads her arm with mine to lead me from the football field.

I can't help it. As if I'm Lot's wife unable to resist the temptation, I turn to get one more glimpse of Tanner. I don't turn into a pillar of salt but do melt into a puddle of longing.

He's still there, just a few steps behind me, and as Ginny leads me away, he moves his head and glances at us. I don't look away immediately, wanting to hold onto the way he looks standing there in the middle of the field. The backwards hat and the navy t-shirt hugging his torso so I can see his shoulders and tapered waist. His arms, which I know are the perfect sinew of muscle, are crossed over his chest. I'm hopeful he might see me, see that I'm not boring, but eventually I have to acknowledge that I have nothing to offer him. I finally turn forward grateful his image is seared in my mind. Maybe if I weren't so boring, like Bella Noble said, Tanner would kiss me again. Though I want to do so much more with Tanner James, and that is very dangerous indeed.

tanner

I watch Emma leave the field with her friends and on a whim say, "You guys want to go get burgers at Marta's?" I'd overheard them, and I know that's where they are going. My body hums with Emma's touch, so I want to chase it. She'd looked back.

It made me think about the wave. She'd waved back.

Which makes me think about junior year. The kiss. I would really like to kiss Emma Matthews again, though I can feel there's a lot more to my want than that.

"Dude," Josh says. "Fuck, yes. I'm starving."

"Danny? Griff?"

They agree, and we leave the field and climb into our respective cars. Danny rides with Josh, and Griff rides with me.

Griff talks about Senior Send Off. "Josh and I are going to pack up his truck tonight with the camping gear. We'll go out first thing in the morning to get our spot. Let's hope last year's seniors haven't taken all the prime real estate."

I don't need to respond, because Griff continues talking, which is a good thing. I'm preoccupied with thoughts about Emma anyway. My hands on her soft skin. I think about her night sky eyes. That kiss from junior year. Her body pressed against mine a moment ago.

"Tanner?"

"Huh?"

"What the fuck? I asked you a question."

"Oh. Sorry. I was thinking about court next week." It's a lie, but I don't feel like sharing my true thoughts with Griff.

"When's that?"

"Monday."

"Nice. One less day to be in school." He doesn't get that I'd rather be in school when it comes to family court. "Can you grab a couple of coolers of ice? Your dad has an ice machine out at his shop, right?"

"Yeah. Sure." I turn the vehicle into the parking lot outside Marta's Diner. I park in a shady spot facing the main road, and Josh pulls his truck next to mine. Griff and I wait at the tailgate for Josh and Danny to get out so we can walk in together. My heart pounds in my chest at the prospect of seeing Emma again. I wonder if she'll think it's weird to see me. I wonder if she'll know I overheard them. That I followed. Maybe this is a bad idea.

The smell of food is in the air, heavy with smoke, onions and spices.

Josh moans and rubs his belly. "I'm gonna get a double with two fries and a giant chocolate shake." He's always hungry. There's no backing out now.

I pull the glass door open by the metal handle and hold it open for my friends.

A bell rings as we enter. Griff and Danny are first, followed by Josh and then me.

My eyes adjust to the different lighting. Marta's is retro even if the restaurant isn't trying to be. It's old, a fixture of our town, and so much time has passed, it's cool again. The dark rock walls mixed with the turquoise tables marbled with orange and green is a throwback to the bygone seventies. Brass pendant lights hang from the ceiling over the tables. The chairs have a space-like curve to them, the bases a mixture of white plastic and brass. There is a marbled horseshoe countertop full of patrons and servers bustling about behind it. A long rectangular window with heating lamps offers glimpses of the stainless-steel kitchen and the short order cooks inside. The rest of the restaurant is filled with tables and turquoise vinyl booths.

I glance around trying to appear nonchalant but not feeling it. My muscles bunch up with tension, and I know I hadn't thought this through.

"There's a place," Griff says and leads us up an aisle past occupied booths.

I glance at the occupants of each one as we pass, hopeful, yet anxious to see Emma.

"Tanner," I hear someone say and look for the voice.

It's Atticus. "Baker." I smile at my friend and head toward his table. Ever since the party at his house, he and I have talked more. He's a cool dude. We shake hands, and then I glance at his companions, assuming he'll be with his basketball friends. The first face I see is Liam. And then Ginny. And finally, my eyes stop at Emma. I can feel the way my smile freezes as my nerves take over. I can't remember the last time I felt nervous about a girl. I look away as Atticus greets Griff, Josh, and Danny, filing for thoughts that are coherent and trying to find words. They're failing me.

Atticus makes sure everyone knows everyone else. "Sorry, we don't have more room," he says referring to their booth.

"It's okay. There's a table over there. We're going to go grab it," Griff says and continues into the restaurant.

Josh and Danny follow him.

I have nothing; my mind is blank, and I've no reason to stay.

"You guys going to Senior Send Off?" Atticus asks as he sits back down next to Liam, who looks salty.

Thank you, Baker. I glance at Ginny, who's smiling, but it doesn't quite reach her eyes. Tough crowd. "Yeah," I say. "Camping. You?"

"Headed out with these guys tomorrow afternoon."

I chance a look at Emma, who's looking at the table. "That's cool." It's all I can formulate. I wish she'd look at me. I'd like to see her eyes. I'd like to know if she still wants to kiss me, but she doesn't look up.

"I'll look for you," Atticus says.

"Yeah." I don't have any reason to stay, so I shake his hand again.

"Later, then." I walk away, my stomach imploding on itself with regret and disappointment. I don't turn around. I can't. It would be so obvious. When I get to the table Griff found, I slide into the seat next to Josh; I can't see Emma from there.

We order.

We eat.

Ginny and Emma pass our table on the way to the restroom.

Josh wipes his fingers with a napkin. "That Ginny Donnelly is hot." He nods his head at the girls' backs. "Emma Matthews is cute too."

I agree, but I don't say anything.

Griff shrugs. "Ah. They're alright. They aren't party girls."

"Is that all you care about?" Josh asks and shoves some fries into his mouth.

"Is there anything else?" Griff asks.

Josh chuckles. "Well, actually, yeah. I think so."

Emma and Ginny walk back a few minutes later. I can see Emma's face now as she passes us to get to her table. She looks at me, just a brief moment, and looks away, but the longer effect of that look sparks a fuse at the base of my spine. *Yeah, Josh*, I think. *I'm beginning to think so too.*

senior year
(7 days to graduation)

"Erickson Dorn glanced from the blood streaked across the back of his hand, up his arm, and then to my nose; I could feel it draining red rivulets, running over my mouth, which tasted like iron on my tongue. He grinned; blood smeared across his face like a madman who'd taken his ounce of flesh. It was a grim reminder of what we'd become: two assholes with ideas of what it meant to be free. The violence a price to pay for the risk of floating in the rainbow. I laughed."

-unnamed protagonist, *Kaleidoscope Concussion* by Saul Annick

emma

The sun slips closer to the golden hour, and the temperate air of early June warms the evening. I leave my house and hop down the porch steps in my low-top red converse, khaki shorts that show off my legs, and black tank. With a bag slung over my shoulder, I skip down the walkway toward my friends who are coming up the sidewalk. They're smiling and talking about the graduation rehearsal the day before, because I hear Ginny mimic our principal Mr. Sanderson's ridiculous directions followed by, "Let's get this right, people." Clap. Clap.

It makes me happy seeing them, Atticus now, too, since he's spent the better part of the last 12 hours with us from school to rehearsal to Marta's for milkshakes. I'm happy for Liam and then think of Tanner the day before, first at rehearsal and then the shock of seeing him at Marta's. What a surprise that had been! I'm terrible with surprises and couldn't wrap my head around my own thoughts. I couldn't even look at him and flush with embarrassed heat just thinking about it.

I shake my head to put myself back into this moment, and to focus on the three people moving toward me. A sunburst fills my heart with loose joy. Ginny's thick hair is drawn back into a haphazard bun and she's laughing. Dressed in a cute yellow sundress over a green and white swimsuit, she waves. "Emma!"

Liam and Atticus, behind her a few steps, walk closely, arms brushing. Both dressed in swim trunks and t-shirts, Atticus's shorts are bright coral orange with aqua flamingos which show off his long, fit legs while Liam's trunks are solid navy. Their sandals smack the concrete as they walk.

"I can be the designated driver." I wag my keys at them.

"No!" Liam and Ginny say in unison with enough force it causes me to sputter step and stall. I have a sense this was a topic of conversation for them on the way here.

Glancing at Atticus, he's smiling as if he'd been warned. He shrugs.

"You'll use it as an excuse." Liam shakes his head, and his carefully styled hair remains in place.

"We're doing this thing together!" Ginny points at me. "TOGETHER!" She emphasizes the word by drawing out its syllables. "That means, we are going all in, both feet, whatever the experience may be."

"I've got it." Atticus holds up his lanyard. "I offered. It's all good." His dark chocolate eyes flit to Liam.

I recognize his look full of hope and wanting. My heart expands in my chest, but my brain also begins spinning. There are a million possibilities of the ways one of us could get hurt. What if something goes wrong? "I have to study," I sputter. "So, I won't be drinking. What time–"

"Emma!" Ginny and Liam cry in unison. Liam's arms flail with exasperation.

"You could fail all of your finals and still ace your classes," Ginny says. "It's time to let go." She links her arm with mine. "Let's have fun."

I notice Liam's glance at Atticus, and the unspoken communication that passes between them.

"What?"

"Nothing," Liam says and takes my arm on the opposite side. He hums several bars of "Please Let Me Get What I Want" as we move down the sidewalk. Ginny and I join him. Then he says, "For tonight, we channel Ferris and Crew. We are invincible. Let's let go and just accept what life offers."

Liam's words soothe and still my overthinking mind. I picture Tanner, who said he'd be there, even though I know he isn't the intent of Liam's meaning. I nod. "You're right."

"We've got each other." Ginny lays a hand on my forearm. "Promise." She curls her pinkie finger for a pinkie swear; I'm transported to fifth grade when we made blanket forts and had sleepovers inside of them.

I wrap my pinkie around hers and nod. "I know. That's never been a question." But the future is. What about in August, when we've all branched out in separate directions? I swallow the fear in my throat. Or in a week when I'm standing on the stage reciting my speech, alone? Though it isn't about being alone, not really. It's about the unknown, the fear of making a mistake, of everyone seeing the real me, the imperfect broken one.

Pastor Green's words come back to me: *It isn't about your attempt at perfection. None of us can attain it. It is a lie to think we can.* I take a deep breath, committed to letting go and doing my best to immerse myself in this experience with my friends. I don't want to be boring and afraid anymore.

When Atticus turns his car onto the highway, Liam turns up the radio to a song we love, and it blasts over the speakers. With the window open and summer air moving through my hair, I sing along with my friends, our voices loud and off key through our smiles. I close my eyes a moment to feel the poignancy, to feel the smile in my heart. I want to remember this exact feeling, to hold onto it, so I can carry it to college with me like a security blanket.

Atticus's car speeds down the road toward the party at the Quarry. A regular spot for amusement when the weather is good, the abandoned quarry turned lake has always been the site for the Senior Send Off tradition the weekend before graduation. Tiered on three sides by giant terraced steps from the water's edge, the walls of the Quarry climb at least a hundred feet toward the sky and trees stretch across the top. The bottom is filled with bright green water. Rumors have always run it's so deep there's a monster lurking in the center. Regardless, it keeps little kids at the edges on summer days. I've spent many summer days with my family there. The fourth side stretches out from the water's edge into parkland. It's here that people picnic and camp. Along the eastern ridge, there's a semi-wilderness in a copse of trees near the water's edge where there's an old swing to launch bodies out into the water. A few yards from there, a short climb up one of the tiers is a cliff where braver souls jump into the water below. I have never done either, but this is where most of the party will be.

Atticus parks his car, and we make the short hike from the lot into the forest toward the revelry. The sun is still up but has just dipped over the edge of the western quarry wall, casting longer shadows. Music, boisterous laughter, the smell of barbecue, the splash of water indicates the revelry started a while ago. Tents are set up along with chairs and fires in pits. Ginny grabs my hand, and I squeeze hers.

Liam and Atticus lead us into the heart of the party. It surprises me since we've never been center-of-the-party people. Heck, we haven't been periphery-of-the-party people. Then I remember, Atticus is: he's well-liked and knows people. Tanner came over to our table the day before because of Atticus. He glances over his shoulder with a smile at Liam and then at Ginny and me that communicates, *I've got you*, as if he were always a part of our group.

"Matthews?"

Corbin from my AP History class waves. "Oh damn! I didn't ever expect to see you at a party, and definitely not this one." He looks around and reaches into a cooler. "Here! This requires a toast." He hands Ginny and me a bottle of beer each. I crane my neck to catch sight of Liam and Atticus who it seems we've lost. Corbin holds his beer up. "A toast to never having to listen to Mr. Groans go on about imperialism ever again."

I offer him a polite smile at his use of the nickname for our teacher and tip the beer up for a sip. "Why not this party?" I ask him.

"It's wild. Every year there's some sordid story that makes the rumor rounds finals week. Don't you pay attention?"

"Not to stuff like that."

"I just wouldn't have pegged you for this party seeing as you don't come to parties. You're like — good."

His assessment stings, and coupled with Bella's *You're boring* knock, I frown. It hurts more, because there's truth in it. I struggle with the part of me that got lost in the back of a limo, another part of me that wishes I'd been braver, a little wilder, and the part of me who's okay with who I am. My brain reminds me that fear is safer, but I'm beginning to wonder if that's true.

"You have to do the rope swing or the cliff jump," he says. "I did it earlier. Oh. Maybe that's too much for you."

"Yeah. I'll look into it," I say without meaning it and listen to the sudden need to get away from Corbin's preconceived ideas about me. "Thanks for the beer. Ginny and I need to find Liam and Atticus. Our ride," I tell him as Ginny pulls me away from him through the crowd.

We wander in the direction Atticus and Liam walked and eventually find them amidst the throng of dancing people. Thankfully, Atticus is tall, and it's easy to spot him. Liam waves at us to join them. "This is intense," he says with a wide smile when we reach them. "I love it!"

"What now?" I ask, feeling out of place, awkward and a little panicky.

"Let's dance," Ginny suggests. "I love this song!"

Like pinballs in a machine, we bounce off other people, until we find a spot to gyrate like fools. We twirl and laugh until our stomachs hurt. It's amazing and wonderful and freeing.

Ginny talks me into hiking the terrace to watch the jumpers. I agree, forcing myself to face the fears that often get in my way, chanting *let go, let go, let go* as we climb the rocky incline. Now I'm huddled next to Ginny near the edge of the crowd that surrounds those brave enough to fly from an outcropping of rock situated between the first and second tier quarry terrace steps. My heart races, and my stomach is unsettled.

"What are we doing up here?" I turn to ask her, but she is talking to someone.

She smiles, widens her eyes at me and tilts her head toward her companion. Check that. She's flirting.

There's no way I'm getting in the middle of that, so I fix my gaze at the edge of the precipice. My heart thumps in my ears with nervous energy watching people risk their lives and limbs. I step back to avoid a kid, a junior I recognize from school, who backs up into the crowd. I could touch his pasty white shoulder and tell him to stop, tell him not to throw away his future, but I don't, checking myself. With a yell, he runs and launches himself over the edge disappearing into the dark. A moment later we hear the splash followed by a cheer that erupts from all of the spectators cliff side.

I shudder.

The energy, however, is intoxicating. It buzzes like electricity around us, humming a tempting song that makes me smile even amidst my nerves. I shudder again with it, trembling with anticipation and maybe even a vein of bravery which propels me to step forward through the crowd. Leaving Ginny's side to give her room to flirt, I take a tentative step toward the edge. Without a specific reason, I'm compelled to stand at the edge of the bluff and peer over the edge. Perhaps it's the adrenaline pulsing through my blood talking to my limbs. Maybe it's the symbolism of wanting to live a little and standing at the edge of a cliff feels like harnessing the fear that is always present in my mind without the risk of actually jumping.

The closer I get, I have the urge to drop to my knees and crawl to the edge, except I know how stupid that would look. Instead, I edge forward and lean to peer over. One foot is in front of me, and the other foot is rooted to the ground behind me. One glance, and my nerves drop through my skin into the dirt with a thud. Though someone has rigged a generator with lights, and there are fires dotting the lakeside, the bottom — the water — is black, obscured by the darkness. Jumping would mean falling toward something you can't see — the unknown. Panic seizes my heart and lungs as a cold sweat breaks out on my brow and a wave of dizziness crashes over me.

"It helps to relax when you're planning to jump," a voice says next to me.

"I have no plans to jump." I straighten, take a cleansing breath, and turn my head to see who's talking to me.

Tanner James — shirtless, board shorts hanging on his hips slightly askew, and the ridges of his chest and abdomen traced by generator light and moonlight — watches me. His hair is wet, curly; he's jumped. Of course he has.

"What?" he asks. "You're already up here. It would be a shame to waste that climb." He smiles, and I feel my rapid pulse low in my belly.

My mouth dries out.

I swallow and look around to reorient myself. "Good exercise," I say and move away from the edge. "I just came to watch."

"Scared, Emma?" he asks me.

I glance at him, confused if I just heard him say my name. He's grinning as if we've been friends for years. Sure. We kissed. But this is Tanner. I'm shocked he remembers my name. Wait. I'm not. I'm Emma Matthews. I'm awesome. Besides, I know his name. We've been in school together since middle school. Except, I feel like he's laughing at me, and irritation rips around inside me. "Actually, yes, I am. I have no intention of jumping into an abyss of death."

He chuckles and looks down at the gravel.

My blood effervesces, heating all the parts of me, and it annoys me more because it feels like I've been struck by lightning. I want to smack myself for even entertaining my infatuation. I just can't seem to turn it off, but if I'm being honest, maybe I don't really want to. I turn to go.

The crowd surges, blocking my path when a burst of sound cuts the din with a noisemaker.

Someone yells into a megaphone, "It's time for the annual senior partner jump!"

"That's a thing?" My heart leaps into my throat. I tense, unable to get through the crowd. I glance at Tanner behind me, but not completely cognizant that it's him. My brain has taken a nosedive into panic mode.

"Oh my god, Emma. You should see the size of your eyes."

"I need to leave." I need to get to a safe distance. Terror squeezes my lungs.

"No. Wait." Tanner grabs my hand, keeping me from disappearing into the crowd. "Be my partner."

An electromagnetic pulse snaps through my muscles. First it stops my heart, and then it restarts so it palpitates in my chest. Panic races through me for so many reasons, but Tanner's hand holding mine — his touch — sends an electric current through my arm. He's talking to me — he said my name after all — so it isn't a mistake. He's asked me to be his jump partner. I'm terrified of both prospects! This is good. This is terrible!

I shake my head even though I hear that little voice in my head, and we go to war:

Why are you here, Emma?

I don't know!

Are you always going to stand on the sidelines?

Yes. It's safe there.

Are you boring?

I look for Ginny, but I don't see her in the crowd. My eyes seek Tanner's. "I—"

He steps closer. My chest eases with him so close, but flutters with a different tension. I forget all the reasons I'm not supposed to crush on him. He says, "I got you, Em. Promise."

"I can't do it." I raise my eyes to his.

His eyes dive into mine, cataloguing the fear, or so I imagine. "Yes.

You can. With me." The look contains the want I noticed in Atticus's look at Liam earlier, as if Tanner has a wish that only I can grant. Impossible.

The megaphone voice asks, "Any volunteers?"

"Us," Tanner has said but hasn't looked away from me, his eyes still and purposefully connected with mine.

The crowd cheers.

He takes my hand. The calluses I noticed the other day tell me a story of strength and accomplishment, hard work; capable hands that draw me next to him. I tremble even as his heat seeps into my side.

We're standing cliffside, and I look out into the darkness. "I can't do it." Fear locks my muscles.

"Matthews — that isn't true." His voice is gentle in my ear. I feel his mouth move against my skin. I cling to his arm, but I can't look away from the darkness beyond my toes. "You can do anything, Em. It isn't *a can't* but *a won't*."

Logically, I know he's correct, but my body, which seems to want to hunch closer to the earth, is saying *can't*.

"Look at me, Emma."

Somehow, I do, and realize how close we are.

"I'd never force you to jump, but I sure would like you to choose to jump with me."

The chaos of the chanting crowd recedes. I focus on Tanner and replay his words: *I sure would like you to choose to jump with me.*

He asked.

He asked me.

Tanner is all I see, all I hear, and in that moment, the fear settles into something less acute like sediment drifting to the bottom of a lake to rest. I nod. "Okay," I say before I can even stop myself.

He smiles and takes my hand, the one cutting blood flow from his arm. He turns. "On three."

"I'm terrified."

"That's the point." He squeezes my hand with his. It sends a strange confidence through my limbs.

"One. Two. Three."

And then I'm stepping off the edge of the cliff and falling through the air. My eyes squeezed tight, my hand in Tanner's, I'm screaming like I've reached the end of my life. Freefalling. Forever. Until feet first, cold wet slams against my skin, and the water of the lake swallows us whole.

I'm disoriented, but I feel my hand still in Tanner's and kick. I break the surface. "Holy shit!"

Tanner still has my hand. He pulls me closer and wraps an arm around my waist. "I told you I wouldn't let you go."

I throw my arms around his neck, press my forehead against his cheek and giggle, adrenaline rushing through me. Our limbs entwine in the water, my bare legs with his, the slip of our skin against one another as we kick to stay afloat. My pulse skips. He draws me tighter, his other hand treading water. I can't help it, I laugh again, giddy. "I can't believe I did that." I'm aware that I'm pressed up against him. "We did that!" So close. I shiver as the adrenaline moves, and my heart jumps ahead of me. "That was fun."

He clears his throat. "We should move before someone jumps on us."

"Yes." My cheeks heat as I think about junior year. *We should stop.* I remember the assumption that Tanner had been embarrassed, even if maybe it wasn't accurate. I move from his embrace, glancing around to find the shore. I'm turned around and inside out in more ways than one, but I reorient when I see the fires dotting the bank. I head in that direction.

Tanner calls after me, "You in a hurry?"

"You just said we needed to move." I roll to my back and swim through the water backward, facing him.

"Yeah, but I just meant—" He stops, leaving the thought unfinished and swims toward me. "It was good, right?"

I test the bottom by sinking under the water. Still can't touch.

"Right?" he asks when I resurface.

He's close again, and it's crossing my logical and emotional connections. I want to press my body against him again. I want to feel his arm around me. I want to feel our legs entwined. My heart skips, and my nerve endings vibrate. I want to take his face between my hands and kiss him, but I don't, a current of something in me that says it isn't appropriate. Random messages cross between what I want and what I've been taught. What it means to be in control.

"What was that?" I ask, trying to reconnect my thinking synapsis with my emotional ones.

"It was good, right?"

I don't know Tanner well, even if I've known him a long time, even if we've kissed. We haven't spent much time together. I don't understand his sounds or his looks. There's a tone of his voice that makes me wonder if he's worried about what I will say. Then he smiles and that moment of vulnerability slips away.

"When I realized I hadn't died, yes." I laugh. "It was awesome." Then inexplicably, I don't censor myself, at war with overthinking and my wants and say, "With you."

His grin deepens. "Let's go closer where we can touch." He clears his throat, realizing what he's said and tries to correct. "Oh shit. I mean the ground." He offers a subdued laugh, a sheepishness I've never attributed to him. It makes my nerves dance in pleasant ways.

I laugh as we swim. "I figured."

"Though, I'm game if you are." His eyes shine in the darkness.

"Tanner James? Are you flirting with me?" I ask, suddenly buoyant and ready to fly. Finally, my feet are under me on solid ground, but my body still floats.

"Would you hate that?" he asks.

But I don't get a chance to answer because someone yells my name from the shore. "Emma! Emma! Where are you? Emma!" It's Ginny, whose voice bounces across the water in the dark.

I look to the shore and see her shadow flanked by the forms of Liam and Atticus. "I'm here," I call, but I know they can't see me.

"Oh my god! You jumped!" Ginny squeals.

Tanner shakes out his hair, which seems to fall perfectly after he does, curling and sticking up at the ends. He's standing up, and I can make out some of his handsome form because of the firelight, but it's shadowed in shades of blue.

I have the urge to reach out and touch him but resist the impulse. My cheeks heat with a blush for even thinking about it, thankful for the obscurity in the dark to hide my true thoughts. Fear steps up again to make me doubt myself. "Thank you." I wish I could impart how much jumping with him meant to me. It hasn't cured my longing to be near him, though. "You know. For being my jumping partner." Intensified it perhaps.

He stretches out his hand to me. "Want to jump with me again?"

I give him a nervous laugh and take his offered hand. "I think my heart can only take that once."

"You might be surprised." He pulls me toward him through the water, drawing me closer, so we're facing one another with barely a breath between us.

He lets go of my hand, but his eyes stop at my lips.

Does he want to kiss me?

I can't breathe.

"Emma?" Ginny's again. "Are you okay? We can't see you."

"I'm good," I call out but remain motionless under Tanner's gaze, afraid to break the spell. The weight of it hints at the possibility of weight in other ways. I can't look away from him, and my breath moves in shorter bursts.

"Are you?" he asks quietly. "Good?"

A little sound of affirmation moves through my nose. My chest tightens and warms, spreading out like hot tendrils inside of me.

"I'd like to jump with you again, Em." I don't think he's talking about jumping. I think of junior year, of kissing him. But instead of kissing me — like I really want him to do — he moves away. He offers me his hand again and leads me to the shore.

So, with my hand in his, we slosh through the water, no words shared between us. I feel steady, sure and secure. The last time I felt that seems a lifetime ago. My insides settle in the silence, but curious about it. I wonder what he's thinking. I've never thought of him as quiet, and the awareness rocks my perceptions like tiny landmines. When we reach Ginny, Liam and Atticus, my friends rush forward, drawing me away from Tanner, and he releases my hand.

"Oh my god! You did it, Emma. You jumped!" Ginny's exuberance rushes around me, and I smile. I glance over her shoulder at Tanner who's talking to Atticus. His gaze flicks to me a moment, with a short smile I'm not sure how to interpret.

"Anyone else want to jump?" Tanner asks everyone but looks at me; it makes me think about Atticus looking at Liam again.

"We're good." Liam's tone isn't inviting.

"Okay." Tanner shakes Atticus's hand. "Thanks, Emma," he says and disappears down the shoreline.

"Bitch!" Ginny yells at me with a huge grin. "My heart stopped when you went over the cliff!" She smacks my shoulder.

I watch Tanner get swallowed by the darkness over her shoulder and turn to my friends with a bright smile. "I can't believe it."

Liam turns to look at me — he was also watching Tanner — "With James?" His eyes narrow. He isn't happy about it.

"Bitch, please," Ginny says. "Who cares who she jumped with. Our girl jumped!"

A smile and laugh bursts from inside me, and I'm transported into the happiness of junior year after kissing Tanner, walking with my friends down the street afterward. "I did, didn't I." The adrenaline wearing off makes me quiver. There's a lot of quick talking, emphatic movements and jostling of my body by Ginny. Liam is subdued, and I'm still thinking about Tanner.

Who cares who I jumped with?

"I wouldn't have done it without Tanner." I say it more to myself than to anyone specifically. It's the truth, though perhaps Corbin's earlier comment about me not being wild, and my own insecurities about Bella's *boring* accusation are in play. Anyone else holding my hand and asking me to jump would have been rejected. Tanner — only Tanner — could have enticed me to take that risk. "I may have agreed to jump but wouldn't have done it with anyone else." I tremble again.

Liam takes my hand. I feel like he wants to say something about it, but he says, "You're cold. Let's get you warmed up."

I follow him along with Atticus and Ginny toward a fire wishing I was still in the warm glow of Tanner.

We walk into a camp where a group of people sit around the fire. "Holt," Atticus says and steps around me to shake another guy's hand. Atticus turns to us. "Played basketball with Tim last year," he says and introduces us.

Tim glances at my wet clothes. "Looks like you need a towel and the fire."

"Yeah." I shiver. "I may have unexpectedly gotten in the water."

A girl next to him gets up. "I've got an extra towel in the tent." She motions for me to follow her. "I'm Anita."

"Emma," I say with chattering teeth now. I've got my arms crossed over my chest trying to keep in the warmth. Without a June sun to dry me, trying to get warm will only happen with dry clothes and fireside.

"You jumped, huh?" She disappears into the tent. "That's brave," she says from inside, and when I don't follow her, she pokes her head back out. "Come in. You should get out of those clothes. Let them dry. Got anything under them?"

"Swimsuit." I step into the warmth of the tent. The plastic floor crinkles under my feet when I move.

"Perfect," she says.

I strip out of my shorts and top. "You graduated last year, right?"

She hands me a dry towel and sits on a cot, the sleeping bag rustling underneath her. "Yeah. It's kind of weird to come home after a year away."

"College?"

She nods. "It's like slipping into old comfortable shoes, sort of, but they're stretched out and don't quite fit right anymore."

I'm not sure about going away to college, but her words make me think about how I've been feeling about church lately, about the life I've constructed in a box of perfectionism. I move the towel through my hair. "How was your first year?"

"Loved it. It's like being able to redefine yourself. High school and all that bullshit slips away. Nobody cares that I'm in the marching band in college, you know." She smiles.

I think about Corbin's earlier comment. "Or if you don't come to parties in high school."

She laughs and stands. "Right. No one gives a shit about stupid stuff that seems to mean so much right now. And if they do it doesn't matter and neither do they. Small minds. All that."

"Thanks for the towel."

"Let's put your clothes near the fire and go listen to Ryan."

I don't know who Ryan is but follow her back outside wrapping the towel around myself. Ginny, Liam and Atticus are situated around the fire with everyone else listening to chords plucked and the streak of fingers moving across the frets of an acoustic guitar — such a beautiful sound. Ginny pats a blanket next to her, and I sit. She hands me a red cup with something suspect inside.

I sip it and look around. Across the fire is a guy strumming a guitar. His playing is hypnotic, but when he sings, it's like magic. The melody of the music moves around all of us. The warmth of the fire mixed with the sound is like a spell doing strange things to my insides. I melt and close my eyes. The anxiety, the fear, the control, everything that usually defines me drips away. It's like freedom has been wrapped up in a ribbon and presented to me in a myriad of ways: the dancing, jumping with Tanner, the glow of adrenaline, and, now, this moment around a fire with strangers. Peace — the absence of fear — is warmth.

Ryan sings a John Mayer song, and I reopen my eyes. He's bent over his guitar, and I notice the sinew of his arms as he works his fingers across the frets. He has a tattoo on his forearm, though I can't make out what it is. I notice the way his brown hair falls forward and shields his eyes. He has a nice nose, and the way his mouth moves as he sings is soft and makes me think about kissing. I imagine kissing Tanner. No. I shake my head. That's the lyrics: bodies and wonderlands and bubblegum tongues.

Overheating with thoughts of kissing Tanner, I stand up and readjust the towel around my body. Ryan looks up, and his eyes meet mine for a second then slide away again to his fingers on the frets of his guitar. I turn away and check my clothes to see if they're dry. Not yet.

Wanting some solitude to ponder the events of the last few hours and about how I'm feeling, I walk down to the water's edge. When the water laps up and over my feet, I take a deep breath, conscious that I need to stay in the moment. If I don't, I'll run the risk of slipping away from the peace and back into the fear.

Someone yells followed by a splash. A cheer goes up from the cliff. I wonder if it's Tanner.

I smile in the darkness remembering all the sensations: the elation, the heady feeling as I flew, my legs and body pressed against Tanner's, my hand in his. My heart speeds up and sputters. There's an uneasy equilibrium running through me, however. An unbalanced reconciliation between what I want and what I think I'm supposed to feel: guilt.

"Emma?"

I turn away from the water at the sound of Liam's voice. Since he's backlit by the firelight behind him, I can't make out his features as he walks toward the water's edge.

He's quiet when he reaches my side, and I can tell he has something on his mind.

"What is it?"

"You okay?"

"Yeah. Actually." I can't help my smile and press my hands to my cheeks. "I jumped. And I'm still alive!"

He doesn't answer me with a smile however and says, "Physically okay. Check." He waits, and we stand side-by-side listening to the lake noises. The distant strumming of Ryan's guitar, squeals of laughter somewhere in the dark, the base of the music pounding from a radio farther down the beach, the hum of voices and the snapping of fires. Then he says, "I mean, you know, about Tanner."

"What about him?" I ask.

"He was holding your hand."

The way he says it makes me think I was powerless in the interaction. "I think that went both ways."

"It's–" He stops and sighs.

I bend down and pick up some pebbles. "It's what?"

"Tanner. Last time. I don't want to see you hurt, again."

I'm not sure if he's talking about *Operation Kiss Tanner James* or the *Junior Prom Incident*. I toss a pebble into the water, and it plunks a few feet away. I decide it's the former, and because I know he's my friend, I recognize he's just being protective. It grates against my awareness in a strange way, though I'm not sure exactly why. Out in the lake, someone yells and there's a bigger splash followed by the cheer. "Tanner isn't to blame for that. I hurt myself, Liam. I attached expectations to Tanner I shouldn't have. He didn't make me any promises. It isn't his fault I liked him."

"But he used you."

"Did he? Because the last I checked, I was the one who got drunk, begged him for a kiss, and then did the kissing. He was actually a gentleman." My cheeks heat thinking about how forward I'd been, but I'm sure I'd make the same choice whenever Tanner is a part of it.

Liam takes one of the pebbles from my hand and throws it. "I still don't like the guy."

"Why is that?"

"He uses women. He and his crew. I don't want him using you. You're too good for him."

We both go through the remaining pebbles in my hand, tossing them into the water one at a time. The water laps against our feet. I understand Liam's concerns. I hear him and his care for me, but it sits uneasy in my mind. As if the protectiveness he shares is rooted in something else. What I don't tell him, because I don't want to hear what he thinks, is that I hear the echo bouncing around in the canyon between Tanner and me. I don't know where it came from or why it's there, but given the opportunity, I want to explore it further.

Liam bends to pick up another handful of rocks as another jumper enters the water. "Maybe you should stay away from him."

Now, I'm defensive. It's the way he said it, as if he's my protector, my dad. I can't keep the bite from my tone. "Remember earlier when you said to accept what life offers, or a few nights ago when you said that you'd be cheering me on with whatever I decide when I decide? Or junior year when you said that you wouldn't get in the way of me doing me?"

"Emma."

"No, Liam. You're being judgy, and you're like the least judgy person I know."

"I can't with him, Emma."

"Well, it's a good thing you don't have to then. He doesn't bat for your team, remember."

He sighs. "I'm saying this because I love you. You're my friend, and he will hurt you."

"It wasn't Tanner who hurt me." I haven't said Chris, but Liam knows what I mean. I turn to him and count off on my fingers all the problems with his argument. "First, you aren't being fair. You don't know Tanner. Second, you aren't my father." I throw all the pebbles in my hand into the water and listen to them plink in succession. "Third, I don't know why we're even talking about this. It isn't like he's asked me out or that I've agreed to marry him. I jumped the cliff with him. We held hands. Why are you so worked up about it?"

I see his jaw tense as he presses his teeth together, his stubborn streak moving through him. He isn't looking at me. I know he loves me. I love him. He's the brother I've never had, my friend since the age of nine. The history between us is rooted in childhood, shared experiences and respect, but in that moment, I'm not seeing him that way. In that moment, his protectiveness feels like something else, like someone else's expectations of me, and I hear my father — my religion — in his words.

"It's my choice, Liam. Mine. Even if it's the worst decision I've ever made. You don't get a say."

He drops the pebbles he picked up, and they plunk against the ground, rock against rock. "Got it." He wipes his hands on his board shorts. "Loud and clear, Emma." He turns and walks away at the same time there's another jumper and a cheer.

I sigh and turn back to the water, my heart pounding for an entirely different reason now. My emotions and thoughts swirl with a concoction of guilt and anger, but justification because I know I'm right. I turn away from Liam, indignant at having lost all of the peace moving through my system, and walk down the beach in the opposite direction.

tanner

On the way back to the cliff, where I know I'll find my friends, I berate myself for walking away from Emma. She'd jumped with me, and like an idiot, I'm walking away. Again. I could make a different choice and didn't. There was chemistry. I'd felt it, and even if it led nowhere, just being in her company was like standing in the heat of the sun on a cold day. I like the way I feel around her, like that she sees the real me; she doesn't have me chained to expectations. The awful truth is that I can't remember the last time that was a truth — other than junior year. I can think backwards through my life and pinpoint a handful of times when I felt free of someone else's expectations, and most of them would involve Emma.

But I climb up the quarry wall anyway, toward my friends and a life that's left me empty.

When I get there, I sit on a boulder off to the side and observe. I can't bring myself to engage, to slip back into the role I usually play. Griff jumps, disappears over the edge and Danny yells something after him. We aren't the only ones up there. A couple — I don't know their names — goes next, and I replay the jump with Emma: Offering her my hand. She takes it. We jump. Her body pressed to mine after. A new loop.

"You okay, T?" Josh asks.

He stands near me, hands on his hips, tattoos on his arms. I hadn't noticed him approach. I look up at him and nod, offering him a slight smile. He watches me just a second longer before launching himself over the edge of the cliff. Under different circumstances, I might wonder about it, but I'm too preoccupied with the drama in my mind. I feel outside and disconnected, like I'm sitting in a different time lapse while everything and everyone moves in fast motion around me. Smiles, laughter, motions. I can't hear; it's just the thoughts swirling through my head that I'd messed up again. That I wasn't ever going to get things right.

"What the fuck has gotten into you?" Griff shakes the water from his latest plunge off the cliff off on me. His dark blond hair sticks up around his head. He's been up and over at least twice since I got back from jumping with Emma.

"Nothing," I say, but it's a lie. How I'm feeling isn't nothing. This antsy feeling is like standing outside of my own skin and watching ants crawl all over me. It's like the January loop, only a new one, more intense and addictive.

Jump with me.

She took my hand.

She chose to take the risk.

With me.

I'm thinking about her hand in mine. I'm thinking about her laugh. I'm thinking about the way her body was pressed against mine after. I'm thinking about her arms around my neck. I'm thinking about her trust. I look up at the sky. The stars. It's like a new story wants to be written, but I'm fighting it.

"Bullshit." Griff pushes me. "You're acting like you've got your panties in a wad."

Pissed, I stand. "Fuck off, Griff." I know I'm acting off. I feel off. "I'll meet you guys at the campsite." Then without waiting for whatever insult Griff can think up to insinuate I'm less than a man, I rush the edge and launch myself into space. I think of Rory. There's a part of me that wishes I could float away. I hang unrestricted for a moment before gravity grabs me and pulls me down and into the water. It's symbolic somehow.

I break the surface. *It's graduation that has me in a funk*, I decide as I swim toward the shore. I'm looking at a future headed toward a black hole of nothing, a box closing in around me, and I'm about to be suffocated. And Emma — gorgeous Emma who trusted me enough to make that jump — just represents a future I wish I had but was too stupid to work harder for because I didn't know it was something I'd want.

I wade out of the water and then collapse on the rocky beach. My throat burns with tears I'm holding in, though I don't know why they're there. I look up at the blackness of the sky and the randomness of the stars dusted across the expanse above me. I swallow the burn. My life feels like that giant black sky. Even if the stars sparkle this far away, I know that space is a giant black nothing.

"Hey? Are you okay?" a voice calls out. I hear the crunch of gravel punctuated with, "Ouch. Ouch. Oh. Ouch," as whoever it is comes closer. "Tanner?"

I sit up and watch the one person I've wanted to see walking toward me with tentative steps down the beach. "Emma." It seems too good to be true.

She smiles. "What are you doing?"

"Contemplating life."

"On your back?"

"I like it that way." It's suggestive, the way I say it. Then I want to kick myself for doing it, because Emma makes a surprised little sound that makes me grin. "Sorry. Bad habits."

"May I sit with you?"

"Yeah." That's an understatement.

Holding the towel she's got wrapped around herself, she sits. "What about life?"

I'm not sure what to say. I realize I haven't been in the business of telling my truth, sheltering the real parts of me in versions that keep others comfortable and myself safe. "Just wishing things were different." I wrap my arms around my legs.

"You too?"

I glance at her. It's hard to see her face. "Too?"

"We graduate in a week. I bet most of us are thinking things like that."

She's right. Atticus and I just had this conversation, though the words were different. "And what could Emma the Great want to change?" I pick up a rock and throw it.

She picks up a handful of rocks. Then drops them and sifts through them with her fingers. "I can think of a few things."

"Care to share?"

"Do you?"

I don't, because what I'd share would scare her away, I figure. I say, "I wish I'd been a better student. Like you."

"And maybe I wish I'd had more fun and had more adventures. Like you."

The silence hangs over us like heavy rain clouds. Her admission steals any words I might say. It never occurred to me that Emma would have noticed me or admired anything about me, but there's a melancholy tone to her words that snags me.

"You okay?" I ask because I know deep down, I'm not. I know that the broken pieces of me I'm beginning to cough up are sharp. I don't know if I can look at them. It would just be easier to stay immersed in the Tanner I've created. Easier. Sitting with Emma, though, I feel like a better version of him.

"Yeah, actually. I think so. I was nervous about coming here tonight, but I'm feeling better about it."

"Nervous?"

"Yeah. I get nervous a lot." She fiddles with the bottom of the towel against her knee.

"Well, I'm glad you did." I surprise myself by saying it. My usual operating procedures have been to be frank about my thoughts and wants but not vulnerable. Saying that to Emma makes my chest tighten, because I feel exposed.

She looks at me. "And are you okay?"

I like her question, but I can't answer it. Instead, I say, "Are you worried for me?" I smile, and the need for her answer feels like a key in a lock that hasn't been turned. Who has ever worried about me since Rory was alive? Atticus maybe. I picture Josh asking me if I was okay a little while ago.

She's having difficulty meeting my eyes, but she smiles. "Sure." She pauses, and her word sinks its teeth into me. Then she adds as though to autocorrect, "I care what happens to everyone."

I can just see her freckles on the side of her face where the light from dozens of fires dance in the trees. "What brought you out here? Where are your friends?"

Her eyes rise to meet mine. "I'm waiting for my clothes to dry." She pauses a moment as if weighing something. Then she asks, "Want to go with me to check on them?"

Yes. Yes. Yes, I do. Though I don't say this. "Okay," is what comes out of my mouth.

She stands, and I follow.

We walk.

I want to touch her.

She struggles over the rocks, crags, detritus along the shore holding the towel closed with one hand, and the other stretched out to her side to keep her balance.

"Where are your shoes? Here—" I ask and scoop her up into my arms. I get to touch her again. It's a little like getting a drink of water to quench my thirst. She makes a cute little noise when I do. It does something pleasant but peculiar inside my stomach. "Where am I taking you, your highness?"

"Follow the music — the guitar." She points. "Everyone is hanging out around the fire with some alumni." She uses her fingers to count them off as she names them. It's endearing. "Know where they are?"

"Nope, but we'll just keep walking until we find them, and then I can demonstrate how manly I am."

She laughs.

I love that sound, and the fact that something I said elicited it. It gives me more energy.

I'm disappointed when I carry her into the campsite a few moments later. Faces situated around the fire turn our way. Ginny jumps up from a blanket. Atticus gives me a head nod; he's next to Liam, who rolls his eyes, though I can't be sure at what, even if it feels like it was at me. There are a bunch of alumni from last year's graduating class, including the three Emma mentioned, who offer me a friendly smile.

"I can walk now," Emma says.

I set her down.

"Hey Tanner, want to join us?" Ginny's eyes bounce from me to Emma.

Emma turns red. It could be the heat of the fire. But–

There's one thing I've picked up in the last several years (even if I'm ashamed to admit it). I may not be great at the school thing, but I've learned a thing or two about the social scene and girls, specifically. The Bro Code and all that. Right now, Emma's blush plus Ginny's look, and I know: Emma is still interested in me.

My world opens up into something more exciting, my chest constricting with anticipation. A new choice. A new story.

I decide to take the risk, smile at Ginny, and say, "I'd love to."

emma

My reaction to Ginny's polite invitation to Tanner is ridiculous. All the awareness of him rushes into my cheeks; I overheat. It shouldn't embarrass me, but it does. What if Tanner says no?

But he says, "I'd love to."

My eyes snap to his. He watches me with a slight smile on his face that makes every part of me tingle. I meet Ginny's gaze. I could freaking hug the shit out of her right now.

I walk away from them before I do something stupid and suppress the urge to glance at Liam, whose approval I want more than I should. But I know it won't be there — so I keep my eyes averted. My need for his approval bothers me; why should I care what Liam thinks? It's just he means so much to me. And suddenly I hear my father, *my perfect girl,* and frown. I recall the million conversations at dinner about saving one's self, remaining pure. What had Liam said? "You should stay away from him." It makes me bristle again, but I cool when I realize Liam isn't doing anything outside the bounds of what any of us have been conditioned to do: protect a woman's maidenly virtue. Make her choices for her. Is my concern about his approval allowing it?

I glance over my shoulder at him.

Liam follows me with his eyes.

I look away, confused but aware. My body. My choice.

And I'm smart.

But there was that one time — Junior Prom — when my choice hadn't been heard. It tries to steal my uncharacteristic desire to take a risk. I shake it off, refusing to give it power.

I don't think for a moment that by hooking up with Tanner it will lead me into a long-term relationship. He's an f-boy for goodness sake. I don't think I'm going to change him. My pop-culture education might have been by John Hughes sticky sweet films but being an over-thinker has sent me into a myriad of online research spirals sometimes into dark and desperate places. I don't think I can save Tanner James from his choices, or that he might, just might change his ways for me. I understand it isn't Tanner who needs changing. It's me: *Operation the Reeducation of Emma Matthews.*

There are so many little things he has shown me over all the interactions I've had with him through the years that don't align with all the ways people have judged him; these have me feeling safe. *I got you, Em. Promise,* rings like a bell in my head. He did. He'd asked. He'd waited for me to say yes. Feeling like I do — jittery and curious and warm and out-of-breath — might scare me, but the attraction climbing through me is like being on a roller coaster and heading into a climactic drop. My nerve endings might be exposed, but neither my head nor my heart are talking me out of it. As an overthinking perfectionist, I usually care more about what I can control, but right now with Tanner somewhere behind me, the opportunity to find the joy I remember from that night junior year has me imagining taking a detour and going off map.

"Are your clothes dry?" Tanner asks.

I turn to look at him over my red cup, unaware he'd been right behind me.

He leans against the picnic table.

My breath catches in my chest, and stalls in the cup as I study him: hair still damp and curling, bare chested — he has a tattoo curling around his ribs I'd like to look at closer — his swim trunks, a nice light blue, resting on his hips. His body is like carved artwork. The weight in my chest free falls into my stomach.

"I need to check." I hand him my cup and walk to the fireside where my shorts and top hang. Dry enough. I collect them.

"I was thinking," Tanner says when I return, "if you're willing — you could walk with me to my camp so I can change into dry clothes." He takes a sip from my cup. My pulse speeds up. He swallows. I notice the movement of his mouth, his jaw, his neck. "Then I'll walk you back here." He sets the cup down on the table and turns his gaze back toward me.

I nod, because I don't think I can say anything. My blood hums through my veins, and for some reason, because I'm feeling bold, I remove the towel. I lean forward and my arm brushes his as I drape it on the table next to him. Now, it's just me exposed in my red bikini illuminated by firelight and lanterns. Not a usual Emma choice; it's bold and vulnerable. Full of risk. I don't have time to overthink the choice, but in the moment, I'm empowered and filled with want.

The look on Tanner's face slides toward something weightier, and his gaze travels my body, which warms me from the inside out. My breath lingers in my chest, as if waiting for something more substantial. He watches me slide into my shorts, assesses as I draw the black tank top over my head. I can feel his regard like a promise. When I allow my gaze to stop on him again, there's a look in his eyes that asks me a question I wish I knew the answer to. The look reminds me of the other day after rehearsal, so I raise my eyebrows to answer him. Though I'm not exactly sure what I've said, he seems to know.

The ease of his smile returns. "Shoes? Or would you like me to carry you, your highness?"

"I'm tempted. But I'll walk."

Grabbing my shoes from near the fire, I slip them on and check in with Ginny before I leave. "I'm going with Tanner. We'll be back."

She grabs my hand and pulls me closer to whisper. "Emma. Don't overthink." She smiles, knowing what she's asked me is like trying to harness the wind. "Let go."

I lean back to tell her, "I think I'll need about five more cups for that. But I have every intention of enjoying myself." I glance at Liam who's sitting at Atticus's side, hoping for a smile, but he won't look at me.

"I've got my phone if you need me. Otherwise, I'll walk back here." Atticus nods. "Got it."

Liam finally looks up at me. "You're sure?"

"I am." I turn away and walk across the campground to Tanner who's waiting where I left him.

"Ready?"

I follow him from the camp into the darkness of the woods. It's shadowy, and we move with slow steps, leaving most of the fires behind us. "Where's your camp?"

"A ways," he says. "Scared of the dark, Matthews?"

"No. Yes. A little." I laugh, having shared an embarrassing truth. I'm not sure I want Tanner to know all the little idiosyncrasies that make me weird.

He stops, and I bump into him. His hand brushes my back and then falls away. "Well, why don't you use your phone and make us a flashlight?"

"Good idea. Why didn't I think of that?" I draw it out of my pocket and swipe up to turn on the flashlight feature; it illuminates a small area. "You're so smart."

"That's your department, Em."

His words, the way he's said them, feel dark and sad. It makes me reach out for him. When my fingertips graze the skin of his shoulder, he slows and looks at where I've touched him. "Being smart doesn't necessarily make you smart," I say. "Ask me. I should know."

"So serious." He takes my hand in his and threads our fingers together. A million butterflies flutter their wings low in my belly and reverberate around the base of my spine. He walks again. "How come?"

"How come what?"

"You're so serious?"

It's a fair question, but one that brings up memories that sting with my need for approval. "I'm competitive," I offer instead.

"Then why not go out for sports?"

"Academics are my sport." When he laughs, I charge ahead. "I'm not very coordinated, or was that not apparent on our jump?"

"I thought you did great," he says. "I think camp's just a bit further."

We pass another fire a dozen yards away. They are singing terribly, drunk and laughing. I smell hot dogs and marshmallows. A few steps later, we almost walk over a couple whose faces are stuck together. All I see are moving hands in the flashlight of my phone.

"Oh," I say and lower the phone. "Oops."

"You two should find a tent." Tanner laughs quietly, at ease with it as we walk around them.

I giggle.

Silence moves in around us. I'm thinking about that couple and wonder if Tanner is too. I'm thinking about junior year. Our kiss. I'm thinking about him and his mouth, his hands, his hips. About my hand in his and how warmth grabs hold of my deep parts and cranks up the heat of them. I take a deep breath and try to distract myself by asking him, "Why do you think smarts is my department?"

"Are you being serious right now? You're the fucking — whatever it's called — for graduation."

I sniff. "That doesn't mean shit in the whole scheme of life, Tanner. You know that's true. It isn't going to determine my success."

"Sure, it does. It's getting you out of this town isn't it?"

He's right, but for some reason it sits like a heavy brick in my overactive mind, slowing things down. "What about you?"

He goes quiet, and continues our trail through the dark, my hand still in his. "Here we are," he says; he hasn't answered my question.

I don't press.

The camp is dark.

"You mind if I change first, Em? Before I start a fire? I'm

freezing." He releases my hand.

"Yeah. Go ahead." I glance around, the nearest fire a speck through the trees, and the darkness feels alive. The idea of sitting alone sends chills up my spine. I shiver. I have my phone, but it doesn't feel like a safety net. I turn off the light to see how dark it is.

Tanner hesitates outside of the two tents. I can't make out his features, it's too dark, but I can see his outline. "You want to come in here with me? Since it's dark."

I don't think; I just follow.

tanner

I know what I'm doing when I invite her into the tent even though I'd spent most of the walk there deciding I wouldn't. *She might like you, Tanner, but that doesn't mean you have to do what you do* I'd been telling myself. But then the campsite was pitch black, and she admitted she's afraid of the dark. What kind of guy would I be to leave her out there by herself?

I walk into the tent and straighten once I'm inside. There isn't a lot of room, so when Emma walks in behind me, I can feel the heat radiating off her body. I point to my right even if she can't see it. "My sleeping bag is unrolled there," I tell her. I say it like it's a secret.

"I can't see anything." There's a smile in her tone of voice I can hear. She's quiet too, like she's in on the secret, and then I feel her hands on my bare back.

I shift, turning to move away, because I'm really trying to be honorable here. Her touch has me thinking about her body, and her smile, and her laugh. That kiss junior year. "Use your flashlight." I choke out the words, because they're caught in my throat.

"Right."

I hear her moving around. Her breath. Her humming. These

sounds are exciting. I close my eyes and clench my fists. You'd think I was an addict, but it isn't the sex — it's Emma. I haven't felt this physically aware of someone since ... junior year. I think of her in that red bikini and watching her get dressed. Excited about seeing clothes put on. I shake my head. Fuck.

The light comes on, illuminating the tent with its gentle glow.

I take a deep breath. "There. The blue one."

She glances at me and then nods. When she sits down on the sleeping bag, it doesn't help my resolve. I squat near my duffle and rummage through it, which keeps me from looking at her. But I'm imagining her gorgeous legs and the shape of her body, the rounded, full, soft places I want to touch.

"Do you need me to shine the light?" she asks from behind me.

"All good." Then because I can't help myself and I'm me, I turn and look at her and hold up my clothes. "You want to watch, your highness?"

It flusters her, like I figured it would, but her laugh skitters like it's a stone skipping over water. She's nervous, and for some reason that makes me feel like my nerves are okay, too. Experiencing them, however, has me leaning to the left, ready to topple. The unsteady feeling makes me uncomfortable but excited.

The light goes out.

"You didn't answer my question," she says, filling the darkness with sound.

"Which?" I strip off the swim trunks and use a towel to dry what's still damp.

"What are you doing after graduation?"

I freeze. I don't want to tell her, but maybe it's for the best. "Nothing." I slide into boxer briefs, moving again. I wish I could tell her I was going to college or doing something worthwhile. It makes me feel shittier about myself.

She doesn't say anything for a while which I figure means that knowing I'm headed nowhere is a huge turn off. *So much for her liking you, Tanner.*

I slip into my clothes: sweats and a t-shirt

"Can I tell you something?" I hear her say.

"I'm done," I tell her. "You know, if you want to turn on the light."

"It's okay. Kind of easier to talk in the dark."

It's a curious statement. Safer to talk in the dark. Instead of taking us outside to light a fire, I use my hands to find the empty spot on my sleeping bag across from her and sit down. With my arms wrapped around my knees, I can feel something pressed up against my foot — her knee, perhaps. "What did you want to say?" I ask.

"I'm scared. About going to college. Actually, I'm terrified about a lot of things. It's pretty much defined my entire existence."

Her admission doesn't surprise me, considering her panic on the cliff, but what does is the way my awareness about her moves when she says it, as if she wants to connect with my admission about being a nobody, somehow. It makes me feel something different, deeper, like when I hear her laugh. "How come?" I ask. It's weird not being able to see her, just hear her words. It also feels somewhat more truthful, which is a silly thought because people tell lies with their words.

"I don't know. It's just always been that way."

I think about her admission on the beach: *I get nervous a lot.* I want to know more. I want to know everything. "What's the bravest thing you've ever done?" I ask.

The silence stretches a moment too long so that I almost reach out to see if she disappeared, but then she says, "Jumping off the cliff at the Quarry with Tanner James."

Fireworks explode inside my chest, making me feel happy, and I can't help but smile. It's a dangerous feeling, because I can't remember a time where happiness warmed me. Other things reaching for happiness, maybe, but not happiness. Then, because I can't help it, I reach out to touch her even though I shouldn't. "Really?" I ask. "Where are you?" I need to feel her.

"Here. Right in front of you."

With my hand outstretched, I'm hoping for her hand, but touch a part of her that isn't fingers. "Em?" I ask.

"Yes?"

"What am I touching right now?"

She laughs, vibrant and sweet, which I think are the only kind Emma offers. "My knee."

My stomach sways with sexual awareness as I run my hand up her thigh. Her breath catches, and she holds it. "Would you come closer, please?"

I hear the whisper of the sleeping bag fabric as she does. I feel her leg shift under my hand — her skin cool to my touch — until my hand is on her hip. "You're cold," I say and find her other hip and draw her toward me until she's between my legs. I imagine she's on her knees, but I can't see her — just the shadowy outline. My heart locks up a moment before bolting.

Her breath is shallow, like mine.

"Emma?"

"Tanner?" She echoes my question with my name.

I open my mouth to tell her I'd like to kiss her, but the words suspend when her hand touches my face. Her fingertips – both hands – running along the ridges of my forehead. One hand is in my hair near my forehead. She explores my eyebrows with her thumbs, and I close my eyes and hold my breath. She touches the ridge of my nose, skims her fingers over my cheeks until they touch my mouth. It's the hottest thing, strangely, and I expel the breath I've been holding. She'll know how much she's affecting me, and that isn't something I allow. Actually, I'm not sure it's something that's ever happened. I can't seem to control it. The darkness, her touch. Usually, I'm the one in control, but Emma has me tripping over myself.

"Tanner?" she asks again.

I hum a response, enjoying her fingertips. I open my mouth when they pass over my lips, and her movement stops.

"Do you remember junior year?"

I open my eyes. "What about it, Em? Just like being a junior? Which classes I had?" I know what she's asking about, but I'm messing with her.

She doesn't respond, her touch disappears, and her heat shifts away from me. I miss the warmth of her fingertips. No, I miss the fire her fingertips ignited in my belly.

I reach out and touch her. She's solid under my hand, but I don't know what I've touched. Her arm? Her thigh? "Yes, Em. I remember."

"You do?"

"Are you surprised?"

"Well, yeah. Kind of."

"Why?" I ask.

"Because... we were drunk."

I hear the lie. There's more to why, but she isn't saying.

She adds, "Did you regret it?"

"Did you?" Her answer is going to mean more to me than it should.

"No."

The confession makes me float, even though I'm warning myself to stay grounded. There was a reason I tried to forget it.

"Your turn to answer."

I know, for sure, I'm about to ruin this moment by suddenly being truthful with her. I could play it, which I would have done in all of my yesterdays, but I think about where all of those yesterdays have brought me. Sure, to this moment, but I'm not sure Emma Matthews is sitting with me in the dark because I'm a player. What had she told me: *I saw you help Connor. That's sexy.* "Honestly, I thought I did."

She doesn't respond, but I feel her tremble under my hand.

She clears her throat. "Thought? Past tense?"

"Emma, when I kissed you that night — when we kissed–" among the other things we did that I haven't been able to get out of mind– "I'd been drunk, but not THAT drunk."

"I don't–" she starts, but I interrupt her.

"I wanted to kiss you then, Em, just like I want to kiss you now."

Then she shifts closer, places her hands on my face, fingertips in the hair at my neck and presses her mouth to mine. Everything inside me dissolves into want.

emma

His mouth. Oh God. His mouth on mine. Tanner's arms shift around me, pulling me closer, so I wrap my arms around his shoulders. He slants his head, and his tongue skims across my lips. I part them, because — oh God — his mouth is heaven. I remember, junior year, his mouth, his hands, the knock at the door to stop it before it had gone any further. Our secret. But this is different. Better.

"Emma," he says my name into my mouth as if it's a prayer, and suddenly he's moving, and I'm shifting, and I'm on my back sliding across his sleeping bag, and his weight is on me.

His hands are on my hips shifting my body. Our tongues' rhythm suggests what the rest of our bodies want to do, and this is better than I remember, ever imagined. I'm not even drunk.

With his hands at the small of my back, he lifts my hips toward his and draws me even closer. I spread my thighs, and his hips settle between them. I can feel him pressed up against me through the fabric of my shorts, and I want him. I'm not even cold anymore because everything happening around me, in me, through me has warmed me. I might be glowing.

Tanner slides his mouth from mine across my jaw, to my neck, and his hands slide up from my hips to my waist and push the hem of my tank top up, settling his hands on the skin of my ribs. I hear myself moan. "Tanner." I sigh his name, and I'm sure I could be more creative, but don't have the confidence, or the experience. What does one say to a guy like Tanner who's been around this block probably more than I want to think about?

Ginny's words: *Emma. Don't overthink.*

Oh shit. I'm doing it. I squeeze my eyes shut just to feel, and it feels so good.

"Yes?" He murmurs it against my collar bone, and then he's up over me, a hand on each side of my head. I know he's looking down at me, but I can't see him very well; I just feel it. "Emma?" He whispers it. It's a question: *what do you want?*

It isn't a difficult question. I know what I want. I want to have sex with Tanner James, but something has shifted in the want. Before, it was infatuation. Before, I thought about Tanner as an f-boy and nothing more, and I could use him as a means to an end in my own personal journey, but the want has drifted. I'm overthinking. Tanner isn't a boy who stays, and suddenly, I'm wishing he was. I know how stupid that is, that it does make me naive. It's because I'm seeing him differently. I'm hearing the silent words said between the spoken ones and aligning the actions with the assumptions. Things aren't adding up.

But I want to have sex — uncomplicated sex — with Tanner James so damn bad.

And I remember, that isn't who I am, even if I want it to be. I'm not uncomplicated. I'm the red wire — the one you cut, and everything explodes.

There's laughter in the darkness outside the tent, and the moment crumbles.

"Shit," he says and drops his chin to his chest. His hair tickles my face. He looks up again and shifts off of me. "It's Griff, Danny, and Josh."

The crunch of their steps can be heard as they move through the woods, and the loud way they talk to one another. I hear a stray "Dude," followed by an "Ouch. What the fuck?"

"Will they come in here?" I ask.

"Probably." He sits up. I hear him in his bag again. He hands me something. "Here. To keep you warm." A sweatshirt. He gets up and helps me stand. "I'll walk you back."

We emerge from the tent. His friends are still half a football field away, but the flashlight beams slice through the night toward us.

"Do you care if they see me?" I ask him. It's all feeling a little like a repeat of junior year.

"What?" He turns and looks at me. Though I can't see his face, I have a sense the question has upset him. "Come on. We'll go around them. This way."

One of them yells from the dark, "Tanner! What the fuck, dude? Where's the fire?" At first, I think it's because they've seen us, but then realize they're just being obnoxious.

They continue to traipse through the forest.

"You think he's passed out?" one asks, and they all laugh. "Maybe he's not here."

"He was acting like a fucking bitch," another voice replies.

I feel Tanner tense, but we keep moving.

I squeeze his hand.

"He's probably with a chick. Bella Noble was all over him earlier."

The comment, as innocuous as it is because he isn't with her, feels like a needle piercing the balloon in my chest. I remember what she said in the bathroom: *I don't think a guy like Tanner would touch you with a ten-foot pole. You're so boring. What can you offer someone like him?* Well, I proved her wrong, but the elation deflates in a slow, steady stream. It isn't because of Tanner. It's because I'm a fool. He doesn't want people to know.

We cross paths with his friends, them never knowing we were there, and continue back across the campgrounds toward the shoreline to find my friends. It's silent between us, tensely so. The earlier ease constricts with something I'm not sure I'm able to identify. Reality, maybe. There are a bunch of things between us not being said, and whatever thoughts that have me wrapped up in overthinking things.

Tanner stops suddenly. Because my hand is still in his, I'm forced to stop too. "What did you mean?" he asks.

"About what?"

We're closer to camps with lit fires, and I can make out the edges of his handsome features. His face is tense, his jaw chewing over his thoughts. Distant fire light flickers, and the sound of people laughing, singing, radios pounding out beats, talking drifts around us.

"If I cared if they saw you?"

I'm right. He is upset. I step closer to him. "I just meant like — I don't know. Like junior year, when you didn't want to be seen with me."

His mouth opens, closes, and then he says with a shake of his head, "Is that what you thought?"

"Well, yeah. You told me to go so no one would see. I thought — maybe — you were embarrassed. Of me."

He sighs, runs a hand through his hair, and starts forward again through the trees pulling me behind him.

It's my turn to make him stop, but I also yank my hand from his. "What else was I supposed to think? You practically pushed me out the door. And then you didn't talk to me again, until a few hours ago, when we were standing on the cliff where you asked me to jump."

"It doesn't matter." He's crossed his arms over his chest, and I can see his profile because he isn't looking at me.

"Tanner. It does. Why you're suddenly upset matters. To me."

His head turns and his dark eyes — reflecting campfires — rove over my face. I see his jaw working in the flickering light. "I wasn't embarrassed of you." His eyes slide away.

"Then fill me in."

His eyes, dark and shiny in the night, find my face again. "Me, Em. Me. My reputation. It's bad. I didn't want that. For you."

There it is again: the unreconciled words, behavior and preconceived notions not adding up. First, it surprises me and catches my breath. He was worried about my reputation. Then it irritates me. "What the fuck, Tanner?"

My response catches him off guard. I know this because his arms drop to his sides and then he puts his hands on his hips. Now, his gaze follows me instead of staring moodily into the distance. Perhaps he's used to girls being like: *Oh Tanner. You're so noble for trying to protect my virtue. Here. You can have it.*

There's a part of me that does think that. The stupid foolish part so infatuated with him that I'd fall into the trap. But there's the other smarter part of me who is suddenly pissed off that he thought it was his decision to make. Like every other male in my life. It's the whole *save yourself to be a valuable woman bullshit, your purity is all you have.* I'm so sick of it even if a part of me feels that same push and pull with my upbringing.

"What the fuck, Tanner?" he repeats, confused.

I stomp past him.

"Wait. What? Emma?"

I turn on him, pointing. "That is the most infuriating thing I have ever heard. You. Liam. My dad." I ignore the limo debacle. I make an exasperated sound in my throat. My finger connects with his chest. "You thought you had a right to make a decision like that for me? I kissed you because I wanted to that night, just like I kissed you because I wanted to tonight. Who are you to determine shit about my reputation? It's mine. Not yours, and if I wanted to be seen with Tanner James — that's my choice. Not yours. Who do you think you are?"

But my rant is silenced under the pressure of Tanner's kiss. His hands frame my face, and his kiss is hungry. "Oh god, Em." Our tongues collide, seeking one another again, and the tense energy earlier explodes with intense physical desire. Hands. Hunger. No space between us. He picks me up, and I wrap my legs around his waist. "That — you — are so fucking hot," he says into my mouth. "I never stopped wanting you."

His words buzz through me: *I never stopped wanting you.* The buzzing energy moves through my body like lightning. A vibration buzzes back but doesn't register. I'm full of Tanner and him alone. "You never stopped wanting me?"

"No."

Buzz.

"I never stopped wanting you."

Buzz.

He moans and kisses me.

I'm lost in it. The sensation of his mouth, his tongue, his hands and arms holding me up, but then he pulls away. Distracted. "I think that's your phone, Em."

Buzz.

tanner

With a sigh, Emma unhooks her legs wrapped around my waist, and even though I don't want to let go of her, I do. She slides down the front of my body back to the earth, igniting all of the nerve endings she grazes on the way. When she's back on solid ground, she doesn't move away, but stays, leaning against me to check her phone; the light illuminates her face. She's looking down so I can see the tip of her pert nose, the sprinkle of freckles and the fan her eyelashes make against her cheeks.

I kissed you because I wanted to . . . I never stopped wanting you.

Her words offer electric shocks to reset the rhythm of my heart.

But I can feel the weight of an impending end. There's always an end, and I don't want this night to end. I don't like it, but I don't know what to do because I'm not used to wanting something to continue. I've never considered it, so I'm out of my element. Emma isn't like the other girls. I know for damn sure; I don't deserve to have her attention. I don't even know why she wants to kiss me. I don't know what to do now.

"It's Ginny," she says. "They're ready to go." She texts something. A gray bubble appears, and she looks up at me. "Would you be willing to walk me to the car instead? A little further toward the park?"

I don't want to because I want to walk her back to my tent. I want

143

to slip inside of my sleeping bag with her. I don't want this night to end, because I'm afraid that when morning comes, it will have all been a dream. She's going to wise up and realize what a near-mistake she's made. And she's going to think: *close call.* And Liam's going to tell her all the reasons to stay away from me. He'll be right.

I tell her, "Yeah. Of course."

She types something on her phone, slips it into her back pocket and steps back.

I take her hand in mine again, interlocking our fingers, and we start toward the parking lot. I want to say something, but for the first time, I can't think of the right thing to say. If I were playing at what's happening between us, it would probably be easy to come up with something, because it wouldn't be real. But this is the most authentic I can remember being — ever. "I'm not ready for this to end," is what drops from my mouth. It's so honest and makes me flinch, but for some reason it's the only way I've been able to be with her tonight.

She squeezes my hand. "So, let's not let it."

"Emma," I say as if she's a child.

"Tanner. DO. NOT. EVEN." She pulls on my hand. "We're graduating in a week."

I laugh quietly, recalling her fire just moments ago, and how sexy she looked. Her admission she wanted to kiss me junior year and tonight. *Who are you to determine shit about my reputation? If I wanted to be seen with Tanner James — that's my choice.* I want to kiss her again thinking about it. I draw her closer, wrapping my arm around her shoulders. The smile slips off my face. "What if you wake up tomorrow, Em, and regret everything tonight?" I hate the question. I hate how desperate it makes me feel. I hate that it makes me feel naked and defenseless. So, I add, "Because maybe I'd like to call you, see if you'd like to go out sometime."

She's looking down at the ground as we walk. "What's to regret? We just jumped from a cliff together, shared some nice conversation and made out a couple times." She looks up at me and smiles. "Why would I regret that?"

Her smile jolts my bones. For the first time in my life, I'm looking up and out, and I'm holding onto someone that feels like she really matters. I'm ill-equipped to know how to keep her there. "Yeah," but the lackluster sound of my own voice confuses me.

I stop walking.

She stops and looks at me.

I hesitate, but the rush of words working from my chest out to my tongue is a new sensation; I can't seem to stop it. I turn toward her and understand what she meant when she said, *it's easier to talk in the dark*. I rush ahead and jump over the cliff. "I'm — I don't — I want–" but I don't finish my thought, unsure.

She reaches out and rests a hand on my arm. "What is it?"

"Junior year." I swallow. I feel like I might be drowning. "It mattered. I tried to ignore it, and I couldn't. I want you to know that."

Emma turns away.

I've fucked up, I think. *Too soon. Not manly enough. She's going to think I'm a pussy, like Griff has always said about guys sharing their feelings.*

She turns and looks up at me, and I see her by moonlight now, the trees thinning out as we near the parking lot. She smiles. "I wish I had something cool to say to that. I don't. It just makes me feel happy."

Elated and relieved that my feeling vomit didn't scare her away (and Griff was evidently wrong), I scoop her into my arms and lift her, so her face is level with mine. "So, I can take you out?"

"Yes. Yes."

I let her go, setting her back down, and draw her phone from her back pocket. "Open this for me," I tell her, holding it out so she can unlock it. Then I open the contacts app, punch my information into her phone and send myself a text. "There." I slip the phone back into the front pocket of my sweatshirt she's wearing and draw her back into my embrace. My heart is still racing, but despite the urgency of its beat, it's accompanied by contentment, or something like it.

I think about Emma being scared and ask her, "Is this something that scares you?"

"You have no idea," she answers and hugs me tighter.

e m m a

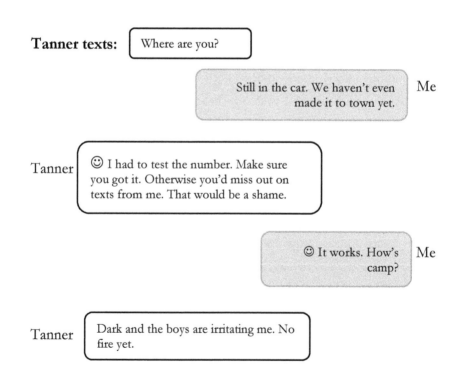

Tanner texts: Where are you?

Still in the car. We haven't even made it to town yet. Me

Tanner ☺ I had to test the number. Make sure you got it. Otherwise you'd miss out on texts from me. That would be a shame.

☺ It works. How's camp? Me

Tanner Dark and the boys are irritating me. No fire yet.

I smile in the back of the car. Ginny sings at the top of her lungs while Atticus drives us back to town. Liam is silent and moody. I'm thinking about making out on sleeping bags. I text him back.

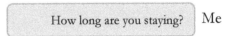

Ginny stops singing. "You're smiling."

"I am, aren't I?" I giggle and cover my face with my hands. I can't remember the last time I felt this relaxed, this excited, this giddy. The last time? I go through my mind files. Senior year. Nope. Junior year. Oh. After kissing Tanner at that party junior year. "Oh my, Ginny."

"I want to hear everything." She turns in the seat to face me.

"I don't," Liam says from the front seat.

"You're being a Steff," I tell him and look at my phone again. It's a low blow because we all hate Steff from *Pretty in Pink*. Those are fighting words if I've ever said them.

Tanner:

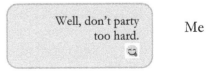

"That's rude, and I'm not. I'm being a realist," Liam says. "And you made it very clear that my opinion isn't wanted."

"You've made yourself clear. I don't think you need to belabor it. Besides, you aren't willing to hear anything different anyway." I lean back in the seat.

Me

I text it — trying to be casual — but it doesn't feel like a joke at all, my insecurities collecting in the dark spaces between my confidence now that I'm not with Tanner.

"Is this spat about Tanner?" Atticus asks from the driver's seat. "He's cool."

Liam crosses his arms over his chest. "He's a known f-boy who exploits women."

Atticus shrugs. "Maybe before. The last party I went to he was there, and he turned down every girl that made a pass at him. I'm not sure if that's exploitation. We hung out talking most of the night." He pauses and then says. "Besides, are any of us the same people we were a year ago? Heck a month ago?"

I'm impressed by Atticus's wisdom. I'm not the same from the beginning of the night to now.

Tanner:

> I'm going to bed. Griff is pissed at me because I don't want to get drunk with him.

Liam makes a noise in his nose.

I want to text Tanner that Liam is mad at me too, but don't. I don't want to tell him why.

"In fact, Tanner helped me find the courage to ask you out," Atticus tells Liam, looking over at him with a tender smile.

I can tell by Liam's face he begrudges the information, stubborn to a fault, even if it surprises him.

Tanner:

> I should leave.

"It's easy to judge someone's journey from the outside, but I don't think we should, not without knowing the whole story. Tanner hasn't always made the best choices, sure, but with his history, it isn't super surprising," Atticus adds.

Ginny and I lean forward. "What? History?"

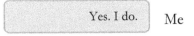 Why don't you? Me

"Do you remember elementary school?"

"We didn't go to elementary with you guys. We were at different schools. Remember? We didn't start together until Middle," Ginny says.

Tanner: | I promised. They're my boys, you know? |

I glance at Liam, who I'm angry with but will always love. I understand and try to connect the dots.

Yes. I do. Me

Atticus clears his throat. "Sorry. I'm not about spreading rumors or anything. Tanner is the guy who should share his history. It's just understandable is all I'm saying; there's always context."

I lean back, taking in Atticus's thoughts.

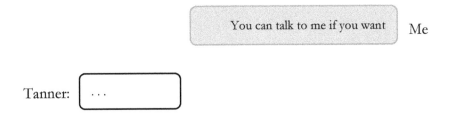 You can talk to me if you want Me

Tanner: | · · · |

He was waiting for my text, and it makes my heart flutter.

senior year
(6 days to graduation)

"The night after my fight with Erickson, I've never felt more alive; the vibrancy of it thrumming under my skin like minor chords on a piano."

-unnamed protagonist, *Kaleidoscope Concussion* by Saul Annick

e m m a

When my eyes open, and I'm in my bedroom, white and pink gilded with morning sun, I roll over onto my belly and scream with joy into my pillow. Tanner James asked me to jump with him. Tanner James kissed me! And Tanner James texted with me until his phone died.

I sit up onto my elbows and look for my phone. A quick check. No new messages. I roll to my back, hold my phone up over my head, and scroll through our conversation. I can't remove the million-watt smile from my face.

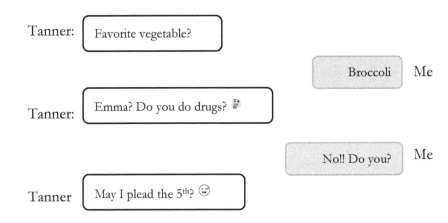

Tanner: Favorite vegetable?

Broccoli   Me

Tanner: Emma? Do you do drugs? 💀

No!! Do you?   Me

Tanner   May I plead the 5th? 😉

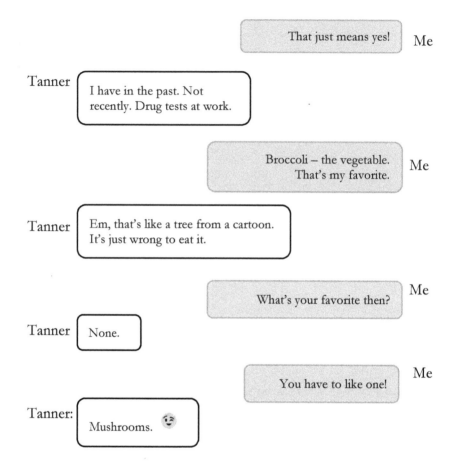

That just means yes! — Me

Tanner: I have in the past. Not recently. Drug tests at work.

Broccoli – the vegetable. That's my favorite. — Me

Tanner: Em, that's like a tree from a cartoon. It's just wrong to eat it.

What's your favorite then? — Me

Tanner: None.

You have to like one! — Me

Tanner: Mushrooms. 😋

The messages go on and on. We talked about food and school, easy memories and then Tanner texts:

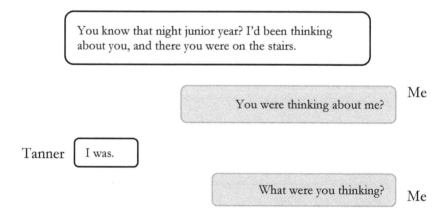

You know that night junior year? I'd been thinking about you, and there you were on the stairs.

You were thinking about me? — Me

Tanner: I was.

What were you thinking? — Me

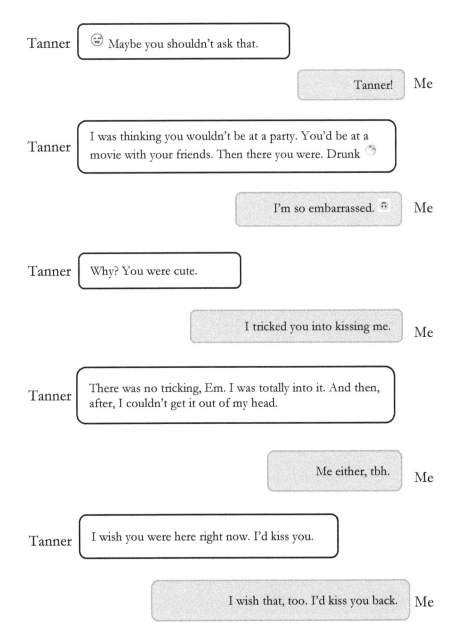

Tanner   Maybe you shouldn't ask that.

Tanner!   Me

Tanner   I was thinking you wouldn't be at a party. You'd be at a movie with your friends. Then there you were. Drunk

I'm so embarrassed.   Me

Tanner   Why? You were cute.

I tricked you into kissing me.   Me

Tanner   There was no tricking, Em. I was totally into it. And then, after, I couldn't get it out of my head.

Me either, tbh.   Me

Tanner   I wish you were here right now. I'd kiss you.

I wish that, too. I'd kiss you back.   Me

I remembered typing it and feeling like perhaps I was playing with fire, as if maybe I'd burst into flames for wanting to be with Tanner. I imagined laying with him in his sleeping bag, kissing him. I replayed kissing him in the tent in my mind, the feel of his body between my legs, and the weight of him pressed against me like comfort and satisfaction. I wanted sex with Tanner then. I want it now. I can feel the pearl of want radiating low in private places which belong to me, stealing my breath.

I'm trying to arrange the Biblical warning of the sins of the flesh around my biology at the same time. Certainly, wanting sex is a fleshly desire, but how is it a sin if God made us? If biology is part of God, then sex is a part of God. Wanting Tanner hasn't made me lose my sense of self or my sense of faith. It isn't as if I've chosen to compromise my beliefs to someone else to the detriment of myself or how I feel about God. I'm unsure how I'm supposed to resolve the natural function of my body with my religion's doomsday warnings that by wanting sex I'm somehow impure.

"Emma! Breakfast!" Shelby's voice calls from somewhere in the house. My guess is she's standing at the bottom of the stairs.

With a sigh, I climb from my bed and after morning routine, enter the kitchen to join my family at the table.

"There she is. Sleeping Beauty." My dad smiles looking at me over his glasses. He's sitting with a coffee cup in hand.

My mom sets the syrup down and sits.

We pray.

I look up at the stack of pancakes. "Blueberry?"

"Yes. With cream cheese," Dad says. We begin the routine of passing plates and dishing out food. "I made them for you, Emmz, because they're your favorite."

I moan around the bite in my mouth. "Thanks, Dad."

"The blueberries aren't fresh, though. Too early, yet. Maybe we can all go picking before you leave for college. One more time."

The realization I'm leaving for college hits me in the chest, knocking out the air. It wasn't as if I'd forgotten. Leaving for college seemed to be the only thing keeping me afloat even if I faced it with a sense of apprehension. Now, though, after last night, finally connecting with Tanner, it feels like a dark tunnel in the distance. I swallow the now too-dry pancake in my mouth. Last night, I'd forgotten anything outside of the moments with Tanner, and though I don't know where that road leads, the idea of getting off of it for college closes my throat.

"How was Senior Send Off?" Mom asks.

"Good."

"I remember jumping from the rock in high school." Dad smiles and takes a bite of pancakes.

"The what?" Mom asks him.

"You know, that outcropping at the Quarry where the kids jump into the lake?"

Mom's eyes grow with apprehension. "You did that?"

He chuckles.

"I bet you didn't jump," Shelby tells me. "Emma's too scared."

Her words hurt, even though I know that's not her intention. It makes me think of *Sixteen Candles* when Samantha's family forgets her birthday because of her sister's wedding. The way they saw her one way and packed her into that box. "I did," I say.

My family suspends, as if I've pushed pause on this breakfast.

"Really?" Shelby asks.

I nod, pressing play.

Family moves again.

"I would, too." My brave little sister takes a bite of pancake.

"That's a very dangerous thing to do." Mom glances from Shelby to me. She's wearing one of those worried looks that places added burden on her eyes and mouth.

"Now, Amy. She's okay." Dad pats my mom's hand. He clears his throat. "But your mother is right." He swallows. "I'm hoping you got that adrenaline rush out of your system?"

I take a bite of my pancake, so I don't have to say anything. I'm annoyed, suddenly, and would like to tell them to mind their own business. They don't get to decide what I get to do. I think if I said, "I kissed a boy named Tanner and wanted to have sex with him" they'd go into shock. Instead of pressing pause, though, it would be the button that detonates the bomb and incinerates everything. Then they'd inform me of all the religious reasons against premarital sex. Warnings that don't sever the desire but only serve to be more confusing, because I can't figure out how religion gets to write rules about that. Why is sex — healthy sex between two consenting people — about morality? Doesn't it fit better in ethics?

"Right, Emmz?"

"Huh?" I ask, because I've lost track of the conversation.

"You won't do it again, right?" My dad's eyes study me. He isn't smiling since he has on his worried dad face that looks a lot like my mom's. Only his look adds a stern line to his mouth pulled taut that makes me feel like I've disappointed him.

I nod. It isn't a lie. I don't plan on jumping off the rock again, but that doesn't mean I'm not thinking about jumping in other ways. I don't need their permission. It isn't anyone's choice but mine.

After breakfast, while we sit in church, Dad, then Mom, Shelby, and me, I tell God how I feel. *I want to have sex with Tanner, God. Does that make me bad?* I think I hear a gentle 'no' reverberate through my insides, but then wonder if I told myself that. When Pastor Green says "1st John tells us to 'not love the world or the things of the world, for it is in the word — the lust of the flesh, the lust of the eyes, and the pride of life — is not of the Father but of this World...for it is passing away, and the list of it; but he who does the will of God abides forever.'"

I open my Bible and look up the verse. John addressed children, young men, and men. Where were the women? I smack the book shut, garnering a look from my mother. *Sorry,* I mouth at her and replace the book, thinking maybe it wasn't the women who needed to be warned away from lust but the men instead.

Later, because I can't stay in the house any longer, I settle onto the front porch swing to study for my finals. That is also a fruitless task since I've been rereading the same text over and over because I'm not retaining anything. I'm annoying myself with my unsatisfied restlessness.

"Hey."

I look up from the book I'm not actually reading, because I've been reliving the moments I shared with Tanner.

Liam stands at the bottom of the porch steps. He looks tentative, which is uncharacteristic. His arms are crossed over his Green Lantern t-shirt, and his dark hair looks unruly. "May I come up?"

I nod.

Under different circumstances, it wouldn't be strange to see Liam at my house, or me at his, on any given day. He lives only a few houses away, so we've spent our lives together. Today, however, after last night, a tension hangs between us like ugly curtains.

His steps thump against the wood as he walks to the swing where I'm sitting.

I watch his white sneakers make the short journey across the porch to avoid meeting his gaze. Then, instead of looking at him, I shift my attention to clearing the papers and books so he can sit. Truthfully, I'm afraid of what I will find on his face; fearful that he hasn't changed his stance about Tanner and our hurtful impasse will remain between us.

The swing groans and sways when he sits.

He leans forward, elbows to knees, then sits back up and runs his hand through his product-free hair. He's frowning, which makes his usually vibrant personality thin and old, as if his soul ages with discomfiture. His complexion is lighter than usual, and his eyes even more droopy behind his glasses than their normal droop. He clears his throat, but then doesn't say anything and studies his hands instead.

"Just say it." I tell him. "We've been friends too long to draw it out." For some reason I'm expecting the worst. More warnings of dire consequences for the feelings I have for Tanner. It's probably me projecting my insecurities on him, because I've been struggling all day with the external expectations of my family and messages at church. But Liam surprises me (which shouldn't be a surprise).

"I just wanted to say, 'I'm sorry.'" He rubs his right thumb over his left palm.

I shift in my seat, sitting a little straighter, still watching his hands out of the corner of my eye.

"You were right." He shifts on the porch swing, turning toward me.

A grin breaks out on my face, because I can't help it, and I giggle.

"Stop that, Emma." There's an unwelcome smile behind his words.

My eyes jump to his. "Did I hear you correctly? Did you say that I

157

was right?"

He can't stifle his smile, now. "Don't get used to it."

I laugh. "And what brought you to this understanding?"

His smile fades away along with his face. His throat works as he swallows, his Adam's apple bobbing. "Being gay is — difficult."

I reach out and lay a hand on his back. "Did something happen?" It's my turn for the smile to fade, and my protective instincts kick up my inner warrior. "Nothing bad happened right?" Because that has always been a worry, especially in this town. "Who do I need to torture?"

"No. No." He shakes his head. "Just let me explain, okay? Listen."

I nod.

"Last night, I wasn't thinking about you as a woman when I said what I said. How you have the right to own your choices. Your body. Your sexuality. I was just thinking about you as my friend — someone I care about and don't want to get hurt. But–" he pauses, but it stretches out. I'm not sure he's going to continue.

"But?"

He turns in the seat and looks at me. His eyes are weighted with a thousand thoughts. "When I got home, I laid in bed thinking about what you'd said. How you'd scolded me that it was your choice, your life, your body. And laying there, running over it in my mind, I couldn't stop thinking about how that's what it's like being gay. How people think they can tell you who you are, who you should be, who you can and can't love; about how for some reason your value is wrapped up in your sexuality."

Tears fill my eyes, and I grab his hand.

"Atticus said we shouldn't judge someone's journey without knowing the whole story, and he's right. I do understand your story, because I live it, too, even if it's different." He takes my other hand and squeezes them with his. "I don't want to do that to you, Emma."

I lean forward and wrap my arms around him as tears slip down my cheeks. "I love you, Liam."

He hugs me back, holds me, his face pressed between the space between my shoulder and neck. "I love you too."

Our hug offers solace despite the heaviness that surrounds us. A part of me wishes we could go back in time to when we were nine and the hardest thing we dealt with were skinned knees. But growing up isn't like that. It just gets more complicated, and now it seems even more important to hang on to one another.

"I'm sorry for calling you a Steff," I tell him.

He chuckles and mutters against my shoulder, "I don't think I can ever forgive you for that."

I laugh too, and just like all that, Liam and I are okay once again.

The cell of us splits. Side-by-side we sit and tell each other secrets about Atticus and Tanner in hushed tones, as if we're thirteen again, insulated by our idealism and one another.

tanner

I'm up early. Earlier than the boys, who I'm sure are hung over from their revelry last night. Griff was pissed at me for not drinking, but for the first time, I didn't really give a shit how he felt about it. I hung out, told him to fuck off and eventually went to bed. In fact, texting with Emma was a great improvement over how things might have been with Griff and his sour remarks about my lack of manhood. Griff's sleeping bag is still empty.

I pack my shit before anyone else is up, which is easy since Griff and Josh brought most of the stuff. I leave one of my coolers still full of food, because I know that Josh will definitely bring it back, and I can get it from him later. The other cooler is close enough to empty. I put it in the back of my truck along with the sleeping bag, my duffle, and the one chair I brought with me.

The campground, not only ours, but the whole of the grounds, is quiet, aside from a few early risers like me. I can smell the fires and coffee brewing on camp stoves. I like the solitude of the morning. The sun just up, and the haze of the cool burning away. Golden light filters like a painting through the trees, and the songs of birds remind me that there are reasons to be grateful. Maybe it's my mood, the happy remnants of a night spent clean. A night where I chose something different for myself, and I woke up to a new story. A night texting with Emma, getting to know her and teasing her about her favorite vegetable. A night flirting with her, wanting to kiss her, dreaming about it. Happiness is addictive, I decide.

"Morning." Josh steps from his tent and walks toward the fire rubbing his eyes. His sandy hair explodes from his head. His red and blue plaid flannel pants are skewed like the wrinkled white t-shirt that reads *F*ck Off*.

"How are you feeling?"

"Fine. I didn't drink that much," he says. "I bet Griff will be feeling it though. Dumbass." He chuckles and sits down in a chair. "You leaving already?"

"Yeah. Work."

"Thanks for the fire."

"Glad you're up, or I would have had to stoke it."

Josh nods.

"Griff didn't come in last night." I indicate the tent with a tilt of my head.

"He dragged Danny prowling for girls. Said something about looking for Bella if you weren't into it."

I sit.

"Probably found a willing partner. Either that or passed out somewhere. Danny probably went to look for some kush."

"How come you didn't?"

Josh leans back in his lawn chair, and it creaks. Lacing his fingers over his belly, he watches the fire. "I'm over it."

His admission surprises me. Josh is cool; we've had good times over the years, but deep conversation hasn't really described the kind of relationship we've had. I engage, however, hungry for it. "Yeah. Me too. For a while."

"I could tell." He leans forward, picks up a stick from the ground, and shoves an end into the fire. "Griff can too. Bitched about it on the way up." The burning wood collapses, shifting and releasing sparks. Josh gets up and adds another piece of wood to the flames.

"You think he thought this would last forever?"

Josh shrugs and looks at the burning end of the stick.

"It doesn't mean I don't–" I pause, not exactly sure how to say what's on my mind, but then remember how easy it was with Emma the night before– "care, you know? I do. You're my boys."

Josh looks up. "Dude. For real." He smiles and pokes at the log again. "It's just growing up. And things are changing. I hope you aren't, like, feeling bad. It's cool."

I find Josh's astuteness refreshing. "Kind of. You know how Griff is."

He scoffs and shakes his head. "You do you, T. That's all you got. For real. You gotta figure out you — not Griff too."

Josh's words somehow reinforce the parts of me I've begun to build. "Thanks."

"We getting together next week? After graduation?"

"Probably." I stand and offer my hand. He hits it twice. "I'll see you Tuesday. Court Monday."

"Oh shit, dude. Sorry about that. What now?"

"Mom's trying to extend child support for college. Dad's contesting because I haven't applied."

"You're not going to college?"

"I can't. No grades."

"Community college?"

"I don't think school's my thing."

Josh nods. "Maybe. Or maybe it just isn't yet. You shouldn't close doors, you know. Maybe check it out?"

He's right. I had closed that door. "I don't really want to join Griff for Bro Code 2.0."

"There are community colleges everywhere, Tanner."

"Yeah." I nod even though it hadn't been something I'd thought about.

"You could come with me to Cali."

I hadn't ever considered it, because it's school, but then I wonder why. Could that be a part of a new story too? It felt too unrealistic, too distant to contemplate. "Thanks."

"And, hey," he says, stopping me as I walk to my truck. "Let me know if you want to talk after court?"

"Thanks, Josh."

As I drive toward town, I replay the conversation with Josh in my head. Maybe by making a different choice, by starting a new story, I opened the door to better things. My interaction with Josh, and even Danny, has been limited. Usually Griff is in the midst, and anything pure gets obliterated to dust with him in the mix. I think about his reaction to my writing, and the way I allowed him to make me feel smaller, or the way he responded to knowing I had to go to court.

Bitterness swells inside me, but I hate that I'm feeling this way about Griff, because he's been there for me the last several years. The shift in me isn't happening in him, however, and I don't know what to do. In times like this, I miss Rory so much more. I know my big brother would have been the perfect person to ask for advice.

I drive into the main office and warehouse yard of my dad's construction company and park my truck next to Dad's car. When I walk into the warehouse, my father is there, looking over paperwork.

"Morning. I wasn't sure you'd been here with Senior Send Off. I thought you'd be camping the rest of the weekend. You didn't need to come in."

"Naw. I'd rather make some money."

"You've got your whole life to make money. Only one Senior Send Off." There's a smile in his voice as he flips the page on the clipboard he's holding.

I don't say anything. What he's offered is more observation anyway. I reach for the forklift keys and the delivery list for Monday morning.

"Everything okay?"

I hum an affirmation.

"Hey, before you set the trucks up, can I talk to you for a minute?"

I pause, waiting, but don't turn toward him. The truth about my relationship with my dad is that there is no relationship other than what

163

we exchange while at work. After the divorce, it became about stupid visitations that were spent at his place, until they weren't because he couldn't figure out what to do with the left-over son. Maybe I just reminded him of Rory. I don't know. Then he married Shelley; his life became about his new wife and the kids they shared. I know my dad in two ways: fighting with my mom and at work. Him trying to talk to me feels like something is up.

"About Monday—"

Yeah. Something is up. I sniff and set my jaw.

"Look, I'm not going to tell you what to say or anything, I just want you to know that if you did want to go to school — to college — I'd cover it."

"That's not what I heard you tell Mom."

"Wait. What?" He's surprised, which I don't understand. I live in that house.

"What was it you said: 'That's all it ever is with you, Marna. Money.'"

He pinches the bridge of his nose and clears his throat. "Well, this isn't about your mom. This is about wanting you to know that if you want to go to school, I'll cover it."

I'm not sure why this feels like razor blades in the back of my throat. I don't look at him, but I nod so he knows I've heard. I walk away to prepare the trucks for tomorrow. *Rory,* I think wondering if he can hear me as I climb onto the forklift. *I wish you were here. There's so much I would like to ask you.* But he doesn't answer me back. He never does. He can't, I remind myself.

senior year
(5 days to graduation)

"Lucy's knowing look read between my lines. I hated it. She made me undone, made me crack apart as if I were dried clay. Or glass. I wasn't that weak. While the villainy of Erickson distracted me from her color, as if throwing fists proved I was strong once again.

And I started sleeping."

-unnamed protagonist, *Kaleidoscope Concussion* by Saul Annick

emma

Monday brings both the giddiness of anticipation but also the anxiety of the unknown. I didn't hear from Tanner on Sunday and was too afraid to text him (afraid to seem uncool or nerdy, even if I'm totally both). It's my last Monday of high school — finals week — and I'm ready, but my mind isn't here. I could take the tests today and ace them asleep, but I'm too busy looking for Tanner. So hopeful that what happened on Saturday wasn't in my imagination, but junior year leaves a hazy residual doubt. What if he isn't into me anymore because we didn't go further? Or what if I was too forward? I shake my head to ward off the conflicting and doubtful thoughts reinforced by a missing apology and a limo disappearing into the night.

I find Ginny at her locker. "Hey."

"Girl..." She smiles knowing all the details about Tanner and Senior Send Off, because I spent part of Sunday on the play-by-play with a need to analyze it again, even after analyzing it with Liam. "Where's your boy?"

"I haven't seen him," I whisper. "And he isn't *my boy*."

She laughs. "Why are you whispering?"

"Gin!"

"Text?"

I shake my head. "Not since Saturday night." I frown.

She touches my shoulder. "Hey." I must look like she needs to worry because her hazel eyes widen with concern, and her brows dip toward them. "Don't overthink this, Emma. Boy is interested."

"How do you know?"

"Uh, sis, everyone at the campfire could see the sexual tension coming off you two like smoke signals." She laughs and continues cleaning out her locker. "Don't worry. Just text him."

But I don't.

He doesn't show up at his locker. He's not at lunch. There's no sign of him. By the end of the school day, I'm worried. My imagination takes over and chastises me for letting my walls down too soon, that perhaps Liam was initially right and worry seeps in to widen the cracks of doubt.

When I get home, my dad is leaning against the island in the kitchen over his computer. "Hey, sweets." He straightens and draws his glasses from his face.

"Hey." I kiss his cheek and walk around the counter to retrieve a glass from the cupboard.

"How was the last Monday of your high school career?"

I offer him a shrug and fill my glass with water.

"Ready for the big leagues, then?" He closes his laptop and looks at me. We resemble one another: dark blue eyes, dark hair, though his is speckled with silver.

I lean against the sink with my glass of water. "I guess."

"What's wrong?"

"I don't know. Just feeling—" I try to find the right word. "Listless." I wish I could talk to him about Tanner, but I know he wouldn't understand. I wouldn't be able to have a real conversation with him that wouldn't resort to Biblical teaching. I need to understand what I'm feeling and grapple with the mixed-up messages that I can be in charge of my mind and choices in one way, but I'm not supposed to when it comes to my sexuality. I can't talk to him because I won't get what I need, and that makes me feel sad and alone.

"The doldrums."

"The what?" I ask.

"It's a sailor's reference to a calm, windless sea where sailing is impossible, and boredom sets in to make them feel dull. Actually, they go mad with it. You didn't read Coleridge's 'The Rime of the Ancient Mariner' in AP?"

"Nope, but it sounds about right." I take another sip of my water.

"This too shall pass." He replaces his glasses and opens his laptop again. "Winds of change are coming. I can't believe my baby girl is graduating."

"Dad. I'm not your baby. That's Shelby."

He looks at me over the top of his glasses. "You'll always be my baby, even when you're thirty-five."

"Only until then?"

"Hmmm." He glances at his watch. "Yeah. At thirty-six you're on your own." He smiles.

"Good to know." I put my glass in the dishwasher. "I better go study for finals."

"Set your watch. Dinner at seven. Mom should be home by then."

I make a show of syncing my watch to his, because he loves it, and I love him.

Once I'm in my room, however, I check my phone again. No text. And then I berate myself for waiting around. *Just text him*, Ginny had said. I analyze all the ways it's a terrible idea, but the only thing that stands out is that she's right. I'm avoiding texting him, because I'm afraid.

I straighten my shoulders. I'm a strong woman who knows her own mind. Why should I wait around like a passive recipient to my own life? I need to be braver. I open messenger, select his name, and text him: *Hey. Are you okay? Worried. Didn't see you today.*

The three dots pop up immediately.

I take a deep breath.

Tanner | Had court. |

I imagine Tanner as a hardened criminal and then shake my head at the stupid thought.

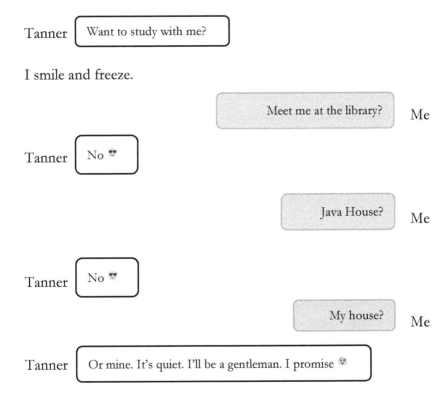

Tanner | It wasn't about me. 😊 Family court. You busy?

Studying for finals | Me

It's a lie, because I haven't cracked a book, but I'm not about to tell him I'm pacing my room worried about whether I should have texted him or not.

Tanner | Want to study with me?

I smile and freeze.

Meet me at the library? | Me

Tanner | No 😈

Java House? | Me

Tanner | No 😈

My house? | Me

Tanner | Or mine. It's quiet. I'll be a gentleman. I promise 😇

My heart races.

I should avoid this temptation at all costs, because I know I won't be studying for finals. But the thought of Tanner's mouth has my stomach dropping through a trapdoor. I begin calculating what I need to maintain my current grades and realize I've already spent a ton of time studying. I don't need to score super high to maintain my grades. It bugs me that I'm considering dropping everything to go to him, but then again, isn't it what I want?

It is.

I text him: *Send me the address.*

Tanner does, and I collect my things. "Last minute study group," I tell my dad on my way out.

"Home for dinner?" He asks.

I check my watch. "Planning on it, but I'll text you if it goes late?"

"Be safe."

I kiss his cheek, rush out the door, and drive across town into a gorgeous neighborhood where the monstrous houses are spaced out between manicured lawns. I've tried to quiet the feelings at war inside me, a study in contrasts. I'm so excited to see Tanner because of how things have developed between us, but I'm also terrified, because what if he has expectations? My limited experience is a juxtaposition between Tanner and Chris, and so far, my experience has been like day and night. While I've realized that I'm not a "just because" kind of girl, it doesn't change that I want to kiss Tanner. I even want to have sex with him, but am I ready for it? I don't know, and yet, here I am driving to Tanner's anyway.

I park my car in a round-a-bout driveway of a traditional Tudor-style home constructed with painted brick and steep gabled windows. It's like a storybook mansion. It isn't how I pictured Tanner's house, though I'm not sure I ever pictured where he'd live at all. The door opens before I even have time to knock, and Tanner steps through. He's dressed in dark navy chinos and a light gray dress shirt. It's unbuttoned several buttons, untucked, the sleeves rolled up, his hands in the pockets of his pants.

"Is this where the wicked witch lives?" I ask as I walk the path toward him. I'm trying to be light because of the weight of unknown expectation swirling around inside of me.

"Sometimes." His tone doesn't match my humor, and his gorgeous face is weighted with whatever is on his mind.

I suddenly wonder if my worry is warranted, as if maybe my subconscious knew something was amiss. "You okay?"

He draws me into his arms. "I'm so glad to see you." He presses his face against my shoulder, and then he steps back so I can walk into the house.

I walk into an expansive entry. It looks like a posh hotel. There's a large circular table with an enormous floral arrangement set on its center dominating the space. To the left, against the wall, a wide staircase curling to a second story landing. He's right. It's quiet. Museum quiet.

"You hungry?" He nods toward the kitchen.

"No. Thanks."

He takes my hand and leads me through the foyer, up the stairs. We take a left at the top and walk down a hallway. Halfway down the corridor, Tanner opens a door, and I follow him into a large room. Besides the normal bedroom stuff — an unmade king size bed rumpled with a blue and gray duvet, an end table stacked with books, bookshelves, a door which I assume leads to a closet, maybe a bathroom — it's a space big enough for its own sitting room with a sofa and TV. What draws my attention, however, are stacks of books. Not just a bookshelf full, he's got stacks lining the wall, on his bedside table, against the wall under the wall mounted TV. I glance at him with my insides stretching toward him. *That* is sexy. Another layer that adds dimension to who he is.

"Welcome to Tanner's Place."

I smile at him. "It's quite a bachelor pad." I nod at the TV, the video game stuff strung out across a coffee table. I want to ask him about the books but can feel he's not in the right mental place to share.

He frowns at the coffee table. Looks up and around the room as if seeing it through my eyes.

"Want to talk about it?" I ask.

He steps past me and sits on the sofa. "Can I say 'no'?"

I follow and sit down next to him. "Sure. You can. I don't think it will help you feel better."

"I know what would make me feel better." He offers a suggestive smile, but it doesn't reach his eyes.

I have the impression that perhaps Tanner is hiding from something. So I say, "Maybe try talking about it first." I lay a hand on his forearm.

He takes my hand in his and draws me closer to his side. His fingers speak against my own, sliding around my knuckles, over the palm of my hand. It's sensual and intimate in a way I could never have imagined. Then he sighs and says, "My family sucks."

I could offer an apology, but I don't think that's what he wants. I stay silent and wait for him to continue.

"We went to court today for a child-support hearing. I'm fucking eighteen, and my mom is asking for more child support. 'For college,' she says. Except I'm not going to college." He stops, and his fingers still speak with mine. "It isn't like she needs it. She just wants to keep punishing my dad."

"How long have they been divorced?"

"Four years, but the fighting started four years before that. This—" he waves his hand, the one not holding mine, about the room— "is the spoils of an awful war between my parents."

The idea hurts my heart. I think about my own family — my parents — and imagine the awful reality of a family under an umbrella of constant conflict, and how terrible that would feel. Eight years of it? I wonder if this is the context Atticus mentioned. Perhaps under pressure like that, I'd find any way to dull that pain. Maybe in partying. I glance at him, seeing him with fresh eyes, and the way his reality has drained him today.

I draw his hand up to my mouth and say against his skin, "I'm sorry, Tanner."

He glances from his hand to my face. "Don't be. It isn't your fault." He offers me a small smile and then wraps his arm around me, drawing me closer. With his lips against my hair he says, "I'm just glad you're here."

"Me too." I press closer to him, relieved I texted. Relieved I faced my fear to be here for him.

"I've been caught in between them. Like today, my dad thanked me for telling the judge I wasn't going to college. Like I did it for him. And now my mom is pissed at me."

I lay my head against his shoulder.

We sit like that for a while, in the silence of his room.

He eventually breaks it. "I'm sorry. I don't mean to bring you down."

"You didn't. I want to be here for you. That's what friends are for."

"Is that what we are? Friends?" His tone of voice is even, but I hear a note of strain. I'm in his arms, but it's as if he doesn't believe the physical matches the words.

"I hope so."

He makes a short humming noise.

I tense. "You don't want to be my friend?"

His fingers continue to caress mine, and my belly responds as I mull the ideas of friendship and sex together. Is that what I want? Friends with benefits? Just friendship? Just sex? No. Red wire. I wonder what he's thinking, and then he says, "I want so much more than that — with you."

I shift so I can see his face. "Only sex then?"

"No." He smiles and shakes his head. "Both."

This makes me smile, and I settle back against him, deciding I need to change the subject to something less serious. "I'm curious about something."

"What's that?"

"It was hard not to notice all of the books. Have you read them all?" I adjust my head so I can look at him again.

He smiles and for the first time since I arrived at his house, his smile meets his eyes; they sparkle. "Not yet, but I've gone through quite a few." He stands up and draws me off the couch after him. "These." He leads me to the bookshelf. "I've read these."

I look at the authors. Kafka. Fitzgerald. Shakespeare. Ducart. Sartre. Joyce. Classics, popular fiction, various topics of nonfiction from memoir to sports leadership to business. "Wow. Do you have a favorite?"

"Yes." He drops my hand and walks to his bedside. "This one." He picks it up and carries it back to me, the weight from his shoulders gone and the Tanner from Saturday returned. He holds out a copy of a book nearly falling apart, stuffed with post-its and marked with annotations. I'm afraid to handle it, but he offers it anyway.

"*Kaleidoscope Concussion* by Saul Annick." I read though I'm sure I've gotten the author's name wrong. "Isn't this a movie?"

"Yes. But the movie doesn't do it justice. Well it does, but it got the ending all wrong. All wrong. Have you read it?"

His excitement makes me smile, and my heart jumps again deciding to race along ahead of me. He looks so handsome and alive. Different in a way I've never seen him, certainly not at school, and then I wonder if he's ever shared this with anyone. His friends, I hope. I shake my head. "I haven't."

His hands go into his hair, and he steps back. "Oh my god, Em. You need to read it."

"I'd love to."

"Oh shit. You shouldn't read this copy though. It has all my notes. All my thoughts. You should read it unadulterated."

Unadulterated. This makes me smile wider. "I think I'd like to see what you think as I read it."

He tilts his head and looks at me through narrowed eyes. "It might ruin your experience."

I shake my head. "Actually, I think it would make it better. But I also don't want to take your copy." I hand it back to him like the treasure it is. "I'll look for it, okay, the next time I'm at Barkers Books downtown."

"We should go." His eyes brighten, but the shift of his head makes me think perhaps he is nervous having suggested it.

"I'd love that."

"Want to go tomorrow? After rehearsal?"

I nod. "Yes. I'd like that."

He smiles– "It's a date–" and returns the book to his bedside. Tanner sleeps on the left side of the bed.

"Are you feeling better?" I ask him.

He shrugs, but his easy smile that lights up his face has returned. "I feel terrible." He looks down at his feet as he walks back to me. When he looks up, I note his mischievous grin, but it doesn't match his words.

174

"Wait. I thought you might be feeling a little better."

"Definitely not." He stops in front of me, so close I'm sure he can feel my heartbeat against his chest.

"How come?"

He reaches up and tucks a strand of my hair behind my ear. "Because, you've been here for so long, and I still haven't gotten to do what I really want to yet."

"Which is?" I ask, but I know because I see it in the hazy way his eyes are perusing my face.

An impish smile touches his mouth. "To kiss you."

I laugh and sidestep him as he reaches for me. "You said you'd be a gentleman."

"I will, Emma. Let me show you." He laughs with me and wraps me up in his arms. He lifts me, and I can't get away, which I don't want to do anyway.

I warn him anyway with a laugh. "Tanner."

"Em," he says, mimicking my tone. Then he stops and releases me so I can stand on my own, but I don't step away from him. His smile melts away. Everything goes still except the beating of my heart and the breath which moves through my lungs like water, thick and heavy. With his fingers, he touches me again, as though he's testing if I'm real. "I haven't stopped thinking about Saturday night. I really want to kiss you, Emma. May I?"

"Yes." I love that he always asks me. It's empowering.

Tanner leans forward, his hand curls around my nape, but he doesn't kiss me right away. He stops, hesitates, and the anticipation of it sits on the edge of something inside of me. My lips part, and then he closes the distance. Finally.

It's slow and sensuous at first. Gorgeous torture, because it feels so good. His lips and tongue move in concert with mine, the only place we're connected. Until I reach out and wrap my arms around him. I step closer. Then our bodies touch.

The rhythm intensifies. I allow him in. I can't help myself; I make a noise that connects the feeling in my belly with the feeling he's creating in my mouth, and it comes out as a needy moan. I draw him closer, thinking about his weight the other night. Wanting it, now.

His hands drop to my hips; he tugs me closer and then he pulls away, his forehead against mine. "Emma — I want to be a gentleman. I do. But–"

I nod, and then admit, not caring how ridiculous I must sound, "I think I was going crazy the last two days." I don't say 'without you' because that might be too much. "It was the doldrums."

"That sounds terrible," he says. "What is it?"

So, I tell him.

"Yeah. That," he says and kisses me again.

tanner

Emma's in my arms, and my body speaks to her because it knows how. My hands caress her, my tongue on fire and lighting her up. She moans, and I light up too because I'm so invested in wanting to make her feel good. My hands on her hips, I walk her backwards until we're both lying on my bed. I settle against her, one of my legs between hers, and I want to do so much more. My chest aches with want, my body tense and rigid everywhere with the need for her.

For Emma.

I'm used to the physical. Bodies. A woman's body. Her sounds. Her pleasures. Mine. These are things I know. But I want to know Emma. For the first time in my life, I want to know THIS woman. I want to know what makes HER feel good. Every touch, every action bound up in Emma's response, her pleasure, and I want to give it to her because for the first time in my life, I see HER. I want her to feel seen and beautiful, like I see her.

She moans again. "Tanner." My name is her breath.

The sound constricts my chest, so I kiss her neck, love the taste of her candy skin on my tongue.

I run my hand to the waistband of her jeans.

She stops me, her hand over mine. "I don't–" are words she says into

177

my mouth, but I don't know what they mean. I lean back to look at her face. There's a line between her eyes, and I'm beginning to understand it. Worry. Fear.

Slow down, Tanner, I tell myself.

I smile. Kiss her nose. "We can stop, Emma. I told you I'd be a gentleman, even if I don't want to be." I kiss her neck and settle onto my back, adjusting her into the crook where my arm meets my shoulder. My body is tight and uncomfortable, but not unwelcome. It makes me smile — a real smile — and there's been so few of those today.

"Tanner?" Emma's voice sounds unsure.

"Yeah?" I turn my head to look at her.

She turns her face toward mine. She's beautiful, but her big eyes droop with apprehension.

I turn onto my side to face her and reach out with a hand to trace the line between her eyes. "What is this, Em? This line? Are you worried?" I settle my hand on her hip, loving the way her curve fits against my palm.

"Kind of."

"What for?"

She glances down at my chest, her eyelashes fanned out across her cheeks. "Are you upset?" she asks and looks back at my face.

"For what?"

"For stopping?"

I move away and sit up. "Whoa. What?" My brain moves with the question. Because I'm experienced? Because it's only about me and my pleasure? I don't understand her question, but maybe I should. I look at her over my shoulder.

She sits up next to me and stares at her clasped hands. The line is there between her eyes, but she doesn't say anything.

"Emma?"

Her eyes jump to mine.

"You can tell me what you need to tell me. I can't read your mind."

"I'm afraid."

"Of me?"

"No. Not you. I'm— I don't — I don't know what I'm doing." She pauses, her face drawn toward something heavy. She looks up, needing something. "I'm confused."

The weight of her words punctures my insides, and I begin to sink. "About?"

She looks away, and I'm afraid now, too. Afraid she's figured out I'm not right for her. I'd hoped because her body tells me one story. I could read it, but then bodies don't always align with mind to tell the same tale.

She doesn't say what I assume: *Tanner, you're not good enough for me.* Instead, she says, "Sex."

Relief plugs up the hole in my heart, and I stop sinking for the moment. Sex. I can talk about that. "What about it?"

"I haven't–" She stalls, takes a deep breath, seems to center herself, nods and says, "I'm a virgin." She blushes when she says it, but her gorgeous blue eyes find mine anyway, demonstrating the strength of her in the way she accepts things as they are.

"Why is that confusing?"

"I'm not confused about you." She reaches over and touches my arm.

All the fear threatening to drown me drains, and I can breathe again. I take her hand.

"It's everything else. All the messages I get about how I'm supposed to feel, and how I'm supposed to act. How I'm not supposed to have sex before I'm married because if I do, I'm somehow less than someone who doesn't. How I'm supposed to submit to a man, but yet be independent. I don't understand how it all adds up." She looks up at me. "Sorry."

I shake my head, stuck on her words. All the ways she's feeling pressure that have nothing to do with me and actual sex. "You shouldn't say sorry. Not for that." I remember her talking about her fears — of letting down her parents and God. "Is it a religious thing?"

"Sort of. The thing is, I don't logically buy into the religious idea that my body isn't mine to make decisions about, but I also can't seem to escape the fear that if I don't do what I'm told, I've somehow disappointed everyone."

I run my thumb over her knuckles, grappling with her words and understanding that just like my struggle with expectations, she's chained to her own. We all are, I suppose. "I don't know about religion stuff, Em, but I can talk about it from my perspective if you want? I don't want to say the wrong thing." I glance at her face.

"I want to hear."

"I don't think less of someone who has sex, but I know the kind of people who do. I don't think it's anyone's business but the people who share it. It isn't something to feel ashamed of, that's for sure, not when it's something you both want. I also think you shouldn't ever feel bad to tell someone to stop, Emma. Ever." I wrap my arm around her shoulder and pull her closer.

She takes a deep breath, as if she's set down the world and turns into my embrace.

I wrap my arms around her. "Whatever is happening between us is about us — not anyone else. And I think you should set the pace, okay? I'm just happy to be with you."

I feel her smile against my chest, and even if I were disappointed to stop because I want all of Emma, her smile is worth it. I want all of her, because she wants it all.

She sits back, smiles a teary smile, and wipes her eyes. "Thanks, Tanner."

"You can pay the receptionist on the way out," I tease.

She pushes me with a laugh, but her laugh fades. Her eyes catalogue my face, taking in the details. She moves closer and sweeps a lock of my hair from my forehead, then runs her fingers through my hair, adjusting the strands. It sparks the base of my spine up with a low fire. "We should probably study," she says, but there isn't any conviction in her tone.

"Is there something you'd rather do?" I ask her and grin as I capture her wrist.

"Besides make out with you?" She pauses, looking upward and then says, "Nope."

I pull her into my lap. "May I kiss you again, Emma?"

"Please," she says, but leans forward, not waiting, and presses her parted lips to mine.

A while later, even though I'm sitting next to her on the floor with a game controller in my hand, I can't keep my eyes off of her. Her back is against the front of the couch in my room an arm's length away, her legs drawn up, and her binder of notes resting on her lap. She's recopying things onto color-coded notecards. She twirls a lock of dark hair around her finger and that cute line is between her eyes because she's concentrating, I assume. All I want to do is draw her into my arms.

I wonder about my parents before the marriage detonated. Did they feel like this? I feel like my insides are too big for my body. As if they are inflating with new feelings, and I might float away. I have the need to touch her, to make sure she's real, even though she's right next to me. The thought unsettles me. I feel content. Happy, actually. My parents must have been happy at some point. There was a time before, before they got married, before Rory was born. Then after. And after I was born. I remember the love they shared. I remember my dad's arms around my mom. I remember them holding hands and smiling at one another when they talked. I remember the way they would kiss. Rory and I would jump between them to push them apart, because it was *so gross*. Then both of them would turn the kisses on us.

They must have been happy then.

Until they weren't.

I feel happy now.

Does that end?

I look back at the video game I'm playing with my heart pumping blood through my body like usual. With these anxious thoughts I've never had before, the unsettled feeling in my belly makes me worried about happiness and endings. I swallow.

It's just family court that threw me off today, I decide. It always feels great when I have to tell the judge that both of my parents are fucked up assholes to one another, and I'm the rope they are trying to hang one another with. Mom had been so pissed; she'd dropped me home and said she wasn't sure when she'd be back. Nothing new.

"You're scowling," Emma says, but when I look over at her she isn't actually looking at me.

"How do you know?"

"I can feel it." She smiles at her book, never looking at me, but she does scoot closer so our legs touch.

I smile. She's wonderful, but that uneasy unfurling in me makes me uncomfortable.

"Don't you have something to study for?" she asks, and then looks at me over her shoulder.

"I am."

She dips her head down so that her chin touches her shoulder, and her eyebrows arch over her eyes with a question. "What?"

"You," I tell her and smile. It's the cheesiest thing I've ever said, and the smile she gives me along with the laugh are so worth it.

"Whatever." She turns her head away and returns to copying shit on her notecards. "You're playing that brain-cell killing video game."

"Studies show that video games increase both motor abilities and visual response time."

She grunts. "I guess there's still some brain cells working."

"You're not done yet, Em?" Now, I'm thinking about sex. Having it. Not having it. Wanting it. Wanting her. "I've been very patient and think I should get a treat."

I lean over and kiss an exposed part of her neck. She makes a little noise that excites me. I curl my finger in the collar of her shirt and slide my tongue lower. Setting the video game controller on the coffee table, I wrap my arm around her waist and pull her closer.

She turns toward me, and her eyes slip closed. She sighs into my touch. "I can't concentrate when you do that." Her head dips forward as she leans toward me.

My heart speeds up. "Em." I continue a trail of kisses down to her shoulder and slip a hand under the hem of her shirt so I can feel the warm skin of her belly. "I think you're still going to college. I think you'll still be giving your speech in five days, regardless." I move my mouth back to her neck and ride my hands around to her ribs just under her bra. "Let me — help you not think."

She turns so that her mouth meets mine, and our tongues speak.

Her binder slips off her legs to the floor making a noise that I'm pretty sure has her worried about her notes. I kiss her more intently and lay down on my back, pulling her with me. She moves up the length of my body until she's draped on top of me. With one hand holding the back of her neck, my other hand teases her hot skin beneath the waistband of her jeans at the small of her back.

"I think I have a really good way we can study for biology."

"I'm not in biology." She trails kisses from my mouth to my jaw. "This experiment–" she adjusts herself so she's looking down at me, and her hair falls around us like a cocoon– "would be purely for personal reasons."

Her phone buzzes.

She shifts to grab it from the coffee table.

That damn phone.

"I've got to go."

I groan.

She looks at me and waves the phone at me. "My family has dinner in thirty minutes."

"Thirty minutes? Can you be a little late?" I grab her hips and bring her back.

"Nope." She pushes my chest and sits up, straddling me. With a look meant to admonish me, she says, "Do not start." But she can't keep the smile from her face.

I grin.

She rolls her eyes, still smiling, and collects her stuff. "Want to come?"

"Yes." We're talking about different things.

"Really?" She looks so excited. When she sees my face, her eyes narrow. The moment she realizes what I've meant, she looks shocked but grins. "Tanner!" She smacks my shoulder playfully.

I laugh. "Thanks for the invite. Another time?"

I walk her to the front door. Then I kiss her against it for a good fifteen minutes. Until she insists that she's going to be late, and that her parents will never let her out again. Watching her walk away hurts. When I close the door to my house, I've never felt more alone.

senior year
(4 days to graduation)

"Erickson challenged me to take the risk. 'What do you have to lose?'
The truth though was that it felt like I had everything to lose, and him, nothing."

-unnamed protagonist, *Kaleidoscope Concussion* by Saul Annick

emma

I'm standing at my locker the next morning before my first final and glance at Tanner's locker. He isn't there yet, but he said he'd be at school today. His text had said: *graduation is a must. I'll be there. Besides, I get to see you.* It makes me feel warm all over thinking about the night before. Tanner's hands on my body. His kisses. His tongue. The way my heart expanded behind my ribs and the want. Oh, the want. My cheeks heat. But it was our talk — his words — that began to fuse my heart and body with my mind.

"So, then the jerk texts–" Ginny stops. "Emma. Stop looking for him and listen to my story."

Liam pinches me.

"Ouch. Sorry, Gin. Go." I turn toward her, my back to Tanner's locker.

"Dean said: 'I think it meant more to you.'" She uses air quotes with her fingers.

"Bullshit."

"He didn't! What a jerk. I'm sorry, Ginny."

Ginny leans against the locker next to mine and looks down at the ground. "The worst part, I knew in my gut, and I ignored my instincts."

She's sad.

"You want me to ask Atticus to get the team to beat him up?" Liam asks.

"Would he do that?" Ginny looks tempted, wearing a mischievous smile.

Liam chuckles and smooths one of his sleeves. "I don't know." His eyes snap back to Ginny. "Seemed like a cool thing to offer."

"Yeah. It was even if we'd never do that." She looks so glum.

I want to do something to cheer her up. "Let's do something after finals are done. Friday night John Hughes?"

"Yes!" Ginny straightens.

"Well—" Liam draws out the word.

"Liam," she warns.

"Atticus and I kind of made plans."

"What!?" Ginny exclaims. "It's our last Friday of high school, and we can't do movie night on Saturday because of graduation."

"I didn't consider that." Liam looks sheepish, his gaze falling to the floor a moment. "I'm sorry."

"Invite him." I put a hand on his arm. "We could introduce Atticus to our Hughes movie night."

Liam stops and tilts his head. "Maybe."

I grab both of Liam's arms with my hands. "The correct answer is yes. Just bring him. You guys can go make out after." I stick my tongue out at him.

He blushes.

"Oh." Ginny smiles and glances at me. "Someone has been holding out on us."

"Shut it," Liam says. "I don't kiss and tell."

"But you'd like to."

I close my locker and look at Liam, whose eyes have grown in circumference.

"Hey," Ginny says to someone behind me.

I spin, and Tanner is standing there with a handful of roses and a cute, boyish look on his face — almost nervous — if Tanner has ever looked nervous.

"Good morning." He steps closer.

"Hi." I can't keep the huge smile from my face but suppress the urge to press my hands to my cheeks.

He looks so handsome — as usual. Those jeans that hang just right. He's wearing a light blue shirt which looks so good against his tanned skin. It reads: *Morally Flexible.*

"These are for you." He holds out the dark pink roses with sprigs of baby's breath. Then he leans in close to me and whispers, "I missed you after you left." He presses his lips to my cheek.

My stomach flies around inside my body as if it has grown wings. I can think of some other things I'd like to add to the day's agenda. "They are beautiful." My face heats with pleasure. If I had any worry I was imagining what was happening with Tanner, this display douses it with sweetness and sunshine. Add to it, everyone standing in the hallways has witnessed it too, including Bella Noble, who's across the hallway with her mouth wide open.

"We're still on, right? After rehearsal? For our date?"

"Yes. I'm looking forward to it." I'd never say, *it's about all I've been thinking about.*

When I get to AP History, Corbin, who sits at the desk behind me, leans forward and says, "Tanner James, Matthews? Damn. I guess I was wrong about you being wild."

I turn in my seat, tilt my head, and narrow my eyes.

His smile fades.

"Are you insinuating that the only reason Tanner would date me is because I might have sex with him?"

Corbin opens his mouth and then closes it looking like a fish out of water. Then he stammers, "Well — Tanner — he's... you know."

"And he's dating me so that must mean, what exactly?"

"I've just heard stories."

My face hardens with anger, because I know what rumors he's talking about, which involve the aftermath of Chris and my rejection of him. "Are you really going there?"

He blushes. "Sorry, Matthews."

"You should be," I say and swivel in my chair to face the front of the classroom. My heart does laps. I flex my hands and then put them in my lap between my knees to stop them from trembling. Corbin's insinuation draws Chris's words back toward the front of my brain. *Everyone says, you know — prom night.* And then behind my back: *Matthews is a frigid bitch.* It's the first time anyone has brought it up to me.

Liam's look seems to ask if I'm okay.

I nod.

"This is it, seniors. Last time in this class with me. Let's do this," Mr. Groans says.

I take my final, but it's hard not to allow my mind to wander to Tanner each time my eyes stray to the roses. But then I imagine dark roses on my wrist. I wish I could say these bright pink roses are the first flowers I've ever received from a boy. Then, I decide that for all intents and purposes, they are. These flowers are the only ones that count.

After a long day of finals, a conscious decision to ignore Corbin's stupidity, followed by another walk through of graduation, I can't contain the butterflies fluttering inside me at the idea of spending the afternoon with Tanner. The minute Mr. Sanderson releases us into the wild of the social scene, I'm moving through the bodies of classmates to look for him. We find one another amidst the crowd. I smile, suddenly feeling self-conscious and hug my flowers to my chest.

"Ready?"

I nod.

He takes my hand in his, calming my insecurities, and we leave the field.

"I thought that would never end," he says as we walk out into the parking lot where his truck is parked.

"Is it just me or has Mr. Sanderson gotten more verbose."

He opens the passenger door for me. "I would have said loquacious."

I laugh.

When he gets into the truck, he adds, "and those florid directions. Damn. You'd think he was Tolkien's ghostwriter."

I laugh harder. "Who knew you were such a word nerd, Tanner? I love it."

"Love it, huh?" He glances at me with a cute smile and starts the truck. "Love it," he repeats again, as if testing the words, and drives from the parking lot. "You know what you're going to love: Kaleidoscope Concussion."

"What if I don't?" I ask. The fact that Tanner loves the book has already ensured favor in my eyes, but I don't tell him that.

"You will."

He finds a parking spot on the street, gets out of the truck and meets me on the sidewalk.

"I wish we could have gone into the city to Booktopia." He grabs my hand, and we walk toward Barkers.

"Oh my. I love that place. It's like heaven. Like when I die, that is where I'll go."

"Let's not think about you dying, Em. About dying in general."

The tone of his voice nearly stops me. The even sound of it, the lack of variation and rhythm. "Hey." I draw him closer to me. "Are you okay?"

He glances at the window of the shop we're outside of and when he looks at me again, he's back. "I'm great, because I'm here with you."

tanner

I open the door to Barkers for Emma and continue to mentally reset myself after her comment about dying. The moment she said it, I couldn't keep Rory from my thoughts. That day, at home, his bed sitting in the living room where it had been for a few days. I thought about the crying of my parents. The way they'd wrapped around one another, giving and needing support. There I was, standing outside their prism, tears streaming down my face, angry, scared, heart crushed into a thousand pieces. I'd run from the room, up into Rory's bedroom and climbed out the window where I'd lost myself. Sometimes I wonder if my spirit is still out in the roof waiting for me to find it.

Now, I follow Emma into the store and shake away the pall of the memory. I haven't allowed myself to think about it, and I don't want to now.

She glances over her shoulder at me. "Where to first?"

I offer her a smile and urge myself to focus on this. On Emma. "Let's ask someone."

She nods.

After checking in with a salesclerk, we follow her through the maze of the aisles. I center my attention on Emma, the way she looks in the cute red dress she's wearing. The hem brushes the back of her thighs. I'm thinking about her in her red bikini, of her sliding on her shorts. I'm thinking about her last night in my room, lying on my bed, dark hair like a halo around her head, my hands on her body and hers on mine. I'm imagining running my hand up her leg, under that dress. *Concentrate, Tanner.*

The clerk points out the book.

Emma thanks her, and the salesgirl leaves us in the bowels of the overpacked bookstore.

I probably stand too close to Emma in the narrow aisle. I can smell her, an enticing mild cotton candy scent. I want to press my lips against the back of her neck. Why did I think bringing her to a public place was a good idea? I just want to touch her.

Emma pulls a book from the shelf. "This?" she asks, shaking the book at me.

"Exactly that." I grab her wrist, the hand holding the book, and draw her toward me.

Emma smiles and acquiesces to my persuasion.

"I've been thinking about kissing you all day," I tell her. My heart moves in my chest like a tethered balloon in a breeze bouncing back and forth, looking for an escape into the sky. It's just Emma is my escape, and I'm sure she can feel it. With my other hand on her hip, I release her wrist, press my palm to her jaw and my mouth to her lips. I kiss her in a secluded aisle of a bookstore like I've combusted. Another first for me.

She wraps her arms around me, the edge of the book biting my right shoulder blade, but I'm thinking about Emma's mouth. I'm thinking about my hands which are now on her hips. I'm thinking about her tongue moving with mine.

Someone clears their throat.

Emma draws away, turns to face the shelf, blushing.

Her shyness makes me grin.

An older guy passes us. He looks at Emma. I notice his gaze drops to her ass, and it heats my insides with uncharacteristic protectiveness.

Then I think about the Bro Code and feel a waver in my stomach that maybe I haven't been much different. When I look back at Emma, feeling contrite and regretting my choices, she's smoothing her dress with one hand and looking at the book at the same time. I glance back at the man as he moves down the aisle way from us and realize I can be different; I don't have to be like him. I don't want to be that anymore. My ire at jerkoff disintegrates as I redirect my energy to what's important, Emma.

"Want to get out of here?" I ask.

She looks up. "If you're ready?"

"Was there another book you wanted to look for?" I ask and lean forward, pressing my lips against her bare shoulder.

She tilts her head to the side and pushes a sound through her nose. "No."

I take the book from her, grab her hand, and lead her back through the maze to the counter where I buy it.

"I could have gotten it," she says, as we leave the store.

The bell rings as it shuts behind us.

"I wanted you to read it, remember? My treat."

She lifts the small white package with Barker's Books stamped across the surface and smiles. "Thank you. I can't wait."

"Where to?" I ask. I want to take her somewhere private where I can kiss her.

"I'm kind of hungry," she says.

When considering it, I say, "me too," though that's the norm rather than the exception. I'm thinking that perhaps a taste of Emma would satisfy me, but she's talking about food.

"Marta's? I'll treat you to some French fries," she says.

"Your wish is my command," I tell her and open the passenger side door. When I close it, I stall and take a deep breath before moving around the rear of the truck. I've never taken someone on a date. It makes me smile that Emma is my first. Now, I can appreciate it.

I climb into the driver's seat and take us to Marta's. Once inside the diner, sitting in a booth across from one another, I love this idea of a date. Looking at her, no distractions. She's so beautiful. She tucks a curl around her ear as she looks at the menu. I find it difficult to draw a breath for a split second, and I wonder why she's here with me.

The waitress takes our order.

"Is Marta's your favorite place?" I ask Emma after the waitress leaves.

"It's been a tradition with Liam and Ginny on Fridays after school. Do you have traditions with your friends?"

I raise my eyebrows at her.

She blushes again. "Oh yeah. Right. Dumb."

"I like that you forgot."

She smiles and leans back when the waitress sets down our drinks. "It's probably weird. That I forgot."

"Forgot my reputation?" I'm not sure why this has me collapse into myself, kind of like remembering Rory. I look at the glass of cola and swirl the straw, watching the ice. I don't want the heaviness to infiltrate my time with Emma; it does, though. "Not sure how anyone can forget that."

"I don't see you that way."

I look up from the beverage and meet Emma's pretty eyes. She's watching me, pulling a straw from its wrapper. She doesn't remove it all the way, just to the tip, then brings the straw up to her lips and blows through it so the wrapper launches at me. I can't help but smile and reach across the table to catch her hand. I need to feel her, reassure myself she's real. "What way do you see me then?" I ask her.

"I just see you. Like right now. Holding my hand. Smiling. I see you that night I coerced you junior year. A gentleman."

"Coerced," I scoff.

She laughs. "I see you cliffside, helping me face my fears. And last night, helping me see a new perspective."

My smile fades. "You make me sound like a good guy."

Her eyebrows draw together, and she tilts her head. "Tanner?"

"I'm not, you know." I release her hand, suddenly realizing I shouldn't even be touching her. I cross my arms over my chest.

"Not what?"

"A good guy." The moroseness is back. I'm thinking about all the ways I don't deserve to be sitting with her. All the choices I've made that will mess all of this up. I consider thinking about ending it before it hurts, because I can already tell this is going to hurt. But when I look at Emma, I can't. I want her so bad. Not the sex part, though I'd be lying if I said I didn't want that. Fuck yeah, I want that. No. I want the goodness of Emma, her sweetness; the way she's looking at me and speaking about me like I'm worth something. I want that.

The waitress returns with a basket of fries and places them between us.

Emma lifts the ketchup but doesn't apply it to the basket until I nod. Then she slathers them with the red sauce. "I guess it all works out then," she says, returning the squeezable ketchup to the chrome rack.

"How's that?" I ask.

She grabs a fry but doesn't eat it. Instead she pushes it around in the ketchup. "I'm a relatively good girl."

"Yeah. I know. How does that work out?"

She's smiling and takes a bite of her French fry. "Like math. We balance the equation." Then she looks at me, her cosmos eyes sparkling.

I can't help but grin.

"So, I was wondering?" she asks. "Would you like to come to my house on Friday?"

"Really?"

"I mean I understand if you're going to be busy with your friends, but I thought I'd see if you wanted to come and watch a John Hughes movie with Ginny, Liam, Atticus and me? It's kind of our thing — usually Saturdays — but it's our last one, you know before Graduation. It would be Atticus's first time, too. I thought I'd see if you want to come too, and–"

"I'd love to," I say cutting off her nervous ramble. "I would." She has no idea how much the idea appeals to me. The alternative sucks. Being without her. Being with Griff who wants to do the same party routine. Nope. New choice. Emma all the way.

"You could bring your friends if you want."

And there is no way I would want Griff within fifty feet of her house and watching a John Hughes movie. "We'll see," I say. "I'm not sure if they have plans. But I'll check."

She smiles and eats another fry.

"So, math? Is that what you're planning on for college? To balance equations?" I ask and hate that I'm imagining her sitting in a different diner eating French fries with another guy.

Her smile falters a moment, but she resets, except that little line is between her eyes — the worry line. She shakes her head at the fries, more focused on the ketchup. "No. I don't think so. I'm not sure yet."

"You excited?"

Her eyes meet mine, and I feel her look low in my gut like a punch. It's filled with anxiety, longing, and something else. She shakes her head. "Not really."

"I bet you're going to do great–" I pause. "Where are you going?"

"California."

Like Josh.

"In California," I say it with a smile, but it feels like tiny pins puncturing my heart and deflating it. I pick up a French fry and hold it up. "Let's toast."

"Fry toast?" She picks up a potato.

"Yes. To Emma Matthews and her complete domination of college in California." I tap my fry to hers.

Her French fry breaks, one half plopping back into the basket. "That looks like a bad sign."

"No. No," I tell her. "That just means you're about to break things." I smile.

"Is this your version of palm reading or fortune telling?"

"Exactly."

She smiles, but it fades. "I'm scared," she admits. "I thought I wanted to get as far from here as I could."

I nod, understanding that more than she knows.

"But now, the closer it gets, the more real it gets. It makes me realize how alone I will be."

I'm sitting across the table from Emma, aware that she won't be alone. When she goes to college, she's going to find a new group. She's going to have guys wanting to hit her up, to date her, to have sex with her, maybe a lucky guy to marry her. She's going to be the amazing Emma like she's always been. But now, as time slips around us, as if we were standing still in a stream, I realize, I won't get to witness it anymore. I think about all the time I've wasted. "I don't think you'll be alone for long, Em."

"Easy for you to say."

"Why?"

"Because you're so good with people. People like you. You're fun and adventurous. I'm a social dud."

"Naw, Em. You're just wise. If I'd been smart — like you — I'd be getting out of here too."

"You can."

"Where am I going to go?" I ask her.

"Anywhere. You can do anything you want."

"Except go to college."

The waitress asks if we want anything else and then drops the bill. Emma reaches for it, but I'm quicker.

"I insist," I say, when she argues that she invited me. "It's my first date."

A smile spreads across her face. "Your first date? With me?"

"Don't let it go to your head."

She giggles. "You can, you know."

"I know. I can pay this bill."

She shakes her head. "You can go to college."

"I didn't make the grade, Emma."

"That's why there's community college."

Josh told me the same thing. "I'm not sure school's my thing." And then I hear the same story I've always told myself and realize everything lately has been offering me the chance to tell a new one.

She nods. "I understand."

I drop in the cash, help her from the booth, and hold her hand as we walk out into the parking lot toward my truck. "You do?"

"Of course."

"I don't think I can do it."

She smiles and watches me open the door, but she doesn't climb into the truck right away. Instead she turns and looks at me. She reaches up and does something to my hair, smoothing a curl away from my temple or something. Who knows; it just causes pleasant flutters inside me. "There's this really smart guy who once told me, 'Matthews — you can do anything. It isn't a can't but a won't.'" She gives me a quick peck on my mouth, and then climbs into the truck.

I close the door, rolling around the familiarity of her words. It isn't until I'm walking to the driver's side that I realize she's used my words against me. It makes me smile.

senior year
(3 days to graduation)

"I'd been asleep too long. The waking up felt like pins and needles in a waking limb. It was painful and frightening, filled with color."

-unnamed protagonist, *Kaleidoscope Concussion* by Saul Annick

emma

"**Emma!**" Shelby whines at me. "Let me have the remote."

I hold it away from her.

She pushes against me, trying to get it. "I don't want to watch this anymore!"

"I like home improvement shows," I tell her. "They're predictable and mindless."

"They're boring."

"I'm the one who's graduating."

"So? What's that have to do with anything?"

I hand her the remote. "You'll be really sad when I'm gone in a few weeks. You'll miss me."

Shelby flops next to me, so close she's nearly in my lap. I don't mind. Being with her is keeping the anxiety fairies from sending me over the edge. After rehearsal, I had to stay after the field emptied to practice my salutatorian speech. I'd watched Tanner leave the football field with his friends, my heart wishing I was with him. Ginny, Liam and Atticus went to Marta's. I met them there after practice but hadn't stopped wanting to be with Tanner, who made me feel like the best version of myself. Then I'd come home, sat with my family for dinner, and thought more about

Tanner, because it was more pleasant than thinking about the impending unknown that stretched out in front of me.

"Emma?" Shelby nudges me with her elbow.

"Ouch. What?"

"I asked you a question like three times. Where are you?"

"Just thinking."

She made a disgusted noise. "You're always thinking. You should stop sometimes."

I know she's right in her thirteen-year-old wisdom, but as her older sister, I can't tell her that. "Maybe you should think a little bit more." I pinch her cheek. "What was your question?"

She pulls away. "You're a butt."

"Yeah. Probably."

"Are you scared? About college?"

My little sister is asking me this question; I'd like to protect her and make her think I've got it together, but I go for honesty. "Yeah, but it's not a reason to not go, right?"

She hums her response. "Are you scared about other stuff?" Her eyes remain on the cartoonish commercial on the TV screen.

"Sure. Why?"

She shrugs.

"Everything okay?"

Shelby looks at me. "You promise not to say anything to Mom and Dad?"

"That depends. Are you safe?"

She rolls her eyes. "It isn't a secret like that. Sheesh."

"Then yes."

She turns so she's facing me, and I mirror her. "So Cassie told me that Mindy texted her that Brian Williams told Derek — you know who that is right?"

I don't, but I nod anyway because I'm not sure it matters. Her middle school drama chain is familiar.

"Well, Brian told Derek who told Mindy who told Cassie who told me that he likes me. And I don't know what to do."

"Maybe you should wait for Brian to say something to you."

She huffs. "It doesn't work like that."

"But maybe it should."

She turns back to facing the TV.

"But you could always ask him yourself," I tell her.

She turns her head to study me.

"You know, if you want to know for sure."

"Like you jumped the cliff." She says this with pride, and it surprises me. She's equated it with facing fears. Who knew? "I told all of my friends."

"You did?"

"Yeah. That's pretty badass, sis." Shelby turns the TV to a teeny bopper show with cute guys and pretty girls. The canned laughter drives me nuts, but I sit there anyway, because I'd rather be with her than alone.

"You know what's badass? Sisters who watch *Sixteen Candles* with me," I say.

She groans. "Those movies are stupid, sexist, and racist."

"And this isn't stupid?"

"At least it isn't racist or sexist."

"That's why we watch them. We analyze them."

"To make fun of them?"

"Sort of. There's good stuff too."

We sit on the couch side-by-side watching Shelby's stupid show.

"I'm going to miss you, Shelby," I tell her.

She glances at me and then lays her head on my shoulder. "Me too."

That's how Dad finds us a few minutes later when he walks in from the garage. "Hey! There are my girls. Family show?"

"Sure." Shelby and I tell him without looking at him.

"Shelby. Go get your mother. See if she wants to join us."

She whines. "Why me?"

"Because you're the youngest. Your legs are freshest." I can't see him, but I know he's teasing her.

She gets up, stomps over to him where I know she receives a kiss on her head and a hug, and then disappears from the room to find Mom.

"Glad finals are over?" Dad asks from the kitchen.

I sit up and turn around on the couch, leaning against the back. "Yeah. Can I ask you something?"

"Shoot." He draws a pan from a cupboard and sets it on the stove.

"Were you scared of going away to college?"

The burner clicks and then whooshes as it ignites.

"Sure, but I didn't go very far away like you'll be. I was driving distance." When I don't say anything he asks, "Are you having second thoughts about California?"

"No. Not second thoughts, but I'm feeling worried about it."

He adds some olive oil to the pan and pours in corn kernels. "I think that's normal for everyone. There's always State U in the city. You could come home every weekend." He smiles at me as he agitates the pan.

This had been a part of our discussion when I'd applied to all of my schools. He and Mom had made me apply to State as my backup plan. The thought induces further tightening of my chest at the idea of being so close, of not finding my way outside of the confines of my family. I turn around and flop back onto the couch. "No thanks. I'm not that worried." But that wasn't true. I was terrified, and now that something was blooming between Tanner and me, new feelings were growing right along with the terror.

Later, after an evening on the couch with my family watching the 1985 version of *Goonies*, we peel away to our own spaces. I'm in my room in bed and trying to sleep. That's when I feel the attack begin, because my brain won't stop spinning. It's thinking about going away, about my speech and graduation, about Tanner, about leaving. The thoughts swirl around and around and around. It's just a pinpoint in my lungs at first, a fear that maybe I'm going to mess up my speech, then mess up everything. Then the feeling expands, a growing whirlpool drawing me into the vortex: what if I get sick? What if I trip? What if I say the wrong thing? What if I embarrass my parents? What if I don't deserve it? What if they made a mistake? I'm struggling with the darkness as it presses in around me. My throat feels like it closes up, and my lungs tighten. I can't do it. I fight for a breath and reach for my phone.

I text Liam. No answer.

I text Ginny. No answer.

I text Tanner: *I'm having a panic attack. I can't breathe.*

The three dots are immediate which slightly eases the tension in my chest.

Tanner — Emma! Take a breath.

Trying. I feel like I'm drowning. — Me

Tanner — Why? Talk? I'll call.

My breaths are shallow and quick. I'm sitting up now.

Can't talk. Yet. I'm scared. For Saturday. — Me

Tanner — Count to 5, Em. Slow. I'll do it with you.
1

1 — Me

Tanner — 2
Remember that time in 7th grade when Cara White kissed David Benning in the caf, and Mrs. Sosa yelled at them? David farted super loud.

My lungs soften, moving air a bit easier. I didn't remember that, but it makes me smile despite the panic.

2 No
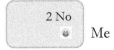 — Me

Tanner

3
I loved giving you roses yesterday, and going to the bookstore, and then sharing fry toasts and seeing you today.

My muscles are still tight, but my breathing slows.

3
I loved all of those things, too. Me

Tanner: Did you start Kaleidoscope Concussion?

Not yet Me

Tanner It's a necessity.

Tomorrow Me

Tanner Procrastinator

I smile and take a deep breath.

Tanner

4
Once upon a time there was this stupid guy who liked a girl who was way 2 good 4 him.

4
Once upon a time there was this really scared girl who liked this really amazing guy who made her feel brave ... Me

Tanner | Em, I wish I was there with you.

The fears recede. They're still there, just less pervasive.

5 | Me

Tanner | Oh yeah, 5.

I wish I was with you, too. | Me

Tanner | You're going to do great on Saturday.

I call him.

He picks up on the first ring. "Are you okay?"

"Better," I tell him. "Thank you."

"I want to be there, Em."

His words are what I need to hear, but they also stop my heart. I'd jumped into this with him a week ago, understanding there would be an end. Now, this roller coaster cart is headed into a turn I wasn't expecting, and I don't want to get off of it. I'm suddenly tearing and sniffing to try and put the tears back.

"Em?" he asks. "Are you crying?"

"No. No. Allergies," I lie.

He's silent for a moment. "I don't believe you. I'm going to call on Facetime."

"Would you tell me a story?" I ask him, changing the subject.

"I think you're the storyteller."

"No. No. I'm the mathematician. You're the storyteller."

"Okay," he says, and I hear his smile. "I'm lying in my bed without any clothes on."

I laugh. "Not that kind of story."

"What, Em? That's the only kind of story that matters." He's definitely smiling.

"A memory story," I say.

He's quiet on the other end of the line for a moment, and then sighs. "I got one. About that night junior year."

"Okay." It makes me smile and blush and wish I were laying with him talking about it. Feeling the plane of his back under my hands, his weight on me, and our legs entwined.

"It's about this idiot boy named... we'll call him TJ, and the night he met this amazing girl named... Ella."

"I like this story."

"Now, Emma, you're going to have to pipe down if you want to hear it."

"Yes, sir."

I eventually drift to sleep to the sound of Tanner telling me our story — the night of our first kiss — and the way the stars exploded behind TJ's eyes when he kissed Ella.

senior year
(2 days to graduation)

"'What does she give you that I can't?' Erickson asked. His jealousy for my attention was a palpable thing, alive and seething, though it existed in the shape of ego; he relished my fists and demanded my devotion to our conflict.

'Besides the obvious?'"

-unnamed protagonist, *Kaleidoscope Concussion* by Saul Annick

tanner

"So," Griff leans over three classmates and places his face in between me and Kendra Jacobs to talk to me. Mr. Sanderson drones on about how important it is to wear something presentable under our graduation gown. "We should go get trashed after this."

Kendra, who's leaning away from him, rolls her eyes and snaps her gum.

"What Kendra," Griff says. "You weren't complaining that time junior year." He winks at her. "Want a repeat?"

"As if, Griff. You're such a douche." She crosses her arms and turns away from him.

"Hard pass, bro," I tell him.

His eyebrows draw together with irritation. "We have a whole day, Tanner! A whole freaking 24 hours before our next pointless rehearsal, and we can show up wasted to that." I can actually see his wheels spinning. He's turning over arguments in his head to change my mind. He returns to his seat and looks down at his phone.

My phone vibrates.

Griff | Dude. Don't b a fucking pussy.

> **Griff** Hang w/ us. Shit. It's almost graduation. U promised.

I frown at the screen. He's right. I kind of did. The three dots pop up on my screen.

> **Griff** U working?

I could lie; it would be easiest. The truth, though, is that I asked Emma to hang out. I asked her to come to my house to swim in my pool because goddam I want to see her in that fucking bikini. I consider lying to him, but then I think of what Atticus said a couple of weeks ago about not being true to yourself is a front. I type: *No. Hanging out with someone today.*

> **Griff** Who!?! Party @ your place?

> No can do. It's a private party. **Me**

> **Griff** 🔥 Wait. This isn't Matthews, right?

I look over my shoulder at him and then send him the emoji of the middle finger. He's given me a rash of shit for the roses stunt. Dick.

Griff narrows his eyes at his phone, his thumbs moving over the screen with speed:

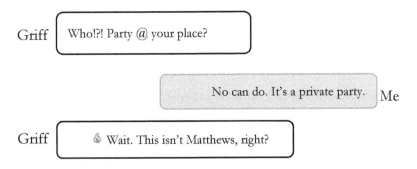

WTF Tanner!?! U R fuckin pussy whipped & she hasn't even given you any.

This pisses me off — not for me but for Emma — so I flip it on him and type: *Bro Code.*

I know it's low and kind of vile. I might not be having sex with Emma, even if I really want to. And probably not today, unless of course she's been enchanted by a sex spell, of which I'd be a happy recipient. But by saying it, I'm implying that's the plan. It makes me feel guilty, because I really like Emma. I'm enjoying talking to her, and being with her isn't only about sex. Griff doesn't need to know that. If he did, he'd give me shit about it. Besides, it isn't any of his business. He's thrown so much shady shit at me lately; I just want him off my back.

He sends a picture of himself with a lecherous grin on his face, and then:

> I see you, T

Just like that, my masculinity isn't in question anymore. It makes me feel kind of dirty, but I want him to shut the fuck up. It may have worked today, but I don't know what I'm going to do about tomorrow and the movie. Getting out from under Griff two days in a row before graduation will be a miracle.

After rehearsal, I wait for Emma just outside the football stadium. I'm leaning against my truck scrolling through IG.

"Tanner!" she calls and does this cute little hop-skip through the gate. She's dressed in short shorts that show off her legs and a bouncy top that reveals glimpses of her bare stomach depending on how she moves.

I can't help but smile, clicking off my phone and stashing it in my pocket. My heart feels all kinds of fluffy, like cotton candy before it sticks to my tongue. "How'd it go, Em?" I ask.

She slows, takes the last couple of steps to me as if she's unsure. "Good. But I had to keep saying it. I kept tripping over this one part because I was thinking about you out here waiting, and I just couldn't wait to see you. I lost my concentration." The bag on her shoulder slips, and she adjusts it in front of her, both of her hands holding the straps. The line appears between her eyes. "What if that happens on Saturday?"

"It won't." I can't wait anymore, impatient to touch her. My lungs are in my throat along with my pounding heart. "I don't mind waiting for you." I reach for the bag, and then I reach for her. I kiss her because I'm not sure I can keep breathing if I don't.

She kisses me back. Her hand slides around the back of my neck, her fingers playing with my hair. I think her fingertips must be molten, because the heat of her touch singes my skin, melting into my bloodstream. I draw back not because I want to, but because I need to or this semi I'm starting to rock will be full-fledged Woodrow Wilson. Besides, I'd like to keep what's happening between us rather than share it with anyone hanging out in the parking lot. "You ready? Will Ginny and Liam be joining us?"

She dips her head a little, and then she bites her lip — which for the record drives me to distraction. "I didn't tell them."

"What?" I'm elated. Perhaps there are sex fairies casting spells.

"I just wanted to spend time with you."

"Perfect."

She opens the driver's side door and climbs in. I get a gorgeous eyeful of her ass and remind myself to calm the fuck down. I follow her in and force myself to drive the speed limit. Okay, five over because there's a cushion, right? I push it to ten.

e m m a

When I woke up to Tanner's text this morning:

> Want to hang out at my house today
> after grad rehearsal? I've got a pool. 😎

I jumped from my bed and did a little celebration dance. He'd been so sweet the night before, distracting me from my panic attack and telling me stories. My heart liquified, turning into mushy goop sticking to all of my insides. And then, this morning, thinking about spending the whole day with Tanner after graduation practice, my mind engaged in all the ways I could imagine his hands, his mouth, and that goopy mess steamed out of my limbs. It will be impossible to hide how I'm feeling about him since I'm wearing it on the outside of my body.

I texted him back: *That sounds like fun. I'd love to.* He'd extended the invitation to Ginny and Liam if I wanted. Nope. No, thank you. An afternoon of keeping Tanner all to myself? Yes, please.

Now, sitting next to Tanner as he drives us to his house, I know I have made the right decision. My nerves flutter and skim through my body just thinking about his kiss. He turns up the radio and then offers me a sideways smile. I want to reach out and touch him (I don't and then chastise myself about overthinking it). While I've spent my life wrapped up, attempting to be a perfect version of who I thought I was supposed to be, sitting here next to Tanner feels pretty perfect. I wonder if I'm supposed to feel bad about that. So, in a tiny rebellion, I reach over and curl my hand around the nape of his neck.

Tanner's smile widens. He reaches over and puts his hand on my thigh.

Yeah. Melting.

After he parks his car in the garage, I follow him into his house. We walk into the kitchen.

"You hungry?" he asks.

"Nope." Not for food. Plus, bikini.

He opens the gigantic refrigerator anyway, takes out two water bottles, then retraces his steps back to me, leans down when he reaches me and kisses the tip of my nose. "Right this way."

I follow him down a hallway into a wide room with a place to change, towels, an enclosed bathroom and a sauna that then leads outside to a gorgeous backyard. The pool is pristine, a hot tub inset in one corner, a water feature offering ambient sound.

"This is like a vacation spot, Tanner," I tell him, following him toward a cabana.

He sets my bag on one of the aqua cushions of the u-shaped couch. "This okay?"

"More than okay." I glance around. "It's perfect." But I'm thinking *you're perfect*. I slip out of my Havaianas and sink onto the couch. "I could get used to this."

He laughs and flops down next to me. His back and shoulder press against my shoulder, and a strong leg is propped up on the couch in the other direction.

My gaze slides over the muscle of his leg, over his knee, to the dark hair dusting his shin, to his proportional foot. I swallow, distracted by his nearness. Okay. I'm always distracted by him no matter where he is, but right now, with him so close, I just want to jump on him.

While I'm assertive about things within the realm of my control, the idea of opening up my hands and offering someone my heart has me hyperventilating. Besides, all of those lessons about submissive wives, and what's ladylike and how men want virginal demureness still taunts me. I know what Tanner said, but I'm still trying to figure out how to apply it to my behavior. Tanner invited me to speak up and tell him what I wanted. It's so confusing, this business of being a woman. I just want to freaking kiss Tanner.

"I'm glad you said, 'yes.'" He leans his head against my shoulder, lying back just a bit more so he can tip his head to look up at me.

"Me too." I think he wants to kiss me, because his eyes dance to my lips, but he sits up, and moves away.

"Want to swim?"

"Yes." I stand up and unbutton my shorts then shimmy them down my legs. When I look up, Tanner fixates on my shorts as I step out of them. He isn't smiling. His eyebrows have shifted. It's slight, but I noticed them just a bit higher over his eyes. When he lifts his eyes to mine, I feel his dark gaze in my chest. Desire. Emboldened with the hem of my crop t-shirt in my hands, I lift it over my head and drop it on top of my bag.

Tanner seems to reanimate when he blinks. Then he offers me one of his bright and practiced flirty smiles. "I wondered if you'd wear the red one — from the Quarry. I like that color too." He nods at my swimsuit.

I look down at the light pink bikini I'm wearing, carefully selected because it's my favorite, and the one I feel the sexiest in. Obviously, a power move. "I love swimsuits. I have like one for every day of the week."

"I guess I'll have to invite you over every day then, so I can see them all." He stands and draws his burgundy t-shirt over his head.

I look away, because I'd like to stare, and busy myself in my bag. "Guess what I brought?"

"What?"

When I look up, he tosses his shirt onto the chair. I notice the way his black swim trunks ride his hips. He has one of those sexy v's with a slight dusting of dark hair under his navel. I raise my eyes to the musculature of his shoulders and arms, the smooth slope of his chest, and the strength that moves through his body differently than mine.

"I like your tattoo," I say, happy that I can look at it closer now.

He lifts his right arm, which flexes gorgeously, then twists a touch. He runs a hand over what looks to be a compass rose on his ribs. I think I might not be able to breathe. Somehow, I draw in my next breath and focus on the tattoo.

"May I?"

"Sure. I got it when I was sixteen."

I move closer and see it is a compass rose, but it's been tipped over as if dialed to the left. North is pointing at Tanner's heart. In the center is an intricate R.

I reach out to touch it but then check the impulse. "It's pretty." Then I reach and touch it anyway, tracing the R with the fingertip of my index finger.

His muscles twitch under my touch; he drops his arms and takes my hand in his, threading our fingers together. "You can't call a guy's tattoo 'pretty.' They have to be like 'bad ass' or 'sick.'"

I laugh, immersed in the invitation of his eyes and his smile.

"What did you bring?"

"Bring?" I've forgotten what I'd said, so distracted by his body, his tattoo, my hand in his. "Oh!" I shake my head and twist away from him to look in my bag. "Kaleidoscope Concussion." I hold up the book. "I thought I'd read. Told you I'd start."

Tanner shakes his head and takes the book from me. "As much as I want you to read that book, it's antithetical to the book. Erickson Dorn — a character from the story — wouldn't want you to waste a beautiful, sunny afternoon poolside with this guy with your nose in a book."

I blush.

"Especially not when you look this good." He licks his lips.

My heart goes into free fall like I've just done a loop-de-loop on a roller coaster. "Is that so?"

"Yes. Read the book."

"You won't let me."

Tanner reaches out and hooks his index finger under the string of my bikini at my collar bone. The touch of his fingertips lights a blaze that moves from the spot across my body like wildfire. Then he pulls me toward him. "I have other plans for you, Em."

Now my heart has decided it's going to stop altogether while the rest of me combusts. "Oh. You do, do you?" I smile.

Tanner leans forward, slowly, and presses his mouth to mine. I lose my sense of direction. My internal compass rose tilts like his tattoo toward my heart. I reach up and put my arms around his neck. He smiles against my mouth, and when I open my eyes to see why, his eyes are curled up with his smile; I realize I've stepped into Tanner's mischief. The next thing I know, he's picked me up, races across the pool deck, and jumps into the water.

I surface sputtering, hair hanging in my face. "Tanner James!" I clear the hair out of my face and look for him.

He's laughing and skims over the water on his back away from me.

"That was dirty."

"I never claimed to play a clean game."

I can't help but smile, annoyed with myself because I do.

He ventures closer, close enough for me to pounce on him and dunk his head. I let go and swim away laughing.

Tanner comes up and shakes his head, the water flying and spraying me with droplets. Then, quicker than I can get away, he grabs me, his strong arms around my middle, pulling me closer. "So that's how you want it?" he asks, that mischievous look on his face.

I somehow slip from his grasp, screeching, but Tanner grabs my hips and drags me back against him (which is fine by me), my back against his chest. He wraps his arms around me again and holds me tightly. His lips move against the skin on my shoulder when he says, "What am I going to do with you, Em?"

"Well, you're stuck now." I smile even if he can't see me. I'm enjoying this game.

"How do you figure? Looks like I'm the one who's got you trapped." His arms tighten around my ribs.

My heart bounces wildly. "Except, the moment you loosen your hold, I will slip through your grasp." I wiggle against his body but love that he's got me.

He draws me even closer, his mouth near my ear. "Hmm. That sounds like a problem. The mermaid that got away."

"Exactly."

"But what if I'm able to talk her into staying?" His mouth brushes my ear, he flicks my earlobe with his mouth, and my stomach clenches while my heart stops.

"I'm not sure it's possible. Mermaids speak underwater languages."

Laughter rumbles in his chest against my back. "Well. That would be a problem, but I have other languages that I speak pretty well."

"Oh. Really?"

"Mmhmm." He presses his lips against my shoulder and kisses a trail up my neck.

My mouth opens at first with surprise but then because I need to gasp for air. I'm so easy, I turn to water in his hands as the nerves in my body relax. "That may work," I breathe.

"I'm pretty adept." His mouth and tongue move over my skin, and his hold relaxes.

Oh. Yes you are, I think and turn to face him.

"See." He offers me a triumphant smile.

"She hasn't decided yet," I tell him and search his face. "She might still escape." As I say it, I know that is a lie. I don't want to escape. I want to be right there, in his arms with his mouth exploring every part of me. I want to press my mouth and tongue against him. I want. I want. I want. And maybe somewhere in there I'm not supposed to. Maybe it makes me sinful somehow, but right at that moment, I don't feel like a sinner. I

217

feel perfectly and wonderfully made. Perfect to share this moment with someone who's tattooing my heart with a new kind of compass.

Somehow, I grasp a hold of the bravery to do what I want. I press my hands against his chest, run them over his skin, watching his muscles twitch underneath my touch and wrap my arms around his neck. I look up into his eyes and say, "After she gets what she wants." Then I press my mouth against his chest.

tanner

Emma's mouth is on me, and for some reason I'm frozen, her words rolling through my brain: *after she gets what she wants.*

What does she want?

What does she want?

What does she want?

Her touch has me overheating. It's all I can do to keep my hands on her hips and let her have her way. This is new and different. My heart surges like a flash flood. My lungs are tight and fight to expand to draw in enough air.

I'm usually the one in control. My sexual timeline has always had me in control of pleasure. The expectation of what Tanner can do. I'm not an idiot. Women talk: *Tanner's good in bed.* How does one become an f-boy? It's the rep. Take a girl where she wants to go and do it well, they'll talk. And all of them stepped into those encounters with expectations of what I could give them, not the other way around, with the exception of Pam, who was my teacher.

Right now, Emma setting the pace and touching me because she's in control is a fucking turn on. She's touching me not because of what I can do for her, but because of what she wants. Her tongue slides over my skin, up my neck to my jaw. Her eyes are closed; her curly hair is wet and clings to her cheeks. Her water-slick body pressed against mine in her stringy pink bikini that took my breath away.

I'm hard as a rock.

She uses her mouth and her tongue to speak to me.

My breath catches, waiting, anticipating what's next.

When her mouth finally connects with mine, I'm ready for it. Kissing her with the pent-up energy that's built up inside of me. Okay, perhaps this isn't letting her completely set the pace, but my blood races, circulating with Emma. I run my hands from her hips over the curve of her ass, all skin-to-skin because that awesome bikini is tiny, and lift her. The water sloshes around us as she wraps her legs around me. I'm sure she can feel how much I want her.

She moans in my mouth, wraps her arms around my shoulders, pulls me closer with her legs and sinks down against my rigidity, knowing instinctively how to drive me wild.

My chest expands with relief with her in my arms. I've won something. Like, I'm standing at the county fair, threw the ball and knocked over the stack of bowling pins. The carnie is handing me the biggest prize and I'm holding it. "Em," I say. Yeah. Emma. Okay, bad analogy. I don't think she's a stuffed animal. *Ugh. Stop thinking, Tanner.*

She hums into my mouth.

I draw away so I can look at her. She doesn't move away, her warmth pressed against my belly. "Emma?"

Her eyes are hooded. She licks her lips. Woodrow jumps in response.

She is a prize.

One I want to treasure.

I kiss her like my life depends upon it, and maybe it kind of does.

Her hands do that amazing thing at the back of my neck that lights my fire. I move my hands to her waist and slide my hand up over her ribs, but I stop, recalling her fear only a few nights ago.

"Please, Tanner," she says into my mouth.

"Please what, Emma?" I draw my mouth away from hers and slide it down her neck.

"Please." She draws a quick breath. "Touch me."

She doesn't have to ask again. My hands move from her ribs to cover her gorgeous boobs threatening to spill out of her bikini top. I remember junior year, remember mapping these curves once before and how the memory was seared into my mind. I'm adding to it; adding to fantasies of her that I won't be able to deny. She's asked for it. *Please touch me.* The deep want I have for her inserted into my veins like a drug.

The buoyancy of the water wraps around us almost as if we've wandered into a world of our own. It defies physics, and we float around one another. Emma releases her legs and floats away. I press my hands at the small of her back drawing her back to me. "I want you, Emma," I tell her.

The line appears between her eyes. "I'm—" she pauses, her breath coming in gasps as I reach down and run a hand up the inside of her thigh. I can tell she's overthinking. I kiss her again, my fingers finding their mark between her legs. "Is this okay?" Her eyes open and a little 'oh' escapes from her into me.

"Yes," she breathes.

The line disappears as I use my fingers and mouth to speak to her body. "Let go, Emma," I say against the skin of her neck. "I got you. I promise." And she lets me. Trusts me. Relaxes against me, into it and I help her find release, kissing her as she finds the magic. Her sounds drive me mad; I kiss her when she gets there.

After, when she needs to find her breath, she moves her mouth from mine to my shoulder. I feel her puffs of air and gentle kisses on my skin. Then she shudders and laughs, burying her face against the space between my shoulder and neck.

"Was it okay? Are you okay?" I ask her, wanting more than anything to know she is happy.

She draws back and looks at me. Her face is bright with a blush and glows with new awareness; she presses her hands to her cheeks. "Tanner.

It was... I'm... goodness." Her eyes are wide with surprise.

She makes me smile.

"Maybe I should have done that a lot sooner."

I narrow my eyes at her, suddenly possessive. The idea of someone else causes my insides to dry up with angst.

She giggles. "Perhaps I was wrong to hit Chris after prom for trying."

This knowledge feels like a forest fire in my belly. I feel my brows draw together. "What? Chris who?" My mind begins turning. Prom? It would be easy to figure out.

She clears her throat. "It's nothing." She leans back again, smiles at me, but I feel like maybe it's way more than nothing. She reaches up and presses her thumbs against my eyebrows maneuvering them from the scowl on my face to force a smile. "It's okay, Tanner."

"If someone touches you without your permission, that isn't okay, Emma." I recall her question the other night. If I was mad she wanted to stop.

Her smile falters, and she presses her face between my neck and shoulder again.

"Chris who?" I ask, suddenly pissed and protective.

"Forget it."

This makes me annoyed. "Chris Johnson. Chris Freeson. Chris—" I begin listing all of the guys named Chris I know.

"Stop. It doesn't matter."

"It does," I tell her and move so I can see her eyes, holding her face in my hands. She's upset and struggles to meet my gaze, but I can tell this isn't about me. It's more important than she's admitting. "It matters because you should never have been forced into slapping someone. Whoever this asshole is, he deserves a bit more of a lesson for crossing a line."

Her eyes finally meet mine. They are full of unshed tears. "I appreciate you wanting to be a knight in shining armor." She smiles through the tears. One slips down her cheek. I follow its trail to her chin and wipe it with my thumb. "I took care of it, and I don't want to relive it." She nods her head, putting an end to it. She wipes her cheek, and then she offers me a coy smile. "And if it had been you in the back of the limo with me, instead of the jerk, I'm not so sure there would have been any slapping." She traces my trap down over my shoulder with a fingertip, and then looks up at me with more awareness in her eyes.

"Did you tell him to stop?" I can't let it go. I can't. I'm so upset that someone would hurt her.

"Tanner." She grasps my face between her hands. "It's done." Her lips touch mine. It's a chaste kiss, just lip to lip. She draws back to look at me. "Thank you." Then she leans forward and kisses me again, each of my eyes, each side of my face, the tip of my nose. Each kiss lingers, gentle and soft and loosens the stopped-up anger that has me tense. "I just want us. Now. Nothing else." Her lips meet mine again, but this time her tongue urges my participation.

I sigh, reset, and need her to breathe. My hands on the small of her back, I press her closer and kiss her with abandon until I'm tense in other ways and in other places. "Emma, I need to slow down." I loosen my hold, not wanting to overstep like some asshole named Chris did. I kiss her nose.

She doesn't move away, shifts and can feel the evidence of how much I want her. With wide eyes, she smiles. "I see." She blushes but also giggles.

Her response makes me feel better, and I can't help but smile as the earlier tension floats away. I wiggle my hips and then I bob my eyebrows. "You ready for that, Emma?" I've never been like this with someone, never playful, but being with Emma is fun and feels perfect. Understanding hits me like an open hand to the chest; I've never cared before. Ever. What I've done now with Emma in my arms was from an emotional place. Warmth floods my chest and the feeling that I'm the champion of all champions because I've won a gift grabs hold. I care. I care about Emma. It's terrifying.

She's still blushing, and I can tell she isn't ready, so I tickle her instead.

She squeals.

I lift her, toss her into the pool away from me, and then give her chase through the pool. She laughs, and I love the sound of it. Throaty, musical, sweet. As we play around in the water, I realize not having sex with Emma actually feels okay. Griff would say something asshole-ish about it, but I hear Josh's words about growing up.

Emma climbs from the pool, and I give chase — thankfully, Woodrow is no longer fully at attention — and follow her into the cabana where she grabs her bag and holds it up between us. Her chest heaves with exertion, and I don't think she realizes how beautiful she looks. Her wet hair, her slick skin, the fullness of her boobs straining against the bikini top, the gentle slope of her belly, her shapely legs. She's fucking hot.

She turns away, laughing.

I catch her around the waist and pull her down onto the couch in the cabana. Then because it's a complete necessity, I kiss her senseless again, reducing myself into an equally senseless mess.

e m m a

I'm still fluttery about what happened in the pool and then on the couch in the cabana, still feeling the sparkles all the way to my toes. Being out of control isn't in my comfort zone — ever — but who knew that letting go would feel so good? And perfect. Tanner's voice was gentle and soothing: *Let go... I've got you... I promise.* Just like jumping at the Quarry. I'm not sure I could have let go with someone other than Tanner (case in point, Chris Keller at prom). Just like the cliff. For a moment, as I slid down from the high, I thought meeting Tanner's eyes might be embarrassing, but it wasn't. Instead, I felt like I'd come home, as ridiculous as that sounds. It was safe.

Even more so now because he knows — kind of — what happened after prom. There'd been a moment when the shame hit me, but it wasn't because of Tanner. Being in Tanner's arms, someone I want to be with whose opinion matters, that perfectionism leaked in and reinforced it. How could he care about me when I've got that awful experience shaping me? But it felt nice to know he wanted to protect me. That shouldn't have been surprising since that's all Tanner has ever done in every single one of our interactions. His character is so much more than people say about him.

Now, Tanner is draped across me, his body wedged in between my legs, his arms around me, his head resting on my belly. I'm leaning against the arm of the cabana couch and though it's scratchy, I could care less. The weight of Tanner on me is a beautiful and welcome anchor. I'm playing with his hair at the nape of his neck with one hand and holding his favorite book with the other.

"Wait," I say. "What's the narrator's name?" He said it was okay to read IF I would read aloud to him. So far, we've made it through one chapter because Tanner keeps distracting me with his mouth and his hands. A welcome distraction. *Kaleidoscope Concussion* will probably be my favorite read by the time we finish it just because I'll have these memories of Tanner every time I read it. I've just started the second chapter.

"He doesn't have one."

"That doesn't make sense." I flip the pages looking for it.

He raises his head. "Yes, it does, Em. It totally does."

"How's that?"

He sighs and moves slightly, wedging himself between me and the back of the couch so he can see me better. "Identity."

"Lack of it."

"Yeah. Or, that it could be any of us, right?"

I nod. "Okay. But, truthfully, this is kind of sad. I mean, he's clinging to Jimmy Gigantic at a funeral where he doesn't belong, crying because it's the only way he can find peace. I don't feel like I can really connect to the nameless narrator clinging to Mooby Jimbo."

"I can totally identify with the joy of clinging to Booby Emma." He presses his lips against the top of my breast straining against the pink fabric. "It will help me sleep at night." He keeps his mouth against my skin but raises his eyes to me and then raises an eyebrow.

I laugh.

Tanner sits up all the way. I miss his weight (and his lips). He dips his chin and tilts his head. "You have to promise me, Em." He looks adorable, his dark hair falling like curling ribbons over his forehead, his eyes wide and pleading with his dark brows arched over them. He has these gorgeous molten gold flecks in his eyes that sparkle.

"What do I have to promise you?" The truth is with that look, I'd promise him anything. Even as I think that, I'm beginning to read my feelings like ticker tape across a 24-hour news channel: *This just in — Emma Matthews is falling for Tanner James. Her red wire is connecting itself to the mechanism and will need a bomb detonation team immediately to prevent self-destruction.* I take a deep breath, my heart suddenly weighted with new awareness, and the fear that goes with it.

"Read it without judging it. Please. Just read it."

I smile at him, willing myself back into a place where my heart isn't involved, and dip my chin to mirror his look. "What if I just offer a teensy-weensy bit of judgment."

He grabs my wrist holding the book and pulls me so I'm straddling his lap. I'm loving the feel of him between my legs, the way his body presses like a puzzle piece I've been missing. And God, I think, which IS a prayer to my heavenly Father who has bestowed these gifts upon Tanner rather than going against one of the ten commandments by using God's name in vain, what Tanner's body can do to me. It makes my heart flutter thinking about more of it. He settles his hands on my hips and squeezes them slightly. "I feel like that would go against who you are, Em."

His dark eyes search my face, and I realize he isn't talking about the book at all. My heart flutters, flaps its wings so that my breath catches, and I wonder what is happening here. Am I the only one feeling the rewiring? The size of my heart adjusts in my chest, almost painfully, but I smile and lean forward, giving him a tender kiss. "Okay. For you."

"T!" The sound cracks the moment like an earthquake.

"Fuck." He whispers it and moves me off his lap. Then he leans back against the couch, his demeanor tightening around him like a coil.

I sit on the cushion facing Tanner, my feet tucked up under his leg, both curious as to what's happening and self-conscious because I don't understand his shift.

Griffin — Tanner's best friend — walks into the backyard. He's trailed by some classmates: Danny and Josh, but also several girls, Bella and her friends, Siobhan, Greta and Cora. Oh. Joy. I look at Tanner, and tension radiates from him like waves. The muscles of his jaw tell me the story. He's pissed, like earlier when he found out about Chris, and that isn't something I expected.

Griffin holds up a cooler. "Figured I'd bring the party to you, since you were such a bitch about it earlier."

My protective instincts kick in; I don't like the way Griffin is talking to Tanner. Rude. Condescending. Disrespectful. And I don't like the way his eyes drift over me as though taking inventory for later use. It's gross. I grab my towel and wrap it around my shoulders.

"That's funny," Tanner says, but I can tell he doesn't think it's funny at all. He runs a hand down his thigh, and the muscles bunch in his biceps and chest. "I think what I told you is that I was spending time with Emma today, and it was private."

"Is that what you said?"

Tanner's eyes narrow. If he presses his teeth together any tighter, I think his jaw might snap.

Griffin laughs.

This interaction confounds me. I glance at Tanner again, who has his hands fisted on top of his legs. I look back at his friends. Danny is smiling, but his eyes bounce between Tanner and Griffin like he knows something is off.

Josh frowns and holds up his hands. "Whoa. What the fuck, Griff? Damn, T. I didn't know. I'm sorry." He looks at me, and his green eyes offer an apology. "Hey, Emma."

I offer him a one-handed wave.

Tanner turns to me. I see the apology on his face, the shift of his eyes as his brow raises over them, and what I think maybe means he's embarrassed. It's not an emotion I would connect to my friends. He leans toward me. "Is this okay? If it isn't, just say and I'll get rid of them."

But there's no way I'm stepping into that hornets' nest. I just look at him, disappointed. It isn't because I don't want his friends around. That's cool. It's because I can tell he doesn't, but he seems to be worried about telling them how he feels. So, I say, "Please don't make this about me. I'm good with what YOU want."

Griffin flops onto the couch across from where Tanner and I sit.

"See, bro. She's cool." He's got a grin on his face that makes me feel like he thinks I'm anything but and makes me want to scratch it off his face.

I don't understand these dynamics. My heart pounds. While it's been going crazy today, this time it's for a different reason. There's something in the undercurrent between Tanner and Griffin that I don't understand, but it threatens to suck me under.

I stand up.

Tanner's eyes follow me.

"I'm going to get into the pool," I tell him. I drop the book on my bag and leave whatever's happening in the Cabana behind.

tanner

I watch Emma walk away, cross the deck and descend into the pool. The anger I feel at Griff is so intense that keeping my eyes on Emma seems like the only way to stay grounded. I can sense I've upset her, and that makes my anger sharper. First, because she's right, and second because it scares me. I don't know what to do. Anger in my world means yelling and accusation — neither of which I want. I want to go back to the ease of a moment ago with Emma's smile, and her kiss. This feels like an ice-cold bucket of water sloshed all over everything, and none of it is waterproof.

"Who knew Matthews was hiding that body under her clothes."

I finally look at Griff across from me. "Shut the fuck up."

He's got this weird look on his face, a strange smirk that I'm not sure I've ever seen before. It's like a challenge. I'm so angry with him, my eyes sting with it, and my heart hammers nails into my ribs. While I've never been a fighter, that doesn't mean I haven't been in fights, but never with one of my boys. Rory and I wrestled and did brother fighting; we were little. This is the first time in my life I've ever wanted to break Griff in half. It's like he's doing everything he can to sabotage me: my changes, whatever is happening with Emma, a future I'm trying to figure out.

Then I'm pissed at myself because I'm letting him.

"Hey, anyone else want to get into the pool?" Josh says, herding the girls away from the Cabana. Danny backs away, and then it's just Griff and me remaining.

Griff tilts his head and studies me. His grin slides from his face. "I don't understand what your problem is, Tanner."

"Really? Seems pretty obvious to me."

Griff holds up his hands. "I thought we were boys."

"Yeah. Me too. And I told you today, this was private."

Griff looks away at the pool.

"In fact, I remember invoking Bro Code. And yet here you are."

"You really thought you were going to get lucky with Matthews? Come on, T." He shakes his head and then snickers.

"Does it matter?"

"Wow T. Forgive me for wanting to spend time with my boy. I can fucking see we aren't wanted."

"You don't seem to give a shit what I want."

We've both played the guilt card. I know all about it having heard it used between my parents for years. The thing is I'm not feeling guilty; I'm feeling so enraged by the person who I thought had my back. My brother. There's a part of me that wants to pummel his face, but I stifle it because I'm seeing the truth. Everything I've done these last few months has been about me keeping the peace with Griff, making him happy at my own expense, instead of just being honest. I stand and shake my head, too pissed, not just at him but also at myself. I can't say anything — not yet — unsteady and unsure how to articulate what's in my head and my heart, knowing that even if I do, Griff isn't going to get it. The thought cracks me down the middle.

So, I walk away from him, cross the deck to the pool opposite the cabana, as far as I can get from him and my anger. I settle at the edge of the pool with my feet in the water. The truth of my anger isn't just because I'm mad, but because I'm hurt. His friendship has been so important. He's been my surrogate brother, and the shift I thought was just something temporary now feels like a seismic rift between us.

Though Griff isn't Rory, it sort of feels like losing my brother all over again.

Pandering to Griff's demands makes me feel weak and unsure, but also confused. I needed his friendship to keep me upright when I was fourteen, but now, at eighteen, I feel flattened under the weight of it. I'm not afraid to speak up myself, to fight for what I want, but the dynamics I share with Griff aren't built with normal materials and instead with shared pain. It's the history of us, the emotional baggage wrapped up, in this package. We were the walls holding one another up, but it doesn't feel like that anymore. Would I turn my back on Rory? How could I know? He's gone. My parents are emotionally unavailable, and Griff has been there for me. I don't know how to solve this problem.

Emma is across the pool, with Josh, who says something. She offers him a tight smile; it isn't like her smiles earlier with her defenses down. I've messed up, but I don't know how to change it. My life stretches out before me like that black hole of nothing. Emma's leaving. Josh and Danny are leaving. Even Griff is leaving. I don't know what I'm doing.

Griff walks out of the Cabana, strips off his shirt and bombs the pool, creating a giant splash and residual waves.

Emma glances at me and disengages from Josh; she swims to the side of the pool where I'm sitting and then leans against the wall, arms folded over the edge. "Hey."

"Hey." I struggle to meet her gaze, worried that what I'll see there is anger, censure, disappointment, because those are the things I'm feeling about myself. I'm also thinking about my own parents and their battles; how they waged war.

"You okay?" she asks.

My heart does a strange dance in my chest at her words, a dip and twist because of her kind tone. The concern for me wasn't what I expected. "I'm sorry." I stare at my feet in the water, instead of looking at her. "I didn't know he'd show up."

Emma hauls herself out of the pool, up and over the edge and settles next to me. Her feet remain in the water like mine. Then she does something I don't expect; she adjusts her ankle to rest on mine like a hug.

She takes my hand in hers.

Now, my heart is in my throat, and I'm willing myself not to let the tears out. First, I don't want to cry in front of her. Second, I'd never hear the end of it from Griff, who's an unwelcome interloper. Third, I don't want to freaking cry. Period.

"You don't need to apologize to me for your friend. It's okay, but I can see it isn't okay with you."

I turn my head to look at her and swallow down my emotions. I have the urge to pick her up and carry her to my room, bury all the feelings moving through me like a raging river in what we could accomplish physically to chase them away. I don't. Obviously. And then I recognize the impulse for what it is — maybe clearly for the first time — running and hiding. I focus on the feel of her thumb moving over the back of my hand, back and forth, back and forth. Her face turns toward me, her pretty eyes looking into mine. "I told him he couldn't come. He did anyway."

She looks across the pool at Griff, who has Greta on his shoulders. They're having a battle with Danny and one of Bella's friends. "Doesn't seem like a very nice thing to do to a friend."

I don't say anything, but she's right, even though I know it's true. I don't know how to tell her he's like a brother, like the only family I've had for the last four years. So, I just turn my hand into hers and interlock our fingers. We sit like that, poolside, for a long time watching the battles. Her wisdom and her presence both rattle me, as if I've suddenly jumped the rails of this roller coaster, but also calm me, burning away my anger. The truth of that awareness settles into my bones. I've spent a lot of time making excuses for Griff, accepting his behavior because of what he offered when I needed him so much. I can't make excuses for him anymore. I can't do that to myself.

Eventually she breaks the silence. "Josh offered to take me back to school to get my car," she says. "So you don't have to leave. Since people are here." She squeezes my hand with hers.

I don't want her to go, but I nod. "I'm sorry. It should be me."

"Stop apologizing," she says and then smiles, looking down at our hands. She covers our joined hands with her other hand. "Things happen. We just have to adjust." Her pretty blue eyes jump back up to meet mine. "I'm going to go get my bag."

She stands, and I keep hold of her hand. I follow her into the cabana, reluctant to let her go. My heart slows as if it's moving through a swamp, but I try and keep it light as she collects her stuff.

"Don't forget this masterpiece." I hand her the book that's fallen to the concrete. "Remember, no judgement."

She takes it from me. "I promise. Though, I think I like reading it with you."

Josh calls from the pool, "You ready?"

Emma nods at him.

"What? Already?" Griff says, but I hear the insincerity in his tone.

Josh climbs out of the pool.

"So about tomorrow," she tells me. "You're still invited."

"I wouldn't miss it," I tell her, no longer worried about any sort of temper tantrum Griff may throw. Now, because of this, he has nothing to say, and I feel no guilt about ditching him.

After Emma leaves, I sit in the cabana where less than an hour earlier it had been a protective cocoon insulated from everything else. While I stare out at the pool and notice what's happening there, Griff hits on one of the girls; Danny and the others are in the jacuzzi; Bella glances at me — I don't really see it. My mind is thinking about other things, mostly Emma.

After Rory died, it's hard to pinpoint a time when I felt happy. That's not true, my friends — Griff, Josh, and Danny — made me happy, or so I thought. After this last week with Emma, though, I'm seeing that perhaps my understanding of happiness has been limited. A skewed version of happiness rooted in seeds of a tree planted with bad choices. I can see it now and have been avoiding it for a while; I haven't been happy being Griff's friend for a long time or found all the things we used to do fun anymore. Today, with Emma, highlighted that even more. Spending time with her is the first time in the last eight years that happiness felt like before Rory was gone. Like real smiles, and real laughter. Like playing hide and seek with my brother. Like sitting under the stars and telling stories. Like being wrapped up in something warm when it's really cold.

"Hey Tanner."

I look up at Bella who's standing a few feet away.

"Hey." I look back at the pool, wondering when Josh will get back. I wonder if Emma said anything about me. I should text her.

"You look a million miles away." She walks into the cabana and sits down an arm's length away.

I sit up from my sprawl to put more distance between us. "Naw." I don't want to talk to her and reach for my phone.

She clears her throat.

I key in the code to open my home screen and glance at her. She leans back on her hands, her body on full display in her colorful bikini. She's a pretty girl, but I'm not interested. I look back at the phone, annoyed, and open my messages. Emma has texted.

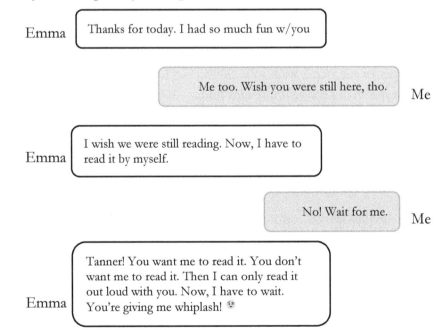

Emma: Thanks for today. I had so much fun w/you

Me: Me too. Wish you were still here, tho.

Emma: I wish we were still reading. Now, I have to read it by myself.

Me: No! Wait for me.

Emma: Tanner! You want me to read it. You don't want me to read it. Then I can only read it out loud with you. Now, I have to wait. You're giving me whiplash! 😜

"Are you looking at funny memes?" Bella asks and leans toward me. My smile slides off my face. "Nope." I keep my attention fixed on my screen.

> I want to read it with you, that's all. I
> enjoyed it. I liked talking about it with you.

"What are you doing then?" Bella interrupts.

Three dots pop up; Emma is texting, and that's where I want my attention, but Bella is irritating me. I sigh and look at her. "Is there something you need? I'm kind of busy." I wave the phone at her.

"I'm just curious is all. I mean, you were hanging out with Emma, and she doesn't seem your type. I'm wondering about it."

The muscles tense in my shoulders. I don't like the way she's said Emma's name, like she's trying to draw me into an inside joke. "And you know my type?"

Bella scoots closer. She touches my leg and runs her hand up my thigh as she says, "Yeah. I think so. I think I'm more your type."

I stand up. "Nope." Eight months ago, she was right, but the tectonic plates that make me have shifted.

Griff laughs from the pool, and I hear him say, "bitch."

It pisses me off. I walk into the house, leaving that bullshit behind and escape to my room, angry and hurt.

Emma | Okay, I'll wait for you

She makes my heart pound with want, but not just physical want; it's a longing to be with her. I love it, but I have to admit that it also makes me unsteady, because I feel like I'm walking over unfamiliar terrain. In the dark. Without a flashlight.

> How was your ride home with Josh? — Me

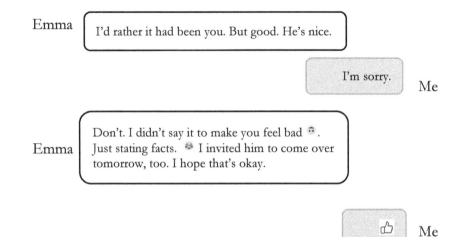

Emma: I'd rather it had been you. But good. He's nice.

Me: I'm sorry.

Emma: Don't. I didn't say it to make you feel bad 😊. Just stating facts. 😊 I invited him to come over tomorrow, too. I hope that's okay.

Me: 👍

There's a knock at my door, and I'm instantly irritated, because I'm figuring I know who's on the other side of it. "What the fuck," I say as I open it.

"Whoa." It is Josh, hands raised in surrender.

"Sorry, dude. I thought you were Bella. Or Griff."

"Too much?" He walks into the room.

I roll my eyes as he passes, and then shut the door behind him. "You have no idea."

"I think I probably do." He flops onto my couch and fires up my video game console.

Me: Josh just got back

Emma: Tell him thanks again.

"Emma says thanks for the ride."

He nods. "Sure. She's cool. You have my approval."

"Like I need it."

The game console sings as it boots up. Josh runs a hand through his hair and glances at me. "You don't have Griff's."

"I don't know what the fuck is up with him."

"I'm sorry, by the way. It was uncool to just show up."

I nod. "I told him I was busy. I don't blame you or Danny." I watch as Josh slides through the apps on the screen and selects the one he wants.

"He's being an idiot, but you're being one too."

I turn my head to look at him. "Whoa. What the hell? Thanks."

He looks at me with a tilt to his head, just a split second before returning his attention to the game. "Clarification: you're not being one because of Emma — she's probably like the best decision you've ever made. She's like a reach, Tanner. You're being an idiot by letting Griff act like that. It's bullshit."

"You're right."

His eyebrows rise up over his eyes in surprise. "I thought I might need to break that down a bit further."

I shake my head. I'm sure he wouldn't say something I haven't already thought. "I don't know what to do about him."

"Stand up for yourself. Dude, Griff is the one being an ass. You don't need to be one. Emma isn't going to put up with that shit for long. But then, maybe Bella is a better fit?"

"Hell no." I pick up the other controller. "Emma said she invited you tomorrow. You want to go?"

"Yep. Not missing that. She said her friend Ginny will be there."

"Dude. Don't mess up what I have going on with Emma to bang her friend."

"Who says that's what I want? Is that all you want from Emma?" He selects the game he wants. The console beeps and loads.

"Naw. I like her."

"Don't assign me the emotional capacity of Griff." He selects his player with a click.

I chuckle and select mine. "Sorry."

Josh smiles. "It's cool. That's what you need to do with him, by the way. Tell him how you feel."

I don't tell him I tried that a little over a week ago. "You know how that's going to go." I watch the screen swirl with graphics toward the beginning of the game and wish that talking to Griff was like talking to Josh.

"Yeah, but so what. You tell him. He acts like an ass, but at least he knows where you stand. Then if he crosses it again, you're justified to knock his ass out."

I nod, but in my heart, I have a feeling it isn't going to be an if but a when, and maybe that's what I'm really avoiding.

senior year
(1 day to graduation)

"'I want you to choose me,' Lucy said.
In the steady climb toward her, I'd gotten winded, and I wasn't sure I was going to make it to the peak without battling altitude sickness."

-unnamed protagonist, *Kaleidoscope Concussion* by Saul Annick

emma

"It's fine. It's just my friends," I equivocate by not delineating which friends are coming over.

My dad shrugs into his blue blazer. "Had I known, we wouldn't have scheduled this dinner and play for tonight." He gazes at me with his bright blue stare behind his wire-rimmed glasses, chin dipped a bit. "I'm always home for movie night."

Mom, looking gorgeous in her little black dress, leans forward to examine her lipstick in the hallway mirror. "Mo." She presses her lips together and looks at him through the mirror. "The thing is, we don't need to be here for movie night."

I nod in agreement. "Yes. I'm eighteen, Dad. I can go to adult prison. I can elect a president. I can fight in a war. I'm going to college. I think I can handle cookies for movie night."

Dad looks like he's going to argue, but Mom grabs his elbow. "There's pre-made dough in the freezer." She looks at me and smiles, her gray gaze teary-eyed. "I can't believe my oldest graduates tomorrow."

"Mom, you're going to ruin your makeup. I'm fine. Great actually. Go have fun."

"Come on, Mo. She's right. She's trying on her adult shoes in an empty house."

Dad smooths his peach tie. "Shelby is at Deanna's. If anything should happen–"

"I'll go pick her up. I got this. Enjoy the city. Have fun on your date. Don't worry about anything but good food and saving your tears for Argentina."

"Clever." Dad chuckles about my *Evita* reference since that's what they're going to see. He pats down his pockets, which I assume means he's looking for his wallet.

"It's inside your jacket, Mo. We don't want to miss our reservation."

"Yes. You're right." He reaches in to make sure and then pats the outside of the jacket.

Mom stops at the door. "Don't wait up. Probably not back until around two."

"Keep the party to a dull roar." Dad kisses my cheek and disappears out of the house after her.

With my back against the closed door, I let out a deep breath. He has no idea how true that might be. If I'm lucky. Then I smile. The house to myself for movie night deserves a quick dance through the hallway — which I do with great flourish. Then I race upstairs to shower and get ready. By the time I return downstairs and start the popcorn, Ginny knocks. I open the door, and she follows me into the kitchen.

"Wow." Her eyes narrow behind some fashion glasses she's wearing. "You look really good. What's up?"

I twirl for her. I did think about what to wear. Something cute, but I didn't want to look like I was trying too hard. "Too much?"

"For me and Liam — yes. You're usually wearing flannel pajama pants and a sweatshirt."

I smooth my hands over the front of my skinny jeans and then primp the cute pastel pink top. "I invited Tanner to movie night."

"Bitch!" She's smiling. "That makes me a fifth wheel." She hops up onto the counter.

"He might be bringing a friend."

She shakes her head. She's left her hair straight. The auburn tresses move with her. "No way. Griffin is awful. Sorry, but I won't stay if he's gonna be here."

I dump the first finished bag of microwave popcorn into a bowl. "Not Griffin. Josh."

"Josh?" Ginny tilts her head and narrows her eyes, trying to place him. She purses her lips, and her eyes drifting toward the ceiling. "Who's Josh?" She smooths the cute navy shorts she's wearing.

"You'll see. Speaking of see, what's with the glasses?"

She looks up. "Wait. The tall one or the shorter one?"

"The tall one. Light brown hair. Green eyes. Tattoos."

She makes a humming noise. "He's cute," though the way she says it doesn't inspire confidence that she believes it. Ginny pinches the glasses and wiggles them. "Step Monster was super annoyed because I insisted I needed to get my eyes checked two weeks ago — you know for college. It may have been a ruse."

"What?"

"She doesn't want to spend money on anything except that stupid fake she-shed she's planned in my room. So after, I bought these babies for ten bucks and told her I got them from Glasses Hut for three hundred. She's pissed because, and I quote, 'that place is a rip off.'" Ginny laughs. "She's been on a penny-pinching warpath since, and Dad's about had it." Ginny laughs and shakes her head. "It's too easy."

"And you're awful."

"Me?! She's the one who's trying to oust me before I even leave."

"That's true. What does your dad think?" I pour in a second bag of popcorn. "How much more of this should I make?"

Ginny hops off the counter. "I don't know. One more?" She grabs a handful and then returns to her seat on the island counter. "He's pretty complacent. I think that's why he and my mom divorced. She wanted more fire."

I put another bag in the microwave, turn and prop a hip against the counter to wait for it. "You know there are stools."

She smiles. "But then I'd be too far away from you." She tosses another popped corn into her mouth and then says, "I guess that's why Karol married Doug. He's a ball of fire. Steroid fire."

I roll my eyes and shake my head. "Maybe you're just too cynical, or you're the textbook kid of divorce who wants their parents back together."

"No way. They were awful together. Always fighting. Well, my mom was." She pauses. "Now that I think about it, Shedevil is a lot like my mom. Did my dad replace my mom with another *my mom*?"

"Why are you such a terror to your stepparents?"

"First, step-monster deserves it. She's an emotional terrorist about this stupid she-space. Doug's okay. I just like to be dramatic."

"That is an understatement."

She eats more popcorn. "Where were you yesterday?"

"Rehearsal," I say.

"After that? Because you didn't text me. And you always text me."

"Tanner's." I say it like it is commonplace, just an average outing, even if inside my heart is bouncing around in my chest like one of those gigantic bouncing balls you buy from one of those displays in a grocery store.

"What?" She jumps from the counter, slides across the floor to me, and grabs my shoulders. "You didn't say a thing, you, sneaky bitch."

I laugh, knowing she's just being her dramatic self. "He invited me over to his house for a swim." My cheeks heat.

Her mouth opens and her hazel eyes widen. "Spill it." She pokes my arm. "You are blushing so hard right now. Did you?"

"What?"

She wiggles her eyebrows. "Did you lose your V card?"

"You and Liam told me two weeks ago that it was an impossibility."

"Perhaps a dramatic overstatement. You're withholding information." She pinches me lightly.

"Ouch! Why are you being so physical?"

"Now who's dramatic?"

"I didn't lose any identification," I tell her, drawing out the words. "But making out with him is like... well, I feel all gooey and buttery thinking about it."

She sucks in a breath, wraps her arms around me then leans back to look at my face. "And you aren't overthinking like you did about that whole prom thing."

"What are you talking about?"

She lets go of me. "When you shared your justified wrath with Handsy McGee."

"He was wrong."

She leans against the counter. "Yeah. He was. Not that part, the part where you second guessed his actions in relationship to yours. Like it was something you did when he'd been the prick to overstep."

"I know that." But she's right. I had done that. I still did.

She rolls her eyes and jumps back up on the counter. "Logically. But emotionally you didn't. It's all that ridiculous propaganda you're taught at church and your hang ups about being 'good' and 'worthy.'" She makes air quotes with her fingers.

The microwave beeps, and I remove the popcorn. "Not." But even as I deny it, I can't help but fall back into that spin cycle. Those keywords that no one can seem to agree about: Submissive. Submit. Good. Pure. I think about Tanner and the day before, the way he waited for me to tell him what I wanted. "Yeah, okay. I mean, I don't think it's a faith thing."

"I didn't say a faith thing, Emma. I said a church thing. All those patriarchs telling women they don't own their own bodies."

"But it isn't just a church thing though, Gin. It's everything. I mean, remember last year at your family reunion — that asshole cousin of yours? Pervy."

She frowns, rolls her eyes and slow nods. "Percy."

"Yeah. He followed us around all day, tried to feel you up. Then you punched him in the nose."

"And I was the one who got in trouble for it."

"Exactly! That's not a church message. It's a social one too, don't you think."

"Yea. You're right. It sucks. Makes me think I will never get married."

Ginny's parents — the two sets of them — definitely have issues. And Tanner's. But Liam's parents are pretty awesome. And my own parents have offered a good example of married life. I've only ever seen them as partners. My mom might be the breadwinning lawyer, my dad a stay-at-home-work-from-home dad, but I knew that when big stuff was decided upon it was together. I also knew that in matters of a tie, and only after much lawyering on my mother's behalf, my dad would get the final vote, but truth be told, I think Dad listened to Mom most of the time, not because she was the breadwinner, but because she was smart and usually right. Perhaps getting hung up on the words wasn't the right approach; perhaps I should be looking at the behavior.

"Anyway." Ginny slides from the counter again until we're shoulder to shoulder. "I think this, with Tanner, whatever it is, is good for you. I was afraid you'd guilt yourself into staying inside the box, but you seem empowered and comfortable. Relaxed." She bumps her shoulder against mine. "Buttery. So, I want the dirt."

I don't want to tell her the details — not because I wouldn't — I just want to keep it locked up just for me, so I evade. "I just enjoyed hanging out with him. We laughed a lot. You know, he's really funny."

One of her eyebrows arches over her eye, and I wish I could do that. "Tanner James is funny."

"Why? Is that surprising?"

"That isn't the usual gossip associated with Tanner's, uh, shall we say prowess."

My smile slips. "Can we not make this about Tanner gossip? I mean, I don't see him like that even if everyone else does."

She nods. "Agreed. Clean slate, then."

I pause. "I just feel happy." I can't help but smile, but then remember Griffin and narrow my eyes. "Then his jerk friend showed up and was a complete jackass."

"Oh? Griff? Do tell."

About that, I fill her in on all the dirty details.

tanner

Josh grabs the collar of a large beast. The dog would be terrifying if it didn't appear to be congenial. The wide-headed animal, black with reddish brown markings, dances around on its four legs; its tailless butt skitters back and forth.

"Indy. Settle," Josh orders.

The dog sits. A wide grin overtakes his whole face, and his tongue lops out.

I can't help but smile. When I move through the front door, the canine closes his mouth and tilts his head, assessing me, tongue stuck between his massive jaws. "Is Indy going to take off my head?" I ask. It's the first time I've ever met Josh's dog, having only been outside of his house. This is a strange realization. How is it possible to be acquainted with someone for years and never hang out at their house? Perhaps my ideas of friendship have been wrapped up in warped boxes. The thought makes me feel like a crappy friend.

"What?" Josh's voice raises several octaves as he bends down closer to the dog's head. "Indiana Jones is a big teddy bear, aren't you, boy?" He makes baby noises as Indy licks his face. Then the dog falls backward exposing his belly to Josh, who rubs the dog's wide chest with two hands. Indy kicks one of his hind legs.

"What kind of dog is he?" I'm smiling at Josh's unguarded affection. I've never seen this side of him.

"This big baby is a Rottweiler." Josh is now on the floor with the dog, who hops up and then jumps on him. Josh rolls and wraps the dog in a bear hug and receives more dog kisses. "He's a trained boy, socialized and super sweet. No worries," Josh leans away, twisting his head to keep his face from getting the brunt of dog affection.

I step into the house and Indy freezes. He assesses me, lunges forward, and shoves his nose into my crotch. "Whoa." I bend to cover the jewels and shift my hips away. Indy looks up at me with his wide grin again. "Good thing he doesn't bite."

Josh laughs, sitting up, and grabs Indy's collar. "Sit."

Indy sits.

"Let him smell you."

I hold out my arm, and Indy strains to smell my outstretched hand. "Are you ready?" I ask Josh while Indy snuffs at my skin. The dog presses his cold, damp nose against it.

"Yeah. Let me put him away." Josh stands and tugs on the dog's collar. "Crate it, Indy," he orders.

The dog's claws slide against the tile as he tries to catch a grip. He tears away and disappears around the corner.

"This way." Josh follows the dog.

I trail Josh down a wide hallway. "This is a nice place."

"Yeah. My parents do okay."

"I was just thinking that it's kind of weird we've never hung out here before." Yesterday at my house was like only a handful of times. "I guess when you're hanging out at parties…"

"True. You're welcome here, anytime, T." Josh jogs across a wide-open room where Indy waits inside a black wire cage.

"That's cool. Thanks." My response seems insignificant to the kindness of his invitation. "You cage your dog?"

"Naw. It's a crate. Think of it like a cave. Makes a dog feel more comfortable. Besides, it won't be long. Just until Chance gets home."

"How is Chance?" I ask, referring to Josh's younger brother.

"A dick, but he's cool. Sophomores suck."

I'd agree, but I don't know that. It makes me wonder if Rory would have said that about me. There were two years between us. He would have graduated like Josh, and I would have been a sophomore. "He's lucky to have a big brother like you." I look around at the family photos on the wall. They are all smiling in one of those posed photos where they all match: Josh, Chance, his parents and an older sister named Brandi, who's almost done with college. The TV and giant couch. Windows that open up to something, but the curtains are pulled. A kitchen with an island. Everything tan and airy and clean.

"You thinking about Rory?" Josh taps the crate with affection as Indy tries to lick him.

I shrug, because I don't talk about Rory.

Josh doesn't push. "I'm ready. I've been thinking about seeing Ginny all day."

I raise my eyebrows at him. "Oh. Really?" I draw out the words so that he knows I'm trying to push his buttons.

He shoves me, and I have to catch myself to keep my balance. I laugh.

"Don't even tell me you haven't been thinking about Emma all day."

He's absolutely correct. I've been thinking about Emma all day, but I don't say it. Josh has got this easy-going-super-honest-say-it-like-it-is vibe, and it works. He's also surrounded by what appears to be a family full of stability and love. I can't find that place; not enough to share, but I allow a smile. That and maybe Griff's ribbing about my manhood — or lack of it — is getting to me.

"You hear from Griff today?"

"Nope. You?"

"Yeah. Said he and Bella hooked up after the pool."

"Perfect. Two birds with one stone or whatever."

Josh chuckles and locks the front door behind us. "So, you didn't have to set those boundaries, today."

We move down the declining walkway to the street where my truck is parked.

"Not today."

"It's going to happen, bro."

I nod. "Yeah. But not today." I press the key fob, and my truck unlocks.

"There's still a few hours." Josh smiles as he climbs in and checks his phone. "Give it some time."

I shake my head and start the truck.

I drive. The radio blasts music while Josh plays DJ. It's comfortable being with him, and in contrast to Griff, I wonder why Griff and I clicked. But I know. We were both knee-deep in struggle with our families. I was dealing with my parents' divorce, and he was trying to figure out how to navigate the difficulty of his single mom trying to hold herself together after his dad went to prison.

"Remember last January when we went to the Tinks?" Josh asks, swiping his thumb through the music app. He selects one of their moodier songs.

Hell yeah. I remember seeing Emma outside. The loop: her laugh. Raising my hand. Her smile. Her wave in return. It's almost as if that moment propelled me onto a different trajectory. "Yes."

"Did you know Emma and Ginny were there?"

I glance at him.

He isn't looking at me, but I wonder if maybe there was something about that night that impacted him too, recalling his comments about Ginny at Marta's the other day. "Yeah. I remember seeing Emma after. Outside."

He doesn't say anything more about it, but it makes me curious. Instead, he changes the subject and yammers about getting a summer job at his Dad's firm. Then he moves on to Brandi coming home for summer, followed by the fact he'll have to drive Chance to all his summer league basketball practices. I wonder if he realizes what a gift it is to have his family. Even as I think it, I'm sure he does.

I park the truck in front of Emma's house, down the street just a bit because I see a couple of other cars. It makes me nervous. Will I have to meet her parents? My mouth dries out. Shit. I totally hadn't thought of that.

I follow Josh to the front door, because he has no concerns about stuff like that. Why would he care about meeting Emma's parents? Why do I? And I realize it's because I want them to like me. But why is that? The answer, which I can see at a distance isn't one I want to think about. Not yet. It's too big and too painful. Emma's leaving.

The door opens.

My heart loses gravity and floats about in my chest.

Emma.

She smiles. "Hi." She steps back to let us in.

I go through first. I want to touch her. I don't.

She follows me with her eyes, and then glances at Josh. "Hey. I'm glad you came."

"Wouldn't have missed it," Josh says.

Emma shuts the door behind him. "Through the hall there, past the stairs."

Josh walks that way.

"Do we get to meet your family?" I ask.

"Not this time," she looks over her shoulder at me. "Everyone is out."

Relief hits me like a refreshing breeze, and I take a breath. Then I shove my hands into my pockets to keep from reaching for Emma. She looks so good. Her jeans hug her curves, the pink shirt hangs off a shoulder, and her curly hair brushes her skin as she talks about stuff I don't catch, because I'm too busy looking at her. Thankfully, Josh is paying attention to the words, because he says something that sounds like white noise in my head.

"Liam, Atticus, and Ginny are already downstairs waiting." She opens a door that leads down a set of stairs. Josh disappears from my view.

I need to kiss her. Bad. I reach out before she disappears down the stairs after Josh and grab her hand.

She glances at my hand holding hers, looks at me and steps closer. "Hi," she says and looks at my mouth.

I lean toward her, wrapping my arm still holding her hand around her back. Just as I'm about to fulfill the fix I've wanted all day, Josh's head pops back through the doorway. "Uh. Can this, like, wait?" He winks.

Such a dick.

Emma blushes. She clears her throat and disengages. "This way."

"Wow. Thanks," I tell him as we follow her.

He laughs.

emma

"Tanner and Josh are here," I announce as I walk into the basement where Ginny, Atticus, and Liam are slopped on the sectional. I glance at Liam and give him a look to make sure we're on the same page. His lips thin, and he raises his eyebrows as if to tell me he deigns to accept Tanner for the evening. For me.

I shake my head and roll my eyes at him.

He smiles.

"Yo." Atticus gets up from the couch where he's sitting next to Liam to greet Tanner and Josh. It's as if a safety net walked into the room even though Atticus didn't need one. They do strange hand rituals and half hugs.

"You guys know Ginny, right?" I say.

Ginny turns around on the couch.

Tanner gives her a smile and a head nod. "Hang out around any campfires lately, Ginny?"

"Not since Senior Send Off when you stole my best friend away. I've barely seen her since."

Tanner pretends to stab his heart.

She laughs. "I'll forgive you."

"Hey," Josh says. His eyes linger on her. When she finally makes eye contact with him, his eyes slide away.

"Breakfast Club is queued," Ginny announces and turns back around on the couch.

"That's an awesome movie," Josh says and moves around the couch to sit next to Atticus.

"The cookies are in the oven," I say. "I have to grab them before they burn." I look at Tanner. "Want to come help me?"

He nods and follows me back up the stairs.

I'm so aware of him behind me, as if he's emitting his own gravitational pull, and I slow.

Then his hand is on my hip, a finger slipped through a belt loop, because I feel a slight tug.

I glance over my shoulder at him. His eyes are darker, intense, and I know what's coming. My breath swirls in my chest.

He catches up as I take the final stair into the great room outside of the basement stairwell.

I turn to face him, and in the space of a breath, his mouth is on mine; his palms hold my face between them. Tongues. Then hands. Sensations. It's fire, hot, and everything in my chest constricts before it melts.

The timer on the oven beeps.

The cookies.

"I better get those," I say against his mouth.

He smiles against my lips.

I open my eyes and look into his; they're sparkling. "Or we'll have burnt cookies."

"Can't have that." He releases me and follows me into the kitchen.

I open the oven and pull out the hot cookie sheet.

"So domestic."

I glance at him. He's leaning against the island. "Would you like to help?"

"Nope. I like watching you."

"Well, make yourself useful anyway, and grab me a plate, third cupboard from the right." I scrunch my nose at him and point to which one I mean.

He moves.

I set the sheet on the stove, set aside the oven mitt, and pull a spatula from the container on the counter.

"Will this work?"

A plate appears in front of my face, and Tanner's warmth seeps through me from behind.

I lean back, against the solidity of his body. "Perfect." I set the plate on the counter.

Tanner doesn't move. Instead his hands conform to my hips, and his mouth presses against the skin of my exposed shoulder. I feel the tip of his tongue. "I'm a little hungry, Emma."

My heart slows, the pulse steady and deliberate, reverberating through my cells like that echo between us. "I could probably find you something to eat." I know we're not talking about food.

He runs his tongue up my neck and nips at the soft spot behind my ear lobe. "This is what I'm craving," he mutters against my skin.

My head drifts to the side to give him better access.

He kisses my jaw, and I turn in his arms. "I want you so bad."

I wrap my arms around his neck and kiss him to show him how I feel. The same. It's slow and sensual at first until suddenly, it isn't. Tanner lifts me onto the counter of the island and stands between my legs. He draws my hips to meet his. I wrap my legs around him, longing to be closer.

Someone downstairs laughs.

Tanner draws away, rests his forehead against my shoulder. "We should probably get the cookies downstairs."

"We probably should."

He pulls back and helps me off the counter.

I slide down the front of his body, every nerve ending lighting Fourth of July sparklers inside of me, spinning and showing off their magic.

He kisses my forehead, watches me plate the cookies and then carries the plate.

"That took a while," Ginny says and sticks her tongue out at me, looking like an emoji.

"We had to wait for the cookies," I say, taking the plate from Tanner and setting it on the coffee table next to the popcorn, chips, and dish of M&M's.

"Start it up," Liam says, and settles against the couch next to Atticus.

tanner

My body is vibrating from earlier, wishing I could just whisk Emma from the room to be alone with her, but I also know that she deserves better than that. She deserves the guy that will sit and watch movies with her. She deserves the guy that will hang out with her friends. She deserves the guy who pays attention to the stuff she loves. I want to be that guy; the one that deserves her.

I sit down on the L-shaped couch at its apex on one side of the L next to Emma. Liam is on the other side of the L across from me. He's offered a polite greeting, but I have a feeling he's only tolerating me. I'm curious since he and I haven't really ever talked. Maybe I just don't understand the nuance of a protective friend who cares about me like Liam cares about Emma. He and Atticus are cozy, sitting next to one another, no space between their touching arms. Atticus glances at me and smiles, then looks at Liam, and I realize what he'd been talking about a couple of weeks ago. *I don't think my boys would get who I really am.* When his gaze slides back to mine, I offer him a look I hope expresses my understanding of what he'd meant.

I lean back and drape my arm over the back of the couch. I don't know what's going on in the movie. I mean, I do. I've seen it. I can track it. I just feel antsy. I bounce my right leg, wanting to move. It rubs against Emma, who moves a little closer. I stop wiggling. She smells so good, clean and sweet. In my whole life I've never sat with a girl like this. I've never wanted to. I take a deep breath and feel a strange brew in my chest, a concoction of desire and — something else that feels dangerous. So many firsts with her and it makes me feel like parts of me are peeling away. Exposed and vulnerable. I'm not sure I like it, but don't want to let it go either.

The bad boy character in *The Breakfast Club* — Bender — switches around cards in a long drawer while they're sitting in the library for detention. It makes me think of Griff moving books around in the library at school. Stupid. I'd laughed but remembered feeling bad about Griff's actions, even if I hadn't done it. I'd let him, like so many things, because I thought that's what you did with your bros.

I look down at my hands and flip them over in my lap.

Emma's hand covers one of mine.

I glance at her.

She smiles and threads our fingers together.

My heart reaches toward her, and I squeeze her hand.

I focus on the movie, but my mind shifts between the heat of Emma's hand in mine to the movie, to Griff again while Bender yells about his old man. Griff has a shit family. I know that because I've been to his house lots of time, met his mom and older brother.

After the movie, we all help Emma by carrying up the dishes and leftovers.

"I don't care how many times you say it, Emma, the best character is Allison," Liam is saying as they disappear through the door back into the kitchen.

"No way!" She's incredulous. "Put the stuff on the counter, here," she directs us, setting down a bowl on the island. "Thanks."

"She's the most normal."

"Liam. That's ridiculous," Ginny says and then flops onto the couch in the other room.

"Why? Because she's weird, she can't be self-actualized?" Liam leans against the counter.

"I think she's the flattest character," Atticus says.

"Thank you, Atticus," Emma says and holds up her hand for a high five. "John Hughes didn't even try with her character. And then, when he did, it was only to make her *look* like a version of Claire. It's insulting."

"I'm not talking about that part. You're right on that, for sure."

"Then what are you talking about?" Ginny asks.

Josh and I are quiet. I'm observing with interest, because my friends have never interacted this way. My friends have existed in jokes and banter that never dives any deeper than the depth of our masculinity and its relationship to our penis and sex, usually both. Sometimes we'd talk about video games, TV, and sports, but it always returns to the first two.

"I think she's like—" he snaps his fingers, trying to find the word— "a gatekeeper. Like all of the characters, in some way, have to go through her to understand themselves."

Ginny shakes her head emphatically. "You are trippin' Liam. No one character does that. It's all of them."

"Agree to disagree."

Ginny laughs.

"Need more help?" Liam asks Emma.

"I got it. You guys leaving?"

"Yeah." Liam blushes, and his eyes move to Atticus.

Atticus smiles. "I promised to take him to that bowling alley where they have a DJ and disco lights."

"Oh. Fun!" Ginny sits up so she's leaning against the couch. "Don't be too late, boys," Ginny warns in a suggestive tone. She wiggles her eyebrows. "Graduation tomorrow."

Liam flips her off but smiles. Then he turns and leads Atticus from the house.

Josh, looking at his phone, says, "Tanner? Have you checked your phone?"

"I left it in the truck."

"Bro. Griff blew us up."

"What?"

He turns his screen toward me. I see a stack of messages. *Where are you guys?* "Told you."

I glance at Emma. "Shit." She looks disappointed. Her lips thin, and she drops her gaze to the counter. "I should deal with him."

She nods but doesn't look up at me.

Ire pops in my chest like an overfull balloon. Griff was around before she was, and then I think if they were reversed, if it were Griff standing in her shoes, he'd be spewing a ton of shit at me for wanting to see her. She's not. I don't know what it is I want from her, but perhaps it isn't about her at all. I'm pissed at Griff, because I don't want to leave her. Why am I?

Boundaries.

"I should go too," Ginny says. "Graduation tomorrow." She does a little dance squeal. "I have to take comfort in my room while I can." She hugs Emma. "See you tomorrow, Tanner. Bye, Josh."

I offer her a half smile, my mind thinking about Griff and how to figure that out.

"Tanner. I'll meet you at the truck," Josh says. "I'm going to go call Danny." He trails after Ginny.

I look at Emma. "I'm—"

She shakes her head. "Don't say 'sorry.'"

I close my mouth and step toward her. She allows me to wrap my arms around her. "Griff's like a brother, you know. When my parents divorced, he was the one who had my back."

She leans back so she can look up at me. "You don't have to explain. You have your reasons. I just don't like the way he treats you. I don't like that you let him."

Her words hurt because she's right.

I let go and turn away from her, annoyed with myself but wanting to lash out. *Grow up, T,* imaginary Rory says, but I hear Josh's voice. I also remember his words of wisdom the day before: *Emma won't put up with that — not for long.* Emma doesn't deserve my anger about Griff. I keep my mouth shut.

"I don't mean to overstep."

I shake my head. "You're not." I turn back to her. "And you're right." I lean forward and kiss her cheek. "I'm going to go and deal with Griff. I'll text you okay?"

She nods. "Okay."

"When do your parents get back?" I ask against the skin of her temple.

"Not for a few hours." She leans back and looks at me. She smiles. "But I'm sure dealing with Griffin will take some time."

"I better go then. So I can come back."

She walks me out.

When I do finally look at my phone, it's overheating with notifications. I listen to the most recent call from Griff: "Fuckin' bitch, where you at? Danny and I are at Grady's. Get your ass here. I can't find Josh either. You two twats are probably together." Click.

I look at Josh, who has listened with me.

"You ready?"

I start the truck. "As ready as I can be, I guess."

I park the truck outside of Grady's townhouse. It's dark, but the housing complex is washed in a yellow light; there aren't any stars here. The party is mild, mostly guys and a few girls. It's quiet, the night faded along with everyone there. Josh and I walk in and those who notice cheer: "Tanner! Josh!"

Somebody yells for Griff and Danny.

Griff's head pops around the corner from the kitchen, drunk, eyes narrowed. "I knew you guys were together. What is this? A gay affair?" He's almost to the point of the ugly slur.

"Discovered." Josh laughs and puts an arm around me; I love how comfortable he is in his own skin. I want that.

"Where were you guys? You left me and Danny hanging."

"I'm good." Danny raises his hands in a sort of don't-lump-me-in-that and smiles. He's sober. "Driving. But Griff here has gone fast and furious since we got here."

"Looks like you're doing okay," I tell Griff, glancing around.

"It's a fucking sausage fest." He pouts and stands, swaying toward

261

me on his feet.

I fiddle with my key fob in my hand. "We had plans."

Griff tosses out a hand and pokes my chest. "Bullshit, T. Twice without me. We're boys." His hand smacks heavily against my shoulder and stays there.

I nod. "Yeah. We can be boys and not spend all of our time together."

Griff makes a stupid face, a grimace mixed with a shake of his head. "No. No. That's not how Bro Code works. We're in it together. Always." He pulls me by the neck and curls his arm around me in a confining hug. "You didn't invite me."

I extricate myself, stepping out of his domineering hold, annoyed. "You've made it clear you don't like Emma." Even as I say it, I know it's futile. Griff is too drunk to have this conversation. I watch him and feel — sad. Embarrassed. I don't think anyone else in the room probably gives a shit, and it isn't Griff I'm thinking about; it's my own behavior. The shit I've done that was exactly like Griff, because he is my bro.

You're changing, growing, I hear imaginary Rory.

Emma and Ginny and Liam are nothing like this. The glow of their friendship, their being together, is still warm in my thoughts.

"She's not for you, T." He swings an arm around my neck again and with his other hand points at my face. "She's an uptight prude, and you'll never get anywhere with her. Chris Keller said she's a frigid religious zealot."

Chris. Chris Keller.

I shrug away from him with a push, having gone from forty miles per hour to seventy. It's about Griff, but now there's more context wrapped up in his statement.

Chris. Keller. That fucking prick.

Griff nearly topples over and hits the wall. Frames rattle on their nails.

"What the fuck did you just say?" I snap. I shake my head and walk out of the house.

I hear Josh say behind me, "Griff. What the fuck man? That's dick."

262

"This is who I am. A dick. Tanner. Dude." He stumbles around behind me. I'm not sure how he makes it down the steps to the sidewalk. "Where're you going?"

"I'm out." I keep walking.

"I'm your boy. Don't go."

I do turn then. "It's pretty clear I'm not yours. Goes both ways, doesn't it, Griff?"

"My job is to keep you from getting whipped. No serious shit, remember?" He sways and grimaces, burping. He's about to lose it.

He's right. We had said that. When we were fourteen and both facing fucked up families. "That was four years ago, Griff. It's time to grow up." I wave a hand at him and turn away.

Suddenly, I'm flying forward because Griff has pushed me from behind, slammed my shoulder blades with both of his hands. I catch myself against my truck and turn ready to fight. "You ready for this, Griff?" I take a step toward him.

"Whoa." Danny jumps in front of Griff and presses him back into the yard away from me.

"You're whipped over a bitch," Griff yells.

I'm angry, but I remind myself he's drunk. "I'll talk to you later."

I hear Danny tell Griff to shut up as I climb into my truck.

Josh leans in on the passenger's side. "I'll have Danny take me home. I'll help him with Baby Griff."

I nod.

He smacks the side of the truck and turns back to Danny and Griff, who's now puking in the bushes.

Disappointed and hurt, I drive away. Anger shoots electrical impulses through me, but that isn't what's driving me. It's the awareness of how messed up my relationship with Griff has gotten. Or maybe it's always been this way, I just didn't have any other means to see it before now? Add to it anger at an asshole who put his hands on Emma, whose name I now know. I drive. Usually, I'd end up at the Quarry — alone — stuck in my own head and heart, but I don't want that. The first place I think of, and the only place I want to be, is with Emma. That's where I drive.

emma

I'm sitting on the couch in the family room of the now quiet house, sipping on tea and thinking about Tanner. Music plays over the speakers. It's soothing and moody and makes me miss him. During the movie he was distant, almost like sitting still was a chore. I'd never noticed him like that before; his mind moving, like it couldn't stay in one place. But then, when he'd look at me, he would come back into focus. Still.

My phone pings.

Tanner | I'm at the front door.

I smile, happy, and pad down the hall wrapped in the blanket from the couch. He's on the other side of the door, facing the street, his back to me. I notice the way his black t-shirt stretches across his back and can't wait to touch him. I open the door.

He turns, and I can see there's emotion on his face that isn't usual, heavier.

"I'm surprised."

"How come? I said I'd be back."

I watch him walk past me into the house. He smells so good, clean and spicy.

"We have a reading date." He smiles. Finally, but it's not in his eyes.

"I'll grab it." I run up to my room to retrieve the book from my bag. When I get back downstairs, I walk into the great room. He's standing at the windows overlooking the backyard, only there's nothing to see in the blackness of the glass but his reflection. "Got it." I wave the book in my hand.

"Can we go sit outside?" He looks at me, and I have the impression that the emotion he's got simmering under his surface is ready to boil over.

"Sure."

"Dark enough to see the stars?" He's antsy again like when we watched the movie. His body tugged by whatever is at war inside of him.

"Yes, but not like out of town."

He unlocks the sliding door and offers me his hand.

I set the book on the counter, take his hand, and follow him out into the night.

Once on the deck, we lay on one of the loungers outside and share my blanket. I'm nestled in the crook of his arm, our bodies pressed together. It's a clear night. The stars are visible, but I know we're only seeing a fraction of them.

"Everything okay?" I ask. His silence tells me it isn't, but I don't know what to say so I remain quiet.

Eventually, he says, "I like to look at the stars. It helps me feel calmer."

"Griffin was bad?"

He stalls and then replies, "He was Griff," without any more.

I can imagine and wait, because Tanner seems to be working out something on his own.

"When I was younger and my parents would fight, I'd climb out onto the roof of my house. It's the best place to go to look at the stars. Now, because I can drive, there's this special place I go when I need to cool off. The stars there are brilliant."

Silence surrounds us again like our shared blanket.

"I should take you." His arms tighten around me.

"You'd do that?" I'm touched he'd want to take me to his special place. I caress his arm under the blanket.

He turns toward me onto his side and slides down so we're face-to-face. His arms draw me closer, the weight of one of his hands on my hip. "Emma. I–" He stops and takes a giant breath. "I figured something out tonight."

"Yeah?"

He nods. "I don't know how to say it."

"Maybe just say it."

He rolls his head away to look at the stars again. He sighs. "I watch the stars because that's what I used to do with my brother."

"Your brother?" I didn't know he had a brother.

He looks at me again, and I can see his eyes are shining with tears. "Rory. He died. When I was ten. Cancer." The sky captures his attention again.

Oh shit.

Context.

My heart suspends and then collapses in on itself. "Oh, Tanner. I didn't know. I'm sorry."

He doesn't respond, but I feel pulled toward him again, as if suddenly I'm the tether holding him to the Earth. "Rory wanted to be an astronaut; he told me he was studying astronomy except he called it astrology instead." He sniffs a laugh. "He built these Lego spaceships and would talk about all the space stuff he was into. Mostly black holes." He pauses. "He was two years older than me, so I was his shadow. One of the things we'd do is make up stories about the stars. The shapes, the colors, the patterns they made. I don't know. We just made shit up." He runs a hand over my back, slips it under my shirt so he can touch my skin as if it's comforting, then makes gentle swirls shaped like galaxies with his fingertips on my lower back. "You know that bright star there?"

I force myself to look away from him, rolling my head so I can look up into the sky. He removes his hand from my skin so he can point. I follow his finger and maybe I can see what he's talking about, maybe I can't, but I'm not sure it matters. I say, "Yes."

"It's actually a planet. You can tell because it doesn't blink like stars. Twinkle, twinkle little star," he recites and then presses his lips to my temple. "Rory used to say that was the brightest of all stars because it was heaven. He said that God made it so bright, so we'd be able to see it and find it when it was our turn to go there. I'd asked him if you could get there on a spaceship. He told me that we probably could."

My throat closes up.

"He wasn't sick when he told me that story, not yet, but it wasn't much later that we found out he had cancer. We didn't stop laying under the stars though, telling stories. Did it as long as we could until he couldn't. He'd point to that bright star and tell me, 'when the time comes, Tanner, that's where I'll be. That's where you'll find me, okay?'"

Tears fill my eyes.

"And then he was gone. And I was alone."

I sniff.

Tanner looks at me and comforts me with his arms even though I'm the one who should be offering comfort. "That's why I like to look at the stars." He presses his lips to my wet cheek. "They settle me because I feel closer to Rory."

I'm thinking about that ten-year-old boy whose brother died and then whose parents exploded. Lost and floating. I wrap my arms around him. When I can find my voice, I say, "Thank you for sharing it with me."

"That's not what I wanted to tell you, though," he says. "I mean I did, but that's not what I realized. When I saw Griff earlier, I tried to tell him how I felt. He was so drunk and stupid. Said dumb shit. It made me mad. Since Rory, whenever I'd get angry, or hurt, or whatever, I would look for the brightest star to tell him. It felt like he was the only one who heard me. And even though I had Griff, we've never had that kind of relationship that I could tell him stuff.

"Tonight, though, it wasn't going to my spot that I thought about after getting into it with Griff. I didn't think about Rory and our star. It was you, Emma. I thought about wanting to see you." He smooths the hair off my cheek. "I wanted to tell you."

My heart.

I lean forward and press my lips to his, eyes open, and exert enough pressure that he rolls onto his back. His hands find my face, framing it. Then my eyes slip closed. I kiss him with my heart, not just my mouth and tongue. I want him to hear the words my heartbeat is saying. My hands on his chest, I can feel the urgent beating of his heart answering me.

His hands move to my hips, and he settles me on top of him. Straddling him, I seek a rhythm with my tongue, and he answers, one of his hands leaving my hip to find the back of my head, to wind his fingers in my hair there. "Emma," he murmurs and draws his mouth away, trailing his kiss along my jaw, to my neck.

I'm panting, unable to catch my breath, so moved, so rocked by his words, his stories, his kiss. I can't find the words to speak.

His hands move, roving like his mouth, returning to the skin of my back, the gorgeously calloused skin sliding up my back to the bottom of my bra. He finds the clasp. "Can I touch you, Em?"

"Yes," I say and feel the strap release. His hands hold me, mold me, offer a kind of praise, and then kisses to set me on fire. I moan something. Maybe his name. I'm not sure because suddenly he's kissing my mouth again, and I'm moving against him, his hands on my hips, helping me find a rhythm with our bodies moving in concert.

He sits up. Stops me. Holds my hips against him. "Em," he pants. "I'm — it feels so good with you. I'm going to lose it."

I want to lose it with him. I lean my head against his shoulder and try to catch my breath. I press my lips, my tongue against his neck. Tanner growls and lifts my head, cups my cheeks with his hands, and kisses me. It's urgent.

Suddenly, I'm on my back, and Tanner is heavy between my legs. He's kissing me like he's fire, and I'm the fuel to burn up. His hand slides from my hip to my thigh and draws my knee up so he can settle deeper between my legs. I know without a doubt, feeling his body there, I want to have sex with him. I've always wanted to, but before I thought it was just physical; now I know it isn't. It's because the wires of my heart have attached to him.

"Emma?"

I'm not thinking. It takes me a moment to register that he's spoken. "Yes?"

"When will your parents be back?"

"Soon."

He stalls and groans but doesn't move. His weight remains, a heavy sweetness that feels like a comforting blanket. After we've caught our breath, spend time touching one another and becoming breathless once again, Tanner adjusts, situating us back on the chair the same way we began, curled around one another. "Now, Emma. I know it's hard to keep your hands and mouth to yourself," he says. "But I'm going to have to insist."

I giggle.

"I'm going to tell you a story instead, since we can't see Kaleidoscope Concussion in the dark."

"I'd like that."

"See the purple star?" His fingertips stroke the skin of my arm.

"Which one."

"Choose one."

"Got it."

"That's where Queen Ella lives."

I shift my head so I can look at him. He's smiling. "Is this a different Ella from smart Ella and stupid boy TJ from the other night?"

"Yes, Emma. Obviously. She's royal." His eyebrows have drawn together, incredulous at my question.

I laugh again.

"Anyway, that's where she lives."

"Is there a King TJ?"

"No. A Knight."

"Oh. As in a Knight in Shining Armor."

"Well, his armor is a little rusty."

"Does Queen Ella help him polish it?"

"I can think of some things Queen Ella would like to polish on TJ, but it isn't his armor."

I smack him on the arm.

He laughs, kisses my temple, and then says, "Thank you, Emma, for being here. I've had fun tonight, with you."

I turn and kiss him, which leads to more kissing, more touching, more want, but also more laughter about Queen Ella and the Knight in rusty armor, TJ.

He leaves before my parents get home.

graduation

"For a three dotted ellipsis, I reached up and grasped the cosmos. It was beautiful, hot and burned, and for that moment, so was I."

-an unnamed protagonist, *Kaleidoscope Concussion* by Saul Annick

emma

I'm sitting in the front row, waiting. The red graduation gown feels like it's cutting off my air as I wait to be introduced for my speech. Adjusting in my seat again, I move so the gown isn't so tight against my neck. I draw the zipper down and realize it isn't the gown, it's my throat, because I've already unzipped it.

Don't freak out. Don't freak out. Don't freak out, I chant in my head. I look around, but no one is around to help me center myself. The lonely road to college stretches out before me. Alone. *Don't freak out.*

My phone vibrates under my leg.

I glance at it.

Tanner | Deep breath. You're going to be great.

I close my eyes, take a deep breath and smile. I type back: *How did you know I was starting to freak out?*

Tanner | Because you're you, and I can see you fidgeting from here. ☺

I shake my head, hoping he can see me, but I can't turn to look, because Principal Sanderson has just started my introduction. "Please help me welcome Bilson Preparatory Academy's Salutatorian, Emma Matthews." He steps away from the microphone and looks for me to walk up the stage steps.

I take a deep breath to calm my tripping heart, my legs trembling, and cross the stage. With another deep breath, I control the panic. *Ferris would own this,* I think. So, I imagine being Ferris. I jumped from the Rock. When I gaze out at all of the faces, I know my mom and dad and sister are here along with my grandparents. I take comfort in knowing that Liam and Atticus and Ginny are out there. I scan the sea of red caps and gowns for Tanner; I know where he is, but I can't see him. I smile so everyone can see, but it's really just for him.

"Somebody thought it would be a good idea for me — Emma Matthews — to give your salutatory address. I'm not sure what you were all thinking, but well, that's probably why I'm standing up here, and you're not."

(Laughter. Phew).

"Graduation has forced me to think about the future even more than my already slightly unhealthy preoccupation with it. But in reflecting about it, I have also had to consider my past. Moving on is like that, right?"

Just like with Liam in duo, the stage, the moment, the practice eases the presentation. I move through my speech hitting the marks with impeccable timing, gathering laughs, and offering words that I hope are thoughtful. As I near the end, I speak with animated confidence, but awareness that I've made a slight change, a change I hope Tanner notices.

"So, here's my final thought. Don't get stuck. Don't get stuck looking backward. You might miss out on something ahead of you. Don't get stuck looking forward. You might miss something beside you. Accept the present like the gift it is. Rip off that wrapping paper of the present and open the box to see what's inside every single day. If we don't, we might miss out on the opportunity to write a new story under the beauty of the stars. It's only when we fully embrace the beauty of now that we'll be able to truly live. So, graduates, here's to living."

My classmates cheer as I leave the stage, my legs quaking under my gown like I'd just jumped at the Quarry.

Then, just like that, after a couple more speeches and getting empty diploma cases, we are graduates, moving our tassels and throwing our caps.

Tanner finds me after. His graduation gown is unzipped over black chinos and a white shirt with a black tie. He smiles, his dark hair curling over his forehead. I'm surrounded by my family, but when I see him, my happiness goes nuclear. I run into his arms, and he folds me into his hug.

"Did you like it?" I say against his neck.

"Want to hear my favorite part?"

I nod.

"The part about the story and the stars."

I pull back to look at him. His eyes meet mine. "I hoped you would notice it."

Someone clears their throat.

Tanner releases me, and I twirl to see my family remembering they're there. They stand in a line watching what just transpired between Tanner and me.

I smile at them with a blush heating my cheeks. "Oh." I clear my throat. "This is my–" I glance at him, not sure what to say, so I go with– "friend, Tanner."

"Hello." He steps towards them, hand extended to my father.

"This is my dad, Mo."

"Mr. Matthews." Tanner's voice is deep and confident.

My dad, usually all ease and friendliness, looks more serious than usual, and takes Tanner's outstretched hand. "Nice to meet you. Congratulations." When his eyes meet mine, I beg him to be nice. I notice his eyebrows shift with his questions.

"Thank you, sir."

I ignore my dad for a moment and continue down the line. "And this is my mom, Amy."

My mom smiles, as usual, and hugs him. "Sorry, Tanner, I'm a hugger. Nice to meet you. Congratulations." She looks at me with an arched eyebrow.

"And this is Shelby, my baby sister."

"I'm not a baby," she mutters at me, and her face turns pink.

Tanner pauses. I notice it and imagine he's thinking about his brother. "Hi, Shelby."

She takes his hand, looking a little like the awestruck eighth grader she is. Dressed in a cute purple sundress and a matching headband to hold back the spiral curls of her dark hair, I can tell she is trying to appear cool. "Hey."

"And these are my grandparents, Pop Pop and Nana." They're both smiling like doting grandparents.

Pop Pop puts a thick arm around Nana and then slaps Tanner's shoulder.

"Congratulations." Nana shakes Tanner's hand.

Tanner smiles, which eases my concern that my family might be too overwhelming. It makes me wonder about his family. I glance around, hoping to get a peek, but he seems to be alone. When I look back, Shelby is staring at me with her giant blue eyes and a subdued smile. She wiggles her eyebrows and then fans herself with her program. I bug my eyes out, frown, and shake my head at her which I hope gives her a proper big sister: *I'm going to kill you if you embarrass me.*

"Where is your family?" My mom asks Tanner looking around for them. "We'd love to say 'hello.'"

"Oh," he says, drawing the sound out. "They left already." The way he says it — like it's a norm of all families — breaks my heart. It makes me wonder if they were ever here.

I notice my dad's brow squish together between his eyes. He glances at me. "We're having a celebration at our house after this. You're welcome to join us. As Emma's friend." He enunciates the word *friend*, and my cheeks grow warm.

Tanner's gaze darts to mine as though seeking permission.

I raise my eyebrows like a question, and then offer him a shrug and smile that says, *it's up to you.*

He nods. "Thank you. That sounds like fun." He hesitates a moment and takes a step away. "It was nice meeting you all. I should — let you–" But his words stall. "I'll see you later then, Emma."

I watch him back away, my heart fluttering that he wants to be with me. "Text me."

He offers me a nod and a smile — one I'm beginning to understand — that tells me a story even if I'm not sure I trust it; Tanner likes me. He turns and disappears into the crowd.

I look at my family.

Every one of them watches me with the same expression — one that communicates their amused curiosity. Their opened mouths curled at the edges like sideways apostrophes and wide eyes with high arched brows. It's my dad who says with his horrible impersonation of Dezi Arnez's *I Love Lucy* voice, "Emma. It looks like you have some 'splaining to do."

"Stop." I shake my head but then am peppered with questions about Tanner and that hug. I shouldn't be surprised. I've never brought a boy home other than going to prom with a boy I thought was just a friend — Chris "handsy" Keller. I've never even shared I might have a crush on one. Then again, why would I have? I've always crushed on Tanner.

"You like him, like him," Shelby says on the walk to the car.

I give her a sideways look and elbow her.

She looks at her feet as we walk across the parking lot and smiles.

"Why didn't you say anything?" Mom asks from behind me. "He's really cute."

"We're friends." Friends who make out and other stuff — but that's my business, not theirs. "What was I supposed to say? Hey family, I have a new friend named, Tanner. Here's his social security number." Add to that, *Hey, fam, here's the boy I like. I let him kiss my boobs.* Yeah. I don't see that going over well. My face heats thinking about the night before.

"Funny, Emma," Mom responds drolly. "That's not what I meant."

"We just like to be a part of your life," Dad says.

"Oh, bosh." Nana sideswipes the conversation. "You didn't tell me every little thing, Morton." Nana never calls Dad Mo. "You were a scoundrel who did your own thing. Emma's entitled to her secrets."

"Mom." Dad's tone holds a warning.

"Don't *Mom* me. Now that she's eighteen, I can say whatever I want. I followed your no-advice-unless-asked rule for eighteen years. And, this isn't about Shelby. You still have four years for her."

My mom snickers.

Nana, who's on my left, leans toward me. "He's a darling. Is he a good kisser?"

"Nana!" Shelby and I say in unison.

"Is he?" Shelby asks wide-eyed.

"Stop!" I climb into the backseat of the van and cross my arms. When everyone is inside and settled, I say, "I will tell you two things and that's it." I hold up my fingers. "One: I do like him. And two: I've liked him for a while. Now, don't be weird about it. Please."

"Ah ha!" Shelby points at me.

I grimace at her.

My dad has gone quiet, and somehow that's the loudest statement of all.

"I remember those *getting to know you* days," Pop Pop says and pinches Nana.

Nana flirty laughs and swats at his hand.

I sigh, drop my head into my hands. It's going to be a long night.

tanner

My phone pings a little while later, after I've left the school and parked my truck in the driveway at my house.

Emma
> I'm so sorry. They can be a lot. You were great.

The thing she doesn't understand is that I liked it — meeting them. It's the first time I've ever met a girl's family. Another first, I realize. I was nervous as hell, which was weird but not unpleasant. Then again, it made me a little sad too, seeing a family like that. Happy. Involved. Invested. They make sense, knowing Emma.

Mine couldn't even be bothered to show up.

I text her back:
> It's all good. They're nice.

Emma
> Hurry! I can't wait to see you. ;)

> Matthews are you flirting with me? ☺   Me

278

Emma

> I'll be right there. Me

The house is empty when I walk in. Surprise. Surprise. I drop my keys in the dish, and my phone pings again. I smile, thinking it's Emma and look at it.

Griff > Where the fuck R U? Party time!

With a shake of my head, I set the phone face down on the counter and leave it there. I don't want to see Griff. Just seeing him at graduation without so much as an acknowledgment of his idiocy the night before leaves a bitter taste in my mouth. What had he said from our seats? *Still being a bitch about last night, T?* He's clueless, or he's being a jerk off on purpose. I'm not sure which is worse.

I take the stairs two at a time, shower, and dress before starting down the stairs. Then, I stop and go back. I brush my teeth again, double up on deodorant, add a splash more cologne and grab a long sleeve flannel in case we're outside later. With my wallet in my pocket, I return to the kitchen just as my mother walks in. She's dressed in her real estate power suit, bright pink skirt, black on the top. She must have been at work.

"Where are you going?"

"Going out." I move around her to grab my phone and my keys.

"Don't you have dinner or a class party for graduation?"

"No. You have something planned for tonight you didn't mention?" I don't look at her. I know she doesn't.

She's silent.

I look over my shoulder at her.

She narrows her eyes. "Did your dad show up to graduation?"

"Why do you care?" I ask. "You didn't. If you had, you'd know."

"Tanner." She sighs and puts a hand on her hip. "You know I can't be around him and his mistress."

"Wife."

"Semantics. He said he was going."

"Well, I guess he didn't want to be around you and your new boy-toy, either. Neither of you were fucking there."

Her mouth drops open. One more thing she can blame on him, I guess, instead of taking responsibility for her own choices.

"I guess you were both too busy with your new toys."

Then she presses her lips together, and her eyes turn sharp.

"Yeah. I know all about Bradley. He called the other day, and I took the message. What? He didn't tell you?"

She sets her shit on the island. "Tanner–" she starts, but I interrupt her.

"Here's the thing, Marna. You have a funny way of being a mom."

"What the fuck is that supposed to mean?"

I shrug. "You figure it out." I start out the door to the garage.

"Tanner! Get your ass back here."

I turn on her, so angry I could break something. "You don't get to tell me what to do. Ever. When you start acting like a mom, then I might listen. Until then, I don't want to hear shit from you." She looks stricken, and I should feel bad. She's my mom, after all, but she hasn't acted much like one, so I don't. "You lost one son only to lose the other. The saddest part about it, I've always been here."

I slam out of the house, my throat bunched up in knots. It's hard to swallow it down as my eyes feel like they're being pierced with needles.

"Tanner!" My mom comes after me.

I ignore her and drive away. The emotion moves through my muscles in tremors. I pull over because I can't seem to see straight and reach to turn my radio up in order to quiet the roar in my head. It isn't working. This is the first time I've ever said that to my mom, even if I've thought about it. Maybe it was poorly done, but the boiling pot of anger inside me overflowed.

I lean my head against the headrest and close my eyes. There aren't any stars to help me settle, there is only the picture of Emma at graduation in my mind. There's watching her walk across the stage. Her speech. Her reference to writing stories under the stars which I know was specifically for me. For Rory. Seeing her after — her excitement to see me. My heart expands, and the rest of me cools off. When I'm calmer, with a deep breath, I pull the truck back onto the road and drive toward her.

A call comes through my car, and I forget to check before answering, thinking it's probably my Mom. Maybe my dad. Maybe Emma.

"Yo!" Griff yells.

My muscles tense. "Griff."

"Come pick me up. There's a party at Marcus's."

"I got something."

"What the fuck? Your parents put something together?" Disbelief mars his voice.

"No."

He's silent as if measuring the information. "Don't tell me you're going to see that prude, Matthews."

"Griff. Wasn't last night enough? Don't."

"Don't what? Tell the truth? She's not your type, T. I know your type. You're going to get bored, bro. Listen, you just need to get your drink on with me and get some fresh box."

"Naw, bro." I enunciate the word bro with as much sarcasm as I feel.

"Matthews must be putting out then, and if she's that good..." Griff laughs as if thinking about it. "I've heard stories about the nerdy ones. Maybe that's why you're spending all your time with your new toy."

My anger surges again, especially at his disrespect of Emma, but also in the wording. I'd just said something similar about my parents. I hear Josh in my head: boundaries. "Griff, you're pissing me off. I'm not in the mood."

"Shit, Tanner. I didn't know you cared about her." He laughs like what he's said is the biggest joke.

But I zone in on his words: *care about her*. My anger dissipates like steam and my chest tightens with something else. Well of course, I care about her, I'm not — I'm about to think *a dick*, but then that isn't true. I have been. I've been selfish and used girls as much as they've used me. I may have made sure everything was reciprocal, but had I ever cared about anyone other than myself?

The timber of Griff's laughter wanes. "No wonder you're acting like a bitch."

I don't have the patience to listen to his insults. "Have fun, Griff." I hang up on him. If Josh were with me, he would look at me sideways and say something about wimping out. I know I need to set boundaries with Griff — to tell him what's what — but it feels like a waste. Besides, his words have me thrown.

Care about her.

I knew I cared about her in one way, but now there's added nuance to the concept I hadn't considered. Feelings deeper than just liking her. Feelings, perhaps, I've never felt before.

When I finally park the truck in front of Emma's, I'm churning with a concoction of excitement, trepidation, anger, and confusion. I'm anxious to see her, but Griff's words are blended with my anger at my mom and dad and disappointment in myself. I wait to get out of the truck, hands on the steering wheel, breathing to find some balance. *Care about her.* He'd said it like he'd tasted something nasty. With several deep breaths I reset myself. Emma is the one good thing in my life.

I get out of the truck.

The house looks different in the daytime, but then it's probably because I'd been so nervous to meet her family the day before, I couldn't see straight. It's a two-story house painted yellow with white shutters and trim and a porch swing. A white picket fence surrounds the pretty greenery of a manicured yard like a picture frame. The property looks like a family of dolls lives there. It isn't far off.

The door opens before I can knock, and Shelby's on the other side of a screen door. "Hi," she says. She smiles, keeping her lips closed over a mouth full of braces. She's so endearing with her curly hair, her deep blue eyes and fair skin. I'm reminded of Emma in 8th grade.

"Hi, Shelby."

Her cheeks shift from a normal pink to a darker shade, and she pushes open the screen door. "Emma's in the back with Nana and Pop Pop. I'll show you."

"Thanks." I follow her inside.

Shelby leads me past the living room and into a hallway which I know leads to the great room at the back. The house is lived in — cozy and alive — so different from the museum where I live. This is what I would want, though the thought pushes me into another loop of this roller coaster I'm on. Considering I didn't ever think I'd want my own family, why would I want a family house? As we move through the hall, I slow to study the pictures hanging on the wall. Last night, I couldn't take my eyes off of Emma. Now, I look for little Emma in the family photos, school photos.

"This way," Shelby calls, drawing me away.

In the bright daylight, the open French doors lead to the deck in the backyard where I laid with Emma the night before. The backyard is outlined with tall trees. Emma's dad stands at a grill at one end, and her grandma sits at a table looking out into the yard.

"Hello, Tanner. Welcome," Emma's mom says from the kitchen.

"Hi, Mrs. Matthews. Thank you for inviting me."

"Of course," she says. "Drinks are in a cooler on the deck. Emma's outside."

"I told him that, Mom," Shelby says, the teenage impatience clear in her tone.

Mrs. Matthews gives me one of those tight smiles, but it isn't angry like I might see from my mom. More like one that communicates an inside joke. She turns to get something from the refrigerator.

I follow Shelby out onto the deck.

"Emma!" Shelby yells. "Tanner's here."

Emma, standing in the grass with her grandpa, looks up. My chest tightens, and my breath catches. She looks so pretty in her blue sundress that makes her eyes look even bluer. Her dark hair is down, and her curls are loose ringlets; she usually pulls it into a messy bun, which I like just as much. She smiles, and I think she must be the sunshine.

You care about her.

Standing there, with my breath caught and my heart stalled, looking at her, then feeling the happiness at seeing her move through me, I realize I do. I care about Emma Matthews, but it's heavy with more than I'm able to acknowledge.

"Hey! Come play with us." She holds up a croquet mallet.

I meet her in the yard, and Pop Pop hands me his mallet. "You youngins play. I'm going to go get a glass of lemonade and sit with my beautiful bride." He winks at me.

I turn to Emma. "You look very pretty," I tell her. I swallow, uncomfortable that perhaps I sound like an idiot. I can imagine an insult from Griff: *When did you grow a vagina, T?* But I realize when I tell her this, I'm just being myself. It's my heart reaching toward hers. Does that make me less of a man, somehow?

She smiles and blushes. "Thank you."

Contentment settles around my ribs. I lean on the mallet toward her and say just for her, "I really, really, really want to kiss you right now."

"I really, really, really want you to." She leans toward me.

"Arm's length at all times," Mr. Matthews yells at us from behind his barbecue. I straighten. Emma rolls her eyes. He chuckles.

I'm not sure what to make of it. Is he serious? Joking? I don't kiss Emma. I don't know what she wants. Besides, we have an audience, and I don't want to mess up my chance to make a good impression. "I don't know how to play this game," I tell her, though I'm talking about more than the game.

"Really?" She doesn't believe me.

"Really." This isn't a game someone plays spending all of their time with friends trying to get laid. I don't say that, however.

"Okay." She steps closer. I can smell her clean scent, like soap and flowers and sweet all mixed together. Her arm brushes mine as she points. "The object is to get the ball through all of the wickets and hit the stakes first. You can attack someone else's ball and send them out of bounds, but don't do that to me."

"Don't listen to her, Tanner," her dad calls out from behind the barbecue. "She's super competitive and will cheat."

I arch an eyebrow at her. "Cheat?" I smirk, tilting my head.

"Dad! You lie," she yells. Then to me she shakes her head, her eyebrows drawing together. "Don't listen to him."

"Listen to him, young man," Pop Pop calls from the deck with his glass of lemonade. He's standing at the railing with his arm around Nana. "She just beat me twice by moving the wickets." He laughs.

Emma puts her hands on her hips, mallet hanging from one, and glares at her dad and grandpa. Then she looks at me — all sugar — blinking slowly. "Not true."

I can't help but grin. "Okay. I guess we'll see." I do not trust that to be 'not true.' Sure enough, I catch her trying to move the wickets a bit later. "Hey!"

She laughs, drops the metal hoop, and dodges my chase. I pick it up and put the wicket where it was. "There will be no cheating, Ms. Matthews, or you will owe me a forfeit."

"Is that an edict from a knight in rusty armor?" she asks so only I can hear her. It makes me smile. "I'd like that forfeit," she whispers.

I hit my ball through the designated wicket, and it stops, resting against her ball.

Her eyes grow with warning. She shakes her head. "Don't do it."

I walk toward her with deliberate slowness. Then, without taking my eyes from hers, set my foot on my croquet ball, and smack it with the mallet. Her ball rolls off through the grass and into the trees at the edge of the yard where it disappears down a slope.

Her family laughs behind us.

She looks at me with wide eyes and an open mouth, fighting a smile. "I can't believe you did that!"

I grin at her.

She turns and stomps down into the trees.

"Emma!" I call after her.

"Oh. I wouldn't want to be him," I hear Pop Pop say as I follow after her.

"Oh really? I think that appears to be a perfectly designed

play," Nana replies behind me; it makes me smile.

I follow Emma down into the trees as Pop Pop laughs, the sound fading behind me. "Emma?" I call. It's darker in the trees, the light filtered in the dark green of the deciduous leaves and pine.

"Here."

I follow her voice, because I still can't see her. My steps crunch through the debris on the ground, and I round a group of tree trunks.

She grabs me and pulls me close. "Oh. My. Tanner. That took you long enough."

Her mouth fits against mine, hungry, and warms up my insides. When my surprise makes way for the desire I've repressed all afternoon, I fully participate, backing her up against a tree.

"Emma," I say against her neck, kissing all the beautiful skin presented in her amazing sundress.

She's breathing like she's run a race, and her hands are in my hair. She pulls my mouth back to hers.

I groan and kiss her with every moment, hope, and dream pent up inside of me.

Her hands rove over my back, kneading the muscle, and her hips meet mine.

My blood is on fire.

"Dinner!" echoes in the distance through the trees and brings me back to reality. Her family is a hop, skip and a jump away.

I open my eyes; my gaze connects to hers.

She smiles, her mouth still pressed to mine.

Then we're both laughing as we untangle ourselves from one another and fix each other's clothing.

We find the croquet ball and walk back to the yard.

I realize sometime later, after Emma cheats me to win the game, that I'd forgotten all about my anger at Griff and my parents the moment I saw her standing in the yard. The moment she turned to look at me, her smile hit my heart, and everything else slipped away.

emma

We eat on the back deck, the seven of us. It's perfect. Mom strung garden lights and set the table in Bilson Prep red and white. My dad grilled steaks. Nana made her famous lemon bars. And Tanner is here. Tanner is next to me, his hand wrapped around mine under the table, and every cell in my body attunes to him.

We tell stories. I'm embarrassed by a few. Tanner loves them, glancing at me with crinkled eyes and a grin every so often.

We laugh.

Tanner helps Shelby and me stack up after the meal, but mom and Nana shoo us from the kitchen, telling us to enjoy the warm June evening. Shelby hangs out for a little while but then goes in to talk on the phone with her friends. Pop Pop and Dad join Nana and Mom in the kitchen leaving me alone with Tanner.

Finally.

We stand out in the yard insulated in the dark though golden light from the house reaches out toward us. He wraps his arms around me, leans down, and kisses me so the world stops rotating. It's a sweet kiss — different and mixed up with something else. It's a kiss that tells me a new story I can feel. I want to hear it, too.

He holds me against him. My ear pressed to his heart, I listen to its steady rhythm, and it gives me life as if it were my own heartbeat.

Everything feels perfect.

Too perfect.

I'm too happy.

But I know that can't be true; nothing is perfect. Fear creeps into my mind, and my chest tightens. "Tanner?" My voice sounds small in my own ears.

He hums a response.

"Tell me a story?"

He leans back and looks at me. "You okay, Em?"

"Too much thinking." I shake my head, hoping to shake the doubts away.

He resettles me in his embrace, and his hands caress my back. I listen to the beating of his heart and the way his breath moves in and out of his lungs in a rhythm. I think that must be what the ocean sounds like though I've never been. Soon enough.

Don't think about it, my heart tells my brain.

"Back to TJ and Ella then," he says, the reverberation of his voice vibrating through his chest into my ear. He tells me the story of Ella who wanted TJ so bad that she lured him into the forest with her magic spell and then attacked him.

"That's not what happened." I have a flicker of guilt, but when he laughs, it effervesces away.

"Oh? It isn't?" His hands swirl across my back. "You tell it then."

"I concede. You're right. She did."

We go quiet, but I continue to listen to his heartbeat. Its steady rhythm mixed with the movement of his hands is the perfect potion and relaxes me.

"What are you thinking about?" he asks, breaking the silence. I can hear that his smile is gone.

"I'm not... it doesn't matter."

"It does. To me."

I squeeze him tighter but don't offer a voice to my fears. We've been seeing each other for a week — I'm being foolish. I knew I wasn't supposed to get feelings for Tanner James, but that is exactly what I have done. The truth is, those feelings have always been there, only now, they've developed into something more permanent. The red wire. Tears press against the back of my eyes. I don't want to scare him away. I don't want this to end, and I know it's headed toward me leaving for college in a matter of weeks.

I swallow down the words, the tears, the fears. Hadn't I just told my classmates not to miss what was next to them by looking too far ahead. It's how I'd been living my whole life. And now, I'm in the arms of an incredible man, and my fears want to lose sight of it.

"May I take you somewhere?" he asks.

"Where?"

"A surprise."

"Yes."

We return to the house where my mom, dad, Pop Pop, and Nana are playing cards. "Tanner and I are going to go for a drive."

Nana discards a card in the pile at the center of the table. "Is that like going *walking* when we were young?" Nana looks over her reading glasses and wiggles her eyebrows. She pats Pop Pop's hand.

"Nana," I warn her and give her a kiss on her cheek. I work my way around the table stopping next at my grandpa, kiss my mom, and reach my dad.

He's looking at me over his glasses, reminding me of Nana, only he's serious. His usual playful humor is gone. He glances at Tanner. "Cars and graduation night are worrisome."

"You have my word that she'll return home safe, sir," Tanner says.

My dad's eyes skip to me. "Be smart," he says and then tells me he loves me.

I kiss his cheek.

"You better get a sweater," Tanner says, looking at my bare arms as we walk down the hallway.

I leave him in the entry and go to my room to grab his sweatshirt from Senior Send Off. I draw it over my sundress. Then I reach for a blanket but stop. My pulse speeds up. It feels like a decision. One easily wrapped up in fear. One I need to conquer by taking the leap into the dark. One I want. With Tanner. I snatch it up and leave my room.

Tanner waits, his hands in his pockets. He looks up at the stairs when he hears me walking down, and smiles. My breath catches in my chest; there's so much emotion coiled up inside of me. His eyes drop to the blanket in my arms, and then jump back up to my face. A story passes between us; it feels like the same one.

I look at the blue and pink fabric of the blanket and then back at him. "I wasn't sure if we'd need it."

"It's always good to be prepared." He's serious, no joking in his tone.

We leave the house, my hand in his.

He opens the passenger side door to his truck for me and then climbs in on the driver's side.

We talk about nothing of consequence as he drives through town. Graduation. Memories. Twenty questions. Tanner's favorite color is blue. His favorite food is pizza, which according to him should have all the meats. He thinks my desire for vegetable pizza is rubbish. His favorite music is anything that makes him feel something. His biggest regret, he pleads the fifth, which I say is against the rules. Then he calls me a rule monger and says I should break them more. This shuts me up, because I know he's right.

Eventually, the lights of town disappear behind us. The dark road stretches ahead of us. I ask, "Where are we going?"

"I told you; it's a surprise." He reaches for my hand. "I like to drive," he tells me. "So, I've discovered lots of places."

"We're going to one of those?"

He nods. "My favorite."

I realize we're going toward the Quarry and recall what he'd told me the night before. I glance at him, my heart swelling when I realize he's taking me to his most important spot. We're going to look at the stars. He turns the truck onto an access road where we climb through the trees until they thin out. The truck bounces over an expanse of plateau. When we get near the edge of the Quarry, Tanner turns the truck, reverses it so the truck bed faces the drop off, and parks.

"Bring the blanket. And when you get outside, look up." He leans over and kisses my forehead before getting out.

I climb out the passenger side of the truck. I hear Tanner open the tailgate, and I look up. If Tanner's smile captured my breath earlier, this cracks open my chest allowing all of the awe to fill me. The sky is brilliant. It sparkles with the ether of gasses, galaxies of planets, suns and stars; a myriad of colors swirling like purple and blue sequined velvet. "Oh my," I say, releasing the breath I'd been holding. *This*, I think. *This is where God is.*

I hear the crunch of gravel under Tanner's shoes as he walks toward me; he stops by my side and looks up at the sky with me. "When you said you wanted a story, I thought of this place." He bumps my shoulder with his. "It's top secret. You're the first person I've shared it with."

My eyes burn with tears. The beauty. His thoughtfulness. Him. "It's so beautiful." When I'm able to, I look at him. "This is the place you talked about last night."

"Yeah." He takes my hand in his and leads me to the bed of the truck. Then he helps me into the back and climbs in after me. "Here. The blanket." He reaches out to take an end.

We lay it out together and settle ourselves on it, laying side-by-side on our backs to stare up at the sky.

The night is heavy with anticipation, with what isn't being said, but my mind won't quiet without saying them. "Tanner?"

"Yeah, Em?"

"Thank you for bringing me here."

"You like it?" he asks. There's a thread in his voice that sounds insecure. I've heard it before; the night we jumped. *It was good right?*

I reach over and take his hand in mine. "Yes, Tanner. I do." I squeeze his hand with mine and turn to look at him.

He watches my face, measuring my reaction. Then he smiles and returns to gazing at the sky. "Ready for a Star Story?"

I return my gaze to the brilliance overhead and revel in the moment. In the feeling of how small I am, but how big this moment is. At the feel of Tanner next to me and my hand in his. At how perfect it all feels. At the sound of his voice, and the texture of the blanket pressing against my legs. Everything is bright despite the cocoon of darkness around me. I'm struck with the realization that this is what I have been missing — the life I'd avoided out of fear. I've been missing out on moments. Jumping from the Rock. Sliding across a sleeping bag while kissing ferociously. Receiving roses and smiles and kisses that imprint the heart. Kissing in a bookstore. Letting go in a pool. Being so hungry for connection, kissing in the woods. With Tanner, I've lived a lifetime. If I'd had them sooner, maybe I wouldn't appreciate them like I do right now. Perhaps I'd have thrown them away. Maybe now is the right time. The understanding fills me up. I swallow and then say, "I'd like that."

"Are you sure? Wouldn't you rather we just make out?" I hear his grin in his voice.

I look over at him. "I would like that too."

He hesitates. When his eyes float to my mouth, I think he might kiss me, but then he looks away. His thumb continues its steady rhythm back and forth over my skin.

"Can I ask you something?"

He clears his throat. "Anything for you."

Usually I can hear the smile in his voice, but for the moment, it sounds serious. I'm nervous to say what's on my mind. How quickly we're moving, but how it doesn't seem strange in my heart because he's always been there. If I think backward in time, it's a truth. Even before junior year when I planned *Operation Kiss Tanner James*. He's been inked into the soft tissue of my feelings like a tattoo. A compass rose pointing to my heart, like Tanner's.

The doubt about my inexperience and my ability to understand my feelings has me mistrusting myself and insecure. Books, tests, academic stuff, speeches, I can do. This is real life, and I've been standing on the sidelines while everyone else has waded into the deep.

"Emma?" he asks when I don't finish my thought.

"I'm trying to figure out how to say it."

His dark eyes are shiny even in the darkness. "Why do you have to figure it out?"

"I'm nervous."

"Why?"

"I don't — I've never — I just–" But I can't get any of the words out that are sitting in my chest. The red wire is wrapped up like a coil that's strengthening the way I feel about him but wrapping me up in it too, tense and insecure. This is Tanner. He's a party boy. He understands and has lived. He's brave and free.

And he's with you now, my inner voice says.

He rolls onto his side toward me, releasing the hand between us and putting his other hand on my stomach. "Now you're making me nervous."

"Are we moving too fast?" I blurt. I struggle to look at him and keep my eyes fixed on the sky above, looking for the brightest star.

"Do you feel like we're moving too fast? For you?"

I cover my face with my hands. "No. And I'm confused."

"How come?"

"Because I'm not supposed to feel this way; my feelings are so big."

"Feel what way?" He sits up on an elbow and looks down at me.

"I'm afraid."

"Afraid of what?"

Of not being good enough.

Of making a mistake.

Of being wrong.

I can't say any of them, because they're all lodged in my throat which has suddenly swelled with tears. I cover my face again as the tears leak out of the corners of my eyes. "Everything."

"Emma." Tanner pulls my hands away from my face and draws me into his arms, rolling to his back. "Talk to me."

"I'm always scared." I sniff and hide my face against his chest. "Always. Scared of messing up and disappointing everyone. My whole speech was a crock of shit."

His hands move over my back, pet my hair over and over, offering comfort. "Naw. It wasn't."

"I'm terrified of living in the now. Look at me, Tanner. I'm crying in the back of a truck with the most amazing guy because I'm afraid! I have all these feelings for you, which seems strange because we only just started talking, and what if I scare you away? What if I get this wrong?"

Tanner's hands continue to offer comfort, but he doesn't say anything right away, until he says, "I'm scared too, Em."

I sniff again and then look up, my chin on his chest so I can see him. "You are?"

"Yeah."

"How come?"

"You asked me what my biggest regret is."

I nod and swipe at my cheeks to wipe the tears away.

"It's watching you walk away junior year. It's shutting down how I felt about you then and wasting all that time, because I've never felt for anyone like I feel about you." He looks at me and offers a tentative smile. "But it's like — I'm not supposed to or something."

"Why?" His words surprise me.

He sighs and runs a hand over my hair again. "Because you're awesome. You're going places, Emma. I'm not. I'm stuck here — in bullshit, small-town America — a dead-end. It's why I let you walk away. I don't have the right to feel like I do about you, because I'm messed up. I've made terrible choices." His touch cascades over my head, alighting all my nerve endings. "But, you're always on my mind. You're the one I want to talk to. You make me smile and feel happy and hopeful all at the same time."

His words crash against me, hearing them but feeling them as they empty out like headwaters into my heart and aligning it with my brain. I reach up to press my hand to his face. "I've liked you for a long time, Tanner. Long before kissing junior year."

He turns his face and kisses my palm. "Same."

"Really?"

"I've been thinking about you, Emma, since eighth grade when you told Cole Butler he was a Neanderthal. Or whatever it was you called him, because he was trying to fuck up the dissection."

I laugh and float toward the stars, but I'm not looking at them. I'm looking at Tanner, leaning against him so I can watch him. He's watching me. "You see that star four quadrants over from the pinkish swirl?"

He smiles and nods.

"There is a girl who lives there, in that galaxy. She's been flying around in a ship all by herself."

"How? Is it small?"

"Yeah. Pretty small." I use my finger to smooth a lock of his hair off his forehead.

"It would have to be, to operate it by herself."

"Well, she has a pretty good computer system."

He nods and tucks a strand of my hair behind my ear.

"Well, the computer system failed, so she had to crash land on a planet." I lay back down next to him so I can look up at the stars. Now I'm nestled in the crook of his arm. "Anyway, she was terrified because she didn't have any survival skills. She'd just been on her ship with her computer. Now, her ship was broken, and she had to venture outside."

"How did she know she could breathe?" Tanner asks.

"Well, she ran diagnostics before she landed."

"Convenient and smart." He squeezes me against him.

"I told you she was smart, right?"

"No."

"Well, she's super smart. As she ventures out of the ship, though, she realizes that being smart isn't going to be enough to survive."

"It's pretty good though, right?"

"Sort of. But if she doesn't believe she can do it, then maybe she won't survive."

Tanner rolls toward me and leans up onto his elbow to look at me. "Emma. You're going to survive. It won't matter what you do."

"She had to leave the ship," I tell him, keeping to the story. "She took the risk to leave it, and then met this... alien boy."

He smiles. "Hmmm. An alien?"

I glance at him and return his grin. "Yeah. An alien who she'd studied but realized she didn't know anything about. And he helped her. Helped her find her way."

His smile fades. "Emma," he says quietly and leans toward me.

My heart moves in my chest, thumps with new awareness, new wants, and races ahead of me. I know I won't be able to catch up. I can't speak anymore, so physically aware of Tanner leaning over me. I hum a response.

"I really want to kiss you."

"Please," I whisper. I reach out and pinch his t-shirt to pull him toward me.

He leans down. His kiss is tender; unspoken words that linger around us in the bright moment. Feelings neither of us seem able to adequately express. It doesn't matter because the kiss says everything we need it to.

Tanner presses a palm against my cheek, his fingers interwoven in my hair near my ear.

His touch makes me shiver.

He pulls away and looks at me. "Are you cold?"

I shake my head. "You just make me feel all the stars — inside." I lay my hand against his chest, over his heart.

He makes a throaty growl— "Oh damn, Em" —and kisses me again, but this time the kiss is different. Hungrier. Wider mouthed, more insistent. I've rolled toward him. He adjusts his body, our legs wrapped up with one another, so it isn't clear where he begins, and I end.

"Oh my god. This sweatshirt." He tugs at it. "I want to touch you."

I help him take it off.

With his hands on my hips, he rolls onto his back while we kiss, and draws me with him so I'm draped over him. My legs framing his hips, my summer dress fans around us. I can feel his arousal against me, and the sparks shooting through me are perfect. I sink against him and moan into his mouth. "Tanner." I say his name like a wish. "I want... closer."

His hands clasp me against him as he sits up. His kiss undoes me.

"Em. God. This feels so good." His voice is threaded with the breathlessness I feel.

I tilt my head as he trails his tongue across my skin. He draws a strap of my sundress down and kisses one shoulder and then the other. I remove my arms so I can grab his face and bring his mouth back to mine.

He kisses me and unzips my dress, freeing me, and his hands find my breasts. "Em, I've dreamed about you." He dips his head, and his tongue moves against my skin like nobody's ever has before. I moan and arch my back to be closer to his hands, to his tongue; my hands are immersed in his hair.

He rolls me onto my back and whispers against my skin, "I want you so fucking bad."

My insides flex and melt. I stop thinking.

He settles between my thighs.

The dress, his clothes, barriers between us. I pull his shirt off, and he shrugs out of it.

Hands on either side of my head, he holds himself and looks at me. "You're so beautiful."

But I think he's beautiful. The moonlight sculpting the ridges and planes of his body in shadow and light. I run a hand over the plane of his abdomen to his belt and begin to unbuckle it.

He stops me, a hand over mine, and searches my face. "Is this what you want?"

I stop and force my mind back into gear. The gears grind as they begin moving again. Is this what I want? The answer is yes. I have wanted this with Tanner for so long, but it's changed. Before, when I wanted uncomplicated sex with Tanner, I thought I wanted the experience, but it isn't the experience I want anymore. It's Tanner. I want Tanner. The red wire is connected to my heart. "Yes," I tell him. "I want you, Tanner. All of you."

He lets my hand go and allows me my way. I remove his belt, unbutton and release his beautiful body from the confines of his clothing. He helps me take the rest of my sundress off and everything else, until all we are is the truth exposed to one another under the brilliant sky.

I feel God looking down on me, but I don't feel His censure. I don't feel His judgement or His conviction. *Am I supposed to, God?* I wonder. There are all kinds of desires wrapped up in me, and I know I'm supposed to be at war with what my flesh wants over what my soul does, but I don't feel like I'm split in two. I feel like I'm just a whole being.

I shiver again.

Tanner covers me with his weight. "Emma. Are you okay?"

"I'm scared."

He freezes. "Emma, you decide. If you want to stop, you tell me. I'll stop. Okay?"

I shiver again. "Are you okay?" My body is high, moving at the speed of light, and I can't control the adrenalin that has me shaking.

"I'm more than okay, Em," he says between kisses. His hands touch and fill me with their worship until I'm hot beneath him. "I'm flying." The tension of him is rigid against the softness of me. He eases his body away, so it isn't as insistent, and then kisses me. "Emma? Are you still afraid?"

I'm terrified, but I'm more terrified of the regret I'll feel if I don't jump. I have spent years regretting not being braver. "A little."

He searches my face. "You're sure?"

Adrenalin pulses through me, and I shiver again. "I want this, Tanner, with you. I want this memory, forever, like jumping from the Rock. I want to hold your hand and jump into the dark."

My words do something to him, awaken something more in him, because he kisses me again with ferocity. "Do you trust me, Em?" His voice sounds raw and full of emotions I can't name.

"Yes. I trust you."

He trails kisses from my mouth over my chest and down my stomach until he settles between my thighs and kisses me intimately at the core of my gender. And his mouth does things. Slippery gorgeous things that make me climb, but I don't know where I'm climbing. I just keep going, because he's leading me there, and my hands feel lost without him, so I grab a fistful of blanket, and I'm making sounds I didn't know I could make. Until I'm at the side of the cliff at the Rock looking over the edge.

Tanner moans against me, "Let go, Em." Just like in the pool. Just like at the partner jump. "I've got you."

And suddenly I jump and am calling out his name as I fall. And he's up with me, sheathing himself in a condom. "Emma? You're still sure?"

"Yes, Tanner. Yes." I take hold of him and pull him toward me. He pushes his sex into me. It feels strange but perfect, like the missing puzzle piece of myself is finally put into place. Every part of me stretches around him, my legs wrapping around his hips, my arms around his torso, my head fitting in the space between his neck and shoulder. I relax. I feel. I love.

He's holding himself up and away, waiting, and then moving. Our mouths meet briefly before finding the need to catch our breath. But I can't find it, because it's moving through me so quickly. In and out like the rhythm of our bodies together. I'm sliding in pleasure until I'm climbing again, but this time holding Tanner. And the sounds excite me — his subdued sounds — as if he's holding back - and my sounds. Together, we are a symphony.

"Oh god, Em," he breathes.

"Jump with me, Tanner," I say, because I'm standing at the cliff's edge again.

"Emma. Emma." He chants my name with his breath until he can't. Until he can't hold himself up anymore.

And then we fall, which is actually like flying.

tanner

"Emma." I breathe her name, drawing out the 'uh' sound. It's all I can do for the moment, but fuck, that was incredible. Amazing. I'm tired, completely satiated and content. Depleted. I roll to my side drawing her with me, holding her tightly as though she's too good to be true and might effervesce into the universe leaving me alone.

I've never experienced something so emotionally heady and physically satisfying.

Another first.

And she chose me.

My heart swells and at the same time it constricts with both pressure and fear.

I squeeze her tighter.

"Oh my. Tanner." She breathes my name.

My Tanner. I know this isn't how she's said it, but I slip into it. I like it. I like her.

"THAT'S what I've been missing? Holy shit. That was like…" Her voice fades.

I lift my head to look at her even though it takes work. I'm exhausted, and content to stay right here with her in my arms, but I need to know.

I want to know if she was as affected by the experience as I was.

She shrugs her shoulders and wrinkles her nose, "Eh." She turns her head to look at me and smiles.

I wrap us up in the blanket like a sushi roll. "Just an *eh* then?" I smile — eyes closed — and slide my arm around her waist to keep her against me again. I know for a fact that wasn't *eh*; I worked hard for that outcome. My throat constricts. Her first time. She chose me. She's chattering about it, and I like having her in my arms, her skin against mine. Her voice talks bubbles.

"Yeah." She's wide awake. "I think I will have to try that again. You know, to make up for the *eh* quality. Maybe it was just because it was the first time. Then again, maybe I need another partner for comparison."

I squeeze her tighter, so her words cut off. "Don't even think about it." Then I wonder where the possessiveness came from; that's new.

She giggles.

I feel her turn in my arms so she's facing me, but my eyes are closed so I revel in the sensation of touch and physical connection. Her legs slide through mine and her arms wind around me until all we are is an entwining of limbs and two bodies pressed together. I smile at her with my eyes still closed.

"Tanner?"

My eyelids peel apart so I can look at her. She looks so beautiful. Her dark hair a shadow poured out around her. Her eyes shiny orbs in the moonlight.

"You know I'm kidding right?" She reaches up and caresses my eyebrows with her fingertips. My nose. My lips.

"I hope so," I mutter, enjoying the feeling of her touch — her attention. I'm enjoying everything about her: the sound of her voice, the texture of her laugh, the way she tells me stories. Like the story of the girl in the spaceship — her star story — for me. I hold her tighter and notice a panicked feeling tighten my chest. Everyone I have ever cared about has left.

"Are you tired?"

I dismiss the thought, content to focus on the moment. On the now, with her. "What gave me away?"

She goes silent, but I feel her kiss the skin near my collarbone. She releases her hold and rolls away.

I moan in protest. "No. Come back." I reach out for her and lay my hand on her belly.

"I want to look up at the stars while you sleep." Her hand is on my arm, her fingertips tracing lines and circles.

"Tell me another story," I tell her, though the first one moved me to kiss her when I'd vowed to be a gentleman. I'd driven up here thinking about what her dad said as we'd left: *Be smart.* All I kept thinking about was how being with me wasn't smart. And then she'd shared what she'd shared; *I have all these feelings for you... I've liked you for a long time.* I lost all ability to think clearly.

She chose me.

I picture her outside of the Revolution last January, the loop that changed my trajectory: her laugh. Raising my hand. Her smile. Her wave in return.

She's quiet for a while, and I drift into the loop until I'm sinking toward sleep. The idea of sleeping with her here is appealing, and unnerving. I've never wanted to do that before — I haven't done that before. I fall into it, darkness sparkling with stars racing up around me, and I float.

Then, though I'm not sure how much time has passed, she says, "You asleep?"

I grunt at her.

"Once upon a time there was a princess — no, a queen — named Ella," she says. "Ella was a very foolish queen who felt the only way to be safe was to lock herself up her tower. One day, while she stood at the window looking out at her queendom watching all of her subjects enjoying their lives, she realized she wasn't very happy. She'd spent so much time in her tower trying to control everything that she'd trapped herself there.

"Then, one day, she left. She ventured out, still afraid, but weary of the tower. Along came a beautiful prince."

"King," I interrupt with a smile and pinch her side. I like the smooth velvet of her skin under my hand.

"It's my story, Tanner." She moves and kisses my mouth before returning to her position looking up at the sky. "Fine. Along came a beautiful king named TJ, and he invited her to…"

She stops.

I open my eyes.

She smiles. "Skydive."

I laugh, though it's muted and subdued, and close my eyes again.

She rolls toward me, because my hand slides across her belly and then rests on the curve of her waist where it meets her hip. "And skydiving was the best thing Queen Ella had ever done in her life, but she decided that it was because of King TJ."

She shifts and presses her mouth to my cheek. "King TJ was kind, you see." Her hand, on my back, moves in soft circular motions over my skin. She kisses one of my closed eyes. "He was funny and made her laugh." She kisses my other eye, and the skin of her body against my chest sparks fires in my belly. "He was encouraging so that Queen Ella didn't feel so afraid." She kisses my nose and then my bottom lip. I'm now fully awake in all areas. "And he was sexy as fuck."

I run my hand from her waist, over the swell of her hip, around to cup her against me.

"Oh," she says with surprise since I'm hard again and pressed against her belly.

I take her bottom lip in my mouth, release it and say, "King TJ decided he needed to show Queen Ella that Skydiving wasn't just *eh*."

She laughs.

I kiss her, silence the laugh and wrap us up in desire. She's got me wound up tight and feeling so many feels I don't know what to do with them. This — her and I — is so farfetched. It doesn't make any sense, but it has happened. I care for her, but it's more than that. New emotions move under my skin when she touches me. They speak in the flutter of my heart when she says my name like a prayer. I feel them in the church of her body. I sigh. I sigh. I let go of all the pain, and hurt, and drop the walls. I sigh. "Emma. Please, Emma." I hear myself — this vulnerable wanting is something I've been looking for but didn't know I needed. Until now. This isn't Tanner the f-boy with Emma. It's just Tanner the man. I want her. All of her. I want her heart.

She's sighing, mewling, making noises that hit me deep with craving.

My heart races. And I can't go slow anymore. In a frenzy that's wrapped up in all these new sensations, I roll her onto her back and go with her where we both want to go.

After, she's the tired one, and it makes me smile. She's curled up in my arms, and my heart suddenly aches because I remember she's leaving. I swallow the ache for now. Be in the now, I think. I saw a speech on the internet about that one time. The speaker spoke about intention, and it makes me wonder about my intentions. I've never thought that far before.

I've thought about my own pleasure. I've thought about giving it and receiving it. I've thought about feeling anything else other than the constant hurt that presses in on my body. I look at her and swipe a lock from her face with my fingertip. But now. This is nothing about using her. It feels like the world finally makes sense. I wonder why it took so long for me to see it. How many minutes, hours, days, months, years I've wasted not having Emma a part of my world. I need her in my life.

"Tanner?"

"I thought you were sleeping."

"Resting. I don't want to waste any of my moments with you," she says, giving voice to my thoughts. It's disconcerting being on the same wavelength.

I kiss her cheek.

"May I ask you a question?"

"Yup."

"Earlier, today, you seemed sad."

"Yeah. I got into it with my mom."

She opens her eyes and turns her face. "They weren't there today were they." She says it as a fact.

"They weren't there today."

She sits up, and the blanket falls. She turns to look at me. She is a beautiful, naked goddess. I'm struck first with how gorgeous she is and second that she chose me. Me!

"What?!" she says, and her arms fly out to her sides. "I can't believe that!"

"Don't worry about it."

She sits in the pool of blanket. "You don't deserve that, Tanner. You deserve the world."

I sit up just as she's shrugging into my sweatshirt. She crosses her arms.

I draw the blanket up around my shoulders and around Emma, who's facing me. We are cocooned together. I pull her into my lap. "Your family was the real MVP. And truthfully, Em, this has been the best day of my life."

She smiles and drops her cheek to my shoulder. "Mine too."

I kiss her.

She smiles under my lips. "How will we ever top this? There's a lot of life left to live."

"I bet we can find a way," I tell her, but even as I say it, fear hits me like a bullseye in the center of my heart. A clock just started to lose her. Everyone I care about leaves.

emma

I don't exactly sneak into the house, but I'm not walking in the front door like I usually would either. I'm not sure why I feel like I should sneak into my own house. When the screen door creaks, I freeze. I tell myself it's late, and everyone is asleep. I'm being thoughtful. The truth, though, is that I want to hang onto that Tanner afterglow which makes me smile and warms me inside out. I don't want words to ruin it, to remind me that I'm imperfect.

I push in through the door, the screen squeaking behind me as I catch it before it slams.

The hall light upstairs comes on and claws at the darkness downstairs.

I close my eyes and sigh.

"Emma?"

My mom.

"Yeah?" I lock the door and start up the stairs.

"Goodness. It's late. What time is it?" I hear the sleep in her whispered voice.

"I don't know." I reach the top.

She's standing with her arms crossed, her sleep shirt bunched up under them. Her dark hair is fluffy and messed up from sleep. She's squinting as she looks at me. "You're just getting in?"

I can't hide it and am not sure why I'd think I needed to other than the whole don't-have-sex-until-your-married thing. "Yes." I wonder if I look different. I feel different.

"Where did you go?"

"The Quarry. Stargazing." I hold her eyes with mine even as guilt moves through me like a storm cloud trying to hide the warmth of the sun.

Her eyes assess me. "Are you okay?"

"Yes." I wonder if she knows.

"You want to talk?"

"Not really," I tell her. I don't see judgement in her eyes or hear it in her voice, but the question is there. I can feel her wondering, but she doesn't ask.

She makes a noise. "Well. I'm insisting. Go put the water on in the kitchen. I'll be right down."

"Mom." I say it with impatience, but maybe the tone of my voice doesn't exactly match how I'm feeling either.

"Emma. Not a negotiation." She turns and disappears into the room she shares with my dad.

I retrace my steps down the stairs, turn on the light above the sink and the stove to keep the light to a soft glow, and flip the switch on the electric kettle. I don't wait much longer before she walks into the room wrapped in a sunny-colored robe and her hair pulled up into a bun. She walks to the cupboard, pulls two mugs, and brings them to the island where I'm sitting.

She stands at the end of the island so we can see one another. "So."

"So." I offer her a stool so she can sit.

"I want to know more about this boy. Are you surprised I'm curious? And now that you're walking in well past curfew, I think asking questions is a parental obligation."

"So lawyerly, Mom."

She smiles. "Well?"

The tea kettle clicks, signaling the water is ready. I get up to avoid having to look at her and retrieve the tea cache and the water. I'm sure the moment I talk about Tanner, she'll see the truth written all over my face. Even as I think it, I realize perhaps if I'm ready to have sex, I should be ready to acknowledge it, though I'm not sure it's anyone else's business.

"I've liked Tanner a long time."

"I know. You told us that in the car after graduation. Why is this such a surprise then?"

I deposit the tea on the counter and pour hot water into our cups. "Did you tell Granny everything?"

"No. I didn't."

My eyebrows raise over my eyes as I replace the kettle. "And you regret you didn't."

"No. I don't regret a thing." She unwraps a tea bag — lemon zest — and dunks it into the water. "But I'm pretty sure Granny knew what was up." My mom's gaze rests on me. "I didn't know there was a young man. It almost feels like a lie of omission."

"I wasn't lying. There just hasn't been anything to tell." I won't tell her about getting drunk junior year but decide I can allude to it. "I've liked him for a long time; we had a tiny thing during junior year, and we just started talking again."

She hums a noise. "Thinking about Granny, I can see now how she might have felt being left outside the loop of my life."

"Are you sending me on a guilt trip?"

She chuckles. "No. Just making an observation, though I'm particularly good at those, having lived through quite a few of them." She looks at me with a smile. "I said that because having met this young man, who is obviously important enough to take you—" she pauses— "stargazing, I just want you to know I'd like to be on the periphery of the loop. I'll always be your mom, and I want to be there for you as you move onto the next phase of your life."

I choose chamomile.

With her hands around her mug, she stares into the cup. "I know,

Emma, that at some point you are going to begin making choices for yourself that your dad and I aren't a part of." She looks up. "That's a normal part of life."

It's my turn to stare at the tea in my cup and grasp the tag to swirl it around in the water. "Are you talking about sex?"

"That, among other things, I suppose. You're going to college soon. I don't ever want you to feel like you can't talk to me. Sometimes those adult kinds of decisions can be confusing, and I want to be there to help you."

"Did you and dad have sex before you got married?" I look at her then.

She nods. "Yes."

I can't meet her gaze. Not because I'm embarrassed about her and my dad, but because I'm terrified she's going to say something that might convict me about the choice I've made. I feel it like a steel trap. Fear climbs up onto the stool next to me and grabs hold. "Are you going to tell me that you wish you hadn't?"

"No."

My eyes shoot to her face.

"I know that perhaps I'm supposed to tell you that we should have waited until there was a wedding. There are people who do, and I applaud their choice, but that wasn't the choice I made with your dad. Do you think less of us because we didn't?"

I shake my head, my chest opening up and air rushing in making it easier to breathe. "But all that stuff about remaining pure and sins of the flesh. It's confusing."

"I don't have an answer about that, Emz. We can read the scripture and take it for face value. Perhaps your dad and I were wrong for not waiting, but we're long past worrying about that. Truthfully, one thing Granny taught me was to own my choices and stand by those consequences without making religion a part of it. I had to look at my actions and align them with my faith. Maybe that's backwards. Maybe it isn't. Whatever choices you make is between you and God. Not you and me or your father or anyone else." She takes a tentative sip of her tea.

"You know what I'm saying?"

I nod and take a deeper breath.

"Your dad was a bit of a mess after you left." I must give her a confused look because she chuckles quietly. "I'm not sure how he's going to handle when you leave for college. Or when you begin making choices that scare him."

I hear what isn't said between her words.

"I like Tanner. He seems nice."

I blush. "I really like him. Like really, really like him."

She makes another knowing humming noise that moves through her nose. "That may complicate things, yes?"

I nod.

After tea, we both go upstairs, and she stops me in the hallway. My mom draws me into her arms. "I love you, Emma. Always. No matter what." Her hug is a reinforcement of her love, her unconditional acceptance of who I am right in that moment. I'm not sure why it makes me want to cry, but for some reason my throat closes with unshed tears. She draws back, looks at me, runs her hand over my hair, and kisses my forehead. "Goodnight."

When I close the door to my room, I lean against it. I look around the dark space, the moonlight outside shading the usually white and pink room under cover of shades of blue. My girlhood is in here, but I feel different. Changed. It isn't like a huge change, like I'm suddenly a woman or something. I feel like the same me but awake somehow. King Solomon's awakening. I think about what happened with Tanner and smile, but then worry creeps in along with a voice that says: *you're no good.*

I shake my head. It's a lie. I could hear it in my mom's voice. My mother who made empowered choices for herself. My successful amazing mother who loves me no matter what.

My phone buzzes, and I draw it from the front pocket of Tanner's sweatshirt. It's Tanner. I can't help but smile.

tanner

Emma texts me back: I wish I was with you.

I can't keep the cheesy smile from my face and send her a bunch of emojis. Then text her: *I'll call you after I shower?*

Emma   Yes

I take the stairs two at a time. Once I'm in the shower, hurrying through my routine, I can't keep what happened earlier from my thoughts. It makes me hard again, so I relieve myself. Emma. Emma. Emma. I rinse, dry off, and brush my teeth. Emma. Emma. Emma. My heart is floating, and when I catch sight of myself in the mirror, my smile slides. Emma is leaving. My heart pops and deflates into its normal position.

Once I'm in bed, I glance at my phone, but don't reach for it.

I'd said I'd call her. I want to call her, but I'm uncomfortable. These vulnerable feelings wrapped up in a box given to me by Emma. The survival Tanner — the after-Tanner — who spent my adolescence keeping my heart protected — suggests I run. Mostly, though, there's the before-Tanner, the one who was buried with Rory, who wants to see whatever is happening with Emma through, even though I know it's going to hurt. The before-Tanner wants back out. I think of Griff: "Let's make a pact. We protect one another at all costs. Bros before everything. Bros before hos."

My phone lights up.

A different choice. I reach for it.

Emma | Ready?

I press video chat.

She answers and smiles. I notice how pretty she looks, freshly showered, her dark curly hair wet. The sight of her makes my chest seize up and fill with desire. "Hey." Her voice is sexy.

"I needed to see you. Is this okay?" I ask.

She nods.

"I wish you were with me, too." It's true. Her presence calms the doubts and the fears at odds with the new version of Tanner inside of me.

She settles down into her bed, her dark hair a stark contrast to the light pillows. "And we just saw each other." She holds the phone above her, and I think about earlier, the same view, only I was buried in her, wrapped tightly in her body. My insides start recalling the memory.

I can't think about that and adjust myself against the backboard of my bed. Suddenly, I'm unsure. When it comes to the sex part — the physical — I've had lots of practice. I know how to make a woman comfortable, to make her feel pleasure, but this emotional stuff is outside of my comfort zone. I'm way out of my league. There haven't been many opportunities for the aftermath of sex. I haven't stuck around, haven't wanted to. Every experience has been transactional, now that I think about it. I'm looking at Emma, wanting so much to be everything she wants and needs, and knowing I'm not. The uncertainty and insecurity I feel isn't something I've faced before. Fuck.

"What?" she asks.

Had I said that aloud? "Huh?"

"Why did you swear?" The little line is between her eyes.

"Sorry. I didn't realize I'd said it out loud."

"Something wrong?"

I can hear the fear in her voice. I'm messing this up. This girl — this amazing and wonderful girl who makes me feel all of these new feelings I didn't know I could — chose me to be her first. Here I am, swearing and tripping over my tongue. "No. It's me," I say even knowing it's going to make me seem stupid and insecure. I don't want her feeling bad. Ever. "I don't want to say the wrong thing."

"Why would you say the wrong thing?"

I shrug. "I don't know."

She smiles, the worry line disappearing, and I want to have sex with her again. "Now look who's overthinking." She rolls to her side taking the phone with her. "What are you doing tomorrow?"

"Work. I help my dad prep the trucks for Monday. You?"

"Church, and we always have my grandparents over for dinner. Want to come? To dinner?"

"Yes."

"Want to fall asleep with me on here?" she asks.

"Yes," I tell her.

She moves. The lamp on her side of the call goes out. I can still see her face illuminated by the screen when she settles back into her pillows.

"You want to spend the night one day?" I ask her.

"Yes." She smiles, her eyes closed.

I slide down into the sheets.

"Tanner?"

"Yeah?"

"Thank you for tonight. It was perfect."

There are words that spring into my thoughts. Three words I'm not sure I'll ever be able to say. Instead, I tell her, "Let's try to make every day perfect." I recognize these feelings sitting in my heart and mind aligning things, as if the railroad tracks are coming together to change direction again. I'm afraid of them. I wonder what it is about Emma, always inspiring things to shift inside of me. It happened junior year, again in January, and now it's happening again. I'm not sure I'm ready or equipped to go on this journey, even though everything in me wants to. I'm terrified, because I know whatever the outcome, this is going to hurt.

part two

countdown: 5

"I felt the little bombs inside my blood getting ready to explode. Except now, instead of just hurting me, I'd leave behind collateral damage."

– unnamed protagonist, *Kaleidoscope Concussion* by Saul Annick

emma

I slide my employee card through the computer and clock out. Second shift down at Java House, and working isn't so bad. After grabbing my stuff, I cross the dining room to Ginny who's sitting at our usual table on the dais in the corner by the window. She makes a pretty picture bent over her phone with the exposed brick wall as a backdrop. Her head rests on her hand, propped up by her elbow on the table as she swipes a finger across the screen.

"Is that Josh Tate's Instagram page?" I ask over her shoulder and slide into the chair across from her holding my hot mocha piled high with whip cream.

She flips her phone over. "I don't know." She shrugs. "Could have been. Just scrolling."

I narrow my eyes. "You're being evasive."

She blushes.

I smile. "Are you interested in him?"

She changes the subject while looking at her iced Matcha Tea. "I'm dying you know. A freaking cryptic text? What the hell?"

My face heats. She's right. The text was cryptic, but I couldn't tell her over a text.

"Oh my god." She laughs. "How far?"

I press my fingertips to my hot cheeks and can't help but smile. I lean forward. "The whole way. More than once."

Her mouth drops open, and her hazel eyes widen. "What?" She reaches across the table to feel my forehead.

I swat her hand away and laugh. "Stop."

"Good?"

I fan myself and nod because putting the experience into words is impossible. I haven't stopped thinking about the heat of what I'd shared with Tanner. It makes me hot all over again and needy. A little guilty, but not as much as I might have thought. The talk with my mom had been surprisingly helpful, but I had wondered when walking into church the next morning, if God might strike me down with lightning and reduce me to a pile of ash on the sanctuary floor. He hadn't. Instead, I sat in the pew with my family like usual, listened to the message and missed Tanner. The only thing that changed was me. While Tanner and I have spent time together since, dinner out, milk shakes and fries at Marta's, movie night at my house with Shelby, we haven't had sex again. The thought of it happening again makes my heart inflate and then deflate, sputtering around my chest, losing air with hope and longing.

"I'm so happy for you. I love that it was–" She stops suddenly. "You were safe, right?"

"Of course."

She takes another sip of her tea and then frowns. "I'm jealous. My first time sucked." She sticks out her tongue. "Who am I kidding? Every time Dean and I had sex, it sucked."

"How come?"

"Let's just say," she holds up her finger, "One: he didn't know how to use his equipment; two: I was too shy to speak up to tell him how and what; and three: he didn't care much about my needs over his own." She puts the three fingers she's holding up in my face. Then she shakes her head and takes another sip of tea.

I blush thinking about how giving Tanner was. How comfortable he made me. "So, you've never had an orgasm?"

"Oh sure," Ginny says. "Just not with Dean."

I laugh, and the coffee I just sipped comes out my nose.

"I had to take matters into my own hands, so to speak."

I'm choking on my coffee now, laughing so hard at Ginny, who loves it.

When I get it under control and wipe things up with a napkin she asks, "Okay. So. What is it then — between you two?"

I swallow and then frown. "I don't know. We haven't exactly defined it." I run a napkin over the table, even though it doesn't need it.

She nods. "Friends with benefits?"

"I don't think that." The thought diminishes my happiness. "I hope not." I realize I need to talk to Tanner about what we are, at least for myself.

Her mouth drops open. "Oh. You have feelings for him?"

I cover my face with my hands, spread my fingers, and peek through them. "Yeah."

"And him?"

I take my hands away from my face. "He hasn't said. But Ginny, what he does say..." These words arrive on a breath of air.

Her look — mouth thinned out and eyebrows drawn together — reminds me what I need to remember. This isn't Tanner's first rodeo. It's mine. "Emma. Be careful."

"Be careful about what?" Liam draws a chair up to the table and plops down between Ginny and me, setting his plain cup of black coffee on the table.

Ginny presses her lips together and motions, locking them.

Liam's blue eyes dart from her to me, and his eyebrows rise over his eyes with surprise before shifting into a question. "With James?"

Again, the cheesy grin spreads across my face, and I look at my mocha.

Liam sighs.

"Was that a judgy noise?" I ask him, defensive suddenly.

"No. It's a worried one."

"What the hell? Both of you. I'm freaking happy, and you're sitting there looking at me like I just told you someone pushed your Ferrari out of a window."

Liam reaches across the table and covers my hand with his.

I snatch my hand away. "No. You don't get to be all judgmental of me and my choice and then offer me comfort."

"Is that what you think?" Liam asks.

"Aren't you? Of Tanner?"

He looks down at his cup and remains silent, which to me is confirmation.

I glance at Ginny who watches me with knowing eyes. "You're right." She nods. "It's judgmental."

"He's never been anything other than respectful and kind to me."

"I'm sorry."

"Me too." Liam looks at me.

I offer them a nod of acceptance. "I understand you don't want me to get hurt. I don't want that either, but I walked into whatever this is with Tanner with my eyes open. I wanted this even knowing that I will leave for college soon." I also know that it's probably going to hurt like hell when I do, but I don't say this. I don't want to give them more to worry about. Truth is, I might be worried too, about feeling so much for him. I'm exposed and in over my head, but I like the way I feel about myself when I am with him. Brave. Fun. More.

They look away from me, back to their beverages sitting on the table in front of them.

"I get it," Liam says. "Like me dating Atticus when we'll be on opposite sides of the country. It doesn't make a lot of sense." He runs his thumb over the handle of his mug, and then adds, "Right now, what does make sense is that things with him are cool. He's really fun to be around, and nice to talk to. I feel like a more complete version of myself when I'm around him, but it isn't because of him, you know?" He looks up at us, his gaze bouncing between Ginny and me. "It's because of me, and how I feel about myself in my own skin when I'm with him." He pauses. "That probably sounds stupid."

"It doesn't." I sit in Liam's explanation rolling it around in my brain.

320

Being with Tanner makes me feel happy. I like the way he makes me feel, but then, sitting here, wondering what we are, it slips away. I question my worth again, my value, what I have to offer him, but these aren't things I can tell my friends. Maybe they would understand, but how can I explain it when I don't exactly understand it myself.

Ginny gets one of her grins laced with playfulness. "The more important question is: how good of a kisser is Atticus Baker, Liam?"

Liam smiles. "I knew you couldn't hold out for long." He chuckles and then blushes so that his ears turn red. "Good, if you must know."

Ginny and I squeal with excitement.

tanner

Work — the stuff I have to do for my dad in the office — sucks. It's not that I mind the work. I like seeing the effort of my labor. Probably one of the reasons school and I didn't get along. I like seeing progress immediately. Load and unload a truck: progress. Carry, deliver, and stack: progress. Sweep a dirty floor until it's clean: progress. Build a wall: progress. On the other hand, sit: boring. Study for a test, take it and guess how you did: a waste of time. But Sam put me in the office today. I'm sitting at a desk looking at plans and learning how to do a material take offs. Reading them is pretty straight forward, but it's so boring measuring line after line with repetitive counting. I'd rather be out on the jobsite, moving. Besides, my dad is in the portable office with Sam for a meeting, and I'd rather be anywhere else, away from him.

Seeing him for my usual Sunday routine prepping the trucks had been hard enough.

Initially, my dad hadn't been in the warehouse when I opened up; I thought maybe I'd dodged having to see him, but he'd arrived with little Will in his arms after I was on the forklift partially done with the first truck. Of course, as soon as Will heard the forklift, my three-year-old half-brother started yelling for me, pudgy arms raised. "Nanner! Me. Up.

Hold me!" I stopped the forklift so Will could climb into my lap and pretend to drive. With a sideways glance, I could see my dad shift on his feet, cross his arms, as if he wanted to say something, but I left my earbuds in because I didn't want to hear his excuses. I handed Will back to him and continued loading the truck more angry and bitter than before. I'm not jealous of Will, but I can feel the envy of what he gets from my dad like an infection in my system. My dad was that man with me a long time ago too, before Rory died. After I finished with the trucks, he began to say something, but then stopped, unsure. I made an excuse about having plans — which was truthful, because I went to spend time with Emma. I didn't stay to hear him out.

Now, I lose count.

Start over.

I keep having to recount because my mind wanders to Emma and having sex with her after graduation. I can't stop the loop moving through my mind over and over. The way she looked in the moonlight. Her ire at my parents. Her laughter. Her kiss. Then I have to measure a stupid line again. My mind wanders over her body. The way her skin felt like moving my hands through water; the sound she made when she was nearly there; the brightness in my chest like I'd just accomplished the most important task ever. I'd felt like Leonidas of fucking Sparta. It makes me smile thinking about her, now. I want to do that again with her.

Soon.

Shit.

Start the count again.

My dad's shoes make a hollow sound as he walks across the floor from Sam's office, and his voice bounces around the portable. "Okay, then. I'm headed back," he tells Sam.

"I'll keep you posted on that change order," Sam replies, and I hear him slip out of the office door to go back out to the jobsite.

I don't look up. I measure instead and start the count. I can see my dad out of the corner of my eye. He's dressed in his president-of-the-goddamn-company suit. Emma slips away from my mind, unfortunately, because I can't keep her there and the anger at him in the same space.

"Um–" my dad breaks the silence I have no intention of breaking–"things going okay, Tanner?"

"Fine." It's all I'll give him.

He sniffs. "Look, I'm sorry about graduation."

I look up at the paneled wall in front of me, away from the plan, and stall to take a deep breath.

"Could you look at me?"

I do.

He must not like my look, because he runs a hand through his hair. I resemble my dad more than my mom. The dark hair, brown eyes, and the height. He pinches his nose and then releases it. "I should have been there."

I look away. What am I supposed to say to that?

"Your mom called, hysterical, and said she's worried about you."

"When isn't mom hysterical?"

He scoffs and then waits several beats before saying, "Well, the point is that, whatever you said to her, pushed her to call me for help."

"A first."

He walks across the room and pulls out a chair next to me.

I remeasure a goddam fucking line.

"I've screwed this thing up, I'm afraid… being your dad."

You could say that again, I think, but I don't say it. Instead I say, "I don't want to hear it."

I see him look down at his hands. "Fair enough. I was hoping maybe — if you still haven't decided about what's next — maybe you'd think about joining the company. Learn to run it. It's why I asked Sam to put you at a desk today."

I turn to look at him. I wonder if he can see how perplexed I feel. "You think that? That I want to learn to run your company?"

"Kind of hoping. I won't be around forever."

"You should give it to Will."

"Will has a lot more time to decide. He's only three."

"Is this your way of trying to buy me off?"

"Is that what you think?"

Yeah. It is. "It's what you've always done. Give money to Mom. Hand me cash."

"I didn't hear you complaining."

"Really? You didn't hear me ask to be with you? Rejection got old, Dad. It's pretty clear that asking for time with you and getting payoffs instead is what you were willing to give me."

"That isn't fair."

"It isn't?" I dare him to tell me different with my face, a hard stare pinning him down.

He doesn't try to. Instead he looks down at the floor. His hands are on his knees, and his arms extended.

My throat closes. I know why. "It's because I look like him. Isn't it? Every time you look at me, you see him." My voice breaks over the last word, and tears fill my eyes.

My dad's eyes snap to my face, and he shakes his head as if to deny it; he even opens his mouth, but no sound escapes. His eyes grow heavy with emotion, and he clears his throat.

He can't deny it.

I stand up. "I don't want anything to do with this company." The words contain no fire, as if the sun is shining and we've only laid out a picnic to enjoy in the park. I set down the pencil and the tape measure I'd been using on top of the plan. "I don't want anything to do with you." I tell him, turn and walk from the trailer out the door.

I hear his footsteps scramble after me. "God dammit, Tanner. Get back here. Let's talk. I'm trying my best, here."

I keep walking and don't look back. Even if I had stopped to look back, I wouldn't be able to see him through the tears. Instead, I get into my truck and drive off the site, leaving him standing at the door of the trailer, his hands on his hips and his head bowed.

I drive, and drive, and drive. I wait at red lights, move at green ones. I turn on the blinker and turn left; I turn right. I don't know where I'm going. I want Emma. I consider setting my course for her house, but I don't want to give her any of this shit. I consider going to the Quarry, but it will make me think of Emma and the other night. It will remind me how much I want her and how dangerous it is to allow someone that much power over you. I don't drive there. I don't want to go home. Josh is working. Danny is doing stuff for his recruiter. Griff.

The thought of Griff cuts me in half. A part of me wants to find my brother, lose my hurt in the relationship we've cultivated the last four years. The other half knows that what I want isn't there. He's proved it over and over, and yet I still turn the truck toward his house, unwilling to look too deeply at the choice to seek comfort in the one place I've been trying to remove myself from the last six months. I park in front of Griff's house, a single-story 1950's ranch-style track house in need of paint, walk the sidewalk to the door, and knock. I'm just about to leave when I hear someone thumping around inside. I look at my watch. It's almost noon.

The door opens.

Griff is dressed in basketball shorts, slightly crooked, his white chest in need of sunshine. His light hair stands up on end. "What the fuck, dude? It's like the fucking crack of dawn." He turns and disappears into the darkness of the house inside.

I open the screen, which creaks, and walk in. "Actually, it's lunchtime."

"What are you doing here? Now, I'm good enough to hang with?"

"Why? You butt hurt?"

He walks into the kitchen ignoring my question. "You on a break, then?"

I follow him and lean against the countertop.

He's got the fridge open with one hand and holds the back of his neck with the other.

"I walked off the job."

He looks at me. "Whoa. Really?"

I nod.

"Your pop is going to be pissed."

"He knows."

"Want to play Duty, then?" Griff gives me the depth I expect.

326

I wonder why I'm here. The normalcy of being Griff's friend? Only it hasn't felt normal for a while. I hear Josh in my head and recall the need to clear the air about what happened before graduation. Now is the time to talk to him, draw those boundaries. He's my friend, my bro. He deserves that. So do I. "Sure."

An hour later, Griff and I are still killing shit with video game remotes from his couch. This feels normal with the stupid, meaningless banter and helps me forget what happened the night before graduation with him, with my mom, with my dad for a little while. The moment I realize it, however, I recognize the truth. Griff makes me forget, helps me run away. This feeling is temporary, because the moment I get back into my truck and drive home, it will all come rushing back.

"Dude! What the fuck. I said to go right!" His phone chimes. He looks at it, sets it down, and resumes playing. "Danny texted there's a party at the Quarry Friday night. Bonfire. Wanna go?"

I do. I don't. I think about Emma and wonder if she'd want to go. "Maybe."

"Fuck, Tanner. You didn't even show up at Marcus's. What the fuck is up with you? You're acting like a bitch."

"Stop, Griff." I press the controller and take out a sniper.

Griff's character moves in front of mine on the screen and uses a wall to shield him from enemy fire. My character is behind his. The character steps out and gets shot.

Then he says, "I'm not the one who's trailing after smarty-pants like she's a bitch in heat. I'd never drop my boys for a chick."

I slam the control onto the table and stand. "Shut the fuck up." My fists are clenched.

Griff glances at my hands and leans back on the couch. "Why are you being so effin' sensitive?"

I turn and walk to the door, afraid if I don't put more distance between him and me, I might throw punches. Pinching the bridge of my nose, I turn around and look at him. "I thought we were friends. You were the closest thing I had to a brother."

"That hasn't changed." He crosses his arms over his chest. The action strikes me as insecure, but I don't get caught on it, too focused on what is on my mind.

"Yeah. It has." It's my turn to cross my arms over my chest. "You've been acting like a dick for months."

"Well if I'd known you'd get your panties in a wad, I would have talked to you more like a lady." He laughs.

I turn away and slam out of the house.

Griff yells at me from the door. "Come on, Tanner! I'm just kidding."

But I don't respond. I don't go back and smooth things over. It's no use. Talking to him was never going to work. I get into my truck and drive away, feeling sick to my stomach. It feels like I've let go of the cliff, and I'm in a free fall.

When I park the truck, I'm sitting in front of Emma's house. I don't even know if she's home, but she's the only one I want to see. I grab my phone to text her, but I see movement from the corner of my eye, and Emma steps out onto the front porch.

I climb out of the truck and walk around the end.

She's smiling.

I'm not.

Her smile fades. "Tanner?"

I climb the steps, stopping a few steps below her, and then I lean forward and rest my head against her shoulder. I can't speak because if I do, I'm afraid I might lose it. I don't want her to see me like that. I don't want to infect her with any of this shit, but I don't know where else to go, what else to do.

She puts her arms around me, and it feels like maybe the fall stops. I wrap my arms around her and hold on as though she is a life raft in the middle of the ocean.

"Come," she says and takes my hand. She leads me into the house, up the stairs where there are more family pictures lining the creamy yellow walls, and in through a door that leads to a bedroom. She shuts the door, and I sit on the edge of a fluffy bed covered in plush white and pink bedding pushed into the corner of the room under perpendicular windows. I can't appreciate it, however. I bend forward, elbow to knees and rest my forehead in my hands.

Emma sits down next to me, and the warmth of her hand heats the skin of my back through the t-shirt. She slides it back and forth across the fabric.

I swallow words, because I don't know what to say. I haven't said anything right today. I'm afraid to break what's happening between us, because I don't have any tools to understand what to do with this vulnerability. But the feel of her hand moving across my back fills whatever I'm needing, cracking open my heart to let the hurt I'm carrying inside out.

"What is it? Is there something I can do?"

I glance at her, embarrassed for the tears pressing against the corner of my eyes. I lean forward, and she wraps her arms around me. "I can't talk. I just need you."

There are different kinds of wanting, I'm learning. I'd always thought needing and wanting were wrapped up in physical packages satiated by the meeting of two bodies. But with Emma's arms around me and her strength to lean into, I begin to understand wanting in a different way. In comfort. In the acceptance when I can't hold myself up anymore. And I realize, this — what Emma is offering — is what I have been looking for, I just didn't know how or where to look. I'd been wrapped up in the Bro Code, thinking that was it.

"Lay with me," she says.

She crawls onto the inside of the bed between the wall and me. I remove my boots and face her, laying on my side. When she situates herself, I draw her against me, connected, but quiet. Her arms are around me, mine around her; we're entwined, and I take her comfort. Eventually, I drift toward sleep. My mind cuts off the hurt and confusion and succumbs to the safety of not being conscious.

Sometime later, I wake up cocooned in the safety of Emma's room as the golden light of a setting sun filters through the windows. Her room is warm. Fairy lights are strung around her bed, and pictures of her friends — Ginny and Liam — and family hang on the walls. It makes me sad that there are none of us because of how important she suddenly is in my life. It's as though she's become a sun around which I'm revolving. It's frightening to allow someone that much power, because I mostly know what it feels like to be a lonely satellite lost in space.

Emma faces me, asleep, her head tucked against my chest. I feel better but weighted with more than I'm able to manage.

I move a lock of her dark hair off of her face. She looks so pretty and peaceful, and it makes me feel better seeing her this way. Relaxed. Her light skin, the sprinkle of tiny freckles on her cheeks and nose look soft. The long lashes of her eyes fan her cheeks. Her rosy lips are full and relaxed as she sleeps. It's the first time I've noticed how perfectly heart-shaped they are. I have the urge to kiss her but don't.

I'm still working through what's on my mind and heart. Facing these things is a struggle because my impulse has been to run away from the strength of these feelings. Feelings hurt. I think about my parents. Their anger and bitterness toward one another. The way they cut and maim with words. They ran. Or Griff with his emotional unavailability and painful sarcasm. I'm not sure how to handle where I've been, where I am, or where I'm headed.

Emma moves, drawing my attention back to her. A hair falls over her face again. I sweep it aside with a finger and watch her wake.

Life presented me with opportunities to see and know Emma. 8th grade, different classes, at school in the hallway or the cafeteria, that night junior year, a few months ago outside The Revolution after the concert, and cliffside when I finally spoke up: *jump with me.* Emma has always been there in the center of things, even if I wasn't ready to see her. Now, I can't see anyone else.

A feeling hits me square in the chest: I want to always see Emma. Every day. I want to hear her laugh. I want to ease the worry line from between her eyebrows. I want to be the one lying next to her when she sleeps.

Those three words — I can't bring myself to acknowledge — illuminate my heart like a neon sign.

My breath catches in my chest, seizing up with panic.

The awareness is so big. I don't know what to do with it.

emma

When I open my eyes, the sun casts a golden light in my room. Tanner is lying in my bed with his brown eyes open and studying me. "Hey," he says.

I stretch. "Hey."

"I'm sorry. About earlier."

"For what? You don't have anything to be sorry about."

"I didn't know where else to go. No." He stops for a moment. His eyes flicker away from mine, then they come back to meet my gaze. "There wasn't anywhere else I wanted to go."

This statement expands my heart. He chose me. Needed me. "Want to talk about it?"

He rolls onto his back. With an arm under his head, he stares up at the ceiling. "I quit my job."

I'm not sure what to say, so I don't say anything.

"I work for my dad. I lost it with him today when he tried to apologize for missing graduation."

"You can't forgive him?"

"There's a lot there between us — him, my mom, and me. None of it very good since Rory died."

"Feel like talking about it?"

"Truthfully, no." He rolls back toward me. "But that's kind of like Kaleidoscope Concussion, huh?"

I laugh. "We'll call this the Tanner James Top Secret Support Group."

He squeezes me tighter. "You know most of it. After Rory died, the fighting started. They divorced when I was fourteen. The fighting didn't stop. My dad remarried. He has a new kid, Will."

"You have a half-brother?"

"Yeah. And a step one, Gregory. Will is three. He's cute." Tanner goes quiet. His fingers slide over the skin of my arm and raise a chill of awareness on my skin. "He told me today that he wants me to learn to run his company."

"Why is that bad?"

"His offer just felt a little too late. More of the same. Like—" He stops speaking, stops moving his thumb across my skin, and swallows down his emotions. "Like I've been here this whole time. Waiting for him to see me." He looks away and presses his lips together. "I told my mom that day after graduation that she'd not only lost Rory, but she'd lost me too. That's why he did it. It wasn't because of me. Rory is gone. It's because he feels guilty."

It's at that moment I see him. The f-boy facade, the party boy falls away, and I see how wrong I was about him all that time, even if that's how he acted. My eyes fill with tears for him and his hurt. Tanner is lying next to me vulnerable and afraid, struggling as much as I am to figure his life out.

"Could there be another possibility?"

His eyebrows bunch up with confusion. "Like what?"

"Like he does love you? Like he knows he's messed up and doesn't know how to fix it? Maybe he's trying to reach out."

Tanner doesn't reply, but his eyes move over my face. He's thinking about it. Then he says, "I don't know what to do."

My gaze skims over his thick dark brows and heavily lashed brown eyes, wide eyes swimming with unshed tears, the strong nose and generous lips, the bottom slightly fuller, his wide jaw. Then I reach out and place my hand on his cheek and caress the skin under his eye. "You don't have to figure it out now."

"I want to be good enough, Em."

I hear what he hasn't said: *I haven't been good enough for him.* "You are."

He shakes his head. "I want to be good enough for you. I don't want rusty armor anymore."

This admission rocks me and stops up my breath for a moment. His words give voice to my own insecurities as if he'd read my mind. When I find my voice again, I say, "You are. You are good. You are enough." Even as I say them, I wonder if I can accept the same for myself?

And suddenly the tears that receded in his eyes are pooling. He closes his eyes, rolls away, and covers his face with his arm. He doesn't cry like I do — it's quiet and just as heart-breaking. I move against his side, my arm draped around him, and I hold tight. Eventually, he moves and presses the fingertips into his eyes, and pinches his nose. He sniffs and rolls back to me, drawing me closer.

"Thanks, Em." He sniffs and kisses my hair. "Maybe the guy in Kaleidoscope Concussion was right."

"What about?"

"Crying. When he cried with man-boob Jimbo at the funeral, and he said that it was freedom."

"Technically, I think he was talking about the release of the emotion being freedom. That crying was looking up into the stars and losing yourself in the cosmos.'"

"Oh shit." Tanner props himself up on an elbow. "I forgot that line. Like star stories?"

I know he's thinking about the stories he and Rory used to tell. About the stories we've been telling one another.

"Where's the book? I need to see that."

"There." I reach over him.

He catches my hips with his hands as I reach for the book on the nightstand, and I settle on top of him. He's smiling with that impish look.

"I don't know where the line is, Emma. Can you find it in the book for me? There are some other things I've been wanting to attend to." He moves so that his lips are pressed to the soft skin of my neck.

"You do too know where–" I gasp when his teeth graze the skin, which sends a jolt of longing through my spine. My head droops forward, closer to him. I finish the thought, though it's fleeting and sounds half-hearted as it leaves my mouth. "You know this book better than I do."

"Nope." He rolls me over, presses a knee between my legs, and continues to nuzzle my neck with his mouth. "You're smarter." I can feel his lips and then tongue working in concert against my skin after he says it.

My belly buzzes, and my breath locks in my chest, but then I sigh. "It's early. In chapter two." I breathe the words.

He pulls away, looks at me, and I can see his demeanor has shifted. We both know where the thirst coursing through us goes.

The heaviness of needing to define this relationship presses against me, but unlike the weight of Tanner, it's uncomfortable. "Tanner?"

"Yes, Em?"

"What are we?"

His mouth opens, but sound stalls because a knock at the door interrupts us.

Tanner looks at the door and then at me. His wide eyes make me smile.

"Emma?" It's Shelby.

"Hold on. I'll be right there." I maneuver my way out from under Tanner and scramble to open the door. By the time I do, he's sitting on the edge of my bed that looks perfectly made. The stretching of my heart fills my chest. I realize what was once an infatuation and then a physical want has shifted again. It's emotional. The red wire. I understand my feelings, and they rock me with both a simultaneous burst of light and fear. This boy I've known of but only have come to know has knocked me sideways. I'm falling in love with Tanner James. No. I am in love with Tanner James.

That red wire. That freaking red wire becomes my mantra as I move down the street toward Liam's house. I need to process my newfound awareness with my best friend. So, after I walked Tanner out to his truck, instead of going back inside, I turned up the street for Liam's. The clarity of my feelings for Tanner has knocked the wind out of me. The fact he's bared his soul for me to poke around inside has only reinforced that darned red wire. I can't help where my heart has gone. I'm in trouble.

Ginny alluded to it. I knew it when I got involved with him. It's like an unwritten rule that boys like Tanner don't change. And even though I'd like to tell myself he is changing; Bella's words keep cycling through my mind: what could a girl like me offer a boy like him? So even if I'm naive enough to hope, my insecurities are making the wiring so much more complicated.

I climb the wide stairway onto the porch of the beautiful craftsman house where Liam lives with his parents and knock on the green door. Liam's dad, Edmund, opens it and smiles lighting up his blue eyes that remind me so much of Liam's. I can't help but sometimes think I know exactly who Liam will be in twenty years.

"Emma. What a pleasant surprise."

"Hi, Mr. Quinn. Is Liam home?"

He opens the door to let me in. "Emma, Ed is fine. I don't feel like my Dad yet." He smiles.

I look down at my feet and cross the threshold. "Did you enjoy graduation?"

"Most assuredly, and Jolene said your speech was the best of all of them."

I smile at the compliment and at the mention of Liam's mom. "Is she home?"

"She's down at the shop. Maybe you'd like to stay for dinner though?"

"I'd like that," I tell him.

He nods at the stairs. "Liam is up in his room. Go on up."

After thanking him, I take the stairs two at a time, skirt around the spindles of the oak banister, and walk down the traditional runner in the hallway. It's a trail I've taken many times in my life. "Liam?" I call out.

His bedroom door is open, because light stretches out into the hall, and his head pops out the doorway. "What are you doing?"

"It's nice to see you too." I walk into his room and flop on his bed without an invitation, grabbing a pillow to hug against my stomach. I groan.

"What?" he asks.

I roll so I can see him. "I'm in trouble."

His eyebrows lift. "What's that supposed to mean?" He looks like he's doing calculations in his head and glances at the pillow.

"Not THAT kind of trouble. It's too soon to know that, and we were safe. I just need you."

His mouth thins out, and I see that he's irritated with me.

"Don't be like that."

"Is he acting like an ass already?"

"No. Actually." I roll to my back and look up at the ceiling. "That's just it. He's perfect. How can that be?"

I hear the chair Liam is sitting in squeak, because he's moved.

He steps into my line of vision. "Scoot over."

I move to the edge of his twin bed.

He lays down next to me, our shoulders stacked because we're both too big to share his bed, and we stare up at the ceiling. He takes my hand in his. It feels like we've gone back in time. Emma and Liam. Liam and Emma.

"I'm scared," I tell him.

"How come?"

I turn my head to look at him then. "Because what if you're right? Liam, I'm falling for him. The real deal. And I'm leaving in a few weeks. And–" but my throat closes up and tears fill my eyes; I can't say another word.

His eyes search mine before turning to look at the ceiling again. He squeezes my hand tighter. "We can't help who we fall for. You're in it, and no matter what, Em. No matter what happens, I'll be here."

I squeeze his hand with mine, and it makes me breathe a little easier.

countdown: 4

"I was afraid."

-unnamed protagonist, *Kaleidoscope Concussion* by Saul Annick

tanner

I love that Emma is by my side driving down the highway. Ginny is
also with us. The radio blasts a song the girls sing to, the windows open,
and strands of Emma's hair whip around her face. Her hand is in mine.
We're on our way to the bonfire, which I wasn't super enthusiastic about
attending because of Griff, but Josh asked. Maybe a different sort of Bro
Code. I knew he was looking forward to seeing Ginny. I liked the way I
felt with Emma and wanted that for him too. But knowing Griff will be
there has me anxious. It's the before me intersection with the after.

When we get to the Quarry, I take an access road to a spot on the
East side where the bonfire is located. By the time I park the truck, the
sun has gone down, but the bonfire, near the shoreline, is bright. There
is a throng of people, more than I anticipated, but the energy is good. I
text the Bro Code thread that we're there and then get out of the car.
Music thumps with the rhythm of my heart and feels good moving
through my body. Besides Senior Send Off, and our first party together,
this is the first time I've ever gone to a party with someone other than
my friends.

My phone pings.

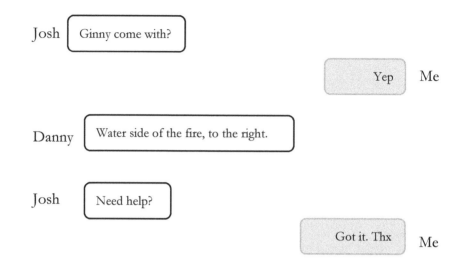

Josh | Ginny come with?

Me | Yep

Danny | Water side of the fire, to the right.

Josh | Need help?

Me | Got it. Thx

Griff has remained silent on the thread since I last saw him.

"Ready?" With a cooler in one hand, I reclaim Emma's hand with the other.

She carries a blanket and a bag stuffed with God knows. She's got that little line between her brows. "I'm nervous."

I pull her next to me and kiss that little worry line. "What about?"

She shrugs. "It isn't rational."

"Note to Tanner," Ginny says over her shoulder as we walk across the grass towards the bonfire. "Emma always freaks out a little bit when it comes to crowds."

"Hey!" Josh waves, closing the distance between us and him. "Thought I'd see if you needed help."

His appearance surprises me. He'd have had to have run to get to us so quickly or been waiting near the lot for us. I glance at Ginny and realize maybe Josh feels stronger than he's letting on. Ginny holds out her bag. "Sure."

Josh — who doesn't even look at me — falls into step with her. They lead the way.

I wrap an arm around Emma and pull her closer. "Need a story?"

"Yes."

I pause, thinking, and then lean closer so that my lips are near her ear. "Once upon a time, there was this queen named Ella. And the heroic King TJ saved her from her tower."

"No." She shakes her head. "She walked out of the tower on her own. She's strong and can save herself."

I chuckle. "Okay. What's the point of King TJ, then?" I draw away to look at her face. The little worry line is gone, replaced by a smile that tells me she's about to say something sassy.

"Skydiving."

I laugh.

"Among other things." She walks forward, pulling me by the hand. "Like dancing." She turns, walking backwards. "Did you know I love to dance?"

"I didn't. But now that you mention it, I think I saw you at a dance doing some weird moves."

"Is that right? Which dance would that be?"

I drape an arm over her shoulder as we walk side-by-side toward the party. "Oh. Probably our sophomore year."

"Did you even go to a school dance our sophomore year?" she asks. I laugh, and she pokes me in the side. "You're awful."

We follow Josh around the bonfire, circumventing the crowd to where Griff and Danny are set up. They've been drinking for a while and yell my name when they see me.

"Hey." I slap Danny's hand. I stop at Griff. He holds his hand out first. I reciprocate. "You guys know Emma."

"This is a first." There's a bite to Griff's tone that runs up against my edges.

"Hey," she says. "Thought I'd try and keep up with you."

Josh and Danny laugh. "No way. Not possible."

Griff hands Emma a drink. "Here then, Matthews. Let's see if you can."

She salutes him with the bottle and takes a sip.

He hands me one too. "Now that we're all here." He raises his bottle. "To being high school graduates!" He takes a swig.

Eventually, Emma and I unfold the blanket she brought and lay it out on the shore. The blanket makes me think of graduation night; I imagine her body wrapped around mine and my stomach clenches. I'm hungry for her; we haven't had sex since, not for lack of wanting to, but for lack of opportunity. I tumble onto the blanket, making it difficult for her to spread out the fabric she's trying to make neat and perfect.

"Tanner." She pretends to be upset, up on her knees with her hands on her hips. Then she pushes at my back, laughing.

I relax, becoming deadweight so she can't move me. "What?" When I can, I grab her and draw into my arms.

She laughs and pretends to be annoyed even though I know she isn't. Emma rights herself and sits next to me. Close. I sit up, wrap my arm around her and kiss her temple.

"So, Emma." Griff flops down on the blanket on the other side of her. "I want to know how you snagged my boy here."

"Snagged?" She asks. "Like caught as if he were an animal?"

Griff looks at me over her head. "Sure."

I shake my head at him.

Josh and Ginny, who've been talking a yard or so away, stop and look over at us.

"I don't think *snag* is the word you're looking for, Griffin," Emma says, bringing my attention back. I look at her.

"Really? What's a better word?"

"Snared. Entrap. Land. Lure." She tips her head away from him with a smile. "I think those are better words for your passive aggressive question."

"Oh, damn." Josh laughs. "Smarts win every time."

Griff's smile fades.

My heart plummets into my belly.

Emma looks at me with that smile. "Do you feel ensnared in my web?"

"Definitely," I tell her and kiss her cheek.

Griff rolls his eyes.

"Em?" Ginny interrupts. "Would you come with me to the restroom?"

"Sure." Emma stands. "Save my spot?" She bends down and kisses me.

When they're gone, I turn to Griff. "What the fuck was that?"

"Being friendly." He stands up and walks past me.

I stand too because everything inside me tells me this isn't Griff being nice. "You call that friendly? I think you were being an asshole. I don't understand what your problem is with her?"

He whips around and points at me, a finger against my chest. "You're fuckin whipped, dude. I think you're going to regret wasting your summer with her."

I push his hand away. "Who the fuck are you to decide that for me?"

"Your best friend." He pushes my shoulder.

"Yo. Dudes." Danny steps closer to Griff and me.

Josh doesn't say anything. I know why. I can feel his reserve, and his understanding that whatever is happening between us needs to happen. I think of all of his advice to stand up for myself, to stand up to Griff. I backed down the other day at his house. I can't anymore. "Well then fucking act like it. My best friend would be happy for me because I'm happy. You don't want that for me?"

"Oh. Is that what I am now? Your best friend? It sure hasn't felt like the last few weeks, you dick. Thing is, you could be happy with us. You could have your pick of chicks all summer long. Instead, you're choosing her."

"Is that what this is about? You're pissed at me because I'm not doing what you want so you can scrape up my leftovers?"

Danny takes a step away and sucks in a breath, which he blows out slowly.

"Oh shit," Josh says.

"That's bullshit." Griff takes a step toward me with fisted hands and gets into my space.

I press my hands against his shoulders and move him back. It isn't aggressive but communicates my need for him to back off. "She makes me happy."

"How does *that* make you happy?" He points the direction Emma

343

disappeared with Ginny. "She's a fucking dead fish. Chris Keller told everyone."

His words light the kindling in my gut and the name adds fuel. "Shut. The. Fuck. Up. Griff."

"Griff!" Danny says. "That's fucked up."

"Griff. Uncalled for," Josh says. "Take it back."

"I won't fucking take it back." He narrows his eyes, and his finger is back, poking at my chest. "Here's the truth, man: in the long run, she's going to fucking leave." He accentuates each of his words with that stupid fingertip. "She's fucking smart, Tanner. And you're not."

I don't think; I swing, and my fist connects with Griff's face. His head snaps to the side, and he falls to the ground with the momentum.

Danny jumps in between us, and Josh grabs one of my arms, dragging me back to create some distance.

Griff sits up and shakes his head, his hand wrapped around his jaw as he tests the hinge. He looks up at me. "Fuck you, Tanner." Then he stands and points at me. "You broke the code. You. You're choosing a bitch over your friends, and you're going to get hurt. Don't come crying to me when it happens, because I'm gonna fucking say 'I told you so.' Then tell you to fuck off." He walks toward the bonfire and disappears into the crowd.

Danny backs away from Josh and me in the direction Griff went. "He'll come around. He just thought summer would be different." Then he turns to go after Griff.

"You okay, dude?" Josh lets go of my arm.

I don't answer him. What can I say? I just hit my best friend— the guy I'd always thought of like my brother. He's right: I did break the code, but I'm not sure the code was ever fair to begin with.

"What he said was bullshit, Tanner. Really."

I turn and walk down to the water's edge. Griff's words echoing in my ears: *you're going to get hurt.*

Griff hit me where it hurt — all the insecurity of not being good enough for Emma. Not Smart Tanner. Going Nowhere Tanner. But being with Emma, feels like some strange convergence of the stars aligning into the perfect story. Even as I have the thought, the rational part of my brain tells me to stop. She's leaving. Everything I have ever cared about has left in some way or another. I shove my hands into my pockets and look out at the water, the moonlight shimmering on the water, the stars reflecting in the glassy surface.

You're going to get hurt.

Griff isn't wrong. I know that. I can feel it every time I look at Emma. Each time I touch her, kiss her, laugh with her. Time is steamrolling toward a goodbye. I glance up at the sky and look for Rory and my star. What's happened with Griff hurts too. He was supposed to be my friend, my brother, and he turned on me because— I don't know why. I don't understand it. Is it as simple as me not doing what he wants? The only thing that feels right in my life at the moment is Emma, and while we might be headed toward an impending ache of a goodbye, maybe it doesn't have to.

emma

Ginny links her arm with mine as we walk from the bathroom. She leans in. "Full disclosure, Emma. I might have a slight crush on Josh."

I smile. "Well, he is cute."

"And nice."

"Is there something you aren't telling me?"

"We might have been talking since the last John Hughes movie night."

"What? I thought you hated him."

"I may have been skeptical, but let's just say his art of flirtation has been swaying me in his favor. He might have also been into the ice cream parlor a few times to visit me at work last week."

I laugh and smack her arm. We walk without talking, until I say, "Play your cards right, you might be able to give your hands a rest."

"Oh!" It's her turn to smack me back and laugh. "I'm not ready for that yet."

I nod.

"But talking to Josh made me realize something about dickhead number one."

"Yeah?"

"I let him pressure me into something I wasn't ready for, and I lied to myself about it."

"What do you mean?"

"I told myself that Dean respected and loved me, but now, getting to know Josh, I don't think that was ever true. Check that, I know it wasn't."

"How can you know that just talking to Josh for a couple of weeks?" I ask her.

"It's the way he talks to me. Even in the first couple of weeks it's different. Weirdly enough, Josh is quality."

"Why do you say *weirdly*?"

"I didn't mean—"

"Yes, you did. You think it's 'weird' because he hangs out with Tanner; you assumed he'd be a jerk."

She looks down at her feet as we walk over the gravel toward the waterline. "You're right. I did think that."

It hurts me.

"And, now I see what you meant from the other day. That Tanner hasn't treated you with anything other than respect. Josh has been the same. I judged him — and Tanner — unfairly. I'm sorry for it."

"It's okay, Gin. I did too. I mean, I have nothing to say. Weeks ago, I was ready to use Tanner." I'm ashamed to admit that, recognizing I would have done exactly what I looked down on him and his friends for doing. I'd judged him, too, just like Griff was judging me.

"Well, I said all that to say that I don't want to rush into anything with Josh. We're both leaving. He's going to California, like you. I'll be in Georgia. I think hanging out and getting to know him seems like something worth pursuing, but I'm not sure beyond that."

"That's smart," I tell her, because I can feel the initial tug of separation anxiety that's beginning to pull at my heart. I fell for Tanner, and that had never been in the plan.

When we get back to the spot where I'd left Tanner, Josh is there. Griff and Danny are gone. At first, I think Tanner is as well, but catch sight of him down by the water.

tanner

"Hey." Emma's arms slide around me from behind. I feel her cheek pressed against my back.

With a hand over hers, I turn so I can put my arms around her. The world corrects. "Hey."

"What's up? You look so serious contemplating the moonlit water."

"Griff and I got into it."

"What?" She leans back, so she can see me. "Are you okay?"

"Yeah. No. I don't know," I tell her and sigh.

Her arms apply additional comforting pressure. "I'm sorry."

"I think we've been headed there for a while."

We stand in one another's arms, the bonfire and party behind us. The music moves around us, but I don't have it in me to join in the revelry. It's another shift. Before, I would have tried to find a way to numb the feelings — lose them, really — in the fun of inebriation and possibility of sex. Now, I'm content to stand with Emma, but maybe that isn't what she wants. "Do you want to dance?" I ask her.

She looks up at me. "Actually, I was thinking that maybe swimming sounded better. Want to swim?"

I lean down and kiss the top of her head. "That sounds perfect."

She slips out of the clothes she's worn over her swimsuit, smiling, laughing and racing into the water.

I shrug out of my t-shirt and run after her, able to catch her about waist deep and tackle her so we both fall. The water swallows us.

She surfaces sputtering and giggling, her hair hanging in her face. She moves her hair so she can see me, splashes me with water, and swims away into the deep.

I swim after her, loving that she's having fun, because it helps me reset my attitude. When I catch up with her, we're shoulder deep, and her arms wind around my neck.

"I thought it would be colder." She shivers.

"Why are you shivering then?" I pull her closer.

"All the feels," she says. "Like the stars in the sky coming out of my body." She takes my face in her hands and kisses me. Her tongue speaks all the words she wants to say, and the meaning is very clear: *I want you, Tanner. I need you. You are enough. I want to be with you.*

My chest tightens, and my belly presses against my spine, as those stars work their way across my skin. I can do all those things her kiss asks for, and I kiss her back with all the words I have on my heart and mind too: *You are everything, Emma. You make me happy. I need you.*

When she wraps her legs around my hips, I groan into her mouth. "It's impossible to stay cold when it involves you."

"God, Tanner. I've been wanting–" she says against my lips but doesn't finish the thought she's started. Instead she kisses me again, and I sink lower into the water, widening my stance, dropping us into the embrace of the water, lapping over our shoulders, now, around and through us with its own hypnotic and sensual rhythm.

With my arms securing her against me, I kiss her, and kiss her, and kiss her until it isn't prudent to do so anymore. "Em?"

"Mmm," she hums into my mouth.

"We should probably stop."

"You feel better?"

"Yes. I feel better whenever you're with me."

She shivers.

"Are you cold?"

She shakes her head. "No. Happy."

She relaxes against me, and I just hold her, content to just be in the moment with her, swaying in the water as if we were dancing. And then the words run through my mind: *I love you.* I bite them to keep them inside, scared of how big the feeling is. They feel unreal and irrational in as little time Emma and I have been — I don't even know what we are. I've never said them to anyone — how can I know they're authentic? But then I feel as though I might be trying to talk myself out of the truth of what's running through my heart.

"You asked me a question the other day we didn't get to finish talking about."

She doesn't move but stays wrapped around me. "Which one?"

"What are we?" I've never had this conversation with anyone before. I'm not sure how this works.

She takes her head off my shoulder and straightens so she can see my face.

I think she looks so pretty. Her wet hair slick, and her skin bright in the moonlight. Her lips are full from my kiss. I take a deep breath to focus. The moon, which juxtaposes light and shadow, illuminates the line between her brows.

"I'm sorry. Should I not bring this up?" I ask. "It seemed like a good time."

"It is. I want to. It just scares me." It's hard to see the details of her face in the shadows, so I'm only able to function off the sound of her voice. She isn't hesitant, and I think about the time she said how much easier it was to talk in the dark.

"How come?" I ask her.

Her fingers play with my hair at my nape. She doesn't say anything for a few seconds and then says, "I'm afraid because I don't want to ruin anything. I'm enjoying whatever this is."

I squeeze her tighter. "You're not going to ruin anything."

Her fingers still. "What if I said: 'Tanner, I think we should go our separate ways.'"

My heart deflates, and my arms relax around her. "Is that what you want?" I can feel the way the words sound walled up when they leave my mouth. Disappointed and harsh.

"No." She gives me a reassuring squeeze with her arms. "Not in the slightest. But see, I could say the wrong thing." Her fingers resume the caress of my hair. She giggles, pressing her face into the space between my shoulder and my neck. "But, now, I don't feel so frightened."

"Why is that?" I'm smiling.

"Because I like you. I like you so freaking much it probably isn't healthy. You consume all of my thoughts. I just want to be with you all the time." She nuzzles her mouth against my neck.

"Emma. I like you too. But I think it's more than that." I pause. "You caught me off guard."

"Me too. This isn't what I expected to happen, but I'm so glad that it has. You make me feel... alive." She goes quiet and then asks, "What do you mean *more than that?*"

I can't go there with her; I can't drop the love word. I don't trust it. I don't trust myself, but I know this is bigger than just liking her. "I don't know how to name it, but the other day, when I woke up next to you in your bed, I had this feeling that is where I want to always be. Waking up next to you."

Every part of her tightens around me. The relief I feel is like a deep breath after trying to hold it and then bursting through to the surface. Then she says two words that add to the relief. "Me too."

emma

We're prunes. When we return to shore, Ginny says Josh is going to take her home, so we gather up what we brought. I'm shivering and wish the latent heat of the bonfire was stronger, but it has died down with the party. What's left are blankets and bodies. I hear the murmur of talking and laughter. Tanner and I walk out holding hands.

"Should I drive?" I ask him when we reach his truck. "I didn't drink more than a couple of sips at the beginning of the night with Griff."

"Sure." He surrenders his keys. "But I need you to understand how significant it is that I've given you the keys to my baby." He backs me up against the truck and places his hands on my hips. "I've never, ever let anyone drive Princess Leia."

My eyebrows arch high over my closed eyes, and I smile. "Did I just hear you say that your truck's name is Princess Leia?"

He nuzzles my neck with his mouth and hums an affirmation. "Double cinnamon roll hair, Leia."

"Why, Tanner," I chuckle but grab his shoulders, enjoying the feel of his tongue working magic on my neck, "you're a big nerd."

He laughs against my skin, and the vibration does things to my insides. "Let's go. Thinking about cinnamon rolls makes me hungry."

I drive us back to town.

"I think Josh likes Ginny," Tanner says after we've driven about ten minutes in the darkness of the cab. Music from the radio is low but fills the silence. I've been lost in my own thoughts about Tanner, aglow with the understanding there's more between us.

"He told you that?"

"Not exactly. Just my observations."

"I may have to ask about his intentions." I smile at the road.

"What exactly are your intentions with me, Ms. Matthews?" He reaches over and squeezes my thigh.

"My intentions are severely sinister, like Darth Vader when he captures Leia and forces the truth serum into her."

"Oh. That actually sounds really sexy." His hand caresses my thigh.

My insides throb.

We find the lone 24-hour market on the way to Tanner's house and buy some cinnamon rolls in a tube. Then I drive the truck into the driveway of his dark house. He unlocks the side door, cuts the alarm with a code, and turns on the kitchen lights.

"Your mom home?" I ask.

"Alarm was on. Nope. She's usually at Bradley's." He calls out for her. No answer. "See."

I approach him from behind and wrap my arms around his torso, laying my cheek against his back. "Are you lonely?"

He turns in my arms. "Not anymore." He leans down to kiss me.

"I'm glad."

His kiss is gentle, warm, and filled with more context than just what is physical between us. Awareness that we'd made a sort of agreement in the water fills me with added layers to my usual desire for him with gorgeous but a worrisome complication. I'm leaving for college, and my heart is invested in him, in us. The knowledge doesn't keep me from kissing him back, however, and instead adds fuel to my need to be with him. Now. I want to unwrap this gift and settle into the beauty of now.

"Cinnamon rolls before or after?" he asks against my mouth.

"Before or after what?"

He lifts me and sets me on the kitchen island. He pushes my damp dress up my thighs, his calloused hands grazing my skin. His eyes sweep over me, and he licks his lips. "Never mind. I can't wait. After." He runs his hands around my hips, under the hem of the dress, and pulls me to the edge of the counter toward him. His mouth meets mine again, but doesn't stay, using his tongue and hands to spin magic spells against my skin.

"That feels good." I lean toward him, wanting to be closer.

He pulls back to look at me. "We haven't gotten to that part yet." His eyes caress me like his hands did, his eyes dark with intent.

I feel powerful. I feel wanted. I feel sexy. I feel bold. "Tanner," I whisper. "I want you." I reach for his waist.

"The condoms are upstairs." His mouth moves against the skin of my neck again.

I tug at his swim shorts. "Let's go get them."

He groans, draws me off the counter, and carries me from the room. One the way up the stairs, he stumbles on a step. We laugh, then kiss some more, undoing one another on the stairs. "Condoms," I remind him, and we're up and moving through the hallway, kissing, touching, stopping to press one another up against walls and doors, until our breathing is in sync. Once we're through his bedroom door, we strip. My dress and bikini, his t-shirt and boardshorts, no patience to separate as we do, hands and mouths still connected to one another, until we're on his bed. He settles his weight between my legs. I've never been more ready to take him in, but he's kissing me again, taking it slow.

"I want to stay here like this with you."

His words do something to me. Ignite a fire and burn like — I can't wait. I push him so he has to roll over onto his back. "Give me the condom."

He hands me the package.

"Show me how to do it."

He takes it from me, opens it, starts it on, pinches the tip and then guides my hand to sheath him.

"I want you," I tell him and straddle him.

"Damn, Em."

"What?"

"I like this. It's hot." He's smiling and runs his hands over my skin.

I shiver, lean over, and kiss him. "I like you, Tanner James. You make me hot."

He grabs my hips and helps me adjust; his body ready to connect with mine. And then I lower myself onto him, take him in, gasping for breath as I do. The connection feels so good.

"Emma. Emma," he chants and guides my hips until I understand the rhythm. And when I do, I'm lost in the sensations. I'm lost in the way Tanner's eyes are closed, but he's lost in it with me. I'm lost in the feel of his hands on my hips. Then suddenly, Tanner rolls me over onto my back. We move, the ebb and flow of the rhythm we create with our bodies, our mouths, our tongues, our sounds, wraps around us and becomes a cocoon we construct together.

After, we lay mixed up in one another's limbs, Tanner's stroking my back with his hand. I'm relaxed and content. "Tanner?"

He moans a response.

"Can I tell you something?"

"Anything, Em."

"You won't tease me?"

"No."

"I'm afraid."

"Why?"

"No. Not that I'm afraid. I'm just afraid to tell you."

His hands stop moving, and he rolls to look at me. "What is it? You're making me nervous."

I let my eyes slide down to look at my fingers on his arm. "I ruined it with all my talking."

"Just tell me."

I hesitate, because I know there's no going back after it's said, but I also know that I can't go back anyway regardless if it's said or not. With as much bravery as I can muster, I force my eyes back to his. "I love you."

He rolls me onto my back and looks down at me. "What did you say, Em?"

"I love you. I love you so much. And I know it seems fast–" But I don't get to finish what I'm saying, because Tanner's kissing me with the fire I'd started a little while ago, igniting it once again.

tanner

Emma's head rests in the crook of my arm. Her hand holds mine, her legs entwined with mine. She's said she loves me. I'm warm with the knowledge that THIS girl thinks I'm enough. THIS girl feels like that about me. When she said it, *I love you,* something exploded in my chest as if there were a supernova, and a new star was created. I couldn't speak. I could only show her. So, I did.

All my heart is wrapped up in her. I'd be lying if I said it didn't terrify me. It does. I've never given anyone that kind of power over me — not since my family disintegrated. It isn't that I don't want to tell her how I feel, I do. I feel the words sitting on my tongue— but every time I want to say them, I swallow them. As we lay here, talking about stuff, I'm struck with the weight of my feelings but also with the awareness that time is moving too quickly.

"What do you want now?" she asks.

I move my arm and pull her against me. "You know what I want."

"I don't mean that, you animal." She laughs. "I mean, in your life — for you."

I sigh. I don't want to think about it, but then again that's what got me to the point of questioning everything I've ever done. I know she's right to ask. "Honestly, I don't know."

Her thumb caresses my palm as she ponders what I've said. I know she's probably got her life all figured out — a life I was never a part of — so my answer probably terrifies her. But she says something surprising, "That must be freeing."

"What do you mean?"

"Queen Ella's tower," she says and adjusts her head so she can look up at me a moment. She lays her head back down. "Too much planning, and you miss out. Feel trapped."

"Not enough planning, and you're lost. Your options are limited."

"So smart. I think you've been holding out on the world. Don't think I didn't notice all of your books."

"You weren't supposed to see those." I smile. "I usually try to hide my word porn."

She rolls over on her stomach. "Do you even understand how hot that is?" She's smiling at me, and crawls upward, draping her bare chest on mine. "You're talking dirty to me."

I don't move; I just enjoy the view, the feel of her, the sound.

She studies me, moving her eyes over my face. I can tell she wants to say something — the line between her eyes — but it softens and passes.

"What about you?" I ask her. "What do you want now?"

Her eyes sparkle. "You know what I want."

"I don't mean that, you animal." I parrot her words and caress her head, submerging my fingers in her hair. I work my fingers through her hair. "I mean for your life."

Her smile fades, she blinks and then lays her cheek on my chest. "I'm not ready to think about it."

"About what?"

"I don't know if it's what I want anymore."

Her voice sounds different.

I move, rolling her so she's looking at me. "What is it?"

"I thought all I ever wanted was to get into a good school, follow the four-year plan, you know?"

"I don't." I laugh, amused at my own fallibility. It makes her smile, but it's mediocre. She turns her head away again, trying to hide the fact that tears are filling her eyes. "Emma. You deserve everything you've worked for, including that four-year college and the success that comes with it." I brush a lock of hair stuck to her cheek.

"I didn't expect that when I took your hand and agreed to jump, I'd feel like my heart is going to come apart thinking about going away." She looks at me, her hurt and confusion are liquid in her eyes. "I don't want to think about leaving you."

My heart constricts, pausing in its beat to make me feel like my chest might implode. But it does restart, and I move, drawing her into my arms.

She clings to me. "I don't know what I thought, but I was so stupid. I want the clock to stop."

"Stupid for jumping with me?"

"No. Stupid for thinking I wasn't going to fall for you."

"Fall for you," I repeat, which strikes me as funny given the circumstances. Her admission makes me smile. "So, you were planning on using me?"

She giggles through her tears and sniffs. "Maybe."

"Damn. That's cold." I hold her tighter, the beat of her heart connecting with mine.

"I thought I just needed to get you out of my system. I'd been crushing on you for so long."

"I'm kind of like that, I guess. Irresistible and addictive."

She giggles and tries to pull away.

"You know what will make everything better?" I ask.

"Skydiving?"

I laugh. "Sure, but I need the next best thing. Food."

When we make it back into the kitchen, the tube of cinnamon rolls has popped from not being put away. We attempt to salvage it anyway and put them in the oven then raid the fridge. Emma — dressed in one of my t-shirts that just makes it to the top of her thighs, a blue one that makes her eyes intensely vibrant — is making me a sandwich. I want to touch her. I can't get enough. I move around the edge of the island and lean against it just to be closer to her. I feel like a lovesick idiot.

She hands me the sandwich.

"This looks delicious," I tell her and kiss her cheek.

We settle around the kitchen island, her on a stool and me leaning over the counter toward her, eating sandwiches and talking. Time spins around us, moving, but I feel as though perhaps it has stopped because being with her is effortless and buoyant. She's telling a story about Liam and trick-or-treating in seventh grade when the oven beeps reminding me that time is, in fact, moving like a rushing river past us. I remove the pan of cinnamon rolls from the oven.

"I didn't realize it was so late. I should get home."

I turn and lean against the counter loath for more time to pass us by. "Do you have to?"

"My parents will flip out. They'll worry."

"Rephrase: do you want to go?"

She pauses and looks down at the countertop, fingers a vein in the marble, and then looks up. "No."

Her admission presses around my heart, because I don't want her to go. "Text them."

"And say what? 'Hey mom and dad, I'm having a sleepover with Tanner.'"

"Sounds perfect." I smile.

She hesitates, but I can also see her mind working it out. The line between her eyes that designates she's thinking but worried. "I'm an adult." She rationalizes and looks at her phone. "I'm trustworthy."

I can tell that she's freaking out a little. "It's okay, Em. I don't want you to worry. I'll take you home. I just have to grab my wallet."

She stops me, looks at her phone, and then at me. "Both feet." She types something on the screen. She sets her phone down, looks at me and smiles.

"Both feet?"

"I'm jumping. I don't want to waste any of our time. I want to wake up with you."

Her phone chirps.

She hesitates before picking it up.

"Them?"

She nods. "My mom."

"What did she say?"

"Be smart."

"Which is no big deal, because you are." I move in closer to her, draw her from the stool into my arms. Then in a singsong voice I sing, "We get to have a sleepover. We get to have a sleepover," and sway with her.

She laughs.

"I can't wait to wake up next to you."

"But what if I have gross breath."

"That's what a toothbrush is for. Speaking of gross breath, we should definitely eat a cinnamon roll."

We do but spend more time with the frosting and places on one another's bodies to remove it with our tongues. A sticky mess, we clean up the kitchen and shower. I show her what skydiving in the shower feels like, which she seems to enjoy immensely. Then we get ready for bed. It's strange that I feel a little shy about climbing into bed with her. I mean, we've had sex, and we napped together the other day. But there's something committed about climbing into bed to consciously sleep with someone else. Committing to the act of staying. I've never stayed.

emma

When I stretch and open my eyes, I remember I'm in Tanner's bed, not at home. I smile. I've slept through the night — not so normal for me — though all of the sex probably helped. Tanner's still asleep. I don't want to wake him, so I slip from under the sheet to use the bathroom and brush my teeth. I creep back into the room to put my swimsuit and dress back on to find coffee, but movement catches my eye. Tanner's hand sweeps the bed, looking for me.

"Where are you?" he mutters, moving his hand over the sheets. "I can't open my eyes until you're here. Otherwise, I won't be waking up with you."

I drop my clothes and crawl back into bed next to him.

He wraps me up in his embrace and pulls me toward him, so we fit together like two matching puzzle pieces. "Better," he mumbles in my ear.

His breathing is even and deep. I think he may have fallen back to sleep, but he says, "What time is it?"

"Almost 8."

"Dear Lord, woman. It's so early. And on a Saturday, too. I'm so glad

I don't have to be at work."

"I'm an early riser."

"Me too," he says and wiggles his hips so his hardness presses against my backside.

I laugh. "I was going to go make coffee."

He tightens his hold. "Not yet. I'm enjoying this." He threads his legs with mine, and I relax against him.

I must drift to sleep again, because the next thing I know, Tanner's getting up from the bed. I roll and grab my phone to check the clock, which reads nearly 9. I scoot up to lean against the headboard to read the bazillion texts from Ginny. I open the thread.

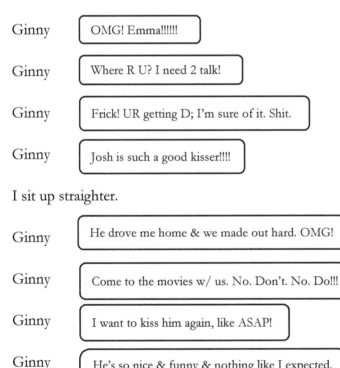

Ginny   OMG! Emma!!!!!!

Ginny   Where R U? I need 2 talk!

Ginny   Frick! UR getting D; I'm sure of it. Shit.

Ginny   Josh is such a good kisser!!!!

I sit up straighter.

Ginny   He drove me home & we made out hard. OMG!

Ginny   Come to the movies w/ us. No. Don't. No. Do!!!

Ginny   I want to kiss him again, like ASAP!

Ginny   He's so nice & funny & nothing like I expected. He can carry a conversation. That brain 🤤

Ginny   That D better B 🔥

Ginny | Text me when you get this.

I smile.

"What are you laughing at?"

"Ginny," I say, wiggling my phone and glance up. Tanner is padding across the room barefooted and bare chested. He's wearing light gray athletic shorts that ride his hips. I notice how lean and fit he is, the ridges and edges of his muscles perfectly proportional. There's nothing extra about him. I remember admiring him in a t-shirt, but looking at him this way, knowing he's spoken to me with his body, catches my breath. My stomach tenses and radiates electrical impulses through my body.

He runs his fingers through his longish dark locks before getting on the bed and crawling over the sheets toward me. When he stops, he lays his head in my lap and rolls over so he can look up at me. I have the fleeting thought of how fantastical this all is — how perfect and temporary — and turn my back on it. I'm content at this moment.

I slide my fingers through his hair. His dark eyes glance up at me.

He smiles. "What did Ginny say?"

"She and Josh kissed."

Tanner chuckles. "That's my boy."

"Perhaps Ginny did the kissing."

"Then doubly that's my boy." He laughs and scrunches up to protect his perfect abs when I reach down to poke him. He grabs my hand.

"What's up for today?" I ask.

"Hmm. I can think of something." He wiggles his eyebrows and grins.

"You're incorrigible."

"You love that about me."

"I do," I say and continue my ministrations of his hair. He shuts his eyes. I love the way his lashes fan across his cheeks. I lean over and kiss his forehead.

He sighs. "I don't want to think ahead of right now. I like being here. With you."

I lean forward and kiss the side of his face and then the other. "I like being in this moment with you too. Though I would like some clean clothes."

His forehead scrunches up. "What? You don't want to just walk around in my t-shirts naked underneath?" He rolls and draws me under him, the t-shirt catching under me. "Because I really like it. It turns me on." He kisses my jaw. Then he kisses my nose. Next, my opposite jaw. His hand on the outside of my thigh moves up to my hip, then pushes the t-shirt hem up higher. I *am* naked underneath, exposed but relishing it because of the way he makes me feel. Because of the way his appreciation shows on his face. He kisses my eyebrow. "I think we can just–" kisses my opposite brow– "stay in bed–" kisses my nose– "all weekend."

My heart speeds up, dancing inside my chest. I like the sound of his plan. "We agreed to go to the movies with Josh and Ginny."

"Fuck it," he says against my lips as he kisses my mouth.

"As much as I like the sound of that," I say into his kiss, and then I take a deep breath, because his fingers have found my center, and he's moving them in ways that move the rest of me. "I should–" but I gasp for breath, grab hold of his shoulders, and arch into his hand, because it feels so good. It isn't as if I've never done this to myself, but... "Oh god, Tanner," I pant into his neck.

"You were saying?" he murmurs in my ear.

"I forget." I breathe the words, barely able to put them together.

With his other hand, he pushes the t-shirt up so he can have access to all of me with his mouth and between his mouth and fingers, I'm on fire. He draws his mouth back up to my mouth and his tongue moves like a prophecy of things to follow. "Jump, Emma," he says, as turned on as I am, because I feel his erection against my thigh. When I do let go, jump toward Tanner, who's waiting for me at the bottom, he's ready. He sheathes himself in a condom and then sheathes himself in me, and I think I might explode. I cry out, and Tanner moves in me. It's fast, greedy, erotic, and this time — different. Unrestrained. I can hear my voice panting his name, loud. I pull at his shoulders with my hands, trying to get closer to him, and I can't get close enough, because I want to share my body with his. I want to climb into his skin.

"Oh god, Emma," he breathes against my neck. "I can't wait." His head falls forward, and he's clutching me against him, as if I might slip through his grasp. When he's caught his breath, he whispers, "I'm sorry."

"For what?" I ask running my fingers through his hair and over his back in a rotation.

"I couldn't hold back. You make me so—" He stops and slides off me to the side, drawing me against him, and then he's quiet. He doesn't speak again.

Anxiety kicks in, twirling around in my brain, trying to find something to grab onto. Maybe I didn't do something right? Or maybe Tanner's upset with me? Perhaps I should be doing something better. My breathing speeds up, and my lungs feel like they might be filled with concrete. "Did I do something wrong?" I ask him.

"What?"

He moves when I turn my head to look at him.

"I don't understand why you would apologize for the way you make me feel. And now my mind is spinning with it."

"Oh, shit. No, Em." He rolls onto his back and looks up at the ceiling. "I felt bad because I couldn't get you there. I just couldn't hold back because, well, I don't know how to describe it without sounding like the dick I've been. And if I do, then I'm afraid you'll run for the hills." He turns to look at me with his own worried eyes and then presses his thumb gently between mine. "You always get this line when you're worried."

"Tell me." I set my chin on his chest.

"I've been selfish, and I'm not proud of the choices I've made."

"I'm not complaining." I smile. "Besides, who am I to judge your journey?"

He glances at me and lays a hand on the back of my head. "I've never felt like this with anyone else. Ever. It feels like I can't control myself. Like I want to tell you things." He caresses my hair with his heavy hand. "And I'm afraid."

"Of what?" I ask.

"Of ruining it by being me. Of hurting you. Of it ending." He rolls back toward me, wraps me in his arms, and then presses his forehead against mine. "You know last night when you were afraid to tell me you loved me?"

"Yeah."

"How did it feel after you said it?"

"It was like jumping from the Rock. Like you can't see the bottom in the dark, and it's scary. Your heart pounds. But then you do it, and you're flying. It's freedom. And after, elation." I bring my hands up to his cheeks. "Look at me, Tanner."

His beautiful, soulful brown eyes slide to mine.

"I'm never going to force you to jump, but I sure would like you to choose to jump with me." I smile at him, using his words.

"I'm terrified."

"A wise person once told me: that's the point."

tanner

"Tanner?" My mother's voice in the hallway draws me back to reality from the haven Emma and I have made.

"Oh shit." I sigh and close my eyes.

"Is that your mom?" Emma whispers, the circumference of her eyes doubling.

I nod. I get off the bed, tug on my shorts, grab a t-shirt, and shrug into it before opening the door to my room. I crack it open.

My mother is standing outside. "Is someone in there with you?"

"Yeah," I say, because I don't care one way or the other if she knows. It isn't something that has ever happened before. So, she doesn't have anything to bitch about.

Her mouth thins out, but she doesn't comment.

"Did you need something?"

"Please come to the kitchen." She turns and walks away.

I shut the door. When I turn around, Emma is dressed in her sundress from yesterday, and pulling her hair up into a messy bun. "Now, I'm really sorry."

"It would have happened sooner or later, right?" She smiles, and I can see she's trying to put on a brave face. Her skin turns pink, and she presses her hands to her cheeks. "She's going to think badly of me."

I meet her in the middle of the room where she's standing, looking like she's wilted. "Does it matter?"

"Well, yeah. It does. She's your mom."

"Only because she gave birth to me."

"You say that because you're mad at her, but if circumstances were better, I don't think you would."

I hug her, but I don't comment. I haven't considered it. I turned my emotions off to my parents as best as I could, but what if she's right? All the ways I've built walls to insulate myself.

"What if she hates me?" Emma sounds the smallest I've ever heard her. It confuses me.

"If there's one thing my mom is," I tell her, "it's accommodating to strangers. Appearances and all that. You're all good." I draw back and look at her face. She's frowning and has that little line.

"It's not that. I mean it is."

"What is it?" Her blue eyes rise to meet mine, and I can see her fear, her doubt, her insecurity. These are things that I don't associate with her. "Talk to me."

"She'll think I'm not good enough. I mean because–" She uses her eyes and eyebrows to suggest that we've had sex.

I lean back and smooth her hair, framing her face with my hands. "Em, you once told me that I'm good enough. So are you. To me. That's all that matters." I press my lips to hers, and she squeezes me with her arms. "Ready?"

She nods.

We walk into the kitchen holding hands.

My mom is standing at the island, and a man I've never met is sitting on the stool leaning toward her. He stands up when Emma and I walk into the room.

"Hi." He holds out his hand. He's good looking: tall, older, dark hair with streaks of gray. My mom has a type. He resembles my dad. "I'm Bradley. Brad. We spoke on the phone." He's nervous. I only know because he swipes his other hand over the backside of his pants.

Seeing him pushes a button of anger in me even if I rationally know it isn't his fault. My broken family flashes through my heart, and everything he represents is a complete breaking away of what I once knew. I realize Emma's right, and that I've refused to look at it before. Deep down, I think I have wanted my family back — the way we'd once been before Rory died. My mom and dad, together. Happy. Forget that Dad is already remarried and has a new family. It isn't rational. Bradley — Brad — is the embodiment of that never happening. I just look at his hand and then back up to his face.

"Tanner." I hear Mom's tone of voice, pleading with me to acquiesce. I should, probably for Emma's sake, but I can't.

Brad turns to Emma. "Hi."

She takes his hand, because she's kind and doesn't have all the history. "Emma." Then she looks at my mom.

"Marna." Mom extends her manicured hand.

Emma takes it.

"Is there something you wanted?" I ask.

"I just wanted to introduce you to Brad. I didn't know you'd have company." My mom blushes. "I thought we could eat a late breakfast if you hadn't eaten yet. Emma, please join us."

Emma looks down at the floor as if she's done something wrong.

"I have to take Emma home." I draw her from the room by her hand. "You got everything?"

She nods.

"Maybe another day?" My mother follows.

"Maybe." I lead Emma out to the truck.

Once we're inside, I take a deep breath. I don't start it right away, my muscles tense and ready for a sprint.

"Are you okay?"

"I don't know." I start the truck and drive away from my house. "You hungry?"

"You didn't want to eat with your mom and Brad?"

"No." My tone of voice is too harsh with her. I turn and look at her and reach for her hand. "I'm sorry. No. I don't want to eat with Marna and Brad. I want to take you to breakfast."

We end up at my favorite diner — one my mother wouldn't go to. The waiter pours us coffee. I'm struggling to center myself, so I focus on the black liquid falling into the cups.

"You want to talk?"

"I do. I don't." I sigh. "I don't want to drag you into my shit."

"Except, that is kind of what happens when you love someone, I think." She reaches across the table to cover my hand with hers. "Jump with me, Tanner."

"Your family is perfect, though, Em. Mine is… complicated."

"You'd be surprised." The way she says it makes me wonder what I don't know.

"I think you were right."

"I'm always right, Tanner. You should learn this now, because it will save you trouble later." She's smiling and takes a sip of her coffee.

I fill my coffee with sugar and cream. She scrunches her nose at me. "Sorry, Em. This is not one thing you're right about."

She shrugs. "Okay. So, what is?"

"It's been easier to run away from my parents, and how I feel about them, than to, like, face it."

She pulls out her phone and pretend texts while she says, "Note to self: consider a psychology degree." She smiles at me.

"I don't know what to do with it."

"What do you want?"

"You."

"Me aside. Take me out of the picture."

"I don't want to."

"Okay, just put me out of the picture's frame. For the sake of this discussion, what do you want from your family?"

"Nothing."

"But that isn't true. If it was, you could have shaken Brad's hand, and you would have considered your mom's invitation for breakfast."

"I want them to hurt." The answer surprises me. The stark truth of it. "Like they hurt me. I want them to hurt too. It's why I told my mother she'd lost me just like Rory. I want her to feel bad." I bury my head in my hands. It's so ugly.

"You know why I think I have anxiety?" she asks.

I look up at her.

"When I was young, my dad used to tell me, 'you're so perfect, Emma. My perfect little girl,' and I think somewhere along the way, I was afraid that maybe if I messed up, I'd disappoint him."

"But he loves you."

"I know that. I don't think what happens in our heads is rational." She fingers the cup handle, staring at it. "I just tried harder and harder to make sure I didn't. All that trying built a tower in my head where I could lock myself away." She looks up at me. "Like you, wanting your parents to feel how you've felt. It doesn't make you a bad person. It makes you human."

emma

Tanner drops me off with a promise to return to pick me up for the movie later. When he drives away, I stand on my porch, unsure if I'm ready to face my parents yet. I know mom sent me a 'be safe' text, but I know there's more wrapped up in the context of that message. It isn't my mom that worries me. I'm thinking of the look I'll see on my dad's face. I know I'm headed into a space where I've declared my sexuality to him. This is certainly not standing on the sidelines, and it certainly isn't in the scope of being their *perfect* daughter.

Telling Tanner about the root of my anxiety was even an eye opener for me the moment I said it. There I'd been, wanting to help him work through what he was feeling, and then I was faced with my own struggle. It hurts to think my fears are rooted in my perception of my dad's love for me, but it has had inadvertent consequences. And they aren't his, but mine. It's all so big and unwieldy. I'm not sure how to walk into the house, so I don't. I turn and sit on the top step of the porch.

I'm changed, my eyes opened to a new way of existing. Open to Tanner and all of the sensations both physical and emotional that he's awakened in me. I used to operate thinking I had to walk the perfect line, to follow the rules. Those would keep me safe and protected, but now they feel as though they were a sort of personal prison I'd constructed. I wasn't living, and now I feel alive. Simultaneously, I also feel shaky and insecure.

But I thought guilt would weigh me down. Guilt for submitting to my desire for Tanner. Guilt for having sex before marriage. Guilt for being less than pure, but the truth of it is, I don't. It's the red wire that's connected to Tanner. I'm emotionally invested in him. If I had tried to do the uncomplicated sex thing with him — or anyone else — for that matter — my feelings would be different. I'm not wired for sex without feelings. And I feel so much love for Tanner, the sex isn't the issue. It's the time.

I watch people walk by, their dogs on leashes or their kids in strollers. I wonder if they can tell I'm different. I feel so transformed, like perhaps it has messed with the structure of how I look. Mr. Collins waves to me as his chihuahua, Rambo, pulls him down the street. I wave back. A few moments later, the screen door squeaks open.

When I look up, it's my dad. He sits down next to me.

"You going to sit out here all day?"

"No."

"You okay?"

"Yeah."

"Did that boy hurt you?"

"Dad! No! His name is Tanner. You like him."

He takes a deep breath.

"Are you mad at me?" I ask, and the words catch in my throat.

He doesn't say anything at first, for a while, and I think I might jump from my skin as well as the porch. Then he says, "No. Mad isn't the right word."

"Please don't say disappointed."

"Not that either," he says. "Powerless. I feel powerless."

I look at him and notice him swallow. My strong dad, my hero, my rock, suddenly just a man. My whole life has been spent in worship of my dad. His patience, his love, his compassion. My chest tightens even though he said he isn't disappointed. I can hear the disappointment in his voice, and it's crushing.

"As a dad, I want to protect my babies, and you don't think of them venturing out on their own."

"I'm 18. An adult."

He holds up a hand. "I know. I know. Your mother and I have already been through it."

I imagine them in one of their conversations holed up in their room. The murmur of their voices as they discuss a topic of importance about me or Shelby.

"I know all the logical stuff, Emma. It's the emotional stuff that's harder."

Don't I know it.

"In my mind I see my baby. And I also imagine your future. And I don't want you to mess it up. Not for anyone. I don't want you to make a choice that could forever change things." He looks at me again. "I know it's your choice to make, but I also know who I was when I was 18."

"It's my choice and my journey. I'm tired of trying to be perfect, and I can't do it anymore."

"No one has ever asked you to."

"Maybe not, but that's what I heard: Emma — you're my perfect girl. But what if I never was? I'm tired, Dad. I'm tired of trying to be her, and I've let a lot pass me by. I want to live, to step into the current and let it take me before leaving for college."

"At what cost?"

"I love him," I say.

"I know that is how you think you feel."

"Because that's how I feel."

"I didn't mean to discount your feelings, Emma. That isn't what I meant. I just mean — you feel what maybe you don't completely understand yet."

I stand up. "You don't know what I feel." I'm crushed and angry.

He stands too. "I'm not saying this right."

"No. You aren't."

"I don't want you to irrevocably ruin your future because of a summer fling."

I hear the truth in his words — or the truth of what once was. I started out thinking being with Tanner would be a summer fling, a way for me to step out of my comfort zone and experience something exciting and new before leaving. Practice. But it had turned into something so wholly unexpected, so wonderful and full; Tanner surprised me. I've fallen in love with him, and the thought of leaving him in a few weeks has me anxious, but I also wouldn't trade it for anything. And what if there is a way to see it further? Would I think about not leaving? Yes, I would, even though I know it isn't the right choice. And perhaps that is what my dad is telling me. Except he has it wrong.

"It isn't a summer fling."

"Emma." He looks down at his feet, hands on his hips, and then at me again. "I'm your father. I'm your covering until you are married."

My fists press against my hips. "That's a ridiculous, antiquated notion and has nothing to do with this situation. I'm a capable person able to make this choice for myself." But even as I say it, I can feel the heavy blanket of religious context weigh against me.

"Are you intimating that our faith is ridiculous?" His face turns red.

I lean forward and sputter at him in anger. "No. Your anger isn't about faith. It's about religion."

His mouth falls open and then shuts again. He knows I'm right. It's a conversation our family has discussed my whole life; our pastor has taught sermons about legalism and grace, but I can see he still wants to fight me on it. I realize this isn't about religion or faith. It's about my dad, and his beliefs about me — his daughter. So, I add, "My body is mine just like my faith is mine. I get to decide."

Somehow his brain reboots, because he narrows his eyes. "This house is mine, which means I get to decide the rules."

Unable to hold myself up under my hero's disappointment in me, under the weight of his fallibility, I turn away from him and slam into the house. I run up to my room where I hyperventilate with emotion. I text Tanner: *Please come soon.* Then I crawl into my bed and sob.

tanner

When I arrive home — which I expect to be empty — it isn't. My mom is still there, but Brad is gone. She's in the kitchen, waiting for me. She doesn't say anything when I walk in, not at first, but measures me with her gaze. I imagine her as a spider waiting for me to hop into her web. Though maybe it isn't fair, and I'm just being a dick.

I'm about to leave her in the kitchen when her voice hits me. "We need to talk, Tanner."

I stop, but I don't turn around.

I hear her sigh. "Can you please come here and sit with me?"

It's my turn to sigh, but I return thinking about Emma and her question. Then about my answer: *I want them to hurt.* I'm not so sure I want that either. It's cold and detached, and it isn't how I feel. I feel redhot pissed. I appease her and take a seat at the table. Then I give her a look that I'm pretty sure pushes her buttons.

She comes around the island and sits on a stool at the counter. "You weren't very nice to Brad."

"What did you expect?"

"Civility, perhaps? I was civil to your — what is she?"

"My girlfriend."

"Ah. She going to last? I've recently been informed of your— uh — proclivities."

"Is that what this is? A fishing expedition on all the women I've slept with. You should ask your friend Pam about it. She taught me a lot."

Her mouth drops open with shock. Her eyes shift away toward the window as she thinks about what I've just told her.

"You want me to keep going? I have an extensive list, and I bet you know quite a few of the names. Is that why we're sitting here?"

She shakes her head as if trying to reconnect to the malfunction in her brain.

"Yeah. I didn't think you'd want to know. Emma is special, so leave her out of your insults."

She comes back online. "She knows about your extensive experience?"

"I'm done." I stand to go.

"Sit," she says in a mother tone I haven't heard for a while.

I sit. "Is this about trying to give me the same speech Dad did? You ask him how that turned out?"

"I know." She smooths the front of her pants. "He called me."

"And you were able to have a civil conversation? That's novel."

"Look. I get it, Tanner. We've screwed up. No one gives you a manual to know how to deal with–" She stops and then her throat works around the tears that are ready to bubble to the surface. When she finds control, she says, "How to be a parent. Throw in stuff you don't expect, and well, it's easy to go off the rails."

"You think?" I press a vein of wood on the table and run my finger along the grain.

"I'm trying here."

"How do you figure? Bringing Brad by to meet your grown son? You think that trying to be involved now changes things? That you get to tell me about how to treat my girlfriend or lecture me about sex?"

She's shaking her head. "I don't know what you want from me."

I stand. "I wanted my fucking mom. I wanted her eight years ago when Rory died. When I was twelve, thirteen, fourteen. Who helped me?

378

Who took care of me? You didn't. Neither of you did." I'm crying now, and it makes me even angrier.

She's crying too.

"You left me to figure it out alone and then used me to punish one another. And now you both think you can fix it? It's too fucking late." I leave her crying in the kitchen and escape to my room, slamming the door.

My phone buzzes.

Emma | Please come soon. |

With fucking pleasure.

e m m a

When Tanner's truck pulls up in front of the house, I'm moving
from my room, through the hallway and down the stairs to get through
the door, so we don't have to face my dad. But I'm a few steps behind
him. Dad pushes through the screen door ahead of me, the door
squealing on its hinges. It snaps back with a hiss, cutting me off, and I
stall on the steps. My breath crash lands in my lungs and stops everything
up. *Shit.* From my spot on the stairs, I can see them. Dad is closer to the
house as if he's a sentry on duty. Tanner is on the top step facing him.

I can hear the mumbling of their exchange but nothing concrete.

I restart my lungs and legs and move, stopping just on the other side
of the screen door. Dad's got his hands in the pockets of his shorts; he
looks casual. Both of Tanner's hands hold a crimson lanyard, and he's
looking down at it as though the comment he needs might be attached
to it rather than his keys. When they hear me push the screen door open,
the creaking of it punctuates something between them like an
exclamation point. Both of their heads snap to look at me. Both smile,
but Tanner's doesn't reach his beautiful eyes.

I glance at my dad and narrow mine.

"Enjoy the movie," he says and steps aside to let me pass. "Can I expect you home?"

He asks me, but Tanner's voice rushes forward. "Yes, sir."

I turn from my Dad to Tanner and feel my face scrunch together with a question.

"I'll have her back by midnight," Tanner adds, looking past me.

I follow the volley of his words and see my dad nod. He leans forward to kiss my cheek, and then disappears into the house. The screen door predictably follows its usual routine. Everything about what just occurred is outside of the norm, however. Something about the exchange sits poorly against my spine. I feel as though I've been removed from the equation, as if I'm a variable rather than a constant.

"What was that about?" I ask, following my dad's retreat with my head. I might be asking, but I have a pretty good idea. The discomfort pressed against my neck feels a little like a knife in my back. I look back at Tanner, who plasters on a smile.

"Nothing." Tanner holds his hand out to me.

I take it, and he pulls me toward him. A step on the porch lower than me, we're still nearly the same height. He wraps his arms around my waist when he draws me close, burying his head against the space between my collarbone and neck.

"I missed you." His lips caress the words against my skin, and the meaning of them seeps into the spaces that need them to be filled.

I tighten my hold of him, turn my head, and press my lips to his temple. "You just saw me." I smile against his skin.

"It was too long."

We stand there longer than necessary, arms wrapped around one another on the steps of my front porch, as though wrapped in a magic spell together. I have the impression we're both afraid. As if the moment one of us moves, the enchantment will disintegrate and leave us exposed.

Eventually, I do break the moment by saying, "Ready to go to the movies?"

"No." He shakes his head. "I just want to go somewhere with you."

I understand his sentiment and offer him a knowing smile.

"But," he adds and draws away so he can look at me, "I also want to take you out." He leads me to his truck and opens the passenger door.

Once he's in and driving I ask him, "You going to tell me what my dad said?"

His jaw contracts with tension and then releases when he says, "He was just being a dad. Don't worry about it."

But I am, because that's what I do. The earlier conversation with my dad churns around in my head, and if he said something like that to Tanner, it has me unsettled. My heart hitches. "Should I apologize for what he said?" I ask.

Tanner looks at me, surprised, and then back at the road. He reaches over and takes my hand from my lap. "Why would you think you should apologize for something your dad says?"

I shrug. It's too much to consider. Reality is I probably apologize too much for everyone around me, thinking I need to make everything perfect.

tanner

She's gone quiet, and I don't like it. Not because I don't like that she's quiet, but because I know she isn't quiet because she's content. She's freaking out over something — over her dad. It's a strange awareness that I can sense this, given how little time we've actually spent together. There's been such a shift in me, I can't seem to shut it off when I'm with her.

Her dad had been a dick, but I couldn't blame him. His words stung, but they were also truthful. He'd only said what I'd already been thinking.

"I don't want you stealing her future."

Could I fault a guy for caring about his daughter? Wouldn't I have wanted my own parents to be that invested in me? Yeah. I would. His words crash around inside me, knocking against my wants. My thoughts are like bumper cars at a fair, stopping me up short. At the same time, she's next to me, her hand in mine. All I can think about is wanting to be near her, wanting her to smile, wanting her to kiss me and make those gorgeous sex sounds that make me feel like the king of the world.

Don't steal her future.

But her dad has hit the nail on the head. I don't deserve her. She's better than me; she's going places I'm not. She has a future. I don't. My insecurities churn in my gut.

"Let's just not worry," I tell her. "You have that line between your eyes, and I know your mind is going a mile a minute."

She glances at me with a small smile; the line disappears. She chuckles. "You know me."

"And I want to know everything." I offer her hand a squeeze. It's the truth, and I know we don't have the time. "Let's just be in the now. Remember?"

She nods and smiles brighter. "Yes." She squeezes my hand back.

When we get to the movies, Josh and Ginny are already there. After buying Emma and I tickets, the girls disappear to the restroom, while Josh and I stand in line to buy popcorn.

"How are things?" I ask my friend.

He grins. "Good. You?"

I stare up at the menu. "I got a coming to Jesus speech from her dad tonight."

Josh's grin fades. "Damn. First one."

I nod. Take another step forward in line as the queue shifts forward. "What was that like?"

"Shitty." I glance at him. "Reminds you who's holding all the cards."

"Yeah. But is he?"

"Maybe not, but maybe he should be." We're silent a moment, watching the sign animate and move with the refreshment ads. "He's got a point."

"About what?" Josh asks.

"She's leaving, and I can't get in the way of it."

"Dude. She's not leaving tomorrow. You're thinking weeks from now."

I nod. "Truth?"

He raises his eyebrows.

"I like her."

"And TJ doesn't like anyone."

I laugh and look away. Hands deep in my pockets, I avoid meeting his gaze. "I don't want to hurt her."

"Might be a little too late for that. Either way — whether it's next week or a few weeks from now — you're walking away hurt because you're invested."

He's right. Fuck. He's right. It squeezes my throat thinking about it. I watch the animation of popcorn pop on the sign above the concessions.

"Griff text you?" Josh asks.

"Nope."

We take another step forward as the line shifts.

"So Red?" I nod in the direction the girls walked.

Josh grins, and it's his turn to shove his hands in his pockets. He shrugs. "She's cool."

"Yeah? You might be in trouble then."

He laughs. "Maybe."

emma

I leave the stall and wash my hands at the sink. "I just don't know what he said."

"Did you expect anything different from your dad?" Ginny leans toward the mirror to inspect her eyes.

"I don't really know what I expected."

She glances at me through the mirror, one of her brows arched as if to say: *come on*. "Emma. Your dad? He's, like, super protective. And über Christian. And loves you like nobody's business. How can you say you didn't expect it?"

She's right. "I guess because this is the first time I've liked someone."

"So, you like him, like him."

"You already knew that. And it's bigger than like."

She freezes and then turns to look at me with her eyes instead of through the mirror. "Love?"

I nod, looking away from her gaze.

"You tell him?"

I nod.

"Wow. What did he say?"

"Let's just say he spoke really loud with his body." My cheeks heat, and I look down at my hands as I wipe them with a paper towel. I can't calm my smile down.

She makes a humming noise in her nose and turns back to the mirror. "Well, no wonder your dad is flipping out. He's got competition for his baby's attention."

"Ew. You make it sound gross."

"I don't mean it like that. Your dad's awesome. I mean, like, you're his little girl, and you've worshiped his every move. Now, he's watching you slip away. Maybe he isn't ready yet, you know? Has to wrap his mind around it."

"But what if Tanner runs?"

Her brows come together. "So? Any guy worthy of you is going to take it. If he runs, fuck him. Like stupid Blaine."

She's right. Blaine from *Pretty in Pink* is a smarmy and gross like that. I know logically she's right. I need to move the spotlight. "And Josh?" I ask her.

"Time will tell." She turns back to me from the mirror again. "Damn, Em. He's a really good kisser. Makes me all swirly thinking about it."

When I see Tanner standing at the counter with Josh, my breath catches in my throat. He's so handsome. He moves, the black t-shirt stretching over his arm and chest as he reaches to return his wallet into his back pocket. Then the fabric stretches again over his back as he grabs something else, and I want to touch him. He nods at something Josh says, his dark hair curling at the edges and caressing the tan skin of his face. Then he looks up, sees me, and smiles. It reaches his eyes this time. I find my breath and release it slowly.

"Hey," he says when I reach him.

"Hey." I wrap my arms around his waist.

He wraps his arms around me, a moment in time when there isn't anything else working its way between us. Then I remember where we are and peel away.

He hands me a giant bottle of water. "Hold this so I can hold you." He presses his lips to my temple, and then he takes my free hand in his.

As we walk into the theater, I can't shake the feeling that maybe the particles collecting between us might be growing into something dangerous. My heart constricts with fear at the possibility. I'd already considered the difficulty of leaving Tanner at the end of summer, but the idea that something different might expose fissures didn't occur to me, or that there might be things to widen them. I squeeze his hand a little tighter, holding onto him with everything I've got.

countdown: 3

"The truth, in all of its rainbow glory, was that everything was falling apart."

-unnamed protagonist, *Kaleidoscope Concussion* by Saul Annick

tanner

The warehouse is quiet when I get there. The giant space stretches with racks stacked from floor to ceiling with materials, tools, and anything else a general contractor uses in the day-to-day operations of running a construction company. I like the smell, a combination of metal, wood, dirt, and oil, though my favorite is freshly cut boards measured to specifications for a job in the warehouse instead of on the jobsite. A dense acoustic captures all of the sound amidst the building supplies housed in its innards. My footsteps snap across the space, and though I've been every Sunday to help my dad for years, I don't think I've noticed the sound — or absence of it — before. The emotions connected to my nerves make everything else more intense and vibrant, though I'm not sure it's in a good way.

Everything feels heavy. How I feel for Emma, which I'm pretty sure is love even if I haven't told her. My awareness that she's leaving for college, and I'm not. The message from her father about stealing her dreams. The fight with Griff. My dad, my mom and Brad. Quitting. I've spent my life avoiding anything real. Now, it's like a dump truck has heaped a load of reality on my head, and I'm buried in it.

"I thought you quit?" My father is standing behind the intake desk looking at the Monday morning clipboard. He looks different, tired.

His voice surprises me since I hadn't expected him. I stall. I'd tried to be the first one in to prep the truck, needing the routine of it, and leave before he even arrived. "Yeah. Where's Will?"

"Not with me today." He flips the paper to read a back page. "Why are you here? Since you quit."

I think about telling him everything that's been going on. About Emma and Griff. About feeling like a failure. About being lost. I swallow the words and clear my throat. "I didn't want to leave you without anyone to prep the truck."

"Thanks, then." He sets the clipboard down on the flat surface and leans his elbows on the counter. His head drops forward, a hand wrapped around the back of his neck, and I notice he looks more drawn. Maybe a little pale. He runs his hand over his dark head, the gray t-shirt stretching across his shoulders. He takes a deep breath, leans back up on his hands, and then asks, "Can we talk, T?"

I shrug.

He must take my response as a sign I'm game to listen, and I suppose I am even if bitterness keeps me unsettled. He moves around to the front side of the counter, leans against it, and crosses his arms over his chest. "When Rory died–" He stalls when I make a sound he must interpret as impatient, but it isn't what I mean.

Rory's name makes it feel like my heart blisters and peels after being burned. I clear my throat.

"I need to tell you."

I nod.

He wipes a thumb over his right eyebrow with his right hand and clears his throat. "I got lost. Losing a child isn't something you can prepare for, even if you know it's coming. It's impossible not to keep the hope, to dig deep for strength to offer your kid. That's what you're supposed to do: keep the light on. And then suddenly, you can't, because you can't fix it. As a parent, and everything I ever thought about being a dad, I wasn't supposed to fail at keeping my kids safe. And I did." He stops. I can see he's battling emotions the same as I am as tears climb up my throat. He clears his throat again. "I know it sounds like an excuse. It is, but it's also the truth."

He takes a few deep breaths, looks up at the ceiling, then back at me. "You said the other day that you thought I avoided you because you looked like Rory."

I nod, tears slipping from my eyes.

"When Rory died, and I looked in the mirror hating who I was because I'd failed my son, a part of me died with him. I didn't have anything alive left for you, for your mom."

"That's fucked up."

"I know. I know it is. It's just another reason to hate myself, T. Another thing to add to the list of all the ways I've failed in this life. I couldn't hold myself together. As much as I tried, I couldn't figure out which way was up. I was drowning and dragged you and your mom into the quicksand with me. It wasn't you, Tanner. I was just too selfish to get out of my own pain." He pauses. "I'm really sorry, Tanner. The other day, when you said what you said, and I realized I'd missed your graduation; I looked at myself in the mirror and realized how much I've fucked everything up." He shakes his head.

I have the urge to tell him it doesn't matter, but it does. I keep my mouth shut.

"I know I can't ask for your forgiveness. I don't deserve it. And I don't know how to begin to make it right."

I'd like to tell him that he can't, but I don't, because I think it's a lie. Even if he can't, I want him to try. I want my dad. I'm so tired of climbing out onto the roof to hide. I'm tired of talking to stars and wishing someone could hear me. I'm tired of trying to hold myself upright. Emma — tangible Emma whose arms fit around me, who sees me and tells me I am enough — has taught me that. I need grounding, my feet firmly attached to this planet.

"If you'll let me try, I'd like to spend the rest of my life trying to be a better man. A better dad. To you."

The dam in me breaks, and tears free flow. I drop my head forward, and my chest cracks open with a sob. My dad's footsteps shuffle in the strange acoustics of the warehouse, and suddenly his arms are around me. The surface of me — the eighteen-year old who has raised himself — wants to flail about with rage, indignation, and tell this man that there isn't anything he will ever be able to do to make up for the canyon between us. The depth of me, however, the boy of me, the ten-year-old still needing his parents, collapses into the man who is my dad, grabs hold, and clings to the comfort of his strength.

emma

Dad has withdrawn since our fight, and my heart is weighted with a two-ton anchor. As much as I'd like to tell myself we will be okay, nothing about the silence between us feels okay. Mom and Shelby can feel it, because I see it in the flicker of their eyes moving between us. That morning, during church, after, and now around the dinner table, the tension is thick like smoke. I'm just trying to get through dinner to escape to my room and wallow in discomfort of having disappointed him. Another part of me is angry though, wrapped up in the belief that I haven't done anything to disappoint him; my choices — having sex with Tanner — have nothing to do with him, or my mother, or Shelby, or anyone else. Not God. Not even my love for God. Just me. Just Tanner.

I push my salad around on my plate, lost in my thoughts until Shelby taps my leg. I look up at her.

She nods at my grandparents across the table.

I glance at them. Both Nana and Pop Pop are studying me with suspended smiles on their faces. Pop Pop's bushy gray eyebrows are elevated over his crystal blue eyes. Nana's head is tilted, her sleek silver bob asymmetrical with the tilt. Nana's eyes narrow, and I see her shrewd mind working. "I'm sorry. Did I miss something?" I ask.

"How does it feel to be graduated?" Pop Pop asks, rolling his pasta with his fork into a spoon.

"It's fine. Just working at the Java House."

Pop Pop nods. "Good. Good. Having a job is a wonderful thing. Lots of things to learn, working. Having money is a nice benefit." He winks at me and takes a bite of his pasta.

"That's true. I like the independence."

"How's that boy we met? Tanner?" Nana asks.

I watch her gaze slide from me to Dad and then bounce back again. My father takes a bite of his spaghetti while keeping his eyes on his plate. I look at my plate. "Good. We went to the movies last night with some friends."

"What did you go see?" she asks.

"That new rom com. The one with Stella Morris."

"Oh. I think she's a good actor," Nana says. "Was it good?"

I shrug. "Yeah. Formulaic, but I enjoyed the company."

Nana smiles at me, and with its vibrancy I feel okay. I feel like maybe I don't have anything to feel angry about.

Dad clears his throat, breaking open a fault line. "Too bad you're leaving in a few weeks."

My gaze darts to him, hot with irritation and tears that press against the back of my eyes. "I don't need the reminder, thanks."

"It's always good to be prepared. You know. For the worst."

"Don't pretend that bothers you."

Dad looks at me, his mouth thin with anger and jaw pressed together. Then he looks back at his plate and twists a bite onto his fork. "That isn't fair. Of course, I'm bothered you're leaving."

"Just not that I'll be leaving Tanner."

"Goodness," Nana mumbles. "I may have popped open a can of worms."

"That's a norm for you, my girl." Pop Pop pats the top of her hand with his.

"I love him." I set my fork on my plate. The metal clanks against the glass.

"You love the idea of him."

"Mo." My mom's voice is heavy with warning.

"Excuse me." I set my napkin on the table next to my plate and push away from the table.

"You haven't been excused."

It's a battle of wills, and I have no intention of backing down. I know I've been taught to honor my mother and father, and I have. I do. But for some reason, this feels different. This feels like standing up for myself.

"I don't need permission to remove myself from an unhealthy situation." I walk away.

I hear the scrape of a chair, and my mother's voice says my father's name again. Then Nana offers words, though I don't catch them, because I've turned up the stairway, and the walls insulate their voices. I don't allow the tears to fall until I've closed my door, lean against it, and then drop my face into my hands.

A few moments later there is a soft knock at my door. "Emma?" It's Nana.

I wipe my face with my hands and open the door.

"May I come in?"

I follow Nana with my eyes as she walks into my sanctuary — or what used to be. Now, that feels like wherever I'm with Tanner. Nana perches on the edge of my bed. Her lavender shirt swirls around her, and she opens her arms toward me. I glide into them and cry again. "He's being such a jerk."

"There. There." Her hands comfort me with gentle movement, a pat here, an adjustment there.

When all the tears seem to have been spent, I lean back and find a tissue to clean my face. "Sorry, Nana."

"Oh shoo." She smiles. "What are Grammies for?"

I sniff.

"When I was your age — oh goodness — getting locked in a battle of wills with your father was unheard of. So, of course, that's what I did."

She chuckles.

I smile through my tears.

She tucks me back into her embrace and continues talking. "There was this boy who I met outside of the soda fountain in the town where I grew up. He'd just gotten out of the military and was just a sight. Goodness." She drifts a moment, remembering. "A bit older. He was working as a builder, and my father caught wind of my talking to him. He forbade me to see him, and well — my father's dictates didn't work very well with me. Being the wily young lady I was, my girlfriend, Audrey, and I devised a way for me to keep seeing the boy. Thankfully, it was summertime and made it so much easier to figure out ways to do it. The summer fair was in town, so every night, we'd meet at the Ferris Wheel and around and around we'd go. Ever kiss on a Ferris Wheel?"

I giggle and shake my head. "Did great granddad find out?"

"Oh. Yes, he did."

"How?"

"That young man wanted to come calling, officially."

"What's that?"

"Dating. Like you going to the movies with your young man; he didn't want to sneak about. My father was furious. Ranted at me, but after some time, cooled off and relented."

"How come?"

"We both were stubborn, like you and your dad. And I supposed my dad knew that if I had to choose, I might not choose him. He went the safer path." She stops, and her hand continues to pet my hair. "Here's the thing I want you to hear, Emma: no one can tell you the value or the depth of the feelings in your heart. Only you. You get one chance at this life. One chance to take the risk. One. We win some. We lose others. We fail. We love. We cry. But every experience — the good ones and the bad ones — shape our stories in all their complex and beautiful color." She goes silent and squeezes me to her. "Do you understand what I'm trying to tell you?"

"I think so."

She grabs my shoulders and holds me at arm's length so she can look at me. Then she frames my face with her soft, weathered hands, and her bright blue eyes search mine. "Every day, Emma. Every moment matters in the tapestry of you. It isn't the choices we make that invalidate who we are as people, but it's not making a choice because we are afraid that will."

I nod. She's right. Tanner — in all of that complexity — has made me a better and stronger person.

"What happened to that boy."

Nana smiles. "I married him."

Ginny leans over the counter at the Java House. "I'm still jealous as hell that you got the prime job."

"You're two doors down." I slide her Matcha green tea across the counter toward her. "How's the ice cream business?"

"Sucks. All the little kids wanting samples. I think I scooped two gazillion samples and sold two ice cream cones. Yesterday, I decided to tell them that a monster spit in all of the buckets."

"You didn't."

"Okay. I didn't. But I wanted to."

"How's Josh?"

She gets a dreamy faraway look in her eye. "He's — just, wow."

"That good huh?"

"We haven't gone that far." She smiles.

I offer her a smile, but it's measured; things just feel so off. Between Tanner who's distant and my dad, who's moody, I feel like I'm being punished somehow. It has nothing to do with God, but instead the human beings in my life.

She sighs. "He's talking about wanting to take me away for the weekend to his family's cabin. Except my dad and step-monster say that I'm still under their rules until I'm paying my own way. Which means: no unchaperoned co-ed sleepovers. How did you — of all people — get away with that?"

I know she's referencing my very Christian parents. "I didn't ask." But I also don't go into detail about the repercussions with my dad, because I did make that choice. A consequence like my mom said I had to be willing to face. I close my eyes and imagine my Nana and her wisdom: *You get one chance at this life. One chance to take the risk.* I refocus on Ginny. "I'm sure you'll find the work around; you always do." The bell rings above the door. "I better get back to work. I'm done here in a couple of hours. I'll come down and see you after?"

Ginny raises her cup of Green Matcha Tea to me.

I watch her leave, and then take up my position behind the cash register once again. I don't hate working. I love that it gets me out of my house and away from my dad, but it's pretty mindless. Unfortunately for me, it leaves a ton of time for my mind to wander and then to wonder and then to feel tight with errant thoughts.

I miss Tanner. Since the movie — or his talk with my dad — he's been busy. I have been too, so I know my worry should be contained to reality, but my overthinking always gets me into mind spirals. His texts are short, our conversations pointed, and though his words are still sweet and endearing, it feels like a pulling away. I miss our stories.

"Hello? You in there?" A voice interrupts my meandering thoughts.

I refocus and recognize the guitarist from Senior Send Off. "Oh. Hey." I snap my fingers trying to remember his name and finally say, "Ryan, right?" He's dressed in a black shirt and khakis, tying on a blue apron like mine. "I didn't know you worked here."

"Yup. When did you start?"

"A while."

"And you've survived Brandon here?" He offers a good-natured laugh at the barista who's been training me.

Brandon tosses his blond dread head — even though the unwieldy group of hair pythons is tied back as best as he can — and grins. "I've been easy on her. Right Emma?"

"All good," I say and straighten the gift cards next to the register.

399

"Now, she's all yours, Rye-Guy, since I'm out." Brandon removes his apron and disappears through the door to the back. His girlfriend, Honey, is walking in the front door when Brandon reemerges. "See you both on the flip side." He throws an arm over her shoulders; the bell above the door rings as they leave.

Ryan takes up the space behind complicated machinery that makes the espresso and begins cleaning it. The morning rush has subsided, and now we're down to two people with laptops in opposite corners with earbuds in their ears. I go through the pastries and the cooler to pull any expired food; there isn't any since I did it earlier.

"So, now that graduation has come and gone, what's next?" Ryan asks me.

"College. Headed to California. Berkley."

"You're a smarty, then."

"No. I work hard."

"Point taken. Didn't mean to offend."

"You didn't. You?"

"I'm at a Berklee too. Berklee School of Music in Boston."

"Wow. A different kind of smarty."

He smiles.

"You are very talented. I enjoyed listening to you play at the campfire."

"I didn't know you noticed."

"Sure. John Mayer."

"You walked away. I thought maybe you hated it."

I smile, walking into the dining area to collect a full gray tub of dirty dishes, thinking about the fact he'd noticed whether I'd been listening or not. "No. It was great. Had stuff on my mind." I carry the tub into the back. Once the dishes are running in the washer, I return to the front. Ryan is making a drink for someone waiting.

"Thanks," I say when he's done.

"Teamwork." He wipes the frother. "What are you thinking about studying?"

"Not sure yet. Something in science, though. I've kind of been thinking about biology."

He nods. "That's cool."

"But I also really like chemistry. So, I'm not sure yet. Keeping my options open."

"That's wise. Things change for sure. You have new experiences, meet tons of people, new teachers and opportunities. It's good to keep your options open."

He sounds like my dad. It takes great effort to keep from rolling my eyes at the echo of my father.

A group of women come into the shop, which then seems to open up the floodgates for a slight rush. A look at the clock, and I'm down to thirty minutes left in my shift.

I wipe things down again in the dining room, put away the clean dishes and utensils, restock shelves and then wait. A girl named Caroline comes in and goes into the back to wait for her shift to start.

"Are we on together again this week?" Ryan asks.

"I don't know," I say.

He slips into the back. When he returns a few moments later. "Yep. Not tomorrow but Friday morning and Sunday evening." He grins, and the bell rings on the door. "I'll get to give you a hard time since Brandon has been going so easy."

"Whatever," I say with a smile and shake my head.

I turn to look at the customer who approaches the counter. My heart flutters with awareness as Tanner stands on the other side of the counter. He's in his work clothes — jeans and a gray t-shirt with his dad's company's logo on the front. Heavy boots. He looks yummy, and I can't keep the smile from my face at the joy of seeing him. "Hi."

He smiles and holds a tiny bouquet of hand-picked flowers out to me. "Hi."

Pretty sure I'm radiating warmth; I take his offering. "What is this for? I didn't expect to see you until later."

"I couldn't wait."

"Can you wait another five minutes?" I ask, glancing at the clock.

"Yeah."

"You want something?"

"Nope. Just you." He glances at Ryan.

His words make me silly grin, and the worries slip away. "Oh. This is Ryan. Ryan, Tanner."

Tanner holds out his hand. "You were a year ahead of us, right. I remember you playing guitar at Senior Send Off. You can jam."

Ryan shakes Tanner's hand. "Thanks." His gaze moves to me. "We're good here. You can clock out since Caroline is already here."

I untie my apron. After hanging it on the peg and clocking out, I grab my stuff. "See you Friday, Ryan." I slip out the door with Tanner, my hand in his. "I'm so happy to see you."

"I missed you." He draws me into a hug and then kisses my temple.

"It's nice to be missed." I press my cheek against his chest and enjoy the sound of his heart.

"Ryan Bishop works with you, huh?"

I draw away at the tone of his voice. It's tight and lacks the fun it usually holds. "Just found out today."

"You guys looked like old friends."

A red flag goes up in my mind, and I think back over what Tanner would have seen. Ryan and I were talking and laughing. Did it look like flirting? "Are you jealous, Tanner?" I ask him, grasping hold of his belt loops and rocking him back and forth even though he barely moves.

The tendon in his jaw works. He looks away for a moment, sighs, and then his eyes return to me. "That wouldn't be smart," he says and then offers a wan smile. "Why would I need to be jealous?"

"You don't," I say and rise up on my toes to kiss him.

We meander toward the ice cream parlor where Ginny works.

"So, I have some news," Tanner says, "and you were the first one I wanted to share it with."

"What is it?"

"I talked to my Dad."

"That's good. I hope." I glance at his shirt.

"Yeah. He apologized. I went back to work."

"That is good, then."

He looks down at his shirt. "Yeah."

"Talk to your mom yet?"

"Not really. But that's not what I wanted to tell you."

"What's up?"

He looks away as if searching for the words. "Dad had this idea that maybe I could go work for an uncle in Hawaii, since I'm not sure what I want to do yet. Turns out, my dad's half-sister's husband owns a construction company out there. Anyway, he put in a call, and they said they'd love to have me."

"Whoa." I stop moving. "Hawaii? That's so far away."

His eyes find mine. "Did you know that it's almost the exact same difference between here and San Francisco and San Francisco and Honolulu. And it isn't a sure thing."

"You checked?"

He smiles and looks down at his feet.

"Except there's an ocean between San Fran and Honolulu." We walk hand-in-hand in silence, and I ask, "Are you thinking about going?" I'm thinking about how far away Tanner is going to be either way, but in my head across an ocean sounds farther and makes my heart seize up. I know it isn't fair; I'm leaving for California. The reality of it has always been rooted in the realization that I would be leaving Tanner behind, that he would be here. Even though it makes me feel guilty for finding comfort in that thought, I did.

He must see the shock I'm feeling in my eyes. "It wouldn't be until after—" he stops and then mutters— "you leave."

I turn away to hide the tears burning my eyes. "I'm sorry. I'm happy for you. I am. I don't want to think about being apart."

He pulls me closer. "One day at a time, right?"

I nod against his chest but for some reason, the comfort I expect isn't there. I'm thinking about Tanner leaving. I'm thinking about Tanner meeting new people, and for some reason the only voice I hear is Bella Noble's saying, *what can you offer someone like him?*

tanner

My nerves are frayed. I'm worried about what's coming. After I park my truck in front of Emma's, I sit in the cab, gulping breaths for bravery. I don't want to face Emma's dad again, but then what kind of man would it make me to avoid it? I'd considered it, scared to see the judgment on his face, because he knows what I've done with his daughter, but Emma means too much to me. It makes me think about what my dad said about facing himself. I don't want to keep looking in the mirror and regret who's looking back at me.

My eyes shift up to the rearview mirror to meet my own gaze. "You got this." I say aloud. I take one more deep breath and leave the safety of the truck cab.

When I knock on the front door, I hope it's Emma who answers the door. It isn't. Shit.

"Hi, Mrs. Matthews," I greet Emma's mom.

She smiles the kind of smile that reaches her eyes and disarms the nukes I'd entered the codes for in my head. "Hi Tanner. So glad you could come to dinner." She steps back so I can pass her walking into the house. "We're in the back. Emma should be down in a few. She just got home from work."

After she shuts the door, I follow her through the hallway. Shelby is standing outside on the deck next to her dad, who's at the grill.

"Anything I can do to help?" I ask her, hoping it takes me away from here.

"Yes. Actually." She picks up a tray with packets of foil on them. "Can you give these to Mo. He'll get them on the grill."

Anything but Mo, I think, but take the tray. "Sure." Then like a dead man walking, I take my final walk before I'm thrown into the barbecue for the human sacrifice.

Shelby turns and sees me. Her eyes light up. "Hey, Tanner."

"Hi, Shelbs."

Mr. Matthews looks over his shoulder. "Hello there, Tanner. Glad you could make it."

I'm not sure if I believe him, but say, "Mrs. Matthews asked me to deliver these."

"Excellent." His voice is clear and vibrant, no anger or censure in his tone. He takes the pan from me and offers a smile.

I think about putting the nuclear bombs back into the bunker but am not ready to let my guard down completely.

"Shelby, would you take these to Mom for me?" He puts the steaks he's grilled onto a plate and holds it out to Shelby. She takes it and disappears into the house.

Now, it's just him and me. The two of us. Alone on the deck.

"How are you doing?" he asks and closes the top of the barbecue.

I'm not sure what to make of his question. *Doing* in what capacity? So, I just say, "Good."

He turns and reaches for a glass on the railing. "Would you like something to drink?"

"No, thank you. I'm good."

He leans against the railing and takes a sip of whatever is in his glass. "What are you up to this summer?"

"Just working."

"Where's that?"

"For my Dad's company."

He nods at the foil on the grill. "What kind of work is that?"

"Construction."

"Useful skills."

I'm not sure how to respond so I don't. I'm not sure if it's because of how I already feel about myself, my own failing and lack of options, or because his tone of voice has implied it. I just feel small.

"Hi."

My attention is drawn to Emma, who walks through the open door, and I feel my chest tighten. Her dark hair is wet from her shower. Wearing a pair of dark denim shorts that hug her curves and a fitted red top, she looks like summer and joy. The smile on her face reinforces my feelings for her, but there's a dangerous undertow caused by how I'm feeling about myself. I hear Griff's words: *she's smart, Tanner. You're not.* I smile anyway. And her father's: *don't steal her future.* Seeing her with Ryan Bishop in the coffee shop the other day started my wheels spinning. Her smile and their laughter. I couldn't help but think he was a guy more deserving of her. It made me jealous as hell and reminded me there would be Ryan Bishops all over her college campus. She was leaving.

"Hi."

She gives me a hug.

I'm stiff, worried about her dad, who's standing there, observing.

When she pulls away, she looks at me. She can feel my hesitancy. "Want to watch some TV with me?" she asks.

I nod.

"This won't be long," her dad calls after us.

Emma ignores him and pulls me by the hand through the sliding door, past the kitchen, and through the pocket door that leads to the stairs down into the basement. When we get to the bottom of the stairs, she turns into my arms and kisses me — a full-frontal attack — which heats me up. I participate, willingly, because Emma is in my arms. My hands settle in the curvature of her back, press her tighter against me.

"I've missed you." Her fingers play with my hair at the back of my neck. Electricity races down my spine.

"It's only been a few days." I smile against her mouth.

"Too long." She draws away, and her eyes move over my face. "Are you okay?"

I nod, but I'm not. I'm not even sure I could tell her why. It isn't her. It's me. So, I resort to my default setting and kiss her again. It's easy and perfect and feels good.

"Emma?" Shelby calls down from the top of the stairs. "Dinner."

"Coming up," Emma says, but her eyes remain on me. Her eyebrows shift to ask me a question. "You sure you're okay?"

She's smart, Tanner. You're not.

I nod and follow her up the stairs.

We sit down to dinner on the deck. The sun is waning, and the evening is comfortable. As dinners go, it's typical. It isn't like her family are cannibals, and I was on the menu, even if my insecurity makes me feel like that might be the case. There's lots of talk about work, and customers, and clients, about Shelby's adventure to the community pool with her friends. Questions about the movie we watched, and what I do for my dad. I do note Emma's strain with her family, the ease of graduation night coiled up into something tighter and tense.

Then her Dad says, "So, where are you headed to college, Tanner?"

And I wonder if we'd already talked about this. Had we? Maybe not. Emma clears her throat.

I glance at her, and she's shooting daggers at her Dad with her eyes. It was a question he already knew the answer to. It makes me feel smaller, because its purpose has been served. *What are your prospects for my daughter*, it asks? *None*, is the answer. I put my hands in my lap. "I'm going to stay here. Work for my dad."

"Oh. That's nice." He offers a smile that doesn't reach his eyes.

I swallow because I notice his eyes shift to Emma. In their depths: *I told you.*

I'm on edge.

Emma is too. "I think it's great." She looks around the table, but her eyes stop on her plate. "Here I am going to be going into debt for a degree, and Tanner is going to be making money." She reaches for my hand under the table, finds it and squeezes.

I can't offer anything emotional in return.

She's smart, Tanner. You're not.

"That is so true," Emma's mom says with extra vibrancy. She shifts uncomfortably in her seat, sends a look to her husband, and then offers me that smile.

"Tanner said he might be going to Hawaii to work."

"Hawaii?" Shelby's voice sounds excited. At least someone is impressed.

"Hawaii," Emma's mom says. "That's exciting."

I glance at Emma, annoyed. It isn't because she's shared it but because of the way she shared it. As if she wanted me to look better for her dad — or maybe it's my own insecurity. But it's too late. The damage has been done, pushing me off course.

After dinner, Emma suggests we hang out. "I better not," I say. "Work is early."

I can tell she's disappointed, but I can't seem to shift the trajectory. I can feel myself withdrawing as if Before Tanner is about to move back into my body.

She walks me out to the truck. "I'm sorry about my dad."

I don't respond, just open the truck door.

"He and I have been fighting. He's just being a jerk."

"I don't want to come between you."

"You aren't." She wraps her arms around me.

I move away.

"What's wrong?"

"I thought you weren't happy about Hawaii."

She's left a hand on my arm. Her touch is burning me. I want it, but I'm angry and insecure.

"Are you upset I shared it? I'm sorry. Was I not supposed to?"

I shrug.

She grabs a hold of my shirt at my stomach with both hands. "Really. I'm sorry."

I can't look at her. "I'm sorry, too. That I'm too stupid to go to college."

Her hands fall away from me. Then she crosses her arms in front of her. "I didn't think or say that."

"You didn't have to. Your whole family thinks it."

"Or maybe it's just you who thinks it." She takes a step back. "I never have, Tanner."

She's right. She hasn't, but I'm not thinking clearly. Instead, I'm thinking about the way her dad looked at her. The way she mentioned me leaving for Hawaii, and how defensive it makes me feel. I want to offer her more, but there's suddenly a canyon between what I want and what I think I deserve. *She's smart, Tanner. You're not.* I retreat further. "I better go."

"Yeah." She turns away from me, but not before I see the tears in her eyes.

I feel like an asshole. I don't know how to stop what suddenly feels like is rolling down hill and gaining speed. I get into my truck and drive away, leaving her standing on the sidewalk. And now I'm angry. I want to be angry at her, but if I look closer at my feelings, it's anger at myself. I don't know what to do with it. Everything I am — wrong. Every choice I've made — wrong. Maybe even Emma, who deserves more than my shit show. And I think about Griff and realize he always saw me for what I am.

When I park my truck in my driveway at home. I text Griff: *You were right.*

It takes a few minutes, but the three dots pop up.

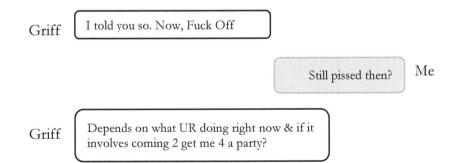

Griff — I told you so. Now, Fuck Off

Me — Still pissed then?

Griff — Depends on what UR doing right now & if it involves coming 2 get me 4 a party?

In my heart, I go through all the reasons to avoid this. I love Emma. But in my head, all I can think about is all the reasons she's leaving for college — she's smart; I'm not on either count. She's leaving. She's leaving. She's leaving.

I text: *On my way.*

emma

It's Saturday night. I didn't work, but Tanner did. I feel the distance between us stretching. I don't know what to do, how to reach him. I spent the day finishing *Kaleidoscope Concussion*, needing some way to feel close to him again. I text him.

Me: *Hey. Guess what?*

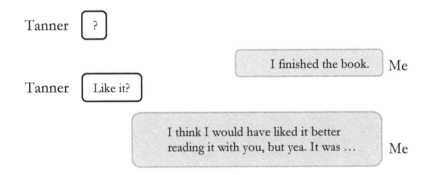

Tanner [?]

I finished the book.   Me

Tanner [Like it?]

I think I would have liked it better
reading it with you, but yea. It was ...   Me

I want to tell him I know why he likes it so much. He's faced so much loss in his life. That quote: *How everything you ever love will leave.* But I'm unbalanced with him, teetering on a tightrope, unsure how to be with him anymore. All the things that make me insecure rearing their ugly faces and growling with power to keep me contained. Things had been so easy and now, it is as if a switch has been flipped.

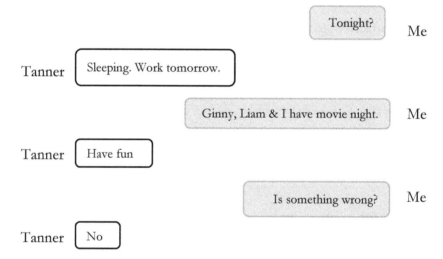

Tanner   ?

                                    Powerful and sad.   Me

I wait for him to text me back, to say something, but he doesn't, and insecurity roars. *See,* it says, *he was never going to choose you.* As if I have something to prove to this inner voice, I text him: *What are you up to?*

Tanner   Work

His answer confuses me.

                                              Tonight?   Me

Tanner   Sleeping. Work tomorrow.

                          Ginny, Liam & I have movie night.   Me

Tanner   Have fun

                                    Is something wrong?   Me

Tanner   No

My throat swells with self-doubt. *You're not good enough, Emma,* I think. I don't know how to navigate these new waters. I don't know if I should text him or if I should give him space. I decide on the latter even though every part of me wants to fix it. I don't want to be right about me not being good enough and Tanner never changing. I want us to be bigger than those boxes.

Sometime later, I leave for Ginny's since she wanted to host movie night to annoy her stepmom. When I get there, Liam is already there. They've set up inside what used to be Ginny's bedroom, the computer on the bed in front of them.

"Emma!" Ginny singsongs when I walk into the room. She adjusts herself on her bed, pulling a fluffy tie-dye pillow tighter against her body and leaning against the bare wall a new shade of pink — so not my friend's taste in colors. The bed sits on the floor, the frame having been dismantled and packed boxes serve as furniture. The effects of Ginny's stepmom are clearly present in the room that was once Ginny's but now looks like a cleaned-out rental.

Her smile fades when she looks at me. "What is it?"

I offer her a smile, because I'm not sure what to say, and I don't have it in me to hear, *I told you so*. Besides, even if it makes me foolish, I still have hope. I'm in love with him, and to me that means working through stuff. "Doesn't your stepmom know you'll be back for Christmas break?" I avoid her question and climb onto the bed to face her and Liam.

"And all of the breaks from school?" Liam adds.

Ginny rolls her eyes. "I don't think step-monster cares all that much about what I want. According to her, I'll have an air mattress for visits." She shrugs and then grins, ready to discuss the real reason we've convened. "Now, updates. Atticus, Liam."

Buster — Ginny's black cat — jumps onto the bed like a stealth bomber.

"Oh shit." Liam clutches his chest.

The cat's tail, tipped white, flicks with a Morse code message. Then he pads across the bed to Ginny with his white stocking feet.

"Can you get that cat a bell or something."

Ginny picks him up. "A bell would be undignified. What is it Mr. B?" She asks him. He begins purring in her arms.

"So, Atticus?" I look at Liam, hopeful he has better news to report than I do. "Everything okay?"

Liam sighs and runs a finger along a line in the fabric of the comforter.

"I don't like the sound of that."

Liam looks at both of us. "We decided to just be friends."

"What?" Ginny sits up straighter. Buster whines at her sudden movement, darts out from her arms, and tears from the room.

"What? Why?" I ask. Panic tightens my chest as I consider this development, because I'm not thinking about Atticus and Liam. I'm thinking about Tanner.

Liam continues to follow the trail of a pattern of fabric in the quilt with his hand as though following the trail to gather his thoughts. When he looks up, he gives a smile meant to bring us comfort, but it does the opposite. Instead of comfort, I feel guilt. I haven't been there for him, so immersed in my own world, my own struggle; I hadn't understood his journey or even asked about his relationship, but he's been there for me.

"Atticus is at the beginning of his journey."

"What does that mean?" Ginny asks.

"I've known I was gay and have been living my truth since I was fifteen." Liam wraps his arms around his legs. "Atticus is only coming out now."

My breath catches, and I swallow, considering how Tanner and I also represent differing perspectives and experiences. "But does that mean it can't work?" I don't know if I'm asking for me or him. Every part of me wants what I have with Tanner to work, but I'm suddenly afraid.

What could I possibly offer a guy like Tanner?

"I think that means that we're just in different places," Liam says. "Like I'm more comfortable in my sexuality because I've lived it longer. Atticus isn't there yet. And it isn't something you can rush because it's a trip you have to take by yourself."

"It can't be taken together?" Ginny asks.

Liam shrugs. "Yeah. I guess it could. It might have a cost though, right? Like maybe we support one another, but what if at the end we aren't even friends anymore because we grow angry and bitter."

"I feel like I don't understand." Ginny scoots back on her bed, leans against the wall, and stretches out her legs. "Like I ship you both so hard.

How come it can't work?" She crosses her arms over her chest and looks as sad as I feel.

Liam sighs. "It's like, I'm ready to hold hands at the movie theater, but Atticus isn't quite there yet. He needs to figure out that part of himself. And I don't want to be upset with him for doing that because it isn't fair to him, but I wouldn't be fair to myself either if I'm ready to be loud and proud about my relationship."

"You don't want to resent him."

Liam nods to Ginny. "I don't. I like him too much."

I think about Tanner's face after dinner the other night. His words about not being smart, about not going to college. The anger and hurt. "Are you sad?" I ask, because I have been.

"Yeah," Liam says, "but it's the right thing. We're both trying to figure out who we are in our own skin, you know? We're both going to college on opposite coasts of the country. Neither of us want the long-distance thing, and we want to stay friends."

"Oh. I see." Ginny smiles. "Friends with benefits."

Liam blushes. "Not my style, Gin. Not my style at all."

"Still have your V card?" Ginny has no shame.

Liam offers her a condescending look, his chin lowered toward his chest, eyebrows arched. "Not that it is any of your business, but I'm the last of us to hold membership. It will take a bit more for me than just a few amazing kisses."

Ginny laughs. "Well, I've been making out like a mad woman with Josh. Other than that, we actually talk a lot. He's really awesome."

"You worried about leaving for school?" I ask, because that's on my mind.

"No. Not really. We are just dating and enjoying one another's company. I mean, we're both aware we're leaving soon. I don't want to go down that road with him and then overthink things like I have with dickhead numero uno."

"But you like him?" I ask.

Ginny looks at me with more knowledge than is comfortable. "Yes. I do. I'm super disappointed in the timing of it. But like you said, Liam, neither of us want a long-distance relationship. So, we'll enjoy this while it lasts, you know?"

I nod and curse my stupid emotions, because I can't keep the tears out of my eyes. I cover my face.

Both of my friends move, and their arms are around me.

"Why did I have to fall for him?" I sob. "I didn't want to fall in love."

"It isn't something you can control, Emma," Liam says. "Even if you wanted to."

"You did. Both of you. Controlled it."

"No. Not true," Ginny says. "Josh and I might have made a decision to not be in a long-distance relationship, but that doesn't mean feelings aren't involved. I really like him."

"And I really like Atticus." Liam swipes a hand over my head, smoothing my hair, soothing my outburst. "I like him so much, but that's why. I don't want to ever resent him. We're going to stay friends. Who knows? Maybe that will lead somewhere one day. I really do like him, Em. A lot."

"Some things, Emma, just can't be controlled, no matter how much you try," Ginny says.

I draw back and look at my friends through a teary gaze. I nod. "I thought it was just going to be a fun summer fling."

"Did you guys decide what to do about you leaving?"

I shake my head. "No. We've avoided it, but–" I stop.

Ginny and Liam exchange glances. "But what?" Ginny asks.

"I think he's pulling away."

Liam presses his lips together but squeezes my hand.

"Please don't say it," I beg him.

"I won't." He pulls me into his arms.

Ginny's hand swipes back and forth over my back. "Why do you think that, Em? Anyone can see the way he looks at you and recognize he's in deep."

I move away from Liam and wipe at my cheeks with my fingertips. "He's acting differently. Withdrawn."

"Have you talked to him about it?" She hands me a tissue.

"Not in those exact words."

"That's probably a good next step." Liam squeezes my forearm.

Ginny nods.

I nod and sniff, using the tissue to dab my eyes. "You're right. Operation: Figure This Shit Out." I smile through my tears. Having a plan makes me feel better. I can make plans. It is what I'm good at.

Liam and Ginny laugh. "There's our Emma."

We collect on the center of Ginny's bed, arms wrapped around one another, our amoeba a welcome distraction.

"You know what always makes us feel better?" Ginny asks.

"John Hughes." Liam and I say together.

I settle in between my friends. Ginny cues up *Sixteen Candles,* and we start the movie. We aren't really in it, however. Ginny is texting with Josh, who's somewhere with his family for the week; Liam is on his phone scrolling Instagram and Twitter. I'm trying to focus on the movie, but my mind keeps driving itself back to Tanner.

I did fall in love with him. I'm not sure anymore what it means. Looking forward, a relationship seems impossible. With California and now a possible Hawaii on the horizon, I don't know how to navigate the distance. Do I want a long-distance relationship? I feel so strongly for him I would do it, but does that mean it's the right thing to do? For me?

What could I possibly offer a guy like Tanner?

"Oh shit." Liam sits up to look at whatever is on his phone. I can't see anything since he's blocking his phone with his body.

Ginny pauses the movie. "What?"

Liam looks up from his phone at me and then at Ginny.

My heart sputters at his wide-eyed worried look.

He turns his phone and presses an IG story — Griff's — and he taps through it until he gets to a throng of people dancing. I look closer, and my stomach twists into a tight knot. A drunk Tanner is at the center of the party, dancing with a group of people — mostly girls — and he's laughing. Like before. Like before us.

What can you offer someone like him?

The bottom drops out from under me. I swallow and avoid looking at my friends. They warned me.

The story continues, Ginny, Liam, watching with me. There's a shift in the throng of people as it seems to explode. Tanner launches at someone, and there's a roar of support from Griff who's filming. He laughs yelling something like, "get it." The camera moves around erratically, but it's clear that Tanner punches someone. When I can see it, hear it, it's Chris Keller on the other side of Tanner's fists.

I cover my mouth. Then I can't stay still. "I've got to go." I scoot off of the bed.

"Emma. Please. Don't," Liam begs, grabbing my hand.

"Yes. Stay. Or let us come with you." Ginny says, scooting off the bed after me.

I shake my head. "No. Um. I need to go." I can't look at them. I can't think, my limbs just moving without purpose. I'm seeing the images. Tanner's smile and then his anger. How did he find out? Then, I remember all the snide comments; he'd only have to have heard one. The worst realization is that he lied.

"Where are you going?" Liam asks.

"Home," I say. "I need to go home." I do. I walk into the house, up to the stairs to my room and close the door. Then I climb into my bed and sink under the covers, drawing them over my head into the safe cocoon. It doesn't feel safe, however. It feels all wrong. At first, I'm in shock. Then I'm angry. So angry. I feel like such a fool. I grab my phone with extra force and angry text him: *you could have told me the truth.*

Then I lay there, waiting with my heart hammering in my chest, struggling to find a rhythm to breathe.

I don't know how long I'm in the cocoon of my room, but a knock on my door draws me out. I climb from my bed and open the door.

Liam and Ginny are outside my door. Both are holding sleeping bags, and Liam draws a pint of ice cream from a grocery bag.

"Now is not the time to be alone," Ginny says.

They both walk past me, settle around my room, bringing familiarity with them. I take a deep breath.

countdown: 2

"I played it like a fiddle in control of those blue grass notes and swinging around laughing maniacally. I was fucking shit up."

-unnamed protagonist, *Kaleidoscope Concussion* by Saul Annick

tanner

I wake disoriented. My mouth feels like it's stuffed with cotton and the meat of my eyes might be squished out of my head. Fuck. I'm hungover; my brain sloshing around inside my head like it's broken loose from its stem. A tentative peek and — I don't know whose house I'm in, actually. I look at my phone and sit up. I'm late. "Shit. Shit." Too quickly. My stomach rolls. There's a notification from Emma, but I don't want to look at it here. I need to get to the warehouse. I've only begun rebuilding a relationship with my dad, and I don't want to mess that up.

With care, because I know the moment I stand, I'll be lucky to keep the contents of my stomach, I get to my feet. I step over other sleepers littered across the room like sleeping bags — Griff isn't among them — and then pause. A wave of dizziness hits me. My head is mush, and the need to puke rises. I swallow. Fuck. The wave passes as I breathe through it, and I move again. I might still be a little drunk. Hard to tell. I mostly just feel terrible. And stupid.

Once out of the house, I get into my truck. Hands on the steering wheel, my knuckles are bruised. What the fuck?

I start the truck and drive to the office, trying to remember what happened. Drinking with Griff, like things were back to normal.

Avoiding the truth of what was happening with Emma. But nothing felt normal. It was like tracing over an already existing picture, but the lines don't line up anymore; I've shifted but can feel myself trying to make the picture fit again. It just doesn't. A girl whose name I don't know danced with me, invited me upstairs, and the only one I wanted to be with was Emma. I was being stupid, but I didn't know how to fix whatever was going on with me. I'd turned that girl down and drank more to chase away the inadequacy resulting in this super hangover.

Chris Keller.

Oh fuck.

He'd been at the party, and I lost my shit. He said something shitty though the specifics are lost. I just imagined him with Emma; Emma telling him to stop, and he wouldn't. Emma having to hit him to get away. Him telling people, blaming Emma like it was her fault. I couldn't stop the loop the moment I set eyes on him.

When I park the truck, I'm shaking. I lean my head against the steering wheel. What if the asshole presses charges? And then I think: who was the asshole?

My dad is already tying down the supplies on the truck. *Shit.* I get out and can't hold back the nausea anymore. I puke. My stomach rolls, and my head swells with pressure. *Stupid, stupid,* I tell myself. I haven't gotten this bad since sophomore year when I didn't know better. Now, I do. And my dad is a witness to it. *Shit.* When I'm done, I straighten and breathe, using my truck as a support and attempting to reorient myself. I heave but nothing comes out, the pain attached to my stupidity coating my insides.

"Truck's done," Dad calls from behind me.

When I'm able, I look over my shoulder at him.

He's standing at the end of the flatbed, leaning against it. He puts his hands on his hips and tilts his head. "You should be at home sleeping that off."

I turn toward him, still holding the hood of my truck to steady myself. "I'm good. I can help. I'm sorry I'm late."

"It's done." He shakes his head. "Are you good enough to drive?"

"Just hanging."

"I'll take you home." He walks back into the warehouse to lock it up. When he reemerges, I can hear his keys jingle in his hands. "Leave the truck here. You can come get it later, or I'll pick you up tomorrow."

I get into the passenger side of his fancy SUV, sink down into the seat, and press my forehead against the cool glass of the passenger window. He's right. I'm bad. I feel like shit, but it's more than just the physical. I miss Emma. I remember she's texted but wait to check my phone until I get home.

My dad climbs into the car. "Good night, then?"

"Not really."

He starts the car and drives from the warehouse lot. "Care to elaborate?"

I look down at my hands in my lap, the bruised knuckles wrapped in the crimson lanyard connected to my truck keys woven through my fingers. It says *Stanford*. I'd thought, when I was ten, that was where I would go, because that's where Rory wanted to go. I didn't even come close. "I–" But I stop. I'm not sure what to tell him.

He makes a humming noise that seems to measure what I don't say. "Going through the party phase is normal," he offers.

I think about my partying, the last three years of it, and think maybe he'd be surprised about how abnormal it has been. I can see it now, understand better what I've been doing: hiding. I remember thinking at one time it was because I wanted to be seen, but that was the lie I told myself. The drinking, the drugs, the women, Bro Code had all been about losing the part of myself that hurt. Maybe he'd understand it if I tried to tell him, but I feel like I don't know him enough to trust him with it.

"I'd offer some fatherly wisdom, but I'm not sure I've got any room to talk." He goes silent, and the turn signal click snaps loudly in the silence of the car. He turns the wheel, and my stomach rolls with it.

Then suddenly, I need to tell him; I need fatherly advice even if he hasn't earned the right. I feel lost and wandering. "I've been partying since I was fifteen. Sleeping with women. Acting like an asshole," I say. I don't look at him, content to look out the window at the passing landscape even if it makes the nausea worse.

"I guess assholes are part of the family tree then?" He chuckles.

I don't smile at his quip, even though I know he's trying to be self-deprecating; it feels too true. "I want things to be different."

"Then what's up with this?" he asks.

I don't have an answer, but I think about Emma. I think about the last dinner we had, and how awful it felt to know what a fuck up I was. How her father saw through my veneer. How painful it was to feel like she had to make excuses for me, and then to disappoint her. I miss seeing her, while at the same time, it feels like my heart is slowly leaking from my chest through tiny puncture wounds because in a matter of weeks, I won't see her at all. She'll be 2600 miles away from me, and I'll be stuck. Here. With my messed-up self. Going out with Griff again suddenly seems like I'm trying to chase away my inadequacy, but it doesn't help anymore.

"A girl," I finally say.

"You get into a fight? With who?" He glances at my knuckles.

I cover my knuckles, embarrassed. "I didn't — wouldn't hit a girl. I hit a guy."

"What did he do?"

"Crossed a line with a girl."

"The girl?"

My silence says everything.

"And the girl?"

I shrug.

He hums again, measuring my words on the scale of his mind. "Speaking from experience, drinking and partying aren't a good way to deal with feelings. Trust me on that one, kiddo."

I know he's talking about mom. About Rory. "I don't know what to do. She's the first girl—" I stop and consider what I'm about to say, and then jump into the honesty of it. "She's the first girl I've ever loved. She's leaving. For college." It's the first time I've said the words out loud.

"You tell her how you feel?"

"No. It isn't going to change things. It shouldn't. She's still going to college, and I'll still be here. Left behind." I think about Rory. Unwanted tears rise up inside of me, but I hold onto them. I think about our stars, our stories. I wish I could rewrite mine, but what would I rewrite it to be?

Dad pulls his car into the driveway and sets the transmission to neutral. "I don't know if this will help, but in my experience, I wish I hadn't swallowed all my feelings — the important ones. I wish I'd talked to you sooner. I know it may not change the outcome of where you're both headed, but maybe it will help you be in a better place?"

I nod at his advice, though I'm not sure how to translate it. "Thanks."

He clears his throat. "I'll come pick you up in the morning, okay?"

When I get into the house, it's quiet. No mom. No surprise. I climb the stairs, shower, and settle into my bed to sleep. Then I remember Emma's text and snatch my phone from the bedside table to read it.

Emma | You could have told me the truth.

I sit up. *Oh shit.*

I call her.

She doesn't answer.

Oh shit.

I realize she's probably at church.

I settle back into my bed and open Instagram and watch the stories. There's a few that show the party, but there's one posted on Griff's story where I'm dancing with a girl, surrounded by a bunch more. I look like I'm having a good time, drunk AF, and then my performance against Chris Keller. My eyes close. I know that she's seen it. I told her I was going to sleep. I lied to her instead of talking to her and broke her trust. Even as I acknowledge my mistake, I resort to anger. I didn't do anything with that girl. Chris deserved what he got. I was defending Emma. I'd only thought about her. What does she have to be angry about?

You lied.

I lied.

I text her: *We need to talk.*

I toss my phone to the bed and slump down into the bedding. When I wake up from sleeping off my hangover, and Emma still hasn't texted me back, I answer Griff's call.

"Yo bitch. Want to go out?"

I hesitate. I don't. I want to talk to Emma. I want to see her, wrap my arms around her and tell her I'm sorry. I want to fix my hurt. She isn't answering. She's leaving. I'm dragged into an emotional whirlpool I don't know how to get out of. My life without Emma begins stretching out in front of me, dark and desolate. What do I have? Nothing. Just Griff. "I don't have my truck," I tell him.

"That's okay. Danny boy can drive us."

"Where are we going?"

"I don't know," Griff says. "But we'll find trouble."

I still haven't heard from Emma when Danny parks in my driveway, or when we're on our way to Griff's, or when we finally walk into his house. He's already drunk and yells our names, playfully slamming the video game controller on the coffee table with emphasis and raising both hands as if he's made a touchdown. Then he's handing us both a cup of something he's mixed. It's strong and good for forgetting. Emma is leaving, and she deserves better anyway. I tank it.

"Atta boy." Griff slaps me on the back and then flops onto the couch.

"Where're we headed?" Danny sits next to him, but he doesn't lean back. He's perched on the edge of the couch, ready and waiting.

"What would be happening on a Sunday?" I sit in the one-man chair perpendicular to the couch and lean back, content to just lose myself. I stare at the bottom of the cup, the remnants of the orange beverage clinging to the white crevices. Considering how hungover I was earlier, there's no wisdom in drinking again, but if anything, my life has proven I've only had a singular event of intelligence — Emma — and I've already messed that up.

Griff passes his concoction to Danny and points at me. "I heard there might be a get together at Noble's."

I refill my cup, drain it, and refill it again.

"Someone wants to get messed up." Griff laughs and grabs Danny to shake him. "Our boy's back! See what happens when you put your faith in a bitch."

"Don't." I tell him, and sip the drink this time, but I can already feel the mellowing and smoothing of my edges while simultaneously feeling keyed up about Griff and his comment. What had my dad said? *Drinking and partying aren't a good way to deal with feelings.* My heart hardens, and I take another gulp of my drink. What the hell does he know? He left me. Instead of grasping onto his wisdom, I try to forget. Everything.

Griff, and I sit there drinking, playing video games while Danny laughs at us since he's our designated driver. Finally, a plan coalesces. It's at Bella Noble's place. I'm messed up as we climb into Danny's car and already feeling like perhaps, I should go home. I can't turn off my head. *Drinking and partying aren't a good way to deal with feelings.* My dad is right.

"Danny? Can you take me home?" I watch the town slide past — store fronts lit with quiet Sunday night lights — through the backseat windows.

"What?" Griff turns around in the front seat to look at me. "No." He slurs the words. I'm not that far behind him, but maybe I'm just a bit less drunk. I don't know. I just want home. I just want Emma.

"I'm going to run into the Quick Stop first." Danny drives the car into the parking lot. "I'll take you after."

I nod.

"No!" Griff says and climbs out of the car once it's parked.

Danny stops on the sidewalk, turning toward Griff's outburst.

I get out of the backseat and lean against the back of the car. "All good. You guys go. I'm done."

Griff shakes his head and side steps with the momentum. "No. No. No," he mumbles. "We're boys. You and me, Tanner. Brothers."

Except I know that isn't true, the words feel off even if I can't exactly remember why. If it were true, Griff wouldn't be mad that I want to go home. He wouldn't insult me. He wouldn't call Emma names.

"Can I go in?" Danny asks.

Griff flops a wave at him.

"I'll be right back." Danny seems to hesitate, but then disappears into the convenience store.

I shake my head. "We were. Brothers." I push away from the car and find my feet. "Not anymore."

Griff looks like I slapped him, his head moving to the side, and then he shakes it as if to reorient.

"Not for a long time."

"What the fuck, T?"

"Things change."

"Why are you being a dick?"

"I love Emma." There. Again. Out loud. "And you don't care like a brother would. Rory would care."

"Rory isn't here." He pushes away from the car and walks toward me.

My pulse accelerates, and my body heats. "Don't, Griff."

"He's dead. And she's a dead fish bitch." He chuckles. "That rhymes."

I'm not amused. I'm drunk, but I'm cognizant of Griff's continued insults. "Take it back."

"No. It's the truth. And if you choose her, you are too."

"Me? Seems like you're the bitch, Griff. Always throwing tantrums when you don't get your way."

He straightens, his eyes narrowing. "Take it back."

"You can dish it out, but you can't take it, huh?"

Griff comes at me, but his drunkenness makes him slow and easy to read. My drunkenness makes me slow but volatile. He scurries to hit me, his hands fisted in front of him, but then slides through the gravel, and I wrap him up in my arms to avoid his punch. Suddenly we fall, slam against the asphalt rolling and punching, a tangle of limbs.

"Shit. Stop!" Danny's yelling and pulling at us. "You idiots."

I push Griff as hard as I can away from me and flop onto my back where I look up at the sky. It's black, and the stars are hidden. "You were my brother, Griff."

"Fuck you," he slurs. "You're leaving."

"Where am I going?" I ask. I don't move, sucking in breaths to calm my racing heart.

"You left a long time ago."

I turn my head and look at him. He's up on all fours. He pushes up to his knees. "Everybody fucking leaves," he says, and I know he's talking about his dad and his brother.

Hadn't I thought something just like that? But my dad was back. "I didn't leave," I say. "I tried to talk to you; you wouldn't listen."

Griff stands and spits. "We aren't friends anymore, T."

I stand up and shake my head trying to put it back in order. "You're right. We haven't been friends for a long time." I take a step away from him and look at Danny. "It's okay." I shake my head. "I'll walk." I back up another step.

"That's pretty far, Tanner. I can take you."

"No." Griff spits. "He isn't our friend."

"He's mine," Danny tells Griff. "I can take you home, bro."

"I'm good." I take another step away from them. "I need to walk." And I turn away and leave Griff behind.

It's dark, and being drunk while walking the side of the road is a terrible idea, but thinking things through has never been a strong suit. I know where I am. I know which way to home. I also know it will take me through the center of town. And Emma is working. Emma.

I look up at the sky again. The stars are fainter among the lights of town, but I can just make them out. "See," I tell Rory. "I've got everything under control."

emma

Work sucks when you aren't in a mental frame of mind to handle it. I'm not. I can't get Tanner and that stupid video out of my mind. The hurt swirling through me is like a forest fire. My imagination makes things worse and my insecurities add fuel to the fire. *Tanner doesn't stay. Remember?* I remind myself, and I'd been foolish enough to think that he might. For me. *What can you offer someone like him?* What an idiot. He lied.

When he called, I didn't know what to say, so I didn't answer. Honestly, I still don't, unsure how to articulate what it is I'm feeling. Then he sent the text: *We need to talk.* That's when I knew it was over. I spent most of the afternoon in bed sobbing, and then dragged myself to work. I'm working with Ryan, who keeps glancing at me. I'm sure I look like trash; my eyes can't hide my misery.

About nine-thirty, the last of the dessert rush rings the bell on the door as they leave. I'm in the dining room wiping tables and chairs to prepare for the closing routine.

"Emma?"

I look up at Ryan. He's standing on the dining room side of the counter looking as though if he says something, I might break.

I continue wiping tables.

"You okay?"

"Not particularly." I scrub at a tabletop even though it doesn't need it.

"Want to talk about it?"

I glance at him. I could talk to him, but about Tanner? It feels wrong somehow, as though I'd be crossing some strange line. Then I think about his text, *we need to talk*, and wonder why I should care. The thing is I do. I care so much my heart feels like it's taking up all the room in my torso, and I can't find a way to correct all the rest of my internal organs around it. I swallow down the tears that are suddenly cutting up my throat and shake my head, because I can't talk.

Ryan returns to the routine of cleaning up the barista station, but I can feel his eyes follow me through the dining room.

At ten, after he locks the door, he counts out the till, and I mop the floor. Eventually, I go into the back to run the dishes through the washer. Ryan turns up the radio in the front, music drifting through the shop, and acoustic guitar settles me for the time being. I suddenly wish I had somewhere to go after this, but Ginny is at her mom's, and Liam went somewhere with his family. I'd foolishly hoped to spend time with Tanner. Now, I'll just have to face the insecurity of my thoughts.

I unload the hot dishes onto the drying mat and then put in the final load of dishes. I slide the door closed, lock it, and push the button.

"Emma?"

I whirl, a hand to my chest, to find Ryan standing at the doorway. "You scared me," I say and then smile. It's then I notice he isn't smiling back. "What is it?"

He nods to the front. "You might want to come see this."

My heart thuds inside me, pushing all those internal organs further out of the way. I walk toward him, my muscles tense with trepidation. When I look through the doorway across the dining room to the front door, I see Tanner standing outside the shop. His hands are pressed against the glass. "Emma!" he yells when he sees me. He's drunk.

"Do you want me to call the cops?" Ryan asks.

"Emma! Open the door," Tanner yells and hits the glass with his hands. It isn't violent or threatening, just loud. "I need to talk to you."

My stomach moves inside my esophagus, and I'm frozen.

"Emma! I didn't do anything with that girl." His voice slurs. "I did punch Chris Keller. I did it."

"Emma?" Ryan touches my shoulder. "Do you want me to call the police?" he asks again.

"Don't touch her," Tanner yells from outside and smacks the glass again.

Ryan removes his hand.

I shake my head. "No."

"Emma! Please. Yes." He's nodding, misinterpreting the movement of my head to Ryan as my answer. "Yes. Please."

"We can't let him in."

I finally look at Ryan, and I can feel my cheeks burning with mortification. "Yeah. I know."

"But if you want to go out and talk to him–" concern weighs his voice– "we're almost done here."

I turn away from Tanner and walk back into the small kitchen storage area.

Tanner keeps calling my name.

Ryan follows me. "I'll stay. Until you need me not to."

I glance at him with tears in my eyes and nod. "Thanks. That's nice. It will be okay." I wipe my eyes with my fingertips to clear them of the tears. "We got in a fight." I don't know why I feel like I have to explain it now when I didn't before, but I do for some reason. I remove the apron, hang it on the peg, and follow Ryan out to the front door, so he can unlock it to let me out.

Tanner, who must have thought I wouldn't talk to him, has his back to the store and sits on the curb, shoulders slumped, legs out straight out in front of him. He looks dejected.

I glance around not sure how he got here. "Tanner?"

His upper body whirls around at the sound of my voice, and he sways as if he's dancing to music only he can hear. He smiles and then it fades as he gets to his feet. "Emma. Emma," he chants my name, as though it will help him keep his feet under him. "Emma. You didn't answer."

I don't answer him now. Instead, I stand under the pergola that runs the length of the shop and wait.

He sways toward me and grabs a hold of a pillar to keep himself upright. "You're mad."

"You're drunk."

He nods. Then he shakes his head. Then nods again. "Yeah. I went with Griff and Danny. They were going to a party. I didn't want to go."

"It looks like you already did."

"I was drinking. At Griff's house. You didn't answer your phone."

"Are you blaming me for your drinking?"

His nose scrunches up, and he shakes his head. "No. No. I did it. I was mad, because you're mad. I messed up. I'm screwed up."

His words press sadness through me, leaving a residue. "Why are you here, Tanner?"

"I needed to tell you. My dad said I should tell you."

"Tell me what?" In my head I know what's coming. He's going to tell me this isn't working. He's going to tell me that we should end what isn't going to work anyway. I'm not the kind of girl Tanner stays with.

What can you offer someone like him?

"How I feel."

My stomach begins a free-fall from my esophagus toward my feet, sideswiping my heart as it goes. I feel sick with it, preparing myself for his drunken break up, and feeling like such a fool because I should have known this was coming.

"I love you, Emma."

Wait. What?

He's got his arms around the post of the pergola in a hug; the post is holding him upright.

Suddenly, instead of feeling sick because he was going to end things, I'm pissed. I'm so angry at him and at myself. "You think that's something you should tell me while you're shitfaced?" I ask him.

He blinks. I'm not sure if it's because he's surprised I'm not more moved by his words, or because he agrees.

"I can't do this now." I hold up my hands and turn away.

"Emma. Please. Wait." He moves too quickly and loses his footing falling toward me. I catch him, because I've turned back around, but he's heavy and his momentum carries us both to the sidewalk.

The door to Java House rings. "Emma!" Ryan's footsteps shuffle across the concrete.

I'm trying to maneuver out from under Tanner, having hit the sidewalk hard.

Ryan tries to help Tanner up or to get him off of me. I'm not sure which, but maybe both.

Tanner flails his hands and connects with Ryan's face. "You prick. You're trying to steal Em."

"Tanner. Stop," I say, but it's pointless. He's turned on Ryan.

"Dude. Emma and I are just friends." Ryan has one hand on his face, the other raised in acquiescence.

"I saw." Tanner turns away. He shuffles to the curb again and flops down. "You're better than me anyway." He mutters it. "Smarter than me."

And that's when I understand, and the tears that threatened earlier leak from my eyes. His insecurity is mine. It's like what Liam said about him and Atticus being in different places, only with Tanner and me, we are the same, neither of us feeling worthy of the other. Those insecurities are festering and will infect whatever might be good between us. The tears move faster when I realize that we can't move forward. Not this way. Maybe not ever. I can't fix him. He can't fix me. We have to fix ourselves.

My heart cracks open.

"Emma?" Ryan gets my attention.

"Do you know how to get a hold of Atticus Baker?" He's the first person I can think of who knows Tanner that isn't Griff and isn't out of town. When he nods, I say, "Could you call him?"

Ryan disappears back into the shop.

I sit down next to Tanner on the curb and recall we'd been like this before only the roles were reversed. Junior year. I'd needed alcohol courage to tell Tanner I was interested in him. He needed it to tell me how he feels. I'd used him for a kiss. He'd been the sober one and tried to protect me from myself. Now, I need to try and protect us both.

"Hi Emma." He smiles when he notices me.

"Hi Tanner."

"How come you're crying?" He reaches toward me and runs a thumb across my cheek.

"I'm just sad."

His hand drops back to his lap. "I needed to tell you I didn't do anything with a girl."

I nod. "I believe you."

"Can I tell you something?"

"Maybe you shouldn't."

He shakes his head. "I've been stupid."

"You shouldn't talk about yourself like that."

"I miss Rory. I miss you. I miss my mom and dad. Griff is right. Everybody leaves. Kaleidoscope Concussion, too."

My chest, which is oozing my heart, tightens with the truth of his statement.

"But I left Griff."

I wonder if he's rambling but listen.

"I went with Griff because I was trying to feel better, but I just felt worse."

I reach for his hand and thread our fingers together.

"He was a jerk. I tried being his friend. We got in a fight, and he doesn't want to be my friend anymore because I'm different. We're not friends. I walked here because I just wanted to see you, Em."

I look at him and see him, truly see him; he is the broken boy I'd idolized. I see myself, the insecure girl. We'd somehow found one another, offering each other what the other one needed to feel whole. I see though, it doesn't work that way. It can't. I can't fill the holes inside of him, just like he can't fill what's missing in me. I have to do that for myself, but it doesn't take away the love I feel for him. I squeeze his hand with mine.

Tanner leans toward me and puts his head on my shoulder. "You're the best thing that ever happened to me."

I squeeze his hand. "Me too."

We sit that way until Atticus parks in front of the shop. He gets out of the car. "Emma? You okay?"

I nod, even though I'm not. My heart is eviscerated and has fallen out of my chest in ribbons of tissue.

Atticus crouches down in front of us. "Hey T."

Tanner lifts his head from my shoulder. "Atticus."

"I came to give you a ride."

"I don't have anywhere to go."

Atticus's eyes bounce to mine for a moment and then back to Tanner. "Well, you're coming with me." With my help, we get Tanner into the passenger seat of the car.

When the door is closed, Atticus turns to me.

"Thank you for coming." I cross my arms and wrap them around my body.

He nods. "Yeah. You sure you're okay?"

I bury my face in my hands and burst into tears.

Atticus puts his arms around me and holds me while I cry.

A few minutes later, with Tanner passed out in the passenger seat, I watch Atticus drive away. When Ryan opens the door to let me back into the shop, I'm embarrassed. "Sorry about that. You okay?"

He holds an ice pack to his cheek. "My first fight. I got my ass kicked." He sort of smiles and then says, "Are you? Okay?"

"No, but I will be. What's left to do?"

"Shop's done."

We lock up the store and offer one another an awkward goodnight. When I get into my car, I allow myself to break.

435

countdown: 1

"Lucy. The way I'd grabbed ahold of her soft parts, and twisted them up with mine, left little room to maneuver. I'd dragged her into my minefield and watched it detonate, only to rain debris around us."

-unnamed protagonist, *Kaleidoscope Concussion* by Saul Annick

tanner

I wake up in a strange house, again, though it feels familiar. This time, I'm in bed. Alone, thankfully. I've blown up, just like the narrator in *Kaleidoscope Concussion.* His spiral, his identity crisis; it's me. One of my favorite lines, even though there are a million: *Everything falls apart.*

"You up?"

I look up, lifting my head off the bed.

Atticus is in the doorway.

"It must be bad if I can't remember how I got here."

He doesn't reassure me.

Everything falls apart.

"My mom made some breakfast."

I groan.

"Yeah. Well, that's the way to cure a hangover."

"What about a three-day bender?"

"Bruh, I can't answer that one. Get your ass up, or I'll make you go on a run with me until you puke. Towels in the bathroom down the hall and some clean clothes you can borrow."

"Thanks." I sit up in bed. I'm not willing to test Atticus, because I know he'll drag my butt out into the street for a run. I look at my phone. The notifications have blown up, and I realize my dad was going to pick me up. *Shit.* I dial him.

He answers the phone and swears under his breath. "You scared the shit out of your mother and me. Neither of us knew where you were. You didn't call. I couldn't find you. Where are you?"

He sounds like a parent. Like a dad, and it's unexpected, and wanted. Tears collect around my eyeballs. "I'm sorry, Dad. I messed up."

"Are you safe?"

"Yeah. I'm at my friend's house."

"I'll come and get you."

"Okay. I'll send you my location."

I follow Atticus's advice and shower, make the bed where I'd crashed, and walk down the hallway to the kitchen. It doesn't smell too bad considering I'm hanging like the dumbass I am. Atticus is sitting at the island in the kitchen, his dad next to him, his mom standing at the stove. He has a little brother — seven or eight — running a truck over the floor, his lips puckered and the purr of the truck escaping from his mouth. Each of them looks my way when I step into the room.

I flush, embarrassed, and wondering if they know.

"No sense hanging in the doorway there, young man. We all were witness to your inebriation. I suppose that makes us family," Mr. Baker says and returns to his paper.

"I'm sorry."

Atticus's mom reaches across the island and taps the paper. "Martin, don't be rude. I'm Stacey," she says and smiles. She's a beautiful woman. Atticus resembles her. She's tall and thin, with a wide smile and dark eyes. Her hair is natural, fluffy spirals that frame her delicate, doll-like features. "I made some French toast."

"He might not want any," Mr. Baker says into his paper.

Mrs. Baker smacks the paper again.

Mr. Baker chuckles and turns to look at me. He's got a serious face, but he offers me a friendly smile. "You're welcome here, Tanner. Anytime, but let's not make a habit of this kind of situation." He pats the stool next to him.

"No, Sir." I walk all the way into the room to take a seat.

Atticus leans back to look at me, shrugs, and then smiles as he returns to his breakfast.

"My dad is going to come and get me."

Mrs. Baker sets a plate of dry toast in front of me. "I didn't think you might be up for the eggs."

I offer her a smile of gratitude.

"And here's some orange juice." She sets down a glass.

"Thank you."

"I'm off to the office." Mr. Baker stands and takes another sip of coffee as he walks around the island. He puts his dishes into the dishwasher and then turns, leveling his dark stare on me. "It was nice to meet you, Tanner," he says. "I'd like a redo, however. Please come and join us for a proper introduction this week sometime?"

My face heats again. "Yes, Sir. I'd like that."

"Look at that blush." Mrs. Baker smiles.

"Don't embarrass the boy, Stace." Mr. Baker leans toward her.

She shifts her cheek, and he leans to kiss her. "I think you already did." She pushes him away with a playful shove and then turns off the stovetop.

Mr. Baker kisses both Atticus and his little brother. "See you later, boys."

"Later, Dad."

"Aaron. Let's get moving," Mrs. Baker says. "You've got summer camp, son."

Atticus's little brother whines but flies out of the room, arms extended.

"Atticus, can you get the kitchen for me? I've got to get Aaron to camp, and then I have a meeting at the firm."

"I got it," Atticus takes a bite of his toast.

"Thanks." She kisses him. "We'll see you later this week, Tanner."

"Yes, Ma'am."

I take a bite of dry toast and chew it. "Can you fill me in on how I'm here?"

"Emma. Well, sort of. Her co-worker Ryan called me."

I close my eyes and breathe through my nose. Oh shit. *Everything falls apart.* "I don't remember what I did, just snapshots–" But then I realize as I say it that it isn't completely true. I'd refused to go with Griff and Danny to a party at Bella Noble's. Griff and I had it out in the parking lot. "That isn't true," I tell Atticus. "Griff and I got in a fight."

"You don't look like you got in a fight."

I look at my hand, the knuckles bruised, the skin mottled red, blue, and purple from hitting Keller. "I think it was more of a drunken wrestling match."

"What happened?"

"We were going to this party. I asked Danny to drop me home, and Griff was Griff; he started talking shit and when I confronted him, he came after me. Next thing I know, we were on the asphalt."

"Damn. Then?"

It's hazy, but I reach for it. "Griff tells me to find my own way."

"Danny listens?"

"Naw. I think he offered, but I just walked away."

"That's a shitty deal."

"I think I knew it a long time ago, just too stubborn to face it."

"So how did you end up outside of Java House."

"I–" I remember the darkness. I remember looking up at the sky and searching for Rory, but I couldn't find him, and in my mind Griff's face was superimposed over what I imagine would be Rory's face now. "I don't remember. I fucked it up, didn't I." It isn't a question, because I already know I did.

"Let's just say the girl was a mess."

I put my head in my hands and sigh. "I'm a fucking mess, Atticus."

He claps a hand on my back, and then stands to take his dishes into the kitchen.

"You got wisdom for me?"

"No. None that you don't already have for yourself but are maybe too scared to admit."

He's right.

Everything falls apart.

440

There's a knock at the front door.

"Probably my dad," I say and follow Atticus from the kitchen after putting my plate in the sink.

Atticus opens the door and stands aside.

Both of my parents are standing there. Together.

emma

As much as I'd like to avoid going downstairs, my stomach won't let me avoid it any longer; it's growling from hunger. I know Mom left for work about an hour ago. Shelby is somewhere, though she isn't who I'm avoiding. That would be my dad. I slip into Tanner's hoodie, because it's a way to feel close to him, and shuffle through the house into the kitchen. Dad's there working at the kitchen island, waiting to pounce, as if he's taken up residence there knowing I would come to the watering hole.

"Good morning, sunshine."

I grunt at him and pour myself a cup of coffee.

"Not a sunshine then. Grumpy better?"

"I don't feel like talking," I say with my back to him.

He sighs. "I'm trying."

I turn and lean against the counter. "Are you though, Dad?"

He just stares at me. Blinks as if perhaps I've grown a second head. "Of course. You're my kid. I always try."

"I don't think you tried very hard with Tanner."

"He's not my kid." He looks down at this laptop.

I make a sound, roll my eyes, and then turn my back to him again.

"You might be right."

"Might?"

"Fine. I wasn't on my best behavior."

"You were judgmental." I look at him over my shoulder. "That wasn't very Christian of you."

"Having premarital sex was?"

I sip my coffee then return to facing him. "Who knows. I may go to hell for it, but I don't think so. I guess it's up to God; I made my choice — right or wrong — and have to live with the consequences."

Dad leans back on the stool and crosses his arms. "It's just—"

I hold up my hand. "Dad. It's my choice, not yours. Not the church's. No one but mine and my partner, and I have to be accountable to God, my faith, on my own. Whether it's dating Tanner, or someone else. The decision is mine. You and mom taught me, but it's my turn. You have to trust me to know for myself."

His Adam's apple bounces in his throat as he swallows. "There's no concise cookbook when you become a parent." His hands move as he talks. "You get a little bit of how you were raised mixed with your own ideas of how you'd do it differently, with a dash of expert advice. Then you hope the recipe works."

"Do you think I'm a failed recipe? A failure?" The moment the question leaves my mouth, I realize how important his answer is to me while at the same time recognizing I need to distance myself from it. He's my dad. He's been my world, my hero. Recognizing his humanity, his fallibility, my own, Tanner's, has pulled me to a stop.

Weeks ago, Bella Noble looked at me and told me I was boring. It bothered me because I wanted to be something different, some version of perfection I thought existed, but it was a lie. I can't escape the person I am, imperfections and all. I am meant to be as I am — red wire included. Seeing Tanner's hurt and insecurity last night helped me recognize it. But I also realize that I have to stand up for what I deserve. I deserve to be trusted. I deserve to be loved, flaws and all. I deserve to take care of myself, and accept myself as the boring, square-peg, imperfect perfectionist, red-wired person I am.

Dad shakes his head. "No, Emma. You are a gift to me, and I love you more than words can express. I'm so proud of you."

It's my turn to swallow thickly, the emotion catching in my throat. "How come you didn't trust me?"

He uncrosses his arms and swipes at something on his keyboard. When he looks up again, his eyes behind his glasses are glassy. "I'm scared." He stands and moves around the island until he's leaning against the counter opposite me. "Right or wrong, I'm watching my little girl drift away, and I know that where you are going, I can't follow anymore to make sure you're safe."

Tears fill my eyes.

"And what is my purpose if not to be the man who keeps his babies safe?"

I step into his arms, and he wraps them around me.

"I love you no matter what Emma. I've always said that, and I mean it." He reassures me with a squeeze, "I'm sorry."

I squeeze him back. "I love you, Dad. Until I'm thirty-six and then all bets are off."

"Nope." He draws back to look at my face. "Forever." Then he hugs me tighter.

tanner

My parents don't wait to be invited in; the moment they see me, they cross the threshold, pass Atticus, and accost me, dragging me into their arms. We look like a pod. Both my parents, strange alien creatures who have developed suction cup arms, encircle me and one another. They are also both talking at the same time.

"Tanner, when we couldn't find you..."

"Tanner. Oh Tanner. My baby..."

I'm shocked by their behavior. Embarrassed, sort of. Relieved too. Unsure how to react. I attempt to break out of their pod and look at Atticus. He's still at the door, unsure whether to keep it open or to close it.

"Mom. Dad." I wiggle away from them. "I'm here. Thanks Atticus." I push my parents away from the house.

My mom won't let go of my arm.

Atticus's eyes move between us and settle on me. "I'll text you about dinner."

My dad shakes Atticus's hand. "Thank you."

I lead my parents down the walkway, somewhere between shock and disbelief. I expect to see two cars, but it's only my Dad's SUV. I turn and look at them, one on either side of me. "Did you come here together?"

"Yes."

My face must indicate my incredulity. "You haven't been able to be in a room together for years."

My dad looks down at the ground, hand on his hip, and his jaw works against itself. He pinches the bridge of his nose.

My mom looks out at the landscape and presses her lips together until they disappear.

Dad looks up at me. "Let's get in the car." He's angry, but there's more to it than that. "We can talk about it on the drive." He walks around the front of the car.

I open the door and get into the back seat; my mom gets into the front passenger seat. It's interesting to me how we fall into the norm of how things used to be even though they haven't been normal for almost a decade.

Dad drives the car away from Atticus's house, and then clears his throat before saying, "You scared the shit out of us." He looks at me through the rearview mirror.

My first instinct is to be defensive. I'm eighteen. I've been running my own life for years. I glance out the window at the moving landscape, the trees, the houses, parked cars moving as we drive past. I feel stuck in here with them, caught in an insulated world where I have to face myself. I have to face them. I want to push them away, be bitter and vindictive, but I also know where that has gotten me. My chest caves in, and I look at my hands in my lap. "I'm sorry I scared you."

Mom bursts into tears and covers her face with her hands; it isn't loud or dramatic, but rather seems to contain the weight of grief she's only just allowing out into the world.

Dad clears his throat again, but I hear the thickness of fear in his voice. "I called your mom when you weren't home this morning, and you weren't answering your phone."

Mom looks at me, then, her eyes streaked with mascara. "I called everyone I could think of: Griff, Daniel, and Josh. I would have called your girlfriend, but I didn't have her number." She sobs this information, cutting it into smaller sound bites with her breaths.

"We were on our way to the police station when you called." Dad puts on the turn signal and slows to a stop. He glances back at me. "What happened?"

"I fucked up." I can't meet his gaze and turn to look out the window. The car moves again.

"And?" His question sounds very fatherly.

It grates against my nerves, but I also remind myself that all I have ever wanted was them to see me. For them to be my parents. Now, in this car, they are both here as my parents. Maybe they are angry. Maybe they are disappointed. Maybe they are terrified. Maybe they hate one another. But they are both here. Together. For me. I could be angry, but instead it makes my throat close up and my muscles fight against the insistent tears collecting in my eyes. "I don't have any excuses. I just–" but I don't know what to say. Until I say, "I'm just lost."

Even though the car is moving, stillness settles in the spaces between us. It's as if what I've said is important. My dad continues driving. My mom continues crying, and I swipe at the tears on my own face.

"I think we all are," my dad finally says.

The tires against the road make the humming sound I find comforting. We're driving. Together. And I think of all the times I've driven away. All of the times I've needed to find solace by escaping in my car. Of running in some ways, whether it was out onto the roof, or in the bottom of a cup of booze, or in the body of some girl, pretending it made me feel better. The truth I see now, was that it was always running from how I felt. And now, ironically, we're sitting in a car forced to face one another.

Mom's tears have faded to sniffing, and she says, "I was so scared." She reaches around the seat and grabs my wrist in a desperate grip.

I look up at her face.

Her eyes bounce from where her hand holds me to my face, a look of intense anguish burdening her features. "I was so scared. I kept thinking about what you said after graduation, that I'd lost both my sons. And then–" She sobs– "You. Were. Just. Gone."

"I'm sorry, Mom."

She shakes her head and pulls me toward her. "No. No. You were right. I was so blind. My grief and pain, and then my anger—" She pauses as more tears overtake her. When she finds a reprieve, she adds, "I had to look closer at — what I've done, who I've become." Silence moves around us at her statement. Then she says in a whisper, "I don't like who I am."

It hits me with the force of a truck knocking the breath from my lungs. Those same thoughts in my head. The same words from my dad's own mouth, and now from my mother. All of us stuck in our own boxes of our grief. Alone.

Then my dad reaches across the divide between them and puts a hand of comfort on my mom's arm. His hand runs the length of her arm, and he takes her hand in his. I glance at his face and see that he's looking at her, his face also streaked with tears. None of us has been spared from the truth of the grief that has pinned our backs against the wall.

"We'll be better," Dad says to her, and then looks at me. "I'll be better."

For a moment, I believe him. A sunburst of hope alights in my chest at the idea that instead of things falling apart, they are actually being put back together. Different. Changed. But new and whole somehow. That I might be able to look in the mirror and I might appreciate the image staring back at me. That I will recognize someone who deserves something more. Like Emma.

You tore everything apart with Emma.

Maybe I'm a fool to hope for it to be true. Hope that perhaps if it can be true for my parents, for me, for us as a family… maybe it could also be true in other ways. A hope that maybe I could find a way to repair what I've broken with Emma.

I study my parents sitting in companionable silence in front of me, my dad's hand holding my mom's, her hand holding mine, and I think that perhaps there is always a way.

e m m a

Tanner texts me that afternoon. | Emma? Can we talk? |

| Yes. | Me

Tanner | When? |

I leave him on *read*. I don't know. I don't know when or where or how. I don't want it to be over. I'm afraid, and yet I know the truth of what's coming. I don't know how to face it.

Tanner | Want to go for a drive? |

I smile. Tanner's optimism of being stuck in his truck with a mad girl amazes me. So, I text him: *Meet at Marta's*. This option makes me feel safe. I can control it and keep a table between us, because I don't know if I have it in me to walk away from him otherwise without that control. I don't even know if I want to.

After we set a time, all I can do with my nervous energy is wait. I'm antsy. I wander the house. I try to read. I pick up *Kaleidoscope Concussion* and flip through the pages to where I've marked quotations with sticky notes. Each one makes me think of Tanner, because now, I can see his searching between the lines. I set it down and wander down into the basement where Shelby's watching TV.

I flop on the couch next to her, close so she's irritated.

"Stop," she whines but doesn't move.

"You love it."

She harrumphs at me; her eyes remain on the screen.

"Want to watch something? You can choose."

She looks at me and narrows her eyes. "Sure? You're not going to argue with me as soon as I choose something you don't want?"

"I promise."

She looks back at the TV. "Okay."

"What will it be?" I ask.

"Survival of the Fittest." She looks at me, waiting for my argument, because I despise that horrible, fake reality show.

I bite my tongue. "Okay."

Her eyebrows arch over her eyes. "Wow. That was a test. I'm impressed."

"You picked the worst show possible on TV."

She smiles and then says, "Let's watch Ferris."

"Really?" I'm surprised, since she hates 80's movies.

"Yeah. Someone is going to have to keep the tradition going when you're off to college. I already told my friends about it."

Warmth spreads in my chest. "Wow, Shelbs. That's one of the sweetest things you've ever said."

"Don't get used to it." She selects the movie.

"I'll go make popcorn."

My sister and I watch Ferris. I recite lines. She pauses intermittently, so she can ask me questions, which we discuss. When the credits roll, she turns and looks at me. "That wasn't so bad."

I smile. "That one is my favorite."

"You're Cameron."

I chuckle. "Yeah. Probably."

Shelby puts her head on my shoulder. "I like that about you."

Her words heat up my heart, aligning with the new understanding I have about myself.

"Who are you?"

"Ferris. Of course."

"Of course." I laugh. We watch some horrible TV, laughing and making fun of it as we do, but the anxiety rushes back in when it's time to go to Marta's. "I'll be back."

"Where are you going?"

"Meeting Tanner."

"I like him."

"Me too." It isn't a lie. It's a devastating truth.

When I get to Marta's, I sit in the parking lot for a few minutes, my heart beating out of my chest with anxiety. *I can't do this. I can't do this. I don't want to do this. Tanner is all I have ever wanted.*

Then I hear a tiny voice inside of me: *You need a story?*

My breathing slows, and my heartbeat pitter pats back to its normal pace as I recall Queen Ella and King TJ. It makes me smile. When I open my eyes, Tanner is standing on the other side of the window. My heart palpitates, and I clutch my chest.

He smiles.

I push the door open. "You scared me."

"I was worried about you. You were sitting in there with your eyes closed."

"Why didn't you knock?"

"I was going to. Then you smiled and I just–" He stops, and then he smiles, but it's shy. I can see the worry weighing the usual brilliance of his eyes.

I suppress the urge to throw my arms around his neck. My rational brain is disconnected from my emotional one.

We walk toward Marta's shoulder-to-shoulder. He smells good, like soap and spice. His hair is still a little wet at its curly dark edges. He holds the door for me, and once we're seated in a booth facing one another, I feel awkward. It hurts to look at him. My attraction and feelings for Tanner aren't gone. Confusion mires everything I'm thinking, and I'm not sure what to say. The waitress takes our order. I look out the window after I've given her mine and wait, watching the cars pass on the street beyond the parking lot outside.

"I owe you an apology," he says after the waitress leaves and draws my attention back to why we're here. "I didn't want to give it to you over the phone or text."

His brows shift over his dark eyes, and the gentle slope of his lips are shaped with regret — a slight downturn when he would usually be teasing me with his smile. He presses his teeth together so his jaw flexes, getting sharper. He moves a hand through his hair. My heart expands just like it always does when I look at him. I see the truth: my love for him is real. It's big and will always be big. It just isn't enough. My insecurities — his too — will only be a sieve, and the love will slip through until we can patch the insecurities making up the fibers of ourselves.

He sighs. "I'm sorry about last night. What makes it worse is I can't replay it all, only bits. So, I'm not sure all of the things I did that I need to apologize for. I'll start with saying I'm sorry for showing up at your workplace."

"You were very drunk."

"Yeah."

"How come?"

He looks at his glass of water and gets lost in it for a time. Then he pulls a paper napkin from the dispenser and begins to fold it. "At that last dinner — at your house — I freaked out. All I kept thinking about was how I wasn't good enough while at the same time realizing I–" he swallows– "I have really strong feelings for you. Those things weren't computing in my head. I got scared and instead of facing my shit, I called Griff."

"And now? Those feelings and your head?"

"They're pinging around like a pinball trying to find the right place to fall."

"You told me you loved me last night."

His eyes meet mine, sliding up from the napkin he's been folding and refolding. I fall into the dark brown softness of them. He bites his upper lip a moment and then runs his hand through his hair again before pinching the bridge of his nose. "Shit." He sighs. "That isn't how I would have wanted to tell you."

I swallow down the sharp taste of threatening tears. "Do you?" I don't look away, too invested in his answer.

"Yeah, Em." He removes his hands from the tabletop and drops them into his lap. Maybe to keep from reaching out for me. Then he leans forward, his chest against the edge of the table and levels a steady gaze at me. "I do. I love you. I knew it when I saw you graduation night playing croquet with your Pop Pop."

I need to acknowledge what he's said and hold my hand out to him over the table. He takes my hand in his and shifts it so his hand rests on the table under mine. His fingers curl around my hand, strong and acquiescent at the same time.

"I love you too." I go to war with myself, wanting to figure this out, to fix it. I want Tanner with every part of myself, but even mistrusting his feelings for me validates why I can't do this. The realization hits me with the force of a hammer in the chest.

I recall Liam's words about Atticus and him.

The waitress returns with drinks.

Tanner studies our joined hands, his thumb moving over my skin.

The feelings — as strong as I feel them — aren't enough. I know this. I remind myself again because it is easy to slip into the feelings of just being with him. I can feel the awareness as concretely as his thumb moving over my skin. "Those feelings pinging around in your head looking for a place to land made me see something about myself."

His eyes meet mine again. He's frowning. "I broke something else."

I offer him a wan smile, and I think of *Kaleidoscope Concussion*, which unsettles me a moment. "No. You said, 'you're better than me.'"

"You are."

I shake my head. "No. I'm not. And you weren't talking about me. You were talking about Ryan."

"Ryan?" He looks down as if trying to place the information. "The guy you work with?"

I nod and stop. I'm not sure how to navigate what I need to say, but I keep thinking about that book — Tanner's book — and suddenly I say, "You remember that part in Kaleidoscope Concussion when the narrator and Erickson Dorn start fighting?"

His eyebrows shift over his eyes with surprise. "Yes." He says this slowly, drawing out the sounds.

"Remember when he says something about how maybe we have to break everything to make something better?"

He swallows, releases my hand, and reaches for the napkin again. He nods.

"I felt it too."

Now his eyebrows pinch together. "What? Like breaking something?"

"No. That you were better than me, that somehow I didn't deserve you."

His confusion is written all over his face. His jaw contracts. "What the fuck are you talking about, Emma? That's a lie." He's angry I've said it. "What is the point of this?"

"The point is I recognized myself in what you'd told Ryan."

"I don't understand."

"I see you, Tanner. I have always seen you, and in these last weeks, you made me feel awake. That's a good thing. But I shouldn't feel like I don't deserve you. And you shouldn't feel like that either. Like it's a fluke we see one another." I'm trying to put it together, to express what I mean, and then suddenly say, "We can't be one another's fighting dummy — we can't break one another." My throat catches. "You mean too much to me."

The waitress returns with our food.

Silence moves in with us after she leaves, each of us chewing on what I've said, and I keep thinking I should have said it better but not sure how.

"What you're saying is that we needed each other in order to break?"

I can't help but offer a wan smile. "Sort of."

"I'm a mess, Em. I realized it before, but I know it now. All the drinking, the stupid choices have been my way of hiding. You helped me realize it, but that doesn't feel like you broke me. I already was."

"Yeah. That. Me too."

"Your dad was right."

"My dad?"

"Yeah. That night, before the movie, he told me not to steal your dreams."

It's my turn to be embarrassed. "I'm sorry."

"Don't be. He's just being a protective dad. But I realized that I need to clean up the mess of me before I step in to try and be something for someone else. I watched that tear apart my parents."

"So, you understand what I mean?"

He nods. "I just don't like it."

"Me either."

Our baskets of food remain untouched.

"Em?"

My basket has blurred, and I'm afraid to look up at him.

"Maybe this is weird, and maybe the timing is bad, but can we go look at the stars?"

I don't hesitate. "Yes."

We box up our food, jump into Tanner's truck, and he drives us to the Quarry. I don't consider the wisdom, or the lack of it; it just feels like what I need. What he needs. He pulls the tailgate open, and we sit on the edge of it, our boxed food in our laps. We eat it as the sun goes down, lighting the Quarry up with gold.

He isn't chatty. Me either. I'm locked up in my thoughts and my struggle, but I need to hear him, not done being a part of what was us. "You got in a fight with Griff?"

"Yeah. I realized I was trying to find Rory, and Griff just isn't."

"He was important to you though. A part of your journey that brought you to now."

Tanner nods. After a few minutes he says, "Not everyone is ready to take the journey, I guess. It sucks."

I close my box of food, set it next to me, and settle on my back in the truck bed to look at the sky as the stars begin to emerge. The sky is orange pink turning blue. Weeks ago, Tanner took me on a journey to find the imperfect version of myself I'd locked away. I found freedom even if I also found heartache, because this hurts. I sniff and wipe at the tears in my eyes.

Tanner remains sitting.

I watch the stars begin to twinkle in the sky as the darkness falls. "It wasn't written in the stars, I guess." It makes me wonder about us. When I consider all of the ways Tanner and I moved around one another over the years, it seemed destined, as if there were a puppeteer commanding the strings to make sure our lives intersect. The truth of it is, I needed Tanner.

I needed him to kiss me that night junior year.

I needed that wave outside of the club.

I needed him to ask me to jump.

I needed him to make love to me under a starry sky.

I needed our star stories.

And in that moment, I realize I'm stronger, more self-aware, more whole than I have ever been because of him. Our star stories were true stories.

He sets his box down and settles in the truck bed next to me, his face open to the sky, and when I look at him, I'm pretty sure I can see the stars reflected in his eyes. "This hurts, Em. Like when I lost Rory." He covers his eyes with a forearm.

I take his other hand in mine. "You see that star there, five swirls to the left of somewhere?"

He sniffs, wipes his eyes, and turns his head to look at me. "Yes."

"You aren't looking at it."

"I don't need to. I know which one you're talking about."

This makes me smile through my own tears. "As the story goes, there was an ogre and a witch that lived there, in different places."

"An ogre and witch? That isn't very romantic."

"It isn't supposed to be." I squeeze his hand.

He smiles. "All stories have to have romance in them."

"Kaleidoscope Concussion wasn't romantic."

"Emma!" Tanner admonishes me and then wiggles his body like he's having a fit. He freezes and looks at me. "You didn't just say that! What do you think the whole Erickson Dorn thing was? And Lucy?"

"Do not tell me you're going to say it was a love story."

"Yes! Erickson Dorn was the narrator's twisted love affair with the parts of himself that he wanted and couldn't find!"

My mouth drops open.

"What?"

"Are you my Erickson, Tanner?"

He laughs. "No Em, you're my Erickson."

"That doesn't bode well for either of us."

We laugh.

"Sorry." Tanner gets me back on track. "The Ogre and the Witch."

"I lost it. I was never a very good storyteller to begin with. That's your department."

We both go quiet.

"Rory never left you, Tanner," I tell him.

He looks at me.

"You've carried him with you." I touch his heart. "He's in your stories. He's waiting for you on your star. And I'm not leaving you. Getting rid of me won't be that easy." I offer him a smile.

He squeezes my hand and holds it against his heart, then looks back up at the sky. "So, the Ogre and the Witch," he begins and then says, "Nope. I can't. Once upon a time there was a Queen named Ella and a Prince named TJ."

"I thought he was a King."

"No. He had to go on a quest first, you know, to earn it." He shifts his head to look at me and smiles, and I know then that even in its difficulty, even in its imperfection, everything really is going to be perfect.

seven months later

"There were dull gray parts of me mixed with a rainbow. I was all of it, and none of it. I was a kaleidoscope of colors, working in concert to make something messy, but incredibly beautiful. Turned out — like Lucy said — we all were."

-unnamed protagonist, *Kaleidoscope Concussion* by Saul Annick

emma

I juggle a stack of library books as I swipe my fob to key myself into my dorm room.

"Need some help?" Jentry, a guy from down the hall rushes forward and pushes open the door. "How are you, Emma? Haven't seen you for a while."

"Thanks," I tell him. "Good. Busy. Biology has had quite a workload this term."

He pushes the door open. "Here."

Jentry is cute — and asked me out a few months ago. I agreed. I mean, why wouldn't I? Single. Available. He's cute. We had a good time. Did I mention he is gorgeous? He's got that great dark hair that explodes from his head in kinky spirals. He usually draws it together with a band, so it sticks up from his head, like a wild, man-bun ponytail, but looks more like a poof. His gorgeous mocha complexion invites touch, but every time I look into his eyes — those incredibly deep brown eyes — I stop in my tracks. They remind me of Tanner every time I sink into their depths. Which isn't fair to Jentry, who is awesome. He has a Tanner-vibe, and makes me laugh, and after our third date he kissed me (and it was good) but I just couldn't stop comparing him to Tanner. So I ended things, and we've remained friends. I have a feeling he'd like it to be more. I think he's hoping for something casual, but I'm the red wire.

"Thanks so much." I lean against the door to keep it open. "How are you?"

He crosses his arms over his nicely formed chest. He plays football for the school and looks all chiseled and sculpted. "Busy. It's good though. Keeps me focused." He glances at my lips and then looks down at his feet, and I know he's still interested.

"Good to see you. I have to study for this massive exam, and I have a research paper due next week." I indicate the library books.

"Yeah. You too, Emma."

I thank him again, and the heavy door slams behind me. "I'm back," I call out, but Karen, my roommate, or better yet, my sister from another mister, isn't there.

I unload the stack of books on my perfectly ordered desk, and glance at my copy of *Kaleidoscope Concussion,* which was another reason Jentry and I just wouldn't work out. He'd said something about hating to read fiction, and he didn't have any books other than his textbooks. Nope. I have decided that a must-have attribute for a future Mr. Emma Matthews must have a love of reading and a book collection.

I pull my phone from my back pocket and text my roommate: *Where are you?*

Karen | I told you! Date. Cute Lacrosse player.

Which one is this? The blonde or the dark haired one? | Me

I smile because I know she only dates red-haired men. It's her wacky rule, which I think is weird and told her is *hairist*, so I tease her that she's going to meet a dark-haired boy who sweeps her off her feet. Any time I mention it, I think about a certain dark-haired boy back home whose curls felt like silk against my fingertips. Then I shake my head and remind myself that I'm working on myself. He's working on himself. And that is probably a never-going-to-happen-again. It was written in the stars for a moment in time, even though sometimes I imagine the stars aligning again.

I wonder how his test went and think about calling him to ask, but I've been pretty rule-oriented about keeping things platonic, even if we still talk once a week. Every Friday, when I get to see him on Facetime to talk about how our weeks went, the ache in my bones from missing him is sometimes too heavy, so I consider suggesting we don't talk anymore. Then he flirts with me, makes me laugh so I forget the ache of missing him and only remember the joy of talking. He insists on Facetime to "keep his face front and center" so I don't forget him.

My phone pings.

Karen | You ARE dead to me. |

| LOL! Have fun. | Me

My Facetime rings. It's Saturday, so I know it isn't Tanner since we talked yesterday afternoon — our one day of the week. A look at the screen, and it's my sister. "Hi Shelbs," I say as her adorable face comes into focus. I sit on my bed decorated very similarly to my room at home with twinkle lights and white fluff. I now have pictures of not only my family, Liam, and Ginny, but also Tanner, Josh, Danny, and Atticus.

She smiles. "Notice anything different?"

Of course, besides the fact she's looking older, I can see she's got her braces off, but I mess with her. "New haircut?"

"Nope."

"New earrings? Did you pierce them again?"

She sighs. "No." She gives me a giant grin.

"No more braces! Wow. That's awesome. Congrats. Still like ninth grade?"

"Way better than 8th," she says. "There's this cute junior. His name is Chance. I'm hoping he invites me to prom."

461

"Stay away from juniors," I tell her. "At least until you are a junior, too. How are the parents?"

"Good. Annoying. Good."

I smile. "Do you miss me?"

"Yes. Dad is like, so, nosey about everything." She makes a disgusted noise.

I laugh, and we talk for another twenty minutes about her last John Hughes movie night, among other high school dramas, until one of her friends calls. "I have to take this. Cassie is having boy drama. Love you."

"Love you too." I disconnect the call, set the phone down, and grab my biology book to look over the chapter again for Monday's test.

I'm unfocused, however, and have to reread a giant section of the chapter, because my mind drifts to Tanner. Seeing him over winter break. Wishing things were different but understanding why they aren't. I sigh. "Focus," I say aloud and get comfortable again, returning to the beginning of that section. My Facetime rings again, and I grab the phone that's face down next to my knee. Without looking at it, I swipe it open to connect, leaning over to highlight a word in the text I missed. "What did you forget, Shelbs?"

"I got gender reassignment."

My heart wakes and stretches inside my chest at the sound of Tanner's voice. If I could hide the smile, I would try, but I can't. "You're a butt, and you're breaking the rules. We talked Friday."

He smiles, that beautiful Tanner smile that connects to the wires in my heart. "First, you love that I'm a butt. Second, you are a rule monger, and sometimes rules are meant to be broken."

He's right, but I don't tell him that. "How was your test?"

"Aced it. Community college is too easy." He adjusts the red baseball cap on his head, and I wish I could see more of his hair, though the edges curl up around the edge of the ball cap.

"Double up on your classes then and finish early."

"Naw. I like working with my dad and making money. I need cash to take girls out on dates." He winks at me and adjusts himself so that he's leaning against the headboard of his bed. He's living at home with his mom which — surprisingly — he seems happy about. I think it probably helps that his family has been in counseling together and individually since summer.

"How are those dates going?" I keep my voice light when I ask. Since our quarry-side chat when we decided to end things, we've cultivated a fun, flirty friendship, but I know when he finally mentions he's met someone, my heart will break. I still love him. I will always love him, but it has grown and changed into something that resonates with who I've become. I don't look at Tanner and think I don't deserve his attention. I don't look at him and think he must not like me. I know he does. He wouldn't keep calling if he didn't. And he's better too, in his skin. His swagger, which was always present but dimmed under all of the hurt he was hiding, is so bright now, because he's healthier. My love for him, full of depth and latent hope, would probably be best served by not seeing him, so I could begin to let go. But I just can't. I'm unwilling to break my friendship with him. Ever. A part of me thinks we were lucky to keep it at all.

"Dates? I don't go on dates, Emma. You know this. I'm saving myself for you." He insists this is true, having told me repeatedly that he has a *no women rule*, which Ginny has confirmed via Josh. Tanner hasn't dated a single woman since me, because he's *working on himself.*

"Then why did you say you needed money for dates?"

He clears his throat, shifts behind the camera, and his eyes slide away for a moment. I think he's up to something. "I'm saving up. Look, I called for an ulterior motive."

"Which is?" I narrow my eyes.

"Why are you looking at me like that?" He tilts his head and removes the hat. He runs his hand through his hair. The strands are unruly and messy, and I wish I could reach through the screen and run my fingers through it. My chest tightens.

"I'm not looking at you in any way. You said you have an ulterior motive, and you called twice this week."

"How was your date?"

I laugh. "You don't want to hear about it." But he always asks. I've been serial dating without involvement. The truth is that the guys are mostly nice, and lots of them have wonderful potential. But none of them are Tanner. It's that red wire.

"You're right. I don't. But I do. Tell me. Is he the one? What was his name? Sloppy Joe?"

I shake my head. "No. It was Steve Jones. Do you think I should tell you if he was?"

"Definitely. It would tell me that I need to drop out to get to California."

I laugh. "Stop joking around."

"Who says I'm joking?" He smiles his million-watt smile. "Tell me, is Sloppy Joe my competition?" His smile fades.

"No. It was a terrible date. I will not be going on another date with him."

"Terrible, huh?" He smiles again and leans back on his arm, so I can see his bicep peeking out of the sleeve of his gray t-shirt. "I want all of the gory details."

I have to look away. "I will not."

"Come on, Em. I'm using this to study. I need to prepare for my foray back into the world of dating."

It makes my stomach clench. "Is that going to happen soon?"

"It is a distinct possibility."

I try to keep my smile, but it's hard, because I'm jealous. Horribly jealous. I don't want Tanner to date anyone. But I have no intention of sharing details with him, so I say, "It was fine. Dull. Not compatible."

"You say that every time. I think you might be holding back."

I sigh. "Is this why you're really calling?" My eyes narrow at him. "Is it really to ask me about my dating life? Which is thin. I'm usually in the library."

"You're sure you aren't coming home for Spring Break?"

"We already talked about this. No. It's too expensive. Summer."

"I just wanted to double check."

"Why?"

Tanner drops his arm, so I'm not looking at his full bicep anymore, and does something off screen that I can't see. "You're so nosey." Then his face is back, and he's looking at me, but it's more serious, reserved Tanner. "Maybe, I wanted to ask you out on a date."

"I'm nosey?" I roll my eyes. "Well, I'm not coming home. Besides, we already have Facetime dates every week with the exception of this week, which included a second, suspect call."

He dips his head, chin to chest, eyebrows arched over his eyes with a look that makes me gooey. "Don't you roll your eyes at me, Em. You're getting full of yourself, and this is not a date."

"What is it then?"

"Girl talk."

I laugh. And I realize this is a lot like a good date. Spending time with him, talking, laughing. All that's missing is the physical connection. But all these months we've focused on just the mental part of getting to know one another.

"There would be other activities involved in these Facetime chats if it weren't girl talk." He wiggles his eyebrows at me then grows serious again after I've laughed.

"Oh really? Aren't you assuming a bit?"

It's his turn to laugh, and I can't keep my eyes from admiring the shape of his neck, the taper of the muscle that connects to his shoulders. The way the hint of his Adam's apple moves with his laughter. "Real talk then." His eyes, still alive with mirth, look at me through the camera, but his smile tempers. "I'd like to ask you for a real, honest to god, face-to-face date." He pauses, and I feel like he's nervous, because he shifts and swallows. "And–" his swagger back– "I need to give Sloppy Joe and Billingsworth Hexagon — that was his name, right?"

"No. Bill Hemming or Hennig or something."

"I need to get my name into this competition."

"Oh. Really?" I sound sarcastic and playful, but my heart has jump started, speeding along a winding road I didn't know was coming. "What would you call yourself? Tennyson Jefferies?"

He pauses, thinking about it; his eyes squint just a touch and look up into a corner I can't see. "I like it. But let's add Lord in front of

Tennyson."

I laugh. "So, you're coming to California then, for this date?" I don't believe him, even if every part of inside me is screaming for it to be true.

His smile drops further, and he looks down while he runs a hand through his hair again. Then he looks up with a very serious look — a Tanner smolder. "I am."

My heart picks up speed. Aside from our Facetime chats, I haven't seen him in person since Winter break and even then — only five months removed from our Quarry talk — we were both very careful to keep things light and friendly. With Josh and Ginny still talking, Liam and Atticus friends, and Danny home on leave after basic, it was inevitable that we'd see one another. Even then, the tension between us was alive. I knew he felt it too, but it was too important to me not to act on it, even if every cell in my body strained toward him.

Thinking about it now makes my cells turn into water. The desire I feel for him has only gotten more intense and acute. The reason every guy I've dated has been compared to him is because no one makes me feel like he did. No one makes me laugh like Tanner does. No one is as effortless as he is. No one is as fun to talk to or listen to or be around as him. No one lights me up like stars. Tanner can do that 2600 miles away over a screen.

I will not tell him these things, however. First, his ego is already gigantic now that he's a working college boy. Second, he's found a healthier kind of confidence since he isn't hanging out with Griff or partying (it's probably the therapy and the relationships he's building with his parents), and third, he's been writing stories, star stories, he calls them. Sometimes he shares them, but usually just the ones that involve Ella and TJ, because he wants to get me laughing.

"Emma? Earth to Emma. Are you still there?"

"Are you being serious? If you're joking with me, I'm going to hang up on you."

"I'm being serious. Atticus has a game on your campus the first weekend of Spring Break, because it looks like they'll either have a play-in for the tournament or an invitation. Josh said I should come out to stay with him, so we could watch the game. I'm taking vacation to come out."

"Really?" My heart is now sprinting in the fifty-yard dash. I can't help but smile. "You're serious?"

"I wouldn't joke about this. I joke about lots of stuff, but not about being able to see you. That's the only reason, really, that I would come out. To see you. I mean I love Josh and Atticus and all, but... well–" His voice drops away. He licks his lips and then bites his bottom lip. "We were planning on driving into town from Davis. If that's okay."

"Are you kidding? Yes." I drop the phone. "Oops." I pick it up and press a hand to a cheek; I can't stop smiling.

Tanner's smile matches mine. "I would like to officially add my name into the dating queue to take you out. Is four weeks enough time to get Lord Tennyson Jefferies on the calendar?" When I don't say anything, his brows knit together. "That's okay, right? I mean, if it isn't, then I don't have to."

For some reason, tears press against the inside of my eyes, and I will them to recede. I nod. "I'd like that."

He sighs, wipes his brow, and grins. "Had me worried there for a moment."

"Tanner James worried?"

"King James–" He freezes, and his mouth makes the shape of an "o," then he smiles. "That's very good. Put a pin in that: King James." He puffs up, and I roll my eyes.

"I take it TJ isn't a prince anymore."

"Yes. He still is, but he's worked pretty hard on cleaning up that rusty armor and is much, much closer to becoming a King. Pretty soon — I'd say — in say about four weeks — Queen Ella won't be able to resist him any longer." He smiles.

"Oh really?"

He offers me that amazing smile that reaches his eyes, and chills race along my skin. "I'm counting on it."

"Lucy took my hand in hers. 'We'll find a way,' she said, and the way she said it, I believed her."

- unnamed protagonist, *Kaleidoscope Concussion* by Saul Annick

it's only the beginning...

afterword

At eighteen—raised in a Christian home with purity values—I walked out into the world naive and unsuspecting. I entered the college campus where I was supposed to spend the next four years pursuing an English degree. My sheltered experience, not only due to my family and church belief system, but also growing up in a small town where everyone knew everyone else, I wasn't prepared to recognize that not all value systems were like mine. I was raised to think my "no" meant "no." So, when I walked into the apartment of my date, said "no" to his advances and then was ignored, my worldview completely shattered.

Did you know that women ages 18-24 are three to four times more likely to experience sexual violence than other women? Men in college are five times more likely to experience sexual assault. These statistics are sobering. The harsh reality is that my *Me Too* story isn't uncommon. According to Rainn.org, someone in America experiences sexual assault every 73 seconds. That's one sexual assault **every minute and 13 seconds**. Both men and women are affected by that statistic, and the most at risk are the young. Stop. Think about that. About 70% of all REPORTED cases are between the ages of 12 and 34. Most are female: 1 in 6 females, while 1 out of every 10 victims are male (and the statistics for transgender youth are even higher).

These statistics are occurring in a culture that promotes "purity." As a culture that advocates for sexual training to be done within the family, could purity be synonymous with suppression and shame? I would pose the question: if promoting "purity" and "abstinence only" is effective, why are the statistics so high?

For most of my adulthood, I couldn't face what happened to me, ashamed that somehow, I'd caused it. When I'd attempted to report it, the message I received from the policeman taking my report was bored indifference. Then he asked me, "Did you fight back?" as if it was my responsibility to have to, and with my "purity" background, I believed I was somehow to blame. So I went silent with shame. Then, in 2016—twenty-four years later—I read a book called *Girls and Sex: Navigating the Complicated New Landscape* by Peggy Orenstein. This book gave me permission to look at my own trauma again—to get angry—to understand that I wasn't alone—to acknowledge it wasn't my fault and it never was. More importantly, Orenstein's book helped me acknowledge how important these conversations are for not only our girls, but even more so for our boys. Our girls get it, but our boys need it.

Both Emma and Tanner face different forms of sexual abuse. We might be more willing to overlook what happened to Tanner because he is male; sexually groomed by an older woman who preyed upon his youth. This attitude, however, demonstrates our willingness to look at male sexuality as a form of exploration and experience-building rather than someone who was exploited and preyed upon. On the other hand, Emma's experience is more typical of sexual assault, and while her date's behavior isn't acceptable, his belief system of entitlement and blindness to his own role in sexuality as a partnership exemplify a skewed perspective that hasn't been challenged in a "purity culture" that practices and supports victim blaming. When churches and other religious institutions place all of the onus on females to "cover up" and "be pure" because males can't control their urges, the males of society have the means to point the finger and disengage from their own responsibility.

The Stories Stars Tell isn't a statement against remaining a virgin until married; it isn't advocacy about being flippant or cavalier about sexuality either. Instead of a singular examination of the ways in which messages of "purity" confuse messages about being sexual beings, this story is an exploration of what it would feel like to be personally empowered. Emma provides a picture of a young woman ready to explore her sexuality, but unable to turn to the very people she needs to understand her biology, her options, her voice; what she wrestles with are feelings of guilt, powerlessness, and confusion, which she grapples with alone. Sexuality in America is seen as "other," in a way. A taboo subject. Our first response is to perpetuate shame. While I don't have statistics to share with you, I wonder if mental health is directly related to this inability to process not only our sexuality, but the inherent shame brought about by purity culture and victim blaming.

Orenstein wrote about the "Dutch" approach to sexuality in her book, that when juxtaposed with the American approach is night and day. Whereas Americans are more likely to preach abstinence and purity until marriage based on religious ideals, the Dutch actively promote early sex education. Orenstein wrote, "Dutch teens [...] remain closely connected to parents [who] are expected to discuss the children's psychological and emotional development including their burgeoning sexual drives. As part of that, Dutch parents permit —wait for it— sleepovers [...]That's not to say it's a free-for-all over there. Quite the opposite: the Dutch actively discourage promiscuity in their children, teaching that sex should emerge from a loving relationship" (222-23). In contrast to American statistics in 2015 which reported 38.5 rape cases per 100,000 reported crimes, Dutch statistics reported 7.1 cases of rape per 100,000 (Knoema.com). Sobering, right?

I wrote *The Stories Stars Tell* because I want *Me Too* stories to disappear. I want politicians who grope women and children to 1) stop being elected, and 2) to stop being allowed to make decisions about whether we can develop a comprehensive sexual education curriculum that teaches our youth to love themselves - body, sexuality and all. I want our citizens ready to excuse male behavior as "boys being boys" and "it's just locker room talk" to hear themselves and see their excuses for what they are: excuses. I want young women and young men ready to understand their sexuality to have resources and clarity about their own choices so they can make healthy ones. I want churches to stop shaming children, women, men, gay, straight, trans for being human with human drives attributing self-worth to suppression of self. And I want parents to get honest about the fact that their kids sexual health is as important as their emotional, physical, and mental health; ignoring sexuality, shaming sexuality, or covering sexuality up under the mask of religion isn't going to support our youth to develop self-efficacy about their sexual rights and responsibilities.

I know there will be people who question my faith because I've written a story that illustrates a young woman making an empowered choice for herself that questions not only how her religion plays a part in that, but also questions the patriarchy as it attempts to control women's bodies. I know it comes with the territory of taking a stance; I am a Christian and have been for my whole life, after all. I know the rhetoric and the vitriol that will happen because I'm not staying in my place and because I'm questioning those precepts. I know there will be people who think I misrepresent God's laws on morality. Maybe that's true, but I won't begin to presume what God thinks on the matter. Here's what I'm wholly acquainted with: God's beautiful Grace and that is what I hope this story communicates. No matter a person's sexual journey, shame shouldn't be associated with healthy biological exploration. That shame won't be associated with sexuality and rigidly structured cultural precepts around gender roles as they relate to sexuality. Maybe by understanding that—all the ways we hurt one another because of sexuality—will then heal. I know, call me an idealist, but THAT is why I wrote this story.

acknowledgements

This book might get me sent to Saturday School. I'm okay with that, but I would like to drag some amazing people with me so we can re-enact *The Breakfast Club*. I'd ask these amazing humans to come with me for our Saturday Library Lockdown so we can talk stories and books: the librarians, the readers and fans, the book reviewers and the supporting artists. Our adventure in the library is rooted in your amazing support and advocacy. I've got a red wire attached to you, and I thank you so much for your support of me, the work and these amazing characters who have my heart. You make the work matter.

After Saturday School, I'm going to play hooky from school like Ferris and Crew from *Ferris Bueller's Day Off* so I can take these amazing humans out on an adventure: Katharine Lamoureaux, Becky Clark, Lavinia Ungureanu, Janine Caroline, Stephanie Keesey-Phelan, Britt Laux, Kori Schlacter and Marcie Ahana. Each of you helped me home in on different aspects of this story to come to terms with its strengths and weaknesses. From helping me look closer at Emma's journey, to offering perspective about secondary characters, to your adoration for Tanner, to reinforcing the ending when everything in me wanted to fight against it, to chatting about what you loved and what moved you, to supporting me with the close editing and making sure the words have power in my note — I am so grateful. Lunch is on me, and I might be having a Cameron level panic attack at the mistakes, but they are all mine.

During the next winter vacation, I'm hoping to get stuck on a cross-country adventure with Sara Oliver, like Neal and Del in *Planes, Trains and Automobiles* because though we've started out as strangers, I count you as a friend. I think you are amazing and am so grateful for your artistry on this cover as well as *The Cantos Chronicles*. You spin magic.

When I'm writing a book, I retreat into my own level of Samantha introversion, but as I resurface, it's going to be time for an epic *Sixteen Candles* party. I thank you for your support of my dreams and the work.

Thank you to my mom, my sister, my extended family, my in-laws in the quiet and not so quiet ways you champion the work and me as an indie author. From reading, to sharing posts, to offering meals, to just providing encouragement, I appreciate you. Thank you to my Girls Crew for your willingness to accept the fact I'm mostly a hermit, and then, when I venture out of the cave, allow me to ramble about creative life. To my students who encouraged me to keep going and offered me adolescent wisdom to understand everything social media. To my English colleagues at Kamehameha, because your support has always made me stronger. Someone start up the Rolls Royce and let's take it for a spin to celebrate!

Like Andie's dad loves her and she loves him in *Pretty in Pink*, I want my children to know I will love them forever. Thank you, Anuhea and La'anui. I hope that someday me chasing my dreams will translate to you chasing yours.

To my partner—Vince—I think we might be *Weird Science*, but somehow, we work, though I'm not sure who the computer-generated hottie is—both of us? Thank you for being my best friend. Thank you for listening, offering sage business advice, and for the support to help me chase the dream which probably costs you more than anyone. That red wire wrapped me up with you a long time ago and still connects me to you forever and ever. We're on our way to dreamland, together.

Finally (and without a magical John Hughes reference), all glory and honor to my Lord and Savior Jesus Christ, from whom all blessings flow. My gratitude certainly isn't enough, but I hopefully honor Him in all I do.

Star Stories Playlist

Here are 15 songs that inspired me while I wrote *The Stories Stars Tell* (you can find a longer playlist on Spotify; just look for the book title)

Please, Please Please Let Me Get What I Want By The Dream Academy	This is on the *Ferris Bueller's Day Off* Soundtrack - it just made me think of Emma, Liam and Ginny
5AM by Amber Run	This song made me think about Tanner and his Bro Code crew
Jump by Julia Michaels and Trippie Redd *Quiet* by EXES	Emma's unending infatuation with Tanner After *Operation Kiss Tanner James*, I thought about how Emma might feel fighting her infatuation for him.
Everything I Wanted by Billie Eilish	This song reminds me of how people struggle with inner monsters, but then someone outside of us offers light. "As long as I'm here, no one can hurt you."
Night Drive by Twiceyoung	This song made me think of Tanner and how he would drive to think and process his life.
Discovery by AK	A song without lyrics, but I couldn't help but think of *Senior Send Off* every time I listened to it. It was on repeat.
Feelings by Lauv	I love how this song explores the crossing between friendship to lovers and that it's mutually explored resonated with the story.
Peer Pressure by James Bay and Julia Michaels	I love the angst in this song. It made me think of both Emma and Tanner.
Cymbidium by WMD	Another song without lyrics, its vibe just made me think about Emma and Tanner being together.
Man Overboard by Ed Patrick	Tanner. Tanner. Tanner.
Stay Still EXES	I actually listened to a ton of songs by EXES and only a couple made the list. This one captures that element of time.
Zero-Sum by JJ Draper	Zero-Sum is the concept that whatever is gained by one side is lost by the other. For me, it connected to where Emma and Tanner are in coming to terms with themselves.
All I Got by Said the Sky and Kwesi	Tanner. Tanner. Tanner, P. II
Maybe, One Day by Hotel Apache	Emma and Tanner.

Look for Griffin's Story
Fall 2021

EXCERPT

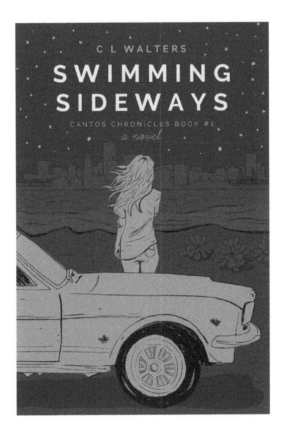

1 WISHING FOR THE AWESOME POWER OF INVISIBILITY

Good Abby has the job of keeping Bad Abby in place on her first day at a new school. I'm hopeful Bad Abby will stay in her cage, though at times, keeping her caged is more work than it's worth. It's important, however, and Good Abby knows this more than anyone. This is a chance to start fresh.

When the teacher says my name, "Abby Kaiāulu?" I cringe, wishing I could throw that in the cage too. My Hawaiian name doesn't allow for anonymity, and that is a rule of Good Abby: *remain anonymous.*

"Here," I say. I've chosen a tone to communicate indifference. Not too loud to express exuberance, but not too quiet to raise any flags of social concern. Instead, an even tone to express, maybe, boredom but without an edge should be neutral enough to be forgettable.

Another rule by Good Abby: *Don't draw attention.*

The teacher looks at me. She's cute with wire-rimmed glasses perched on the end of an upturned nose. Her white skin is dotted with freckles, and her auburn hair cut short and fluffy around her face. "Did I pronounce your last name correctly?" She smiles. Classic teacher move: disarm with a smile.

I nod — even though she's butchered my name — in an effort to steer the center-stage light onto whatever awaits us in US History. While being at a new school is a positive thing, Good Abby knows how important it is to make a good first impression. It is imperative to hide the truth of what I did, to keep what happened at my last school from happening here too.

Next rule established by Good Abby: *Stay under the radar.*

Freckle-nose teacher says, "Would you say it please?"

I sigh. "Abby Kaw-ee-aaawww-oo-loo."

Teacher makes a note on her clipboard.

I return to doodling waves in the margin of my clean notebook, wishing I was in the waves at Makaha with perfect sets of four to six faces rolling in on a clear and calm, sunny day. I imagine the azure water stretching toward the horizon, the *kai* wrapped around my body like a hug. Sitting inside a school room for lessons about US History would be pointless.

But pixie-teacher isn't thinking about waves at Makaha Beach like I am when she says, "Such a pretty name, Abby. What is the ethnicity? It's so unique."

I blink and force myself not to roll my eyes, keeping Bad Abby in check. Every pair of eyes in the room, at least twenty of them, are now on me at this third, pointed question. I sink a little lower in my desk chair and answer her. "It's Hawaiian."

"Hawaiian. Wow!" Her eyes grow to nearly the same circumference as her glasses, and her smile is extra bright. "I want to travel to Hawaii," she adds.

Bad Abby offers the following snide observation: *you and a majority of the rest of the world.*

Good Abby is able to keep Bad Abby's snarky comment internal, however, and focuses on Tinker Bell teacher's words.

"We'll study the overthrow of the Hawaiian monarchy later this year, the imprisonment of the Queen, and the annexation," she says.

Guilt bubbles up a little at Bad Abby's ill-manners, and I wonder if Perky Teacher will teach that annexation was illegal?

"Welcome to Cantos, Abby," Good Fairy Teacher finishes.

I force a slight smile to acknowledge her comments, but not too flashy. I don't want to encourage this interrogation any further.

Even though the teacher finally moves on to today's lesson about how to take notes for the lecture, I can still feel the eyes of the other students in the class boring into me, trying to mine me for secrets. Everyone else has had nearly two weeks to acclimate to the school year, and for many of them a lifetime of knowing one another. It's my first day as a junior at Cantos High School. Right now, I'm wishing that CHS stood for Camouflage High School, a place where I can blend into everything around me due to my awesome power of invisibility.

2 THIS VERSION OF ME

I escape into the first bathroom I find. Water on my face feels good. *Don't cry*, Good Abby coaxes. *Don't you dare cry! There's no reason to. This is a good thing!*

I take a breath to send oxygen to my tear ducts, to dry the threatening tears. I imagine sitting atop my surfboard rolling with a swell, the ocean a home of comfort. I miss it even if I don't deserve it. In my mind's eye I see Poppa: his dark Hawaiian skin, a deep golden brown, his wet silver-black hair sparkling in the sun. He lays down on the board, hands in the water, paddling as another wave rises behind us. With a look back at me, his gleaming white teeth bared with his smile, he calls, "Come on, Tita!" Then he's standing on his board, gliding away from me through the water.

Not that memory, Bad Abby scolds. *That one's sure to start the water works.*

I haven't surfed since Poppa died.

A glance in the mirror and I see the ocean in my eyes threatening to fall. I can never go back there. Poppa is gone. I'm ruined.

No one here knows, Good Abby reassures. *We'll keep it that way.*

Cantos is my new home like it or not. The new chance.

I stare at my face in the mirror and feel the self-induced insults:

481

You're so stupid.

Why did you have to ruin everything?

Everybody at home knows what you did.

While I'm present, standing in this high school bathroom with my reflection staring back at me, my mind travels a million miles away. I'm on a cyber superhighway logged onto a Twitter of my memory. My shame waits there for anyone to search. All anyone has to enter is the right key words, or the correct hashtag to ruin my life here too. Forever waiting.

A gaggle of girls enters the bathroom giggling. They see me and stop. They are blond and beautiful, such an exotic contrast to the monotony of my brownness: skin, hair, eyes - all of me. I look away from them down at the sink and hide the tears that have slipped from my eyes. The group's conversation resumes though in quieter tones.

Good Abby rule: *Avoid eye contact.*

I'm successfully ignored. I wipe my eyes. Bad Abby thinks a smart-ass remark wanting them to feel as bad as their dismissal of me does: *basic, haole bitches.* Good Abby bites her tongue.

Another Good Abby rule: *Don't speak unless spoken to.*

I slink out of the room, head down, and run right into somebody walking through the hallway. Ass on the floor and Good Abby can't contain the bad one any longer: "What the hell!" I snap. "Watch where you're going!" I look up at the culprit. The anger catches in my throat. I've bumped into a boy the size of a wall.

"I could say the same thing about you," he replies. His voice has the lure of the ocean surf in the distance, a gentle and relaxing rumble. His bright blue eyes are the Hawai'i Pacific Ocean, intensely bright set in the golden glow of his bronze skin. His black hair is longish, curly, hanging over his sharp features though his lips are soft and full. He holds out a hand, the sinew of his muscles hinted in the exposure of the brown skin at his wrist.

He helps me up.

Someone in the hall passes and jostles him with a shoulder. The Wall loses his balance and knocks against me as I stand, but I don't fall

482

a second time. His arm wraps around me and keeps me from falling to the floor again. We're so close that I smell the clean scent of him like soap and a hint of something spicy. My hand still in his, an arm around his solid and unforgiving shoulders, electricity winds up my arm straight to my heart and flutters with the current.

"Freak," a passing voice in the hallway says.

I pull away regretting the loss of the connection but unwilling to go back to the social dump. Been there. Done that. This is me starting over.

Good Abby rule: *Selectively choose your friends.*

The Wall looks at me. His eyes have narrowed, the color now flinty, and the energy I thought I felt retreats somewhere safe. I notice the knowing look on his face, and it's a knife in my gut. His jaw tightens. He recognizes this current version of me all too well. I identify his awareness because I was him, after all, the one they called names. It may have not been *freak,* but *slut* or *whore* did the same kind of damage. I knew a version of this new me too, and it makes me feel ashamed.

"Sorry," he mutters and pulls his black hood over his head as he walks away.

Good Abby coaxes the bad one not to look back, not to watch him walk away. Bad Abby wants more than anything to turn around, say she's sorry and let him know she's been there. But she listens to Good Abby and goes to her next class. I walk away wondering which one is good Abby and which one is bad?

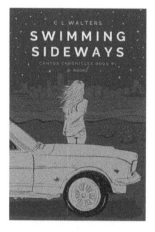

BOOKS

CL WALTERS
Author

Available
wherever books
are sold

about the author

CL Walters writes in Hawaiʻi where she lives with her husband and two children. She's the author of the YA Contemporary series, *The Cantos Chronicles* (*Swimming Sideways*, *The Ugly Truth* and *The Bones of Who We Are*), as well as the adult book, *The Letters She Left Behind*. *The Stories Stars Tell* is her fifth novel. You can stay connected by signing up for her monthly newsletter. Visit her website at www.clwalters.net and follow her writer's journey on Instagram @cl.walters.